I0685129

Black Recluse

Anna Bowman

BLACK RECLUSE

OUTKAST

BOOK ONE

WITH A BONUS SHORT...
THE BOY WHO TRAVELED THROUGH DREAMS

Anna Bowman

Printed in the United States of America
First Printing: 2019
Rivet Wing Press
ISBN: 978-1-7331279-3-6

For my amazing husband, You are one hundred percent awesome.

DISCLAIMER

THE AUTHOR IS in no way responsible for the views, opinions or actions of the characters in this book or the predicaments they get themselves into. They are rebellious and do what they want. She just wrote it down.

CHAPTER 1

SOLOMAND

CAPTAIN BLACK WAS not having a good day. The saloon's working girls wanted him to buy services at Racketrath. His throat constricted at the thought of it.

God knows what I'd come away with!

"Sorry, I have an urgent meeting," he told the smoky-eyed woman, straining his eyes to the doorway in search of his First Mate.

"Ah, come on, Captain Black—no time for fun?" She gave him a heavy-lidded wink, pursing deep-red lips toward his face.

"Sadly, no," he said, ducking beneath her grasp. He stood, shoving his sweat-stained cap on his head. "There he is now. Next time."

He blew her a kiss, stifling a gag, and hurried in an almost desperate pace to meet the man at the door.

"About damn time, Will," he said, taking his cap off to run a hand through his coal-black hair.

Will, a head taller than Solomand, glanced over his shoulder into the saloon. A group of women wearing low-cut blouses and hiked skirts waved at him. He looked back at his Captain.

"Sorry. Didn't realize that was something you couldn't handle."

Solomand lit a cigarette, his fingers shaking as he struck the lighter multiple times before returning it to the pocket of his navy overcoat.

1

"They are becoming more insistent—one even offered herself for free." He shuddered. "And no useful knowledge about the airman's movements for all my trouble, either."

It was becoming more difficult to weasel his way out of 'relations' with the unsavory bar women. There had to be a better way to get information besides talking with them.

He pulled his cap down over his eyes as he walked away from the dingy saloon at a hurried pace. Neon lights flickered in the window of closed shops advertising everything from solar pocket watches to lightweight dusters imported from the Continent Argos.

Solomand casually sidled up to the wall of a building plastered with wanted posters. Wanted: Black Recluse—For crimes against the Coalition. The faded words were barely legible and were followed by an even less discernible drawing of a man dressed in black—a mask over his face.

Tearing it down, Solomand balled the poster up and threw it into a water fountain as he passed by. Running a finger under the leather eyepatch over his left eye, Will gave him a sideways glance. Solomand blew out a puff of cigarette smoke, looking straight ahead.

Newsprints were not popular here anymore. If anyone cared to know the current events elsewhere, they could view it on the moving screen in the town's center. Most people in Racketrath didn't care about whatever the Coalition had to say these days, especially if it was old news.

Today, there was the usual small crowd of people, looking in shop windows and paying little heed to the propaganda that sounded overhead. Solomand would have walked straight through and on his way to the docks, but he heard a familiar voice on the viewing screen. Anyone else might have thought it the deep, assured tone, a pleasant voice. Solomand, however, froze in place, feeling cold as his eyes were drawn involuntarily to look on the face of Stefan LeFrost, governor of the Plains city, Corcyra.

"Our citizens are safer today, thanks to the fine men and women of our 201st Airborne," LeFrost said through the moving screen.

A banner ran across the bottom of the screen, saying 'Live coverage: Public Execution of War Criminal, Stanley Simonson.' The screen split to show a view of the unfortunate Simonson. He wore the green uniform of the insurgents. Rope bound his arms to posts on a pavilion surrounded by a crowd of spectators. His eyes were filled with terror as the savage barking of dogs interrupted the governor's speech.

"Governor LeFrost suffered the loss of his own daughter six years ago when the war came to a close."

The banner came across again.

Solomand frowned. They made it out like the man was some sort of tragic hero when he was a sadistic, calculating, bastard.

One spectator checked his watch, while a lady fanned herself in the sun. Six years. That was how long Simonson must have been a prisoner unless he was recently caught. Either way, that crisp uniform hid details of lengthy torture that always preceded LeFrost's condemnation. It would soon be torn and bloody when the dogs were released to carry out the final sentence.

Solomand tensed. Screams flooded his mind and blood soaked the cold stone of the pavilion, even though the governor had not yet given the word to release the dogs. A hand gripped his shoulder, and he jerked, ready to draw the revolver hidden under his coat. It was Will. Solomand relaxed, allowing his friend to maneuver him away from the square.

"Yeah…" Sol cast a hateful look at the face of the governor and spit on the ground.

Your time will come, LeFrost, Sol thought. It was more of a promise to himself than anything. Aloud, he muttered, "You'd think they'd let a thing go after six damn years."

Will's hand tightened on Solomand's shoulder before he let go, his brow furrowing for an instant.

"Jank didn't pass his flight assessment," he said, keeping close to Solomand as a group of strangers walked past.

3

"Eh well," Solomand shrugged, glad Will did not comment on LeFrost and shove him further down that road of painful memories. It was better to ignore it for now. "I'll just manufacture him a license then. Like I did with mine." He gave Will a sly grin.

Adjusting his eyepatch again, Will remarked. "I think you should have taken the test. We are lucky no one has noticed yours is a fake. They look at those things closer than identification cards."

"Why, Will, if I didn't know any better, I'd think you have an issue with my flying."

"You know I do," Will said, not missing a beat.

Solomand pretended not to hear. The docks of Racketrath came into view. It was one of the few towns actually on the ground and not perched on a cliff or mountain. The red brick buildings had panels on the roofs for collecting the sun's power for electricity. In the Western desert landscape, there was plenty of sun to be harnessed.

Racketrath was neither respectable, like the great Coalition cities to its east, nor disreputable, like many of the one-horse towns scattered throughout the Plains. The constant thrum of noise from radios and communication devices swelled like the rumbling of thunder. Sleek, two-wheeled ironhorse bikes buzzed as their riders shot through the streets, weaving around everyone on foot. Solomand glanced around, feeling like the world was pressing in on him. Sometimes it was easier to hide within the bustle and noise, but he couldn't fight the urgent need to leave.

Pacing, he placed a hand in his coat pocket as he sucked on his cigarette. Among the advertisements papering the wall of the station platform, there was a prominent poster displaying a firebolt catcher dressed in robes with all but his eyes covered. His gloved hand seized lightning from a storm cloud with a dramatic desert background. A stack of empty firebolt cores were stacked at his feet, presumably awaiting to be charged. The various sized cores were marked with red lightning bolts of Sky Enterprises. *Fly, with a piece of the Sky!*

Solomand rolled his eyes. *What an idiotic slogan.* "I hope someone was fired over that," he muttered.

Everyone that could afford the lightning-powered cells already used them. Here, on the continent Lyonese, they were mainly reserved for airships and some motorized vehicles. Anything else was too expensive. People resorted to what power was available: steam, solar, electricity, whatever was cheapest.

White lights flashed at the end of the runway. A small sky rail tilted as a gust of stale air blew across the skyport. The left wing lifted slightly as the wheels touched down and the aircraft pulled to a stop. Flaggers waved orange banners, motioning the sleek, two-man craft to a halt. Further down the platform, a girl of twelve and a young man of around eighteen walked toward them. The girl was holding an ice cream in one hand and a piece of paper in the other.

"Sol!" The girl raised her hand, waving. She ran up to him. "I passed!"

Solomand flicked the remains of his cigarette away.

"Impressive, Zee!" He grinned as she held out the license to him and read the name from the fake paperwork he had given the administrator. "I mean, Tenzin Forge."

Zee took a lick of her ice cream and stuffed the paper in the pocket of her baggy trousers.

"Good job." Will ruffled the girl's short, silky black hair. "Knew you could do it."

The unhappy engineer scowled, his hands stuffed in his grease-stained overall pockets.

"Why so glum, Jank?" Solomand asked, motioning for Zee to give him a taste of the ice cream. After one lick, he handed it back and wiped his mouth on the back of his hand. "The legal way is overrated. You should get one like mine."

"No thanks," Jank scowled. "That's not what's bothering me, anyway. I can't get the fuel cell here. At least, not for a reasonable damned price." He muttered something about bastard pirates.

5

Solomand ran his finger underneath the chain around his neck as he glanced up at the sky. Dusk in Racketrath was always heralded by orange and red streaks of cloud that looked like a paintbrush had been dragged across the sky. One way or another, they had to have that fuel cell. They would not survive another encounter with the 201st Airborne Division if it wasn't replaced.

The transmitter on his wrist gave off a series of low beeps. He looked down as red and blue lights flashed in a series of long and short bursts.

I-know-what-you-are-hiding.

When the message finished, another low tone sounded.

Damn that woman. Solomand rubbed the back of his neck.

"What's wrong?" Will asked.

"We have to get to Ashbury once this fuel cell is settled. That damned woman knows too much."

Jank stiffened, his already pale face whitening.

"I told you she was more trouble than she was worth!"

Solomand turned his collar up, wishing it would rain. The people here were too cheery for his liking.

"So, we don't have enough money for a fuel cell." He started down the platform toward Dock 6, where his airship was waiting. "We'll just have to annex one," he said, as the others hurried after him.

"By annex one, you mean?" Will asked.

"Misappropriate," Zee spoke up as she finished her ice cream.

Solomand smiled over his shoulder at her proudly. "That's a new one. Haven't used that yet."

Zee let her long sleeve slide down to her elbow. "I don't know why you even ask, Will. You know how we always end up getting everything we need."

Will shook his head. "She may be starting to fit in too much," he told Solomand.

Solomand caught Zee's gaze, and she gave him a crooked grin.

"You say that like it's a bad thing." He took off his Captain's cap and put it on the girl's head. "You're flying this one," he said as they walked up the ramp to his docked airship.

"Where to first?" Jank gave him a dubious look.

"Where else? Port Bilboa." Solomand felt his gut tighten as he said it out loud. Going there always seemed to end in a frantic, death-defying departure.

CHAPTER 2

RAYN

WHAT IF I stowed away on one of those airships docked outside?

Rayn sat on a stool, leaning forward onto the bar, tracing ringed stains from beer bottles on the mahogany wood. A tin cup of water rested within arm's reach. She didn't come here to drink, nor did she care for the company. But today, the deep sting of loneliness pressed her to be anywhere but by herself.

The shadow of the low ceiling fan swept across the room in a steady pattern, stirring the cloud of cigar smoke, which stung her eyes. The bartender, a fat, balding man called Absalom, stood behind the counter, drying dirty glasses to prepare for the crowd of customers that would soon swamp the High Flyerz Saloon.

Rayn gripped the cup of water, her fingerless gloves soaking in the condensation as she took a drink and glanced at the clock over the bar. Through the fogged, broken glass she read the time: 1400 hours. Inane, chipper laughter sounded as girls dressed in corsets and high-heeled boots descended from the stairs, preparing for their nightly work.

Hunching her shoulders, Rayn lowered her head, her long braid of red hair drooping onto the soiled bar. *Idiots.* She couldn't stand women who were too stupid to make a living doing anything that involved actual skill. Her thoughts returned to the airships again and the impossible problem of not having traveling papers. The problem with that plan was, eventually, she'd be found out and likely turned in to the authorities for illegal and suspicious activities. That would lead her back here where she started, or—at worst—branded a sky pirate. It was all impossible. She sighed heavily.

I'm tired of waiting, she thought.

A creaking noise sounded as the door opened and a tall man walked in. Rayn glanced sideways as he walked up to the bar without making a noise, dust falling from his black overcoat. Uncomfortable silence settled on the room.

"Haven't seen you in a while, Stranger." Absalom's voice wavered as he set an empty glass in front of the man. "What'll it be?"

The man pushed his sweat-stained hat up, revealing dark eyes. There was a thin scar underneath his right eye, barely visible in the dim lighting.

"The usual." His voice was low and steady. There was an edge to it. He never looked at Rayn, and she still had the apprehensive feeling he was watching her.

Absalom poured water into the glass, spilling some onto the bar. "Here on business?"

The stranger picked up the glass with a tanned hand, swirling the water around as he stared at the bartender.

"I know. I know. None of mine."

Tense, Absalom turned and went back to drying his glasses. The stranger tipped the cup, and his sleeve fell down, revealing the thick, dark lines of tattoos on his wrist. Trying not to stare, Rayn's curiosity piqued.

He was not like any of the others who came and went. Nothing here seemed to interest him, aside from the glass of water in his hand. Water? An unusual choice in a bar. No one drank water here, except for her. She had a nagging feeling that there was something familiar about him, though she was sure she had never seen him before.

But what if I have? She thought.

What if he was from before she lost her memories? Lifting her gaze to carefully assess the stranger, she found his dark eyes fixed on her in an appraising way. A chill worked its way up her spine, and she glanced away.

Pilots streamed in, along with other gentlemen passengers, and Rayn forgot about the stranger. This new crowd all had the familiar, tired, yet hungry for new experiences look about them. Rayn rolled her eyes as the saloon girls led them to a table. *The STDs are beginning to outnumber the people in here.* She gave an unsavory glance around the room before digging two copper coins from her pocket. Placing them by the empty cup, she stood to leave, noticing the stranger was gone.

Oh well. She dismissed him from her mind. He probably had one of those faces that everybody thought they'd seen before. Adjusting her overcoat, she made for the door, passing a stocky pilot with a worn look about him and a younger man wearing a bowler hat.

Port Ashbury was a rest stop for these passengers. The man in the bowler hat should have stayed on his airship. As Rayn passed him, his eyes slid up and down her, and, with a stupid grin, his hand reached out.

She spun around. Who the hell did he think she was? One of these bar trollops? Her hand caught his wrist before it reached her, and she twisted. The bowler hat man's face contorted in pain. A look of anger spread across his face, and he raised his other hand. Rayn pulled her coat open and drew her revolver, sticking it in the man's gut with a forceful jab. She gave his other wrist one more jerk before releasing him, his hands raised, his face whitening. Rayn spoke through gritted teeth.

"Go on. Try it."

She shoved him away from her with the barrel of her revolver and gave him one last savage glare. The man's companion grabbed him by the collar and dragged him away from Rayn, shoving him along his way into the saloon. He gave her an amused grin before tipping his cap and following his dazed passenger.

Rayn re-holstered her revolver and pushed through the double doors out into the streets.

The next person who tries to get handsy is going to get a knife in the leg. These idiot people that passed through were all the same. Steering clear of the stream of travelers from the newly arrived airships, she started down the cobbled street. Her shop was situated outside of town, nestled in a small grove of oak trees.

Turning the wheel-lock, she flipped the toggle switch on the side of the wall. With a grinding sound, the generator kicked in and the lights flickered on. Rayn took off her overcoat and slung it over her workbench, sending a cloud of sawdust flying. Files and hammers lay amidst piles of springs and metal shavings. On the far side of the room stood a small drill press and a bench grinder covered in dust; she hadn't needed to use any of them in the past six years.

A sleek, black rifle stood in the corner. Rayn laid it on her workbench, sat down on a chair, and removed the bolt. She wasn't sure how she'd come by the original gun, but most of it she had modified over the last twelve months, putting her time into it whenever she was bored or angry or miserable.

Now, there was nothing left to do but clean the already immaculate components. Rayn sighed and splashed a squirt of oil into the trigger-well.

The door burst open, and she looked up in annoyance. A scrawny teenage boy ventured forward, his blonde hair as wild as his eyes.

"Ever heard of knocking?" She wiped her hands on a rag.

"S-sorry," the boy stammered. A spray of black powder covered his clothes, and there were a series of scratches on his pale face. "I was wondering if-if you might have a look at this?"

His hands, shaking, lay a short-barreled rifle on her bench.

Rayn stood, her eyebrows raising as she surveyed the weapon. The ruptured barrel was twisted in a thoroughly ruined way she had never witnessed before.

11

"What the hell did you do to it?" She was astonished the inept boy could inflict such damage.

The boy's hands were in his pocket, no doubt to hide their shaking. "I, well, I was practicing for the entrance exams for the 201st Division," he stammered, trying to sound proud.

Rolling her eyes, Rayn put her hands on her hips. The 201st Airborne recruitment posters were all over the docks these days, brandishing pictures of young men and women looking heroic in their uniforms as their famed attack ship hovered in the clouds behind them. *God help us if they're taking idiots like this sod.*

The boy cleared his throat under her hard stare and tried to continue. "Well, I fired a shot, and it didn't do anything."

"Didn't do *anything*?"

"Well... it went off, but I don't think it came out."

A squib-load. Rayn looked down at the rifle and pinched the bridge of her nose. "Where d'you get the ammo?"

"Off a pilot." The boy was looking more sheepish, if possible.

No wonder. It was probably twenty-year-old ammunition the man unloaded to stupid kids like this one.

"What did you do next?" She had a feeling she already knew.

The boy ran a hand over the back of his neck, looking uncomfortably at the floor. "I shot another round through it," he mumbled.

And there it was.

"Did you really think it was a good idea to fire another round through a rifle that has one already lodged in the barrel?"

The boy had no respect for the weapon at all!

He stared at her, looking frightened and ashamed.

"You're lucky that wasn't your hand. Or your face!" Rayn spared him no sympathy.

She pointed at the split iron, evoking a flinch from the sixteen-year-old. Reaching under the tool bench, she pulled out a brown ledger and slammed it next to the rifle. The boy jumped.

12

"Fine Airman you'll make one day," Rayn said, shaking her head. "You'll have to leave your rifle with me. Sign here." She tapped her index finger on a blank line.

Stepping forward timidly, the boy gulped and scrawled in careful letters: Gabriel Glass. Rayn took the book back and snapped it shut.

"Come back in three weeks. Afraid you'll have to practice something else for your entrance exams until then. I'd recommend intelligence, for starters."

"Yes, Ms." Gabriel nodded and tripped over his own feet in getting out the door like he thought Rayn might change her mind or assault him for his stupidity. *Would serve him right.*

Shaking her head, her hand moved to her pocket and closed around the medallion which held the secret of her past. She didn't want to fix the boy's rifle. She wanted to leave and never look back.

CHAPTER 3

SOLOMAND

NO ONE WHO came to Port Bilboa wanted any part of law and order. If you knew of the seedy port's existence, you were on the wrong side of the Coalition of Cities, or you were looking for someone whose bounty was high enough to warrant risking your neck.

It was built on the top of a secluded plateau, shielded by the green outline of the Wakashall Mountains. The only way to reach it was by air, though many left via a one-way trip to the broken rocks below; that is how a typical argument was resolved in Bilboa. This was also the reason a wake of buzzards circled the plateau like a permanent cloud of broken black, perching in the trees of the surrounding cliffs.

Only desperate or degenerate people ever came there; Solomand liked to think himself a little of both. Too much rested on getting the engine fuel cell. He would leave with it, one way or another. And if anyone got in his way—well—the vultures were always hungry.

Angry gray clouds swirled in the sky. Everything looked wrong here. The buildings were constructed of whatever cargo was available to steal. It was a mismatched conglomeration of tin and pine boards on one side and steel beams on the other. The shoddy craftsmanship reflected the horde of ingrates that dwelled within.

Solomand stepped onto the platform of rusted steel and looked around with distaste. Other ships were docked here, all of them unmarked and untraceable. One of them was an angular craft with rust-colored sails; only airships from the Continent Argos were of that design. Argos was the main importer of firebolt cores, the primary power source for those with enough capital to purchase them. However, their primary trade good, and the only one anyone docked at Bilboa would deal in, was slaves.

Zee stepped out of the Osprey with Will and Jank, her soft-soled boots noiseless on the metal. He turned to her, shaking his head.

"No, Zee. Wait here." He lowered his voice, trying to sound stern. It was too dangerous for her. The Argos slavers were always on the prowl for young girls in particular.

Zee pushed up her gray cap.

"But, Sol." Her golden eyes grew wide beneath her bangs. "Last time you said I could go with you."

Solomand's gaze turned to the slave ship, then back to the girl, his frown deepening.

"And you also promised you wouldn't try to weasel out of it." Her lips pursed together into a pout.

Solomand ran a hand along the bottom of his bearded chin. She probably wouldn't catch anyone's attention, dressed in unflattering boy's clothes like she was. He sighed.

"Oh, alright. Stay close, though."

Smoking helped him think. A cigarette hanging from his mouth, he spun the cylinder of his revolver, checking that it was loaded.

Will hooked a thumb in his belt, his wide-brimmed hat tilted to the side, a lever-action rifle in his other hand. Jank wore a head-lamp strapped to his forehead. He looked nervous, as usual. They both looked at Solomand, waiting for orders.

"Right." Solomand secured the revolver in his holster. "You know the plan. Get what we need and get the hell out without getting caught. Or shot. Or maimed. Ready?"

15

Jank gave Will an uncomfortable look before muttering a half-hearted, "Yeah," and scurrying to keep up with Will's stride. The two disappeared down the street, going around the back way to the warehouse.

Solomand was going to distract Bazel, the underhanded goods collector who they were going to rob. The old man's warehouse was filled with accumulated supplies, purloined from other miscreants he'd fed to the vultures.

It was his time to get the shady end of a deal, Sol reasoned. Bazel deserved no sympathy or concern. It was those Argos slave traders, however, that worried him.

"Stay close," he whispered to Zee, gripping her by the arm and pulling her to his side as an Ironhorse sped by.

Shadowy figures dressed in rags and trench coats eyed them suspiciously before disappearing down alleys. Less-fortunate souls leaned against the grunge of the buildings, looking like living skeletons; junkies, unable to care about anything beyond their next fix. A fire slowly rose inside Sol as he looked at them, and he quickened his pace to be rid of the scene.

Clouds formed like gray mountains on the horizon, giving the town a bleaker appearance than usual. Thunder rumbled in the distance, and Solomand felt a drop of rain cool the back of his neck as they reached the door of patchwork tin. It rattled as he brought his fist down on it.

"Bazel! Come on out. I need a word with you."

There was the sound of shuffling within the building, followed by the sound of breaking glass and swearing. Solomand knocked again.

"I know you're there, old man."

Another ironhorse buzzed by, raising a spray of dirty water as it tore through a puddle. They crossed the street and Zee's hand grasped his. Solomand's fingers closed around hers. Raindrops battered on tin like an off-tempo drumbeat. Indiscernible grumbling sounded as the door cracked open and a man wearing thick-rimmed glasses and a droopy scowl peeked out.

"What d'ya want, Captain Black?" Bazel asked in a gruff voice. Thinning white hair drooped over the sides of his face.

"A word," Solomand said, pulling Zee by the hand as he shoved his way into the warehouse.

Bazel made a noise like a low growl as he stepped out of their way. "Word about what then? I expect it's about that friend of yours, eh?" He coughed behind a knobby hand.

Solomand had not gotten as far as thinking up a reason to talk to Bazel. He pushed his cap up.

"Well now, what else would it be about?" He asked, trying to sound nonchalant. He had no clue what the old man was talking about, but would not let on that they didn't.

Bazel shut the door, shuffling to a chair lit by a single electric lamp. It illuminated the ghostly shapes of the junk he collected, stretching back to the extent of the thirty-foot building. He sat down in his chair and coughed again, his eyes bulging even more through the lenses he wore.

"Well now, what's that know-how worth to you, Captain? Information ain't free, you know?"

It could be. But Solomand was not thinking of loose-lipped female gossips this time. Bazel had piqued his interest. He bent down and produced a dagger from his boot.

"How about I cut off a piece of your ear to make it match the other one, eh?" His voice was humorless.

Bazel glared at him, a hand going to his scarred left ear. "Alright," he snarled, eyeing the blade as Solomand used it to clean his fingernails. He settled back into his chair, looking resigned to the fact he'd let a venomous snake into his den. "Came in 'bout a month ago. Looking for, well, I expect you know."

Solomand didn't. His eyes narrowed. "How do you know he's a friend of mine?"

"He has that look about him. You can't mistake your type. What's more, he's got that tattoo on his neck." Bazel pointed to the side of his own neck as he spoke.

No.

17

Solomand knew now who the old man was talking about, and the room spun. For a moment, the steady pattering of rain on the tin above them was all he heard. Then, his blade was up against the old man's throat, his eyes flashing with anger.

"Where. Is. He?"

Bazel held his shaking hands over his head. "Someplace down in the slums where those sorts go—Booker Street!" He shouted.

In the back of the building, something clanged to the floor. Jank better have found what they needed. The constriction in his chest would not allow Sol to stay any longer.

Solomand released Bazel and shoved the knife back into his boot. "Thanks for being so... accommodating." He forced a smile and turned away from the old man, fighting to keep his breathing under control.

The old man spit. "You'll get yours soon enough, Captain Black."

Solomand loosened his collar, giving Bazel a grim smile. "Won't we all?"

The old man hobbled to the door and slammed it behind them. Solomand looked up at the pouring sky as they went to meet the others. He shoved his hands in his coat pocket to conceal the slight tremor.

Booker Street.

Zee's boots splashed in puddles as she worked to keep up with his pace. "Sol, who was he talking about?" she asked, pressing her cap down on her head as a gust of wind threatened to pull it away.

"I don't think you'd remember him," Solomand said. Jank and Will were nearing the Platform up ahead. The engineer lugged a burlap bag, almost as big as he was. Solomand lengthened his stride, not wanting to answer any more of Zee's questions.

Not yet.

Rain crashed down like a heavy curtain all around, making the docked airships challenging to see. Jank was already up the ramp to the *Osprey*, bent under the weight of the fuel cell. Will stooped to give him a hand.

Solomand turned to make sure the girl was still at his side. To his horror, she wasn't.

"Zee!" he yelled, his heart in his throat.

A cry rang out—quickly muffled by the rumble of thunder. Lightning cracked across the sky, lighting up the platform long enough for Solomand to see Zee being dragged toward the Argos airship by a scarfed man in mud-colored robes.

He didn't draw his revolver or stop to think. Tearing down the platform, a sudden, deadly feeling rose inside of him like a violent storm. Before the slaver had time to react, Solomand pulled Zee from his grip. With one swing, he laid the man out on the docks in front of his ship.

Zee was shaking, her eyes wide with shock. Solomand drew his knife. "Get to the ship," he told her, turning his dark gaze to the man on the ground.

She turned and ran. Solomand's vision went red. Will was standing next to him, and he heard himself give an order. "Hold him."

Will dragged the slaver to his feet, and Solomand took a step forward. There was a defiance in the man's black eyes that he couldn't stand. He'd meant to steal the girl away to a life across the oceans of subjugation and misery, after all she had been through already!

"You should have stayed on Argos," his voice was a low rumble, and his hand flashed forward.

The man's screams raised above the thunder. His hands moved to the gaping hole where his right eye was moments before. Will let go of him, and he fell to his knees, still shrieking, red staining his soaking clothes.

Rain dripped red from Solomand's knife as it washed the blood away. He pointed it at the man once more and stooped down, yelling, so he was sure to hear. "You tell the rest of your slave-trading bastards, this is what happens when you cross Solomand Black!"

Returning the knife to his boot, he strode away, leaving the man to his misery. He walked slower, letting the rain cool his temper. If he was honest, the savageness of his action frightened him. But not enough to regret it. If faced with a similar situation, he would do it again.

Will walked next to him, his face blank, unjudging. Solomand was grateful for this. He wanted to put this mess behind him as soon as possible. Will spoke through the noise of rain. "We're heading straight for Ashbury, Captain?"

Solomand wanted nothing more, but Bazel's revelation preyed on his mind. He couldn't go yet, or he would never forgive himself.

"I… there's something I have to do before we leave." He took a shaky breath. "Will you go with me?"

Will's hand gripped his shoulder. "Of course, Sol. Where to?"

Solomand swallowed. "Booker Street," he said. It had to be now, or he would lose his nerve.

The human skeletons they passed earlier were still lining the streets, not caring about the downpour. Solomand cringed, afraid of what they would find on Booker Street. Soaked to the bone, his skin felt icy. But that was not what made him shiver.

As they reached a broken wood sign with the street name on it, a man in a trench coat and top hat greeted them. "You Gentlemen looking for quality merchandise?" He asked, his beady, blue eyes hungry for new customers. Solomand grabbed him by the throat and lifted him from the ground.

"No, actually. We're looking for someone."

Through choking sounds, the man squeaked, "I don't know names, Cap'n! It's all part of anonymity—gah!" Solomand squeezed before lowering him to the ground.

"He has a spider tattoo on his neck," he said, wiping a handful of water from his face.

The flicker of fear passed across the dealer's face. "Ah. Him. He's holed up down the street in number seventeen." He pointed to a ramshackle house in between two low garages.

Solomand pushed past the man without another word. The door was ajar, and no lights were lit in the building, or anywhere else on the street. Holding a hand across his mouth, he stepped inside. Broken glass littered the floor where dead rats were strewn casually about the room. The smell reminded Solomand of things he'd seen in the war, filling him with insistent desperation to leave. If Will had not stood at his side, he might have.

Then, he laid eyes on what he feared; the shadow of a man he once knew leaned against the wall amid a pile of tiny shimmering bottles. His head, where there should have been brown hair, was shaved. A rolled-up sleeve revealed dark puncture marks.

He's done it to himself. A bitter voice inside Solomand whispered. *He doesn't want you interfering.*

Even if it was true, Solomand could not honor such a wish. Not anymore.

"Ivan?" Solomand's boots crunched on debris as he took a step towards the man.

Cold eyes opened, stabbing at Solomand with an accusing look that made his stomach turn. Solomand knew he deserved it, but that didn't make it sting any less.

"What the hell have you done to yourself?"

There was no answer. Ivan's head tilted back against the wall, and he slurred something in his native tongue Solomand couldn't make out. He decided.

"You're coming with us," he said.

Ivan's eyes did not open. "I will not leave this place. Except maybe in coffin," he muttered.

"That will damn well happen if you stay here any longer." Solomand rang the water from his cap before returning it to his head.

"Better to go in coffin than with you, *Captain* Black." There was no small measure of contempt in his voice.

Solomand stood over him, wanting the Ice Wolf to stand up. To fight him. Anything.

"To hell with you then, you Slavik bastard!" He slung a piece of the rotting board from the collapsing ceiling over Ivan's head, expecting him to dodge it and knock him across the room. Instead, Ivan fell to the floor, unconscious.

21

"Shit." Solomand's shoulders slumped, staring at his friend's limp form and fighting back a rising sickness.

It couldn't be Ivan laying there, more dead than alive. Breaking himself from the thoughts he knew would send him over the edge, he turned to Will.

"Let's get him back to the ship."

Will lifted the Slav over his shoulders and carry him alone, something he never would have been able to do six years ago. "We taking him to Ashbury?" he asked Sol as they walked back out into the rain.

"No. I'll have Zee take him back to the Castle in the Sky Rail," Solomand said. He saw the dealer approaching another junkie, slipping him a small vial.

The bastard.

He couldn't force it on his hapless clients if they didn't want to take it. The still voice of reason was smothered under a blanket of fury. Falling behind Will, he circled back and came up behind the man. He'd ruined enough lives to give up his own, and only one life was too many for Solomand to stomach.

The dealer did not cry out when the blade slit his throat. He slumped to the ground as Solomand cleaned his knife on the black coat and then walked away without sparing the man another glance.

CHAPTER 4

RAYN

RAYN WATCHED THE colors of the sky fade and transform as the day, like all the others before it, drew to an end. Once again, she had broken the promise she made to herself that today would be different. The air filled with the smell of exhaust as passenger ships and scout skiffs came into the dock for the night. Tattered flags of orange and red fluttered in the breeze, markers for pilots. A flagger waved the last airship in, steering it clear of the smaller skiffs. It docked at the port with a heavy clank, blocking the smooth flow of purple and orange clouds around the setting sun.

As a mid-class vessel, it was sad looking even among the smaller airships. *Osprey* was painted in letters that looked like they were melting off the rust-tinged shutters. It was oblong with the standard three-decks. These ships could support a few passengers for longer trips, but their primary purpose was delivering supplies to more isolated outposts. The *Osprey*, however, looked like it would not survive another run. The massive propellant fan on the back let out a whine that sounded like nails scraping against metal. Rayn cringed as she turned and shuffled away with a sigh. There was no point in watching the sunset if that depressing piece of machinery was blocking the view.

A group of women dressed in corsets and long skirts laughed together, waving and blowing kisses at the pilots on the docks.

Rayn scowled and crossed to the other side of the road, shoving her right hand deep in her pants pocket. Her fingers clasped around the medallion she always carried, and the restless stirring inside her grew a little more intense than the day before.

Every dusk as the ships docked, crowds of bored villagers flocked to the platform, hopeful of stories and supplies or spendthrift sailors eager to buy a night's company. Everyone involved was rather stupid and Rayn hurried away from them, to the outskirts of the dull little sky port. Shouting and laughter drifted through the alleys behind her, along with the faint sound of boots thumping on the dirt path. The footsteps grew louder, rising above the noise of people cavorting through the town, but Rayn did not turn around.

Tomorrow I'm leaving, she promised herself again. This was not her home, and it never would be.

Her pace quickened until she reached the small shop on the village's edge, nestled between two large trees. The battered sign blazoned with 'Gunsmith' shifted on its hinges in the warm breeze. She stared at the word for a moment, then sighed before turning the lock and pushing the door open. There was no work, except for the rifle of that idiot boy Gabriel Glass, which she was in no rush to fix.

Tomorrow would be the day she'd walk into one of those airships and never looked back. Except, there had been countless tomorrows where she couldn't quite follow through. She bit her lip, mad at herself for being such a coward.

The smell of oil and metal mingled with the scent of grass as she stepped inside. The door slammed shut, then burst open again. Someone staggered into the shop, causing Rayn to jump with alarm. She spun around and backed against the tool bench, drawing her revolver in one fluid motion.

"Are you the gunsmith?" the man asked, then jerked his hands up. "Easy." He gulped, backing away, his steel-blue eyes fixed on the gun-barrel inches from his face. "I don't want trouble. I have a business proposition."

"Who are you?" Rayn asked. Her eyes narrowed. "What kind of proposition?"

The choking smell of tobacco filled the room. He looked to be in his mid-twenties, the same as her, wore a navy-blue overcoat and calf boots in the fashion of an aviator. His sleeves slumped down, revealing a leather cuff around his left wrist with a flat dial and flashing buttons on the front; it was a transmitter; pilots often wore these to communicate with their crew.

"My name is Solomand Black." He inched his hands down. "And I am in rather urgent need of a gunsmith aboard my ship."

An airship Captain. Rayn lowered her revolver. "What could you possibly need a gunsmith for aboard a passenger vessel?" Her head tilted back.

The Coalition prohibited airship guns since the end of the war, but that didn't stop marauders or pirates from equipping themselves, and it was risky business getting involved with those sorts of people. Once you were on the wrong side of the Coalition, it was impossible to go back—or so she'd overheard.

Solomand ran a hand through his disheveled coal-black hair. "Well, it's sort of a, refurbished, passenger vessel. Sensitive cargo is more my line of work." His brow furrowed. "It's for defense." He glanced out the window at the settling dusk, a nervous look crossing his face again. "I can pay you whatever you want, but I have to leave here in." He dug out a pocket watch and glanced at the ticking hands. "Ten minutes ago."

Rayn returned her revolver to the holster on her thigh. "Whatever I want?" She tucked a strand of auburn hair behind her ear and reached into her pocket. The metal was warm against her palm as she clasped the medallion again. She didn't believe in fate, but this could be her chance to find the answers she needed.

"Yes!" Solomand leaned forward on his toes, his eyes searching the darkening sky out the window. He stuffed the watch back in his pocket. "We'll be gone for about two months—what do you say..." His eyes trailed up and down her body. "I'm sorry, I didn't catch your name." He took a step closer and flashed her a smile she presumed he meant to be charming.

Rayn crossed her arms, giving him a disenchanted look. "Rayn." She eyed him with suspicion, although he wasn't unattractive.

"Rayn. What a beautiful name," Solomand leaned forward, trying to catch her gaze. "Just Rayn?"

"Yeah." Her lips pursed together in a tight line, annoyed for having allowed the previous thought to slip into her mind.

Solomand abandoned his ill attempts to be suave and pulled out his watch again. His eyes grew wider when he saw the time, and his gaze darted back to the window. "Well then, what do you say, Rayn? Do we have a deal?"

Rayn's bag was already sitting on her bed, packed and waiting. She had, however, acquired no travel papers or passports. It was a complicated legal process, and she doubted whether she could get them at all. If any of her legal certificates existed, she had yet to locate them. There had been a fire, she was told, and most of her belongings were destroyed. Her only option to leave without those papers was to stowaway or find a Captain who wasn't keen on asking too many questions.

Solomand Black seemed like every other pilot in one respect: ready to flirt with anything but probably harmless. Rayn was confident she could handle his type. And he was unlikely to ask about her identification.

"Two months." She ran her fingertip along the narrow scar under her chin, thinking.

"At the most. I need an answer soon—I should have already left." He glanced over his shoulder at the door as he tugged nervously on his sweat-stained shirt collar.

Rayn had no intention of coming back, but she was enjoying making Solomand Black squirm. Besides, she wasn't about to let him know how eager she was to accept his offer. She chewed on her bottom lip and breathed out.

"I might be able to spare the time," she relented.

Solomand's shoulders relaxed as he let out a sigh of relief.

26

"Thank god. I was afraid I'd have to take you at gunpoint," he chuckled. Then he winked. "Just joking. I'm not a pirate."

Rayn gave him the scathing look that always worked to silence smart-mouthed customers who had anything to say about the price of her work. Solomand cleared his throat, averting her gaze.

"Alright, well, best get your stuff so we can get the hell out of here."

He pulled a cigarette case from his pocket. It slipped from his fingers and clanged on the floor. Solomand scrambled to pick up the scattered bits of black tobacco before hurriedly rolling a cigarette.

"Fine by me, Captain Black." Rayn stepped behind the bench and pushed open the door to her room.

The chirping of crickets drifted in from an open window. Rayn stood by the unmade bed and paused. The room was bare of any personal items, except for the black rifle leaning in the corner.

Rayn looked around. A little voice inside her head tried explaining the insanity of her actions. There was nothing for her here, except the gun of that asinine adolescent. It would probably do the town a service if she didn't finish that job.

Am I really going to leave? She didn't know the man who waited outside her room, yet she wasn't worried about jumping aboard his ship and leaving town.

He's like all the other idiot pilots.

Solomand Black was nothing she couldn't handle.

Still, she had more or less decided this was a permanent move. If anyone else had done the same, Rayn would have been the first one to point out how idiotic the plan was. But something inside her told the voice of caution to be silent.

She pulled out the medallion and traced her fingers along the missing triangular piece at the bottom of the oval. Around a small compass in the gold-tinged metal was the inscription *I will come for you- S.L.* The S and the L were on either side of the missing triangle's point. Aside from the rifle, this was the only clue to her past. The words on it made her more determined than ever.

Rayn squeezed her fingers around the medallion before shoving it back in her pocket.

"No more waiting," she muttered and snatched a pair of fingerless leather gloves off the bureau. She pulled them on to her elbows and slung the satchel from her bed over her shoulder. She grabbed the rifle and ran her hands over the smooth, black stock before hooking it over her shoulder with a belt of ammunition.

Time to leave this place behind.

She glanced around the room one more time, her heart beating with excitement as she pushed the door to the shop open. A low, ringing sound rose above the noise of insects outside the window, and the airship captain's transmitter emitted a frantic beeping.

"Get down!" Solomand jetted across the room and slammed into her before she had time to react. They both crashed to the floor as bullets splintered the walls over their heads. Her rifle slid from her shoulder, the bolt digging into her side as she hit the ground.

It took Rayn a moment to catch her breath.

"Get off," she gasped, coughing as she wriggled from beneath Solomand.

"Keep down! He pressed her closer to the floor as another round of bullets broke out, hitting lower this time.

"What the hell is going on?" Rayn yelled, her nose against the floorboards.

The demoralizing ring gave her the panicky feeling of being underwater.

"Shit!" Solomand rolled onto his back, sliding closer to her. "That's the 201st Airborne Division out there."

"The *what*?" Rayn's heart pounded against the floor. "What's a damned Coalition unit doing all the way out here?" She turned to glare at him. "Just who the hell are you?"

Avoiding a legal matter of travel papers was one thing. But dealing with the 201st Airborne was another.

What the hell was I thinking?

She realized too late she should have kicked him out the moment she set eyes on him. Or shot him.

A deafening boom silenced Solomand's reply. The shell tore a massive hole through the roof, and wood fragments and plastered showered on top of them.

"Those bastards are fast," Solomand remarked, spitting out a mouthful of white dust

Shouts rang out in unison with pounding feet on the roof. The 201st's airship, *Pandora*, whirred overhead. Rayn coughed as she breathed in the debris-filled air.

I'm going to die here.

Her thoughts were on the medallion again. There was a nudge in her ribs, and she turned to Solomand. He brought his face closer to hers, and Rayn could see the growing terror in his eyes.

"We have to get out of here!" He gasped for breath between coughs.

Something fell through the hole in the roof and clanked on the ground a few feet away. More muffled shouts sounded out as the object fizzled, and the shop filled with pungent white smoke. Rayn curled her legs into her stomach, gagging as her lungs filled with a burning sensation.

Solomand coughed again.

Sounding more collected than he should have been, he announced, "Time to go."

Hurling a metallic object over his shoulder, he yanked her to her feet and held her by the arm as he sprinted to the door.

There was a "clank" on the wall as the 201st jumpers descended through the roof. A fiery blast followed shouting. Something hot ripped through Rayn, and her side erupted in pain. Fighting nausea, she forced herself to run alongside Solomand Black under the cover of a heated smog among the noise of shouts and gunfire. The shadow of the airship Pandora loomed over them.

CHAPTER 5

Rayn

FIRE SPREAD THROUGH Rayn's chest as she pushed herself to keep up with Solomand. He dragged her alongside him as they sprinted through the billowing smoke, breathing in the sulfuric air. Her eyes burned in the swirling blackness as Solomand maneuvered through the volley of bullets that whizzed past on either side of them. Their boots kicking up bits of gravel, they tore down the path toward the center of town and out of the thick air.

The unusual commotion shattered the peaceful evening in Port Ashbury and brought the town's residents to their doors. When they saw the imposing shape of the *Pandora* above, they retreated, barring their windows and doors. Not one of them was crazy enough to risk getting involved with the 201st. The airmen were legendary for leaving a wake of destruction behind wherever they went, no matter how neutral the territory was.

It felt like water filled her ears and her vision blurred. She made out the outline of Solomand's airship docked at the sky port.

Oh hell.

Her spirit sank, realizing it was the sad ship she'd seen earlier. Not a match for a three-legged dog, let alone an S-Class attack ship. The *Pandora* drifted closer, the noise it generated drowning out the sound of the passenger vessel's turbines. Still pulling her along, Solomand clambered up the grated metal ramp and they both dove into the open doors of a cargo bay. Sprawled on the cold steel floor, Rayn coughed up a mix of mucous and grime.

"What the hell, Solomand!" An agitated yell carried through the hull.

Wiping her mouth with the back of her hand, Rayn looked up to see a wiry young man in an engineer's jumpsuit running toward them. Lines of grease streaked his brown hair. Swinging a wrench in the air, he stared murder at Solomand. Dark circles underlined his light brown eyes, making it look like he hadn't slept in days.

"You didn't waste any time bringing those bastards on our heels! I just got these damned engines working properly!"

"Then we shouldn't have anything to worry about, should we, Jank?"

Solomand jumped up and clapped a hand on the young man's shoulder before running past him, yelling, "Will! Get us the hell out of here!"

He cleared the stairs two at a time and disappeared.

Jank stabbed his finger at a panel by the doors, muttering obscenities before dashing away. Rayn rolled to her side and glimpsed the approaching *Pandora* before the bay doors slid shut. With its menacing, black airfoils and sleek, crafted nose, it looked like a dark cloud in the sky moving towards them, unstoppable. For a moment, it reminded her of a fierce eagle before it snatched up its prey in readied claws.

And we're the prey.

She thought of Solomand's ship, dwarfed by the mighty Pandora. There's no way he can outrun them. There was a sickening feeling of dying hope in her stomach as she sat up.

"Brace yourselves. We're about to shake these pelicans." Solomand's voice sounded over the intercom.

The little airship shot forward. With a jolt, Rayn skidded across the floor, grabbing for something to cling to. The wall came straight at her.

I never should have gotten out of bed today!

She slammed into the hull, pain exploding in her head as everything went a starry black.

When Rayn came to, she thought she was dreaming.

"You've finally done it."

She heard the low rumble of a man's voice. The sound of boots clanking on the metal flooring drew nearer.

"After six years." She recognized Solomand's gruff tone. "And I'll be damned if I'll let those—"

He stopped mid-sentence as he arrived back in the cargo bay. The man he was with was a head taller than Solomand, skin a deep, olive tone. A jagged scare peeked out either ends of an eye patch over his left eye. Solomand wore a panicked expression when he saw her. He ran to her side, while his companion walked behind him at an unhurried pace.

Rayn sat up, untangling a hand from her hair and stood. She doubled over as a barrage of stabbing pains jabbed throughout her body.

"Are you alright?" Solomand's eyes widened as he dropped to one knee.

He looked her over, searching for any injuries. As she realized this was not a dream, all Rayn could see when she looked at Solomand was the smoke and flames billowing from her shop. He was the one responsible for it.

You weren't planning to go back. A chiding voice reminded. Her anger intensified. *That's not the point!*

"Rayn!" He took her head in his hands. His fingers were callous against her skin. "Are you alright?"

He tilted her head from side to side. Rayn was too groggy to protest at first. She stared for a moment, her thoughts beginning to settle, the pangs becoming duller.

She jerked her head free from his grasp.

"I'm fine," she snapped, unable to hide her flinch at the acute pain surging through her head. She slumped back, falling into the other man's arms. The belt of ammo she had been carrying slid from her shoulder and clattered on the floor. Rayn looked down, the fog on her mind lifting as a horrifying realization set in.

"My rifle."

It was the Medved, a Slavik design. Her second most prized possession could not have withstood the blaze. The vision of the black stock, twisted and scalding, flashed before her.

"Your rifle?" Solomand's look of worry passed for a moment and he laughed. He actually *laughed*. "Don't worry. I'll find you another one."

He attempted to look her over again.

Rayn's lips pursed together, her face growing hot. She could hear a hammering noise in her ears as adrenalin rushed to her head. She thought of the work she had put into restoring the Medved. She polished it for hours, coaxing all the dents and scratches from the barrel and receiver. The protective coating of velvety slow rust-blue took weeks to complete. And most of all, the stock was from the Black Ash, an almost impossible wood to find.

"It. Was. Irreplaceable!" She said through clenched teeth. Her hands were shaking now as they balled into fists at her sides. "That means there isn't another one!"

"Look, I'm sorry." In his defense, Solomand sounded apologetic. But it didn't matter.

"Sorry?" She shoved free of the other man's grasp, drew back, and punched him in the nose. Her hand throbbing, she glared at him.

Solomand staggered backward with a startled expression, his hand moving to his bleeding nose. A tear rolled from the corner of his eye as he stared at her with a shocked expression. The *Osprey* shuddered and lurched to one side.

"Take her to a cabin, Will."

Solomand darted back down the corridor, his head upturned as he clutched his nose. Blood trickled down the sides of his face. Rayn stared after him, her heart still racing.

"I'm sorry, but you're liable to get a concussion if you stay here—the way Sol flies," the man called Will said.

His tone was steady, almost void of emotion. Rayn turned her eyes to him, tilting her head back to meet his gaze. His muscular stature made him look like his last job was something to do with intimidating people. He wore a gray, button-up shirt with the sleeves rolled up past his elbows—clean and tucked into his trousers. The light in his single eye made it appear several shades of brown, ranging from reddish to the dark color of earth. There was a kindness in his expression that seemed unfitting for his stature.

With an amused grin on his face, he asked, "Are you coming, Rayn?"

Rayn could tell he wanted to keep his distance, but would also have no issue throwing her over his shoulder. She had no desire to experience any more of Solomand's piloting skills from the cargo bay, anyway. She nodded, biting her tongue, still too furious to speak.

Will picked up her bag from among the scattered tin cans and boxes.

"This way."

He motioned up a spiral staircase of twisted iron, and Rayn followed him.

The hopeless airship shuddered again, and Rayn reached her hand out, catching hold of the riveted walls of the narrow corridor. Will leaned against the wall and kept walking. His broad-shouldered frame nearly filled the hall. They turned down another passage that had four doors on either side. They all had wheel locks like the kind on Rayn's shop door. Will opened the furthest door on the right and stood clear as Rayn stepped inside the cramped cabin.

"Sorry," Will looked sympathetic as he sat Rayn's bag down inside. "Sol will be along after we lose the *Pandora*."

The *Osprey* swayed to the left, causing Rayn to fall sideways. She landed on a bunk. Will caught himself on the door frame with little effort.

"This is going to be harder than the last time," he said. Then, after a pause, "It always is."

34

Last time? It always is?

"Terrific," Rayn muttered.

Her shoulders slumped as she ran her hand on the rough fleece blanket, watching the gears on the lock turn, sliding the bolts into place with a clank. As Will's footsteps faded from earshot, she sank onto the flat pillow.

Another bolt of pain shot through her side.

"Owe!"

She looked down and saw blood seeping from a tear in her vest. Groaning with annoyance, she undid the four clasps and opened it the rest of the way, her hand shaking the entire time.

Her cream-colored shirt was torn and soaked red; blood still oozed from the gash in her side.

It's not that bad, Rayn told herself.

She hoped it wasn't, anyway. She felt ill. Her head throbbed and her nose still burned from the odorous gas the 201st had dropped. Light-headed and sick to her stomach, she slumped back onto the bed, tearing the blanket loose. She closed her eyes and feebly pressed the fleece into her wound. It probably wouldn't matter. As the airship tipped from side to side, she didn't see how such a horrible pilot as Solomand Black could ever evade the Coalition's most elite airship.

⚙

Silence hung in the town square like a heavy summer fog, filling the air with an uneasiness, even a girl of ten could feel. Rayn hid behind the crates, covering her nose with her sleeve to shield it from the scent of rotting vegetables and fish. Easing up on tiptoes, she peeked through the wooden slots to get a glimpse of the scene playing out.

Her heart pounded with fear as she watched the officers drag the barefoot boy into the midst of the crowd. He looked to be about ten; the same age as Rayn. His skinny arms were tied behind his back. His clothes were patched, frayed and filthy. The constables forced him roughly to his knees. One cracked a short whip across his

35

neck, saying something in a sinister voice. Rayn sucked in a breath as she heard the whip tear at the boy's skin, but the boy didn't make a sound. Her heartbeat seemed to be the only noise in the horrible silence.

'Why don't they do anything? She thought in anger of the crowd.

Her fingers trembled in rage, and she snatched up a chunk of rock from the ground. She wanted to help the boy, but someone had told her to stay here. Someone important to her. Glaring savagely at the gray-uniformed backs of the coalition officers, her eyes fixed on the boy again.

He stared up at the men through uneven, black hair that fell over his eyes. One man raised his whip again, but the boy gave a defiant grin, and his reply broke through that harrowing quiet of compliance.

"Do what you want, Choiro!"

The word was in another language—an insult—and Rayn recognized it, though she didn't know what it meant. The man raised his hand to strike the boy, but he did not flinch, the defiant grin still on his face.

The image faded.

Damn it, no!

Rayn tried to hold on to the dream, desperate to remember more. Who was the boy? Was he the one she was looking for? She felt confident with a little more time she could remember, but the dreams were always cut short. Warm fingertips touching her skin jarred her awake. Solomand stooped over her, his hand slipping beneath her shirt.

"Get off me. Pervert!" She said, jerking her handgun from the holster and smacking the startled captain across the head.

"Gah!" Solomand fell backward, holding his head, his face twisted in pain. "Will, grab her."

36

Will took hold of Rayn's wrist and wrenched the pistol from her hand.

"You sure this was a good idea?" he asked, eyeing Solomand's bleeding head.

Solomand gave Will a dark look. Will shrugged but kept his distance as Solomand turned to Rayn.

"Alright, you're going to stop this crazy bashing me in the head shit right now! You're hurt, and if I don't do something about it soon, you'll not be able to lift that damned oversized pistol of yours!"

Rayn glanced at the medical kit on the floor, the stabbing pain in her side reminding her of the bleeding injury. She realized Solomand had been trying to help her, not feel her up.

He was probably enjoying it, she told herself to extinguish the growing shame.

"What are you, a doctor now?" She scooted away, which made her dizzy.

Solomand massaged the bleeding welt on his temple.

"No. But I've patched enough wounds to know what the hell I'm doing." He cringed as he raised himself to one knee. "Now, are you going to let me do this the easy way, or does he have to hold you down?"

He thumbed a finger toward Will. Rayn thought he looked like he wanted to say something to Solomand but was holding it back. Her hands shook as she tried to prop herself up.

Do I have a choice?

She considered the unpleasantness of being held down by the giant, but what was the point? Solomand was right. She nodded as she lay back down, not wanting either of them to see how weak she really was.

Solomand took her wrist. His touch was gentler than she expected. As he frowned, worried lines formed around his eyes, somehow making the steely blue more intense.

"Will." Rayn was relieved when Solomand looked away. "Bring some water, will you?"

Will nodded, lumbering across the room in two long strides. Rayn gazed at the door as it closed behind him, dreading being left alone with the airship captain who had destroyed her world in a manner of hours. Her heart was racing so fast her chest ached.

Probably dehydration.

She licked her lips as she glanced back to Solomand. He was rifling through the med-kit. Rayn felt a twinge of guilt as she looked at the bloody welt on the side of his head. It would have been easier to dismiss the feeling if he showed any sign of a grudge. He didn't.

She inhaled, holding her breath as Solomand's hand touched her side. His eyes lingered for a moment on a scar over Rayn's stomach; the discolored lines of smooth skin cut into a black, irregular shaped birthmark. It looked like someone had tried to piece her back together after an accident. Rayn often traced the outlines, wondering what happened to make her skin look that way. Solomand, to her best estimate, appeared to turn a shade lighter. He looked up, wearing a weak smile.

"This will probably hurt like hell."

Rayn gritted her teeth and laid her head back against the bed. "Just do it."

She glared at the ceiling and twisted fistfuls of blanket in each hand as Solomand eased a giant splinter out of her flesh.

"Sorry." His eyes narrowed as he concentrated on getting the rest of it out. "That's the worst of it, though."

He set the tweezers down and picked up a bottle of antiseptic, which he splashed on the wound.

"Ahh!" Rayn yelled, jerking upright as the searing sting spread across her side.

Solomand placed a firm hand on her arm and eased her back down.

"I lied."

"Bas—tard!" Rayn gasped out in two breaths as Solomand packed clean gauze into the side and skillfully bandaged the wound.

"Sorry."

"Liar!"

Solomand grinned and sat back on his heels. His eyes narrowed into an intense gaze as he stared at her again. Rayn felt the uneasy sense that he was searching for something, then light rushed to her head before she collapsed back onto the pillow. The last thing she remembered was the strained frown on the airship captain's face before her eyes drooped shut.

⁓✷⁓

Solomand stumbled out of the cabin where Rayn lay unconscious but stable. His hands shook as he turned the lock to close the door and stopped, staring at the blood on his fingers—Rayn's blood. As the *Osprey* rocked wildly, he doubled over, unable to keep down the contents of his stomach.

Shit.

He wiped vomit on the back of his hand and slumped against the hull of the ship. Bolts digging into his back, he fought back memories.

No. He forced them from his mind. *Not here. Not now.*

The gradual tightening around his chest felt like someone was trying to squeeze the air from his lungs.

Get up!

His legs refused to listen, and he started crawling forward, breathing quick gasps of air. Glimpsing the bloodstains on his hands, he clamped his eyes shut and dry-heaved.

Solomand didn't hear Will until he clamped his hand on Sol's shoulder.

"Sol."

"Yeah?"

Solomand slowly breathed in, jerking his head up. Will didn't have to say it. He could already hear the high-pitched hum of the *Pandora's* engines. The 201st hadn't taken long to catch up. They would soon be within distance of engaging his airship with their

39

long-range guns. Hopefully, Jank had gotten the new fuel cell in with his own adjustments to increase the power ratio.

"Don't worry." Will squeezed his shoulder. "I'll lose 'em for you."

His boots clanged on the floor as he sprinted away.

"Thanks," Solomand mumbled.

He gulped against the taste of bile in his throat, forced his eyes open, and continued to crawl down the corridor. There was an explosion outside, and the airship violently tilted. Solomand crashed into the hull.

"Son of a…" He rubbed his bruised forehead.

And he talks shit about my flying.

"I'll be right there." He called to no one in particular as he crawled, inching his way toward the flight deck as the corridor light flickered out.

CHAPTER 6

SOLOMAND

HEAT DISTORTIONS ROSE from the engines as the turbines eased to a stop, the whine they emitted sounding like the cry of imminent death. Solomand's hands shook as he lay against the wall where Will's last-minute maneuver had thrown him from his seat. Fuses on the broken control panel popped, sparks flying from frayed wires. The whirr of the *Pandora's* engine dwindled as it sped after the fake stream of gray exhaust—a tracer Jank had rigged for such an occasion. The clouds provided a perfect cover for the *Osprey* to drop into the shadow of trees on a remote landing pad while the Pandora raced after the concocted trail.

This was the third time Jank's clever trick had saved their skin. That and the wooded hills, which spanned for hundreds of miles. They had never failed to escape the Coalition's so-called Hounds of Hell. The only target they never sniffed out was the battered airship no one else would give a second glance.

Solomand slowed his breathing as the 201st's ship faded from earshot.

Safe. For now.

He sat up, groaning as he pressed a hand to his head.

"That was too damn close."

A voice crackled over the intercom.

"That's the sound of the engine *dying*, Sol." Jank's voice became garbled for an instant. "A lot of damn good that fuel cell did!"

41

Solomand rubbed the back of his neck, giving Will a sideways glance.

"You don't think he thinks I was flying, do you?" He was unhappy to admit that even with one eye, Will was a much better pilot than him.

"Give him a minute." Will unclipped his harness and slid from the cracked, leather control seat. "He probably had his sense knocked out."

He offered Solomand a hand.

"Yeah. Might be best to steer clear of him for a while."

Sol took Will's hand, and Will pulled him to his feet.

"You going to check on Rayn?"

Solomand's stomach tightened.

I can't.

He cleared his throat, pulling his gaze away from Will's.

"You do it. I've got to check on our other guest."

He gave his stoic first mate a meaningful look and turned to leave. Will grabbed him by the arm.

"Are you afraid?"

Solomand paused, his eyes locked with Will's scrutinizing stare.

"You see how she is. Damn right, I'm afraid."

Will released his iron grip, his head leaning back as he laughed. Solomand didn't waste any time darting from the door.

"Good luck," he said over his shoulder as he scrambled down the grated planking—careful to avoid meeting Jank—and out the emergency exit.

The light of approaching dusk greeted him as a summer breeze stirred the forest. Solomand's boots thudded rhythmically on the wooden walkway that wound up the valley to the ruins of a castle nestled in the hill's side. It was once an imposing fortress set high in the rim of the surrounding hills. Overgrown vines and trees claimed it now, pulling it back into the wild, hiding it from view by land or air. Memories of himself playing here among the rocks as a boy slipped into his mind as he strode through the ruins, crunching crumbled stones beneath his feet. A man with tattoos on his arms showed him the tracks deer had made in the damp earth as a myst falcon circled the ruins overhead.

No.

Solomand buried the images in a dark corner of his mind where smoke and the smell of blood were locked safely away. Memories like those were dangerous. They might make a man long for something that didn't belong to him, hampering resolve when it was most inconvenient.

Crows ascended from the ground, cawing in indignation as they took to the trees. Solomand spared them an apologetic grin, wiping sweat from his forehead. He breathed easier here as he walked beneath the crumbling exterior of the castle. The last place of freedom; for him and his companions.

At the back of the ruins stood a more modern building, made of wood and concrete; it was not huge, but it was sturdy and well hidden under the remains of the fortress.

A thick, wooden door swung open, and Zee ran out.

"Sol!" She threw her arms around him. "Did you get what you needed from Ashbury?"

Solomand returned the girl's embrace, breathing in as his arms closed around her.

"More or less." His eyes narrowed. "Is that... cigarette smoke?"

Zee laughed, ducking past to go outside.

"Probably from your own coat."

"Right..."

Solomand's brow wrinkled, doubtful, but he had too much on his mind to interrogate her at the moment.

"Where's our guest?"

"In the cellar. Tristan said that would be the safest place. We had a hell of a time getting him down there."

She handed him a small vial.

"Tristan said to give him this."

"Watch your mouth, girl."

43

Solomand frowned at her, staring with contempt at the bottle as his fingers closed around it.

"Sorry," Zee called over her shoulder, already running down toward the dock to meet Will and Jank.

Walking into the door, Solomand made his way down the cramped hall to the far end of the building. His hand paused on the metal doorhandle before he turned it and went inside.

Stairs covered in dust groaned as he trekked downward into the basement. He distracted himself by imagining what kind of hell the *Pandora's* pilot was going to catch when his superiors found out he had lost them. There was a cruelness in his chuckle.

Wish I could be a fly on the wall listening to that conversation. Well, Sir, they just vanished.

His shoulder pressed against the dirt wall, his feet growing heavier as he took the last step onto the basement floor. A tall window cut into the earth let light stream into the building. His throat went dry as he squinted through the iron grates of a makeshift cell in the cellar's corner.

Ivan lay on a cot inside the cell. His ragged shirt was filthy and torn, revealing the black outline of a spider tattoo on the side of his neck. His arms draped over the sides of the cot, grazing the floor. Solomand felt a pang in his chest as he breathed in, wishing he could look away. There was a welt over the man's right eye, which Solomand was responsible for.

Not my fault.

The Slavik's stubbornness was to be reckoned with. Still, Solomand regretted having to take him by force and hated even more that he could. Ivan should have been stronger than he was.

Recalling their conversation in the rotting slum he'd dragged Ivan from made Solomand cringe.

He's going to be pissed.

Dragging a hand through his hair, he breathed out quickly and then unlocked the heavy door. Chains rattled as he undid the lock and threw back the iron-grating. It creaked on its hinges as it opened and shut. The man jerked a hand to his forehead. "Solomand…" he mumbled.

Bloodshot eyes of icy gray shot open. Ivan licked his chapped lips and eased himself off the cot. Stumbling forward on bare feet, he hurled himself at Solomand with a murderous snarl. "I… kill… you!" he rasped.

Solomand grimaced and stepped aside. Ivan crashed into the grating before falling to his knees. The man's dirt-encrusted fingers clung to the grating as he rested there, breathing in loud, labored gasps. He forced himself up and spun around, lunging at Solomand again. This time Solomand threw him back against the door.

For god's sake, Ivan.

There was a time when he would never have been able to beat Ivan in any kind of combat; he was an Ice Wolf, an elite assassin from the North Continent. Ivan had proved that the group's legendary skill was not idle rumors.

Sweat soaked his clothes and was already dripping from his face. Solomand could smell the pungent scent of the drug that had consumed his life. Most people who did not wean themselves off were dead within two days.

Sol's fingers tightened around the small, glass vial in his hand and he wanted to destroy it. He saw a mere shell of the man he used to know—reduced to nothing by this unassuming liquid in his hand. A growing tightness in his chest reminded him whose fault he believed it was.

"Ivan, look what you've done to yourself, you idiot," he said.

"*Zyat!*" Ivan cursed in Slav, shaking the grating, saliva dripping from his mouth. He pulled himself to his feet.

"I've left you alone in that shithole long enough."

Solomand squared his shoulders.

"I'm not letting you kill yourself with that damned Furi any longer!"

Ivan jerked his head up. Dark circles under his eyes accentuated the gauntness of his features.

"You… you bastard son of Kree whore!"

That's it.

Solomand's jaw tightened. He answered this insult with a blow to the face that sent Ivan sprawling against the far corner of the cell.

"You'll not bring my mother into this!" he exclaimed.

Blood seeped through Ivan's fingers as he cupped a hand over his nose, still staring menacingly at Solomand.

"Well, now. I think that's cleared the air, hasn't it?"

Solomand shook his throbbing hand and set the vial on the floor by the cot.

"From Tristan. To help with the withdrawal."

Ivan's eyes widened. His head tilted to one side.

"Tristan?"

Solomand regarded the contents with contempt.

"Yes. He's still alive—more alive than you've been the past five years."

His hand leaned on the door while he looked back at Ivan, locking his gaze with that stony expression. He wanted to say he was sorry—for the blow to the head, for Tristan, for everything. But all he could do was clear his throat and walk away.

A cigarette burning in his hand, Solomand watched from the stairs as Ivan slid forward on his hands and knees until he reached the bottle of furi. His fingers tightened around the vial. He opened it and raised it to his lips. With a furious snarl, he hurled the bottle against the wall. It smashed, the contents nothing more than a dark splatter on the metal. Gnashing his teeth, Ian ran a hand over his head, leaving a smear of blood before collapsing back on the cot.

Solomand felt a mixture of relief and fear as he eyed the glistening liquid dripping to the floor. If anyone could quit Furi like that and survive, it would be Ivan.

Hang in there, Ice Wolf.

He took a shaky drag on his cigarette and crept up the stairs.

CHAPTER 7

RAYN

THE DARK-HAIRED BOY fell to the ground as the guard struck him across the face. He stood over the boy and raised his hand. Rayn stood up, not caring if anyone saw her. Her heart pounded, and she took a step towards the square. The whip cracked through the air, but instead of the boy's face, it wound around a wooden staff.

"Leave him, Ranger," a gruff voice demanded.

The man who it belonged to towered over the guard in a menacing way, his back toward Rayn. Her shoulders relaxed as she breathed out a sigh of relief.

"He's a thief! And you shouldn't interfere in matters that don't concern you," the guard snarled but shrank away.

The man took a step forward, his staff directed towards the guard.

"You go back to your own jurisdiction and leave crimes in The Mud to me."

Rayn didn't hear the rest of the conversation. Her eyes were on the boy. He rolled over, inched forward on his stomach, and slipped away down an alley before either man could stop him.

"Wait!" Rayn tried to call after him. "What's your name?"

47

Rayn was awake long before she opened her eyes. The pain in her side was still there, but at least the headache had dulled. Hot and sweaty, she rolled over. Solomand sat at the foot of her bunk, an intense gaze fixed on her.

It felt like a knife stabbed into Rayn's side as she jerked herself upright.

"What the hell are you doing here?" She kicked at Solomand, catching him in the ribs with the heel of her boot in spite of him throwing up his hands in defense.

It felt like sandpaper had been scraped down her throat.

Solomand fell off the bunk, catching himself with one hand and grabbing his ribs with the other.

"Shit." His face contorted in pain. "I only came to check on you!" He retreated a few steps. "And... I only just got here," he added, as if he knew what she was thinking.

With an injured look, he pointed to a fresh pitcher of water sitting on the table by her bunk. Rayn gave him one last glare and snatched it up, water drizzling down the sides of her mouth as she tipped it back and drank.

Solomand took a cautious step toward her.

"Here," he said, drawing a paper packet from his vest and holding it out. "It's for the headache."

Rayn's eyes narrowed in suspicion.

How did he know I had a headache?

"The gas the 201st dropped in your shop can cause them for days after you're exposed to it," he said.

She set the empty pitcher down and wiped her mouth on the back of her sleeve. Not breaking eye contact with him, she took the packet. Solomand jerked his hand back like he was feeding a lion a slab of meat. He studied Rayn while she swallowed the bitter-tasting powder.

"Why are they after you, anyway?"

Solomand shrugged. "It's really a simple case of mistaken identity."

"Mistaken identity?"

Rayn cradled her head in her arms.

"Yes. Their dimwitted jackass of a commander has me mistaken with someone else. Apparently."

Rayn threw one leg over the side of the bed. "Who does he mistake you with?"

Solomand's brow furrowed.

"Someone from the war. Someone he never caught... because he's a dimwitted jackass."

His face clouded, and he crossed his arms. Rayn decided not to ask anymore, for now.

"Hungry?"

Captain Black seemed eager to change the subject.

"Yeah."

Rayn ran fingers through her tangled hair, trying to recall the last time she ate.

"Feel up for a walk, or shall I have something brought to you?"

"I can walk," Rayn said, scowling as she forced herself to stand.

The room felt like it was spinning, but she would not let him think she couldn't handle herself.

Solomand raised an eye.

"You sure?"

"Yes."

Rayn pressed a palm against her forehead. Talking made her head hurt worse.

Solomand held his hands up, shrugging at the same time.

"Alright, suit yourself. Follow me, then."

Rayn stepped out into the narrow corridor and followed him, her hand trailing against the wall for support. The smell of Solomand's tobacco, combined with the lack of air, made the pounding in her head grow worse.

"You can meet the rest of the crew—well, most of them, anyway," Solomand said over his shoulder as they made their way down the dimly lit passage.

Rayn wished he would be quiet. It was hard enough to concentrate on walking. A cold, dizzying feeling worked its way through her body, and she broke into a sweat. Leaning on the wall with her shoulder, she paused, pressing a hand to her head.

"Are you alright?" Solomand asked.

She glanced up to see him shaking his head at her.

"I'm fine," she mumbled, not as assertive as she would have liked.

"Here." She tried to jerk away as he took her by the arm. "Would you rather pass out and me have to carry you back to your room?"

"No." Rayn scowled in defeat and put her arm over his shoulders, leaning her full weight on him.

"Don't worry, I promise I don't bite—hard, anyway."

Rayn's murderous glare caused Solomand to drop the playful look he was giving her. He threw his head back in laughter, which had an almost pleasant ring to it.

"Alright—no more jokes."

His hand on her waist, he started down the winding staircase toward the cargo bay.

Beneath the layer of strong-scented tobacco, Solomand's coat carried hints of engine grease and the kind of antiseptic odor that never washed out. Rayn closed her eyes, focusing on breathing in the fresh air. Sunlight warmed her face as she felt wooden planking beneath her boots, and she opened her eyes to see the dock.

The scaffolding built into the side of the cliff swayed with the breeze, and the aged planks creaked as they walked towards the path.

"Where the hell are we?"

Rayn allowed herself to press into Solomand a little more.

"The Lubafell Valley." He nodded to the crumbling building on top of the hill. "The splendid garrison there is Castle of the Wind, what's left of it, anyway. We call it The Castle."

"Castle?"

The hulking stone building looked like it had given up long ago and was swallowed by the thick vines and trees that sprang out from its courtyard.

Leaning sideways so he could see her face, Solomand winked.

"Good place to disappear when you need to."

"I can see why."

Rayn allowed herself to lean more on his arm. So that was how they had escaped from the 201st.

"Need to disappear often, do you?"

There was a feigned look of bewilderment on Solomand's face as he glanced at her from the corner of his eyes.

"Watch your step through here," he said.

Unsalvageable ruins littered the grounds. Bits of crumbling stone lay in heaps, and vines slithered every which way. Solomand's hideout was a much smaller building constructed in the center of the Castle. The thick tar-blackened wood gave it the dismal appearance of a bombed bunker, but it was solid and well-concealed within the shell of Castle of the Wind.

Rayn took one look at the building and groaned.

"You're nothing but a bunch of third rate smugglers."

"I think we're at least second rate." Solomand held the finger of his free hand to his lips.

"Don't tell anyone, will you?"

He pushed the door open, and they stepped into a corridor. Rayn remembered all the tales pilots relayed after having one too many drinks about the ruthless air pirates and smugglers who'd attacked their ships. And here she was, alone and unarmed in a place where no one would ever think to look for her. Not that there was anyone who would notice she was gone. The entire town probably thought she had died in the fire.

Reclaiming her revolver would be the first thing to do. For now, she still had her boots on. A trapdoor in the heel of each concealed a sharp blade that would spring out if she stomped her heel hard enough.

If Solomand tried anything, he would be on his knees before he knew what hit him.

The mouth-watering aroma of stew interrupted her thoughts. Laughter and talking echoed through the corridor as they turned a corner and came to a cracked door. Solomand pushed it the rest of the way open with his foot and the scent of fresh bread and cooked vegetables spilled out.

The kitchen was small. A stove and cabinets with peeling white paint were on the far side, a wooden table and benches were bolted to the floor in the center. The engineer who Rayn had met earlier sat with his back to the door. Will stood by the stove, sleeves rolled up as he ladled stew from a pot into bowls. A girl who looked to be eleven or twelve sat on the counter by the stove, swinging her bare feet. She had a light complexion, her cheek smudged with dirt, and silky-black hair that hung over her eyes. She stopped chewing when Solomand walked in and fixed her peculiar golden eyes on Rayn.

"Move it, Jank," Solomand's booming voice made the skinny engineer jump.

He promptly slid over as Solomand eased Rayn onto the bench.

"Will, some dinner for our guest here, if you don't mind."

Will nodded, crossing the floor in one step, and placed a bowl of steaming stew in front of her. Rayn glanced uneasily around. The room had gone awkwardly silent.

"As you were! You're bothering the lady." Solomand's voice was louder than necessary, but broke the silence in a welcoming way. He set a glass of water in front of Rayn as he sat down across from her. "Sorry, we don't get visitors much. And when we do, they're usually not the most desirable company."

Jank snorted, his mouth full of food, and mumbled, "Phtubid coalithin prophtitute!"

Rayn's squinting as she tried to understand what he had said.

Solomand laughed nervously.

"Never mind him."

He reached across the table and smacked him across the back of the head. Jank choked on his mouthful of stew and leaned over, coughing.

"Where are my manners?"

Solomand grinned, ignoring Jank's coughing.

"I never properly introduced you to anyone. This," his hand motioned to the Jank, "is Jankyn Fleet, our resident engineer. We just call him Jank. He's great at his job, but never mind much of what comes out of his mouth. Right, Jank?"

Solomand took another swipe toward the engineer's head, but Jank ducked this time.

"That's my first mate, Will Ennea," he said, thumbing toward Will. "And that's Zee over there. She's somewhat of a navigator." He motioned to the girl. "And that's almost everyone."

Rayn looked sideways at Jank, who had retreated to the counter and was shoveling spoonfuls of stew in his mouth while giving Solomand hateful looks. "Almost?" She asked.

Solomand leaned back in his seat, lacing his hands behind his head.

"Yeah. Almost."

He motioned to the food in front of her.

Rayn shrugged, the savory-scented steam drifting into her face. She no longer cared about the curious looks and shoveled the soft chunks of potato and beef into her mouth. While she ate, Solomand went to the counter and spooned some stew into an empty bowl before passing it to Will.

Will ducked out of the kitchen, taking the stew with him. Jank left, yawning and dragging Zee by the arm; the girl kept her eyes on Rayn until she disappeared with the engineer. Solomand leaned against the counter, cleaning his fingernails with a pocket-knife. She scraped the last bit of food from the bowl and looked up to see him staring at her.

"Look, Rayn, I'm sorry about your rifle." He closed the knife before returning it to his pants pocket. "The last thing I wanted to do was drag you into any of this."

Wait.

There was that alarm going off in her head that sounded too late.

"Drag me into what, exactly?" Rayn asked.

Guilt dug its hooks in again as she saw the traces of dried blood on his face and his nose of varying purple shades. She almost thought of telling him it was alright. She had, planned on leaving the dismal little ridge town, anyway.

Of all the crow-headed things to do.

She leaned back in her seat, a hardness setting in. No, she would not let him take away her desire to hate him just yet. She wasn't even sure how much of a mess he'd dragged her into.

"I know we never really got the chance to discuss payment for the job." He cleared his throat. "Obviously more would be in order after what I've put you through."

"Obviously," Rayn said between bites.

"But, along with your payment, what can I do to make it right?" His eyes bore into her, unblinking.

Rayn licked her lips and downed a glass of water. Her head was feeling much better now. Her hand moved to her pocket. Aside from any doctors, she never spoke of her lack of memory with anyone, and she did not particularly want to reveal her secret to Solomand Black, who seemed to have attracted the interest of undesirable people.

Her fingers closed around the rim of her most prized possession, and her insatiable need to know swelled, drowning her desire for anything else. If anyone could help her find the answers she craved—even a man like Solomand Black—Rayn was willing to take the risk.

Eyes hardly set on him, she dragged the medallion from her pocket and slid it across the table.

"I need you to find someone for me."

Solomand reached for the medallion, and Rayn's fingers held it for an instant before allowing him to pick it up.

"Have to do with this?"

He squinted, working his thumb across the tarnished metal as he turned it over.

Rayn hesitated.

"Yes."

54

"S. L." Solomand looked at it one last time before handing it back to Rayn. "So, who is this S.L.?"

Rayn's fingers tightened against the medallion like it was a part of her and not merely a trinket she was getting back.

She turned away, her head lowering as she mumbled, "I'm not actually a hundred percent sure on that."

Solomand's eyebrow raised.

"How sure would you say you are, then?"

Rayn scowled.

"Can you find him, or not?"

You owe me, you rifle-murdering pirate!

Rayn was not good with people, but she thought the last thought was best kept to herself.

Solomand crossed his arms, looking like she had challenged his reputation.

"I can. But I'll need to know everything about the person to make it an easier search. Otherwise, it could end up being a bit of a needle in a haystack search."

"So, you'll do it, then?"

"Of course." He looked slightly offended. "I told you to name your price, didn't I?"

"Alright then." Rayn cleared her throat. "I have no idea who S.L. is."

Solomand's shoulders slumped, and he was quiet for a moment, his eyes locked with hers.

"Right. Needle in a haystack search, it is."

Rayn rested her elbows on the table.

"Truth is, I'm not sure who I am, either."

It sounded strange saying it out loud after so long. She felt certain Solomand would squirm out of his agreement now. He leaned back, scratching the stubble on his chin as he listened to her explanation.

"I remember nothing past six years ago. I woke up in a bed in Port Ashbury. There was a doctor there. He told me I was in an accident and that my memories were not likely to recover. The shop

I was in was mine, he said. After I recovered, I started working as the town gunsmith."

Solomand leaned back.

"You don't believe that story though?"

Rayn traced the grain in the wood with her fingertips. Ashbury had been intolerably dull. Everyone eyed her as though she were some dangerous viper. There was not one person she could say she missed. The only solace she ever had there was when she was working, which wasn't often; there wasn't much call for fixing guns in a peaceful port like Ashbury. More than that, there was an emptiness there she couldn't explain, and it felt at times like it would swallow her.

She shrugged.

Solomand raised his head, a distant look on his face.

"Ever been to Corcyra?"

"No."

Was that true, though? She could never be sure.

"Well, not that I know of. Why?"

Shrugging one shoulder, Solomand leaned back in his seat.

"Shitty desert city in the Plains. A lot of nasty weapons manufactured there during the war. I don't suppose you remember any war though, do you?"

Rayn shook her head. She'd heard of it well enough from passing travelers and bar-hoppers that drifted in and out of Port Ashbury. In the beginning, plenty of dodgy-eyed veterans came into her shop asking her to fix the service rifles they couldn't bear to part with. They were illegal, but Rayn repaired them anyway.

Solomand seemed to take her story well. She thought he would believe she was ace-high mad.

"Wait… what kind of weapons? Did they affect a person's memories?"

Her eyes narrowed.

Solomand sprang up.

"Questions better answered by a friend of mine."

"Who?"

Rayn's hand moved to her side as she stood.

"The rest of my crew." His face scrunched like he remembered something. "Well... almost."

CHAPTER 8

RAYN

RAYN LEANED AGAINST the gritty plaster of the wall as she followed Solomand up the stairs. He was telling her that there was a room for her on the second floor. She was only half listening, her hand pressing against her side as the burning sensation intensified. At least her head felt clearer. Solomand hurried past a half-open sliding door and arrived at the end of the hall. Without bothering to knock, he turned the knob and shouldered the door open.

Rayn took in the room with a quick glance. It was much larger than she expected. Alphabetically ordered books lined most of the shelves, others contained unusual devices that looked like they belonged in a hospital or laboratory. A desk sat in the corner, a neat stack of paper and an odd-looking machine with switches and levers Rayn supposed was a typing machine.

Solomand stepped up to the bed where the man she guessed was Tristan lay. His eyes were closed. Sunlight spilled in from the propped open skylight, pooling on the olive-green blanket, making Tristan's fair hair seem almost white. He had a narrow face, with angular cheekbones. A leather book with cracked pages lay open at his fingertips. Even in his sickly appearance, he looked younger than she and Solomand, but not by much.

"Tris, you awake?"

"Ah, Solomand!"

Tristan spoke in a warm, steady voice, much stronger than Rayn expected from his frail appearance. A smile formed on his lips, but his eyes did not open right away. "The very instant I saw you, did my heart fly to your service."

Raising one eyebrow, Solomand glanced at the title of the open book and Rayn followed his gaze to the golden, embossed letters: *Shakespeare.*

"Save that garbage for your lady stalker," Sol said.

"Come now, you know I only have eyes for you."

Solomand rolled his eyes as he leaned over the edge of the bed. "You're an idiot."

"Have you found someone else? After everything we've been through?"

Solomand leaned over and flicked his friend on the forehead. Tristan jerked a hand to his head, chuckling. Eyes as blue as the sky opened and fell on Rayn.

His pale face brightened, and he gave Solomand a knowing look.

"I believe I shall manage to get over you."

A guarded look on his face, Solomand crossed his arms.

"This is Rayn."

Tristan eased his legs off the bed and grabbed the cane leaning against the wall. He leaned forward, both hands gripping the curved handle.

"A pleasure to meet you, Rayn."

He glanced out of the skylight as a breeze stirred the trees overhead. Rayn felt a strange fluttering in her stomach when he smiled at her.

"I have always thought Rayn to be a wonderfully poetic name."

"Know a lot of Rayns, do you?"

She sat on the bed next to him. His charming smile made her feel at ease, like she was talking with an old friend.

"A lot? No. Just one now."

Solomand reached over and jabbed Tristan in the side, causing his friend to double over with a pained groan.

Solomand's annoyed look dissolved to an expression of horror. "God, I'm sorry, Tris. Are you alright?"

He grabbed Tristan by the shoulders, pulling him up. Tristan raised his head, a sly grin spreading across his face.

"Of course."

He held a hand to his mouth as he coughed. Solomand's face flushed red as he stood rigid.

"Ass."

Tristan tilted his head back as he laughed.

"Oh, Sol. I truly am sorry."

Rayn couldn't help but notice that his hands, white against the cane handle, had a slight tremor.

Solomand glared at him and ran a jerky hand through his hair.

"Rayn has a rather unique problem," he said, avoiding Tristan's gaze.

"Oh? May I guess what this problem might be?"

The corner of his mouth turned up as he glanced at Solomand, a mischievous glint returning to his eyes. "I'm good at guessing." His glare intensifying, Solomand crossed to the other side of the room. Tristan gave a resigned sigh and shrugged.

"Perhaps it would be best if you told me yourself."

He turned his attention to Rayn.

Rayn had been rather enjoying how Tristan was getting under Solomand's skin.

"Alright."

She cleared her throat. She didn't mind retelling her story to Tristan, who appeared deep in thought the entire time. Every breath he took seemed forced. The slight way he leaned forward and the quiver in his hand made it look like he was drained to the core and trying to hide it. Stopping herself from syncing her breaths with his, Rayn was unnerved.

"You can remember nothing at all before six years ago?"

The recurrent dreams of the dark-haired boy and others she didn't recognize entered her mind. No matter how much she longed for them to be pieces of her past, she realized, with a twinge of sorrow, she couldn't be sure they were anything more than the unconscious workings of her mind.

"No," she said, clearing her voice as it cracked. She ran a finger along the worn edge of her holster.

"Except that I've never got a gun I couldn't fix, and I don't remember learning the trade."

"That is a rather unique skill set, isn't it?"

Tristan's fingers drummed on the cane, which made the tremor in his hands less noticeable.

"Do you remember having any neck pain when you first awoke—any puncture, a mark which might be mistaken for an insect bite?"

Rayn rubbed the back of her neck.

"Maybe." Her throat felt dry again, and she swallowed. "Sorry, I don't really remember."

Tristan breathed in again, closing his eyes as he pinched the bridge of his nose.

"E. X Solution... nicknamed Empty by the ones who tested it. It was a favorite weapon towards the end; administered by a tiny dart."

He held his thumb and forefinger up to show the size.

"Empty?" Cold fingers of dread tightened around her.

"Yes. Because it's intended purpose was to empty a person's mind." Tristan tapped on the side of his head. "In the early stages, it did its job far too well."

A distant look crept into his eyes as he spoke.

There was the sound of breaking glass, and Rayn turned to see Sol fumbling with a pile of broken glass on the shelf closest to the door.

"Do I need to send you into the hall to keep you from tampering with my things?"

Solomand dismissed Tristan with a wave of his hand, muttering to himself inaudibly.

"Anyway," Tristan turned back to Rayn. "There was a counter solution for the empty, which allowed the Coalition forces to administer their own desired memories... sort of recreating that person, so they would work to the Coalition's end, rather than their own moral convictions."

A chill run up Rayn's spine like an icy wave. The thought of anyone having their life stolen in such a way, and then turned into a weapon against their will, was horrifying. Her heart pounded faster, wondering if it was possible.

"The Doctor said nothing." Her voice betrayed a horror at the possibility.

Tristan reached out and lay his hand on hers. His fingers felt like ice.

He said gently, "Even if he knew, he would not have mentioned it. E.X. is still a secret the Coalition would rather not have exposed." His hand fell away from hers.

"Who would even think up such a weapon?"

Rayn felt even less sure of who she was now.

Tristan's brow wrinkled, and he drew his hand away from her.

"I am sorry. Still," he brightened, "there is the chance that yours is an unrelated case of amnesia and everything I said has no bearing on your past at all."

She could tell he didn't believe this. Her lips pursed together as she thought of her shop, the scar on her stomach and the dreams. Maybe it was the shock of hearing everything at once that made her shrug. What the hell. It's not as if it would change anything, would it?

"Yeah. It could have been anything."

Except it all happened a little too close to the war's end to be a coincidence.

"Yes." Tristan smiled weakly.

He broke into a fit of coughing that drove the discussion from Rayn's mind. She stood as Solomand rushed to his friend's side, staring at him with such seriousness that Rayn's heart sank with alarm.

"You should rest," Sol said, taking the cane from Tristan's hand and propping it against the wall.

His face strained, Tristan slumped onto his pillow without argument.

"Only because you asked so nicely, Captain." The joking expression returning as his eyes drifted shut. "Rayn?"

"Yes?" Her voice was little more than a whisper.

Rayn stood up, an unfamiliar tingling sensation in her chest.

"I enjoyed seeing you. Please come again—and don't let my jailor keep you away, eh? Promise?"

"Of course."

Would he be there later? Her chest felt suddenly heavy.

Tristan opened his eyes one last time to smile at her.

"I shall count the minutes 'til we meet again."

Rayn forced a smile back.

"I'll be back later," Solomand said, reaching into his pocket.

"Bring me a cigarette, will you?"

"No."

"Such cruelty." Tristan shook his head, then added. "Sol?"

"What?"

"I shall count the moments until you return, as well."

Solomand rolled his eyes and shoved the foot of the bed with his boot, so it moved diagonally under the skylight. He and Rayn left with the sound of Tristan's laughter in their ears.

"You should rest too," Solomand said as they made their way down the creaking staircase. "Tomorrow, I'll show you the gun."

Rayn was halfway aware that he was talking about the job she was hired for, and he said something about showing her to a room. She kept thinking about Tristan's morbid way of toying with Solomand and his harrowing cough.

"What's wrong with him?" she blurted out.

Solomand stopped walking. In agonizing silence, he took a cigarette from his pocket and lit it. In the hall the flame of his lighter flickered, showing a veiled terror in his eyes. He allowed the smoke to curl over his lips and looked away.

"Nothing," he said in a gravelly tone. "I'll come for you later." Smoke trailed through the air after him as he strode away.

CHAPTER 9

SOLOMAND

SOLOMAND BURST THROUGH the door and slammed it shut. Twisting the lock, he whirled around. Tristan bent over his desk, scrawling on a sheet of paper with his fountain pen. The words were in perfect, even rows, artistic and flawless.

"Civilized people have been known to knock before entering a room not their own," Tristan said without looking up. "I may have been in the company of a beautiful woman."

"Civilized people. Like you, swank. Not me." Solomand grunted as he crossed the room in three strides. "Well? What did you find out?"

He paced in front of Tristan's desk nervously.

Tristan's left hand paused in his writing, leaving a thick spot of ink which interrupted the meticulous flow of words. He glanced up at Solomand.

"Her condition appears to be consistent with the E.X. solution. Except..."

"Except what?" Solomand slammed his palms on the desk and bent over.

Tristan tapped the end of his pen on his lips. "I'm not sure. It rather seemed like there was something more she wanted to say." His eyes narrowed in that scrutinizing way that was vastly annoying and asked, "Didn't you notice?"

64

Throwing his hands up, Solomand went back to pacing. His throat felt dry as he forced the words out.

"Will they ever return, you think? Her memories?"

Tristan leaned back in his chair.

"I'm afraid I cannot tell you anything you didn't already know, Sol."

There was a sadness in his voice, and Solomand felt his chest tightening. He hated that apologetic tone more than anything.

Tristan coughed into his fist. "Although, that all ties in rather neatly with your perfect plans of martyrdom, now, doesn't it?"

The tightening worsened, and Solomand felt like it would squeeze the breath out of his lungs. The pressing urge to run into the valley, and keep running until the strangling feeling left him, was hard to fight. He loosened his collar as a cold sweat broke over his skin. He crossed the room so Tristan would not notice. Shoving one hand in his pocket, his fingers tracing the edge of his cigarette case.

"She asked about you," he said.

"Oh?" Tristan tilted the chair back, raising the front legs from the ground.

"What did you tell her? That I am a walking corpse whose days are numbered." He lowered his voice dramatically.

Solomand scowled.

"Would it be too much trouble, My Lord Highcourt, to cease the morbid death jokes?" he said, mimicking Tristan's highborn manner of speech.

Tristan chuckled.

"Sorry, they sort of come out without my even thinking about it anymore."

Solomand glared at Tristan and spoke through his teeth.

"Practice. Ivan won't take them as well as I do. He might kill you himself."

Any sense of humor Ivan may have had was frozen out of him in his icy homeland.

"Ha!" Tristan leaned his head back. "No. He might take it out on you, though."

"More likely," Solomand sniffed in agreement.

"While we are on the subject."

Tristan eased the front legs of his chair back on the floor and opened the top desk drawer. He reached inside, pulled out a small vial of clear liquid and tossed it to Solomand.

"It's less potent than the last batch. One drop should still suffice."

Solomand glared at the bottle before slipping it into his pocket. He hated sneaking the drug into Ivan's food.

"You know what he'd do if he knew?"

Tristan sighed sympathetically.

"His determination is admirable, but not even he can escape the ramifications of Furi." His voice lowered. "You know what it does to those who don't ease off of it, Sol."

He knew. The gaunt corpses that littered the seedy minor trading posts were only slightly less disturbing than the savageness that overtook the addicts before they finally succumbed to death. Even before the war, in the slums of Corcyra, Solomand remembered all too well the crazed spectacle of those he had seen running through the streets on all fours, smeared in their own feces. He shook his head.

"Yeah. He's still going to be pissed, though."

Fighting back a cough, Tristan grinned. "He'll forgive me."

"Yeah," Solomand agreed. "But not me." The constrained feeling around his chest grew tighter. "I'll be back later," he mumbled and left.

66

CHAPTER 10

RAYN

RAYN WRINKLED HER nose as she walked into her room. It was small and smelled of must. A gas lamp was mounted on the wall by the bed, and specks of dust swirled in the soft yellow light. There were no windows. Rayn much preferred the smell of oil and metal. She shrugged and shoved the door shut with her elbow. Her belongings sat on the bed, including the revolver she'd been missing. Rayn unsheathed it, pushed out the cylinder and ran her thumb along each bullet primer. Solomand did not appear to have tampered with any of them.

She sighed and returned the gun to its sheath.

I guess Captain Black isn't afraid I'll shoot him.

She ran her hand over the course green blanket, expecting her fingers to come away with a layer of dust. They did. She didn't really care. She had her revolver back, and the room had its own bathroom with a shower in it.

Her clothes had a grungy, sticky feel against her skin, and she peeled them off, careful to avoid doing any further damage to her injury. Leaving them in a pile on the floor, she stepped into the stone-tiled shower and pulled the chain to the drain. She jumped a little as the steaming water streamed over her hair, then sighed with relief as the warm water trailed down her body. The chain fastened on a hook, so the water ran freely, and Rayn scrubbed the sweat, blood, and dust from her body. Feeling each smooth groove

67

of the scar around the lines of a distorted birthmark, she wondered if she would ever be anyone other than just Rayn. A new worry worked itself in; what if she didn't like what she found out?

Soapy foam washed down her side, soaking her bandages. The stinging in her wound turned into a burning sensation.

"Shit!"

Rayn pealed of the bandage, biting her lower lip as the warm water washed the soap away. She sucked in her breath and slung sopping hair out of her eyes as she released the chain and hopped out of the shower. The stinging burning subsided as she patted the wound dry. She dried the rest of herself and spotted a stack of bandages and a bottle of antiseptic near the washbasin.

"Thought of everything but the morphine, didn't he?" she grumbled.

Then, because she would rather deal with pain than an infection, she gritted her teeth and splashed the clear liquid onto her wound.

As her side caught fire, Rayn flattened against the wall, making a mix of guttural and high-pitched noises in her throat. With tears at the corners of her eyes, she told herself to stop acting like a baby and wrapped on the fresh bandages amid another round of winces and groans.

She put on some fresh clothes before easing herself onto the bed.

"Well..." she gasped, "that was a hell of a day."

Her hair, still a dripping mess, soaked the pillow. Rayn raised her head and looked at the towel on the floor by the bathroom.

Not worth it.

She sank her head on the already damp pillow and fell asleep.

She didn't know how long she was out, but no dreams interrupted her this time. When she woke up, she fixed her eyes on a spot of peeling paint on the ceiling. The hollowness inside her grew a little more, like a canyon carved a little more with every rainfall.

Empty.

That was what she felt. Her fingers curled around the edge of the blanket. What would it mean if she'd been in Corcyra during the war?

Rayn kicked the blanket off and got dressed before tying her still damp hair back. She strapped on her gun belt and went to find Solomand.

He wasn't in the kitchen, but she found a basket of warm rolls. The lingering smell of their baking made her stomach growl. She picked one up and, in a very unladylike fashion, finished it in three bites. Soft buttery crust was filled with meat and vegetables. She grabbed another one before hurrying outside and down the debris-littered path out of the Castle.

The walkway was built into the cliff, splitting off into two directions: one angled down toward the dock, the other snaked left, down into the grassy valley.

The sun sank below the mountains amid layered streaks of purple and orange clouds painted across a gray sky. A warm breeze jostled the trees, and a handful of birds swooped past as she stepped onto the path, diving from the branches and chirping. There was another sound too: the gentle rushing of water. Rayn breathed in the smell of damp moss and peace settled on her.

Why couldn't I have been dumped in a place like this?

The Lubafell valley was infinitely more appealing than Port Ashbury, with its constant stream of travelers coming and going and the never-ending cycle of small talk and tedious people.

Shouts and a girl's laughter came from the dock, and Rayn's thoughts snapped back to reality—and Solomand. She took another bite of the roll and wiped her mouth on the back of her hand as she strode toward the dock. Solomand was sitting on the railing, bracing himself with his hands. His untucked shirt fluttered against his chest as the wind tugged on it. He stared down toward the valley with an unfocused gaze.

The wind masked the sound of her steps on the wooden planks until she was right behind him. He turned to look at her, a darkness in his eyes.

"Hello there, Rayn... storm."

As he grinned, the unsettled expression was gone from his face, making Rayn question if she saw it at all.

"It's just Rayn."

She scowled and shoved the last of the roll into her mouth.

"Right. Sorry. How're you feeling?"

He toyed with a silver chain around his neck.

"Better."

Rayn hooked her right hand on the hilt of her revolver.

"Good." Solomand's eyes flicked to the gun at her side. "I would have come for you earlier, but I thought it'd be best if you slept it off."

Clouds reflected in his eyes as he looked back into the valley.

Rayn followed his gaze down the winding trail along a stream, to the fields of high grass panning out below. The movement of the wind through the stalks looked like waves of the ocean. Patches of purple and yellow flowers sprouted across the field like splashes of paint on a canvas.

"It's beautiful," she said.

The smells of earth and trees wrapped themselves around her.

"Yeah. You could say that." His jaw tightened, and he looked like he was going to add an alternative view.

"How did you end up here?" Rayn asked.

"It's where my father and mother met," Solomand spoke in a faraway tone. "My father was a pilot. He crashed in the valley near the Kree camp."

"Kree?" Rayn tilted her head to the side, leaning over the railing next to him to see.

She brushed against his arm, and the scent of his tobacco encircled her like an invisible cloud. Solomand glanced at her arm before motioning across the expanse of mountains in the distance.

"The nomads that travel throughout the region. My mother was one; a member of the Crow Clan."

"Was?" Rayn regretted the word as soon as it left her tongue.

Small talk was awkward enough without bringing up a potentially uncomfortable topic. What if his mother was dead?

She added hurriedly, "Are they still here? The Kree?"

"They come and go," Solomand said. "They'll be back in the valley before the month is over." He swung his legs around and hopped off the railing next to Rayn. "Feel up to having a look at why you're here?"

Rayn had almost forgotten.

"Sure."

"Alright, let's go." He shoved his hands in his pockets and ambled back toward the dock.

Jank was standing by the *Osprey's* side, drawing in a battered leather sketchbook. Now and then his eyes flitted up to the airship, then back to his drawing. Zee sat on Will's shoulders, slathering navy-blue paint on the flint-colored hull. Blue droplets splattered all over Will's clothes.

"Time for a change," Solomand winked at Rayn as they stepped up the ramp and into the open bay doors.

"This wouldn't have anything to do with the 201st, would it?"

"Of course not. I'm simply tired of gray and manufactured rust."

Manufactured rust?

"What?"

Rayn raised an eye and squeezed past a pile of wooden crates behind Solomand.

"Nothing."

"So, how often do you tire of your ship's appearance, Captain?"

They started up a winding staircase of black, riveted metal.

Their voices mixed with echoes of their footsteps on the stairs.

Solomand grinned over his shoulder.

"Once. She wasn't the *Osprey* last time."

Rayn rolled her eyes.

As they climbed, Rayn surveyed the inside of the airship. There was a catwalk on each of the three decks they passed, lined with closed doors. It was smaller than she expected it to be. There was a rounded door at the top of the staircase, peppered with dents and tinged with rust. Solomand grunted as he turned the wheel lock, hanging on it with his full body weight to make it budge. It rolled with a groan, and he heaved it open on its hinges. He held his arm out for her to go ahead of him, bowing slightly.

Rayn stepped into a small room overlooking the topside of the airship through a porthole. Black cases of ammunition lined the walls. Rayn put a hand on her hip.

"Nice armory you have for a passenger vessel."

Solomand leaned against the doorframe.

"I prefer to call it an emergency projectile storage compartment. Sounds nicer. More legal." He nodded to the metal pieces that lay in a black, bulky heap on the floor. "That'd be the gun. Needs a bit of work, but I don't need to tell you that."

Rayn eased to one knee and examined the three barrels protruding from the firearm. Her mouth hung open as her eyes fell on the open case of six and a half inch shells.

"Defense?" she burst out. "This is a damned anti-aircraft cannon, Captain Black."

Solomand crossed his arms.

"No more than that pistol of yours is."

"Ha-ha."

Rayn unscrewed one barrel from the mount. She had to rest it on her shoulder as she held it up to the light.

"Not a pirate, huh?"

One eye squeezed shut, she stared down the end of the cylinder. Flecks of gunpowder and gunk lined the barrel. Pits had already formed, little pockets of corrosion slowly eating away at the metal.

Solomand pretended to look out the window. "I told you, it's all a massive misunderstanding."

"Yes, you said that."

Rayn sat the barrel down. Her hands came away black and greasy.

"You might not know this, but a twenty-millimeter triple cannon is highly illegal."

No wonder he didn't want to bring it into the shop.

"So is a certain black rifle in your possession—err, well." Solomand cleared his throat and peered out the porthole, avoiding Rayn's gaze. "Does it matter if it's illegal?"

A wave of anger rose and fell over her at mention of her rifle. She considered the question while she waited for the heated feeling to dissipate.

"No," she said, pushing her hair back over her shoulder as she stood. "But I don't have what I need to fix it." When she dusted her hands off on her pants, black streaks smeared across the carob-colored material. For starters, it would take massive amounts of rags and ammonia to stave off the corrosion. She couldn't tell straight off what was wrong with it, but she didn't have any tools or raw material to make springs.

"I can get you anything you need. I have to make a run to Trader's Cove in one week, depending on how fast Jank can finish with the airship. Make a list for me."

He ran a hand over the back of his neck.

"I'll be able to ask around about your S. L. while we're there."

"Oh." It was strange how the matter had slipped her mind after being her only consuming thought for so long.

"Sounds good," she said.

"Alright then." Solomand leaned towards her and held his hand out. "Allow me to officially welcome you aboard, Rayn." A smile played on his lips. "Just Rayn."

Rayn hesitated, lost for a moment in his eyes. They almost looked like dark-blue storm clouds, drawing her in. She took his hand, returning a smile.

"Thanks. I think."

His hand was rough and damp with sweat as his fingers tightened around hers. With a quick jerk, he drew his hand away.

"If you need anything, let me know."

He cleared his throat and hurried out of the room, flexing his fingers at his side.

73

CHAPTER 11

RAYN

ON REFLECTION, A week's worth of waiting was not good at all. Rayn didn't know what time it was when she awoke to the darkness in the windowless room. She was wide awake, so she assumed it was morning. Rolling over, she switched on the lamp and slipped into her clothes. She strapped on her gun belt, laid her coat on the bed, and left the room, creeping downstairs.

Darkness forced her to feel her way along the hall until a dull light from the kitchen guided her the rest of the way. As she stepped into the doorway, she saw the engineer bent over a sketch-book on the table, eyes squinted as his hand moved back and forth. His hair was messier than usual, and his baggy undershirt was un-tucked. His bare feet were crossed under the table.

Rayn wasn't aware of how little noise she'd made walking in until Jank looked up from his drawing. Eyes washed over with ter-ror as his entire body jerked, then relaxed.

"You gave me a damn scare, Rayn." His pencil dropped to the table.

"Sorry." Rayn took a step inside. "Where's your Captain?"

Jank flipped the leather-bound book shut in a hurried sweep of his hand and reached for a cup of coffee.

"Sol?" He looked as if she'd asked him something ridiculous. "He'll not be up for hours."

His head motioned to the clock on the wall, and Rayn looked to see the time. It wasn't even four in the morning yet. Her shoulders slumped. This was going to be a long week.

She turned back to Jank.

"What are you doing up at this ungodly hour then?"

The engineer yawned.

"I usually am."

Rayn looked back at the clock, breathing in the scent of coffee and pondering the stillness.

Won't be up for hours, huh?

That wouldn't do.

"Where's Solomand's room?"

Jank choked on a sip of coffee and set the cup down, wiping his mouth on his sleeve.

"Oh, you can't wake him. Not now."

A devious smile etched itself on her face, and Rayn asked innocently, "Why not?"

Jank's sketchbook scooted across the table as he grazed it with his arm. He lowered his voice as if he was afraid to wake someone else, "He'll kill *me* for starters!"

"Oh, come on." Rayn crossed her arms, inching toward the door. "How will he know it was you that told me?"

"He'll damn-well find out. He always does."

Jank sprang to his feet, desperation filling his wide eyes.

"It'll only be this once. I promise," Rayn tried to make her face look sincere.

Janks' swallow was audible in the morning's stillness.

"Alright," he said in a whisper. "Up the stairs—the last room down the hall." He turned stiffly and began pulling ingredients from the cabinet. "And you didn't see me!"

"Thanks," Rayn said, grinning. Jank waved her away.

Knocking would have been the appropriate thing to do. Rayn twisted the handle and opened the door to Solomand's room, easing it open one inch at a time to avoid making any noise. A dented oil lamp burned on a bedside table. The bed was more of a cot than a bunk, and there was little room for anything else in the cramped space.

A pile of dirty clothes was heaped in the corner and papers littered the nightstand: maps, scrolls, and letters written in a language she couldn't read. Solomand lay on his stomach, buried under a pile of sheets and green blanket, one arm draped over the side touching the floor.

One thing seemed out of place in the room: a painting hanging directly above the cot. A late summer-blue sky was marked with lazy white clouds and framed by trees. Invisible wind jostled grass along the bank of a mirror-like river. A man stood on a green hill, holding the hand of a small boy. Standing by the river, there was a woman wearing a brown dress with beads woven into her dark braid who waved at the two.

Rayn crept closer to get a better look at the scene. The toe of her boot found Solomand's finger instead. In a wild leap, he was out of bed, revolver drawn from under his pillow, cocked and pointed at her head.

Her breath caught in her throat, and Rayn saw a dark look of alarm give way to horror. His shaking thumb lowered the hammer, and he threw the revolver into a heap of laundry in the corner and sank to his bed.

"What the hell, Rayn!"

He pulled a shirt over his head and sank his face into his hands, taking long, deliberate breaths.

Looking up at her through his fingers, he asked in a quiet, out-of-place tone, "What. Do. You want?"

Aware of her heart racing, Rayn recovered enough to clear her throat. "I couldn't sleep."

Solomand's hands dropped to his knees, and he gave her a trenchant look.

"Funny. Neither can I."

He glanced at the cigarette case, which lay on the floor by his boots, and took a pronounced breath.

"Well, Rayn... since neither of us can seem to sleep, care to join me for a cup of coffee?" He gestured to himself. "I should probably put some clothes on first."

Rayn's cheeks became hot as she realized the shirt that he so hastily pulled on came just past his thighs, and he wasn't wearing any pants.

"Fine. I'll meet you in the kitchen, then."

She tried not to sound flustered as she hurried out and shut the door.

⇥ ✿ ⇤

Bacon sizzled in a skillet on the stove as Jank poured milk into a mixing bowl. He looked up at Rayn as she entered, then quickly back to the batter he stirred. Rayn sat down at the table and braided her hair to one side as she waited.

Ten minutes later, Solomand walked in. She noticed he did not wear his gun. Jank offered him a cup of coffee, and he took it without a word, eyes jabbing at the engineer.

"Coffee?" Jank asked Rayn, his back to Solomand.

He gave her an 'I told you he'd know' expression.

"Yes—thanks," she said.

Solomand picked up the pot before Jank could and poured her a cup, all the while giving Jank a sideways stare. He handed the mug to Rayn and sat down across from her.

"Tell me." He took a sip, his gaze catching hers. "Is there a particular reason you wanted to... talk to me at," he glanced at the clock, "bullshit-hundred hours?"

Rayn was waiting for him to lose his temper or tell her off. There had been something different in those steely eyes as they were on the other end of a gun, something cold and lethal. Now,

77

there was no trace of that haunted, determined look, and no reaction came.

Rayn took a gulp of coffee and ran a hand along her forehead.

"A week is too long to wait," she said. "I need something to do."

The line around Solomand's eyes seemed to draw in. Otherwise, he offered no reaction. "Need something to do," he said in an almost wistful tone as he drank his coffee. "Well, I've just the thing for you."

He sat his cup down and stretched.

"Oh, and I have no objections to you paying me a visit in my quarters—but next time, I'd appreciate it if you'd knock first."

The sound of a spatula clanging on the stove mixed with the popping of grease. Rayn tried to look nonchalant. She finished her coffee and nodded.

"Sure thing." She had no intention of intruding on him ever again.

CHAPTER 12

SOLOMAND

HIS NERVES SHREDDED, Solomand kept replaying the scene in his mind; Rayn standing there and his revolver aimed at her—*his*—hand poised to fire.

I might have killed her!

His hand moved to his left side where his shirt hid a small, black tattoo.

She might have seen that too.

Sighing, he trudged down the hall to Zee's room and pushed the door open.

The girl slept on a loft bed. Solomand built it for her when she was nearly eight.

A silvery orb replica of the Moon Breman gave off a soft glow on her desk, casting light against a pocket knife and a stack of books. Solomand walked over to the bunk and shook the girl's hand.

"Zee."

She sat up, awake in an instant.

"What is it?" she asked, rubbing her eyes.

"Get dressed," he said. "We're going hunting."

"Really?"

Enthusiasm carried in her voice, and she swung herself from the bed, landing on bare feet.

"Yes, really." Solomand scowled at her acrobatics. "Bring your rifle. I'll be out front."

He shut the door as he left the girl to get ready and went back upstairs for his coat.

In his room, he knelt down and dragged two long guns from underneath his cot. He opened the drawer on the nightstand and grabbed a box of shells. The revolver, which he felt unnerved without, remained in the corner, the thought of what might have happened still fresh in his mind.

Outside, Rayn was waiting, the full moon reflected in her eyes of summer green. Her mouth twisted into a doubtful frown.

"Hunting?"

"Yes." Solomand handed her the longer of the rifles. "Meat costs money, which we're running low on. Here, it's free for the taking. If you can shoot it."

Rayn clutched the gun in one hand and loaded it with the other.

"What are we hunting?" she asked.

"Mostly those annoying tree rats. But if you see anything larger, take it."

Rayn's eyes widened.

"Squirrels? With this?" She looked from Solomand to the rifle as she lodged the last round in place. "They'll be blown to hell."

Solomand wanted a cigarette badly. He fumbled with the ammunition box, trying to load his own gun, and shells spilled on the ground.

"*You* wanted something to do." He bent to pick up the ammunition, feeling jittery and agitated. "And since we are awake at this ungodly hour, we are doing *something*."

Rayn shrugged, to his relief. The door slammed shut as Zee skidded out of the Castle, a lever-action in a smaller caliber carefully pointed at the ground.

"Let's go," he said and started the long walk down into the valley.

They settled into a quiet spot, nestled by the creek overlooking the valley. Solomand let Zee hunt here by herself sometimes. Now, as the three of them waited, the horizon gleamed with the first light of dawn. Squirrels skittered through the trees, barking and scuffling with each other, leaping from branch to branch.

Rayn scowled upwards.

"There's nothing to them," she muttered as Zee aimed for one.

"They're better than nothing." Solomand bit back his agitation. "Look!"

Zee tensed up and lowered the barrel of her gun. Inching forward on all fours, she pointed into the open fields below. A sambar doe made her way across the dew-wet grass. It would be at least a two hundred and fifty-yard shot.

Rayn rested the long rifle against a tree and pulled the stock into her shoulder. Solomand squinted into the valley, holding his breath as Rayn's right eye opened as her finger closed around the trigger.

There was movement in the grass behind the doe as she stopped and turned. Two fawns moved from the cover of brush to follow, and Solomand's heart sank.

Damn.

Why did she have to have babies? She would have given them meat for two months.

"Never mind," he leaned over to tell Rayn. "She's got—" the word 'young' didn't make it out of his mouth. The crack of the rifle ruptured the silence, and the doe dropped in place.

"What a shot!" Zee was on her feet, looking at Rayn with the same awe she usually reserved for Solomand alone. Solomand was aware his mouth was hanging open as he stared at Rayn, eyes wide in a frown kind of shock.

"What the *hell*? Rayn." He found his voice.

"What?" She pushed the safety lever in place and laid the rifle on the ground. "You said if I saw anything bigger to take it."

"She had *young*! There is such a thing as ethics when hunting, you know."

81

Rayn tore off her coat and tossed it down by the rifle.

"Their spots are gone. They can fend for themselves, or did you prefer to eat mangled tree rats?"

"Well, no, but…"

Rayn shook her head at him.

"That was amazing!" Zee said, eyes wide.

"Thanks," Rayn gave the girl a smile and started down the slope where the deer lay.

Solomand lit a cigarette, a slight tremor still present in his hand. He gave Zee a sideways glance.

"I don't think you should hang around Rayn too much."

"Why not? She's awesome," Zee laid her gun down.

Solomand let the smoke fill his lungs and nodded at her.

"That right there. That's why. She brings out a devil in you, girl."

Zee, laughing, said, "Ah, come on, Sol. She's not that bad, or you never would have brought her here."

She scampered after Rayn. Solomand trailed after the two of them.

He did not mind the girl's admiration for Rayn. But Rayn would not always be here. For a moment, he'd let himself forget that. Misery welled up inside him, remembering; she had to go.

CHAPTER 13

RAYN

FOR ALL HIS looks of disapproval, Solomand helped Rayn gut the deer, something she couldn't remember doing before but got the hang of rather quickly. Zee was eager to help, carrying all three guns as Rayn and Solomand hauled the doe back to the dock.

The girl puzzled Rayn. She looked nothing like Solomand, so she doubted he was her father. Still, the way he acted he may as well have been: the way she looked up to him and his watchful eye as she grew careless with a knife.

Rayn didn't want to ask, especially after this morning. Solomand hadn't scared her, but she was more wary of him. She'd seen plenty of Coalition veterans in Ashbury, all with the same tense stare. They might brag about kicking the Insurgents' ass, but most of them didn't want to talk about what had happened when it came down to it. But Solomand was an Insurgent veteran, and there was something different guarded just beneath the surface of his sarcasm.

Crouching back on his heels, Solomand slung blood from his hands as he finished scraping fat from the hide with his knife.

"What are you going to do with it?" Rayn asked him, as she continued to cut chunks of meat off the animal's hind leg and place them in a crate

"Salt it. It'll be good for trading with the Kree."

He glanced up as Will walked down the hill towards them.

83

"Will! Send Jank out here with some salt," he called, and with a nod.

Will turned back up the walkway.

"Give the little weasel something to do," Sol muttered.

He turned to her, his hands held out in front of him, covered in a mix of fresh and dried blood.

"Well, Rayn. I trust dealing with this is enough to keep you busy for a while."

He gave her a grim smile and started back towards the Castle.

It did keep her busy. Maybe more than she realized it would. For the rest of the day, she helped Will and Jank cut the meat and turn it out on racks for drying; some of it they salted, and some they smoked. By the day's end, she washed all the grime from herself and fell asleep with ease.

⚙

It wasn't morning yet. She knew it when her eyes opened, and the stillness carried through the Castle louder than noise. Uttering a curse, she kicked the blankets off and sat up. After yesterday, the thought of harassing Solomand was not an option. After ten minutes, she got dressed and dug out a cleaning kit from her bag and went to the kitchen.

Not even Jank was up this time. The clock ticked away, showing the nearing time was even earlier than the previous night. Rayn sank to the table and disassembled her revolver before scrubbing at the pieces with her brushes and files. It wasn't like there was any debris to be cleaned off, but it calmed her to have something to do.

She hadn't been at it very long when someone walked into the kitchen. Looking up, she saw Jank, a glazed look in his eyes. He looked past her and walked to the sink.

"Morning," she said.

He didn't answer, just got a glass from the cabinet and filled it with water. Rayn's eyes narrowed.

84

"Jank?" she said, but the engineer was already walking from the room without acknowledging she was even there.

Rayn shook her head and started reassembling her revolver, yawning. Her eyelids felt heavy.

She wasn't going back to bed, though. Leaning forward to rest her head on folded arms, she closed her eyes.

The smell of coffee and bacon caused her to wake up two hours later. Lifting her head, she saw Jank standing by the stove.

"Saw you sleepwalking last night," she said, rubbing her eyes.

Jank tensed, and he whirled around, a horrified look on his face.

"What?"

Rayn stretched her arms overhead, wondering what his problem was.

"Last night. Well, a couple hours ago," she said, glancing at the clock. "You walked in here, still asleep."

"I don't sleepwalk!" Jank snapped and turned his back on her as Solomand walked in the room.

Giving the engineer a curious look, Solomand poured himself a cup of coffee and sat down by Rayn. He nodded towards Jank.

"What's that about?" he asked.

"No idea." Rayn shrugged. "I saw him sleepwalking last night and said something to him about it."

"Ah." Understanding registered on Sol's face. "That would be why." He leaned forward, lowering his voice. "You can't mention sleepwalking in front of him. He gets seven kinds of... touchy."

He took a sip of his coffee and leaned back.

"Why?"

Rayn tucked hair behind her ears, casting a confused look at Jank.

"I'll explain later," Sol said. "Not right now. Not while he's around."

Rayn let out an exasperated sigh.

What the hell is it with everyone having secrets?

"Are we going hunting again?" she asked.

"Why? You want to go back and finish the job, do you?" He stared at her over the rim of his coffee cup.

"Their. Spots. Were. Gone." The man was impossible!

His vague smile was hard to interpret. "Sorry. No hunting today." He pulled out his silver tobacco case and began rolling a cigarette.

"I have other things to attend to. You'll have to entertain yourself."

Rayn pressed the palms of her hands on the table. "I don't need to be entertained," she said.

Of all the stupid ideas.

"Sorry," Solomand said again. "You're welcome to mangle as many tree rats as your heart desires." He cleared his throat. "Just don't wander down into the valley and slaughter a pregnant coyote or anything."

He stood to leave.

Angrily, she snatched her revolver from the table and stood to leave. "Did anyone ever tell you, you're a jackass?"

"Lots of times," he laughed. "But you're the first today."

CHAPTER 14

SOLOMAND

IVAN WAS LESS like a walking corpse than when Solomand had first dragged him here. A faint outline of cedar brown hair covered his once-shaved head, barely hiding the shape of his skull. Every time Solomand looked at Ivan, it brought that day to his mind. Then the pain would start to stab and tighten in his chest until he thought he would suffocate. The thought made him inadvertently tug on his collar. He might have called that day second worst day of his life, but the past all ran together as one searing wound branded on his mind. He couldn't blame the Slav for wanting to forget everything. But it was time for him to face reality, as the rest of them had.

Solomand placed a plate of cold rolls on the floor and eyed the half-empty bowl of stew.

"Thought you wanted to kill me, Ice Man," he said, louder than necessary; the following silence carried more weight than a threat would have.

Ivan made a growling noise and moved his arm from where it had been draped over his face. His eyes flashed open.

Solomand flipped over a wooden crate and dragged it directly across from Ivan's cot before sitting down. The overbearing smell of his burning cigarette somewhat masked the scent of sweat and urine in the stale air of the cellar. Without turning to look at him, Ivan reached out a filthy hand toward Solomand. Solomand noted how steady his fingers were before passing him what was left of his cigarette. Ivan breathed in the smoke, his eyes fixed in a furious glare at the cobwebs on the low ceiling.

"You call me Ice Man again… I tear off your head."

He sounded calm, almost like his old self.

Solomand grinned. "You're welcome to try."

His elbows dropped to his knees, and he laced his hands together, resting his chin on his thumbs. His nose burned as he breathed in the room's smell. Ivan needed fresh air and sunlight. This fetid hole of a makeshift jail cell wasn't doing him any good.

Solomand frowned.

"What are the odds a room up top would keep you from breaking out and trying to murder me in my sleep?"

Ivan's chest fell as he breathed out a circle of smoke.

"Not good."

Solomand shook his head.

"Thought as much. Tristan wouldn't approve, you know."

Ivan's jaw tightened, the flicker of fire in his eyes growing more intense. This was the only emotion he offered.

Solomand scraped the heel of his boot across the floor, leaving a trail in the dirt.

"He wants to see you," he said, his voice less antagonizing.

Ivan hungrily took a drag until the cigarette was close to burning his fingers.

"No."

He dropped the glowing butt to the side of his bunk. His eyes shut as he raked a hand over his face and scratched at a month's worth of stubble.

"Not yet."

Solomand rubbed his arm; his face hardened. The words were on the tip of his tongue, but he swallowed them back. If he thought for a moment, Ivan would accept his apology, he would not have hesitated.

He won't.

The knot in his stomach tightened, and Solomand kept quiet once again. It was the fear of admitting his mistake, spilling out his heart to his friend, and being told in all sincerity to go to hell, that Solomand feared. He had lost too much already to bear the thought.

"Alright. I don't sleep that much, anyway." He stood up with a heavy sigh and scooped up the half-empty bowl. "Tomorrow me and Will are going to escort you to your new room—willing or not."

Ivan grunted.

"Don't worry," Solomand said. "I'll have Jank install some special reinforcements to the door."

"Will not be strong enough," Ivan said in a matter-of-fact way.

Solomand rolled his eyes as he turned away.

The chain rattled as he unlocked the door. Before he started up the stairs, he saw Ivan sit up on the cot, place the plate of rolls in his lap, and begin to eat. Solomand could only imagine what was going through his mind as he fixed murderous eyes in his direction.

Probably thinking about a creative and painful way to kill me.

Solomand darted back up the stairs. A grin on his face. It was a start, at least.

CHAPTER 15

WILL

ZEE'S EYES PEEKED from over the top of her cards; her amber stare surveying Will as she carefully laid three cards facedown on the table. She leaned back in the chair, swinging her bare feet back and forth as she clutched the rest of the pile to her chest.

"Three aces," she said.

Will ran a finger under the edge of his eyepatch. The ticking of the clock was pronounced in the silence of the kitchen.

"You're bluffing."

Zee's shoulders slumped, and she let out a groan as she collected the cards back into her ever-growing stack.

Will spread out his last four cards.

"Queens."

Zee's eyes narrowed as she leaned forward, as if getting closer to him would reveal whether he was telling the truth.

"Bluff," she said.

Will flipped over the cards one by one; the first three were queens. He paused on the last as Zee's eyes widened in hope. She groaned as he took his time flipping it over to reveal a queen.

She tossed her cards down and leaned her elbows on the table, slumping her head onto her right hand. "You cheated."

Will gave a faint smile. "You can't cheat at Bluff." He gathered all the cards back into a pile and began shuffling them.

"Oh yeah? Then how come you always win?"

Will tapped the deck on the palm of his hand, edging all the cards back into a neat stack.

"Because I'm better at it than you."

He reached over and flicked her on the forehead.

Zee scowled.

"Why?"

"Just am."

He shuffled the cards one more time and began dealing them out between the two of them.

Because I'm an Olbian.

He didn't bother to say this to the girl. She wouldn't understand, anyway. Memories like passing shadows crossed his mind of growing up in the bustling desert city. Expressing emotion was a sign of weakness, and not suitable for the forces of Olbia's 'Iron Knights.' That was all a lifetime ago. But it came in handy at times other than card games.

He settled back into his seat, fanning his cards out to look at them.

"You go first."

Lines formed on Zee's brow and she leaned back, biting her lip as she selected four cards from her pile and lay them in front of her.

"Fives."

Will fixed his speculative stare on her once more.

"Bluff," he said.

Zee's lips pursed together as she flipped the cards over one by one: all fives.

"You knew I wasn't bluffing," she pouted.

Will grinned, collecting the cards into his pile.

"I thought you wanted to win."

"Yeah—I didn't want you to *let* me win." She waved her hand in exasperation. Her too-large sleeve sank to her thin elbow.

"Sorry. If we had three, it would be a better game."

Zee sighed and set her cards down.

"Jank's no good. Even I could tell if he's bluffing. Do you think Rayn would play with us?"

Will shrugged, stacking his cards atop hers.

"Maybe."

Zee shoved her hair from her eyes, her head tilting to the side again.

"Who is she *really*, Will?"

"Talk to Sol about that, Zee." He slid the cards back into the box and set them down.

Zee leaned forward across the table.

"Sol's scared of her."

Will bit back a laugh. That was a hard statement to argue with.

"I think he likes her," Zee added.

Will stood as the girl continued to chatter. This conversation had the potential to veer down a path he did not want to take.

"I like her too. She's not like that...witch." Zee stood up as he did. "Do you like her, Will?"

Will didn't look at the girl. "Yeah, Zee."

The girl's feet slapped on the floor as she trailed behind him.

"I think you have a better chance than Sol does. She seems like she wants to knock him out most of the time."

Will shook his head as he took longer steps to avoid her questions.

"Go talk to Sol about this."

He pretended like he was going to shove her away, but Zee ducked from his reach.

"Too slow."

She scampered down the hall, and he heard the door slam behind her. Zee rarely spoke a word to anyone beyond their crew, but she always talked the most around Will. He didn't mind, but Rayn was not a topic for discussion. That was up to Solomand, who would dodge the girl's questions like he did everyone else's, which only complicated things. Will didn't like complicated.

He followed Zee outside and stopped short to see her walking along the railing of the walkway, her arms out for balance. He resisted the urge to yell at her to get down as he saw Solomand traipsing up from the docks, hands stuffed in his coat pockets. Rayn was with him. The sun streaming through the trees played on the different shades of red in her loose braid.

She was rolling her eyes as she talked in an argumentative tone.

"*Spry* is a stupid name for an airship," she said.

"That so? Well, it so happens that it's easier to alter existing registration papers than fabricate new..."

Solomand stopped short of what he was saying, his eyes falling on Zee's acrobatic display.

"Zee!"

He jerked his hands out of his pockets and ran, pointing at the girl.

"How many times have I told you not to do that?"

Zee teetered to one side, and Solomand dashed toward her.

Zee caught herself cartwheeling to the side and sprinted into the woods, grinning over her shoulder at him.

"Go climb a tree!"

Solomand called after her, his shoulders relaxing as he breathed in relief. Rayn laughed at him behind her hand, then cleared her throat when she caught his sideways glare.

Solomand shook his head as he passed Will.

"I've told her a million times. She's going to break her neck one day."

Will nodded in agreement.

"Yeah. She's hard of hearing. Kind of like you sometimes."

His glance moved to Rayn and then back to Solomand in a meaning way he hoped his friend would understand.

Sol's spine stiffened, and he shoved his hands back in his pockets, giving Will a reproachful look.

"Et tu, Ennea?"

"Et tu?" Will raised an eyebrow.

"Never mind. You Olbians don't read much, do you?"

"No."

93

Sol shrugged. "Not that I do either. Tristan's endless quoting sinks in sometimes. Don't suppose you could talk Rayn out of going to Trader's Cove with us?"

Will glanced at Rayn. Her jaw was set defiantly.

"Sorry." She tucked her hair behind her ear. "But if I gave you a list, you'd muck it up, and then I couldn't fix your cannon, now, could I? I'm going with you." She wrinkled her nose.

"Well, when you put it like that, I don't have much choice, do I? Unless Will can sway you?"

That was one quarrel Will would never take part in. He clapped his friend on the shoulder.

"Sorry. I'll leave that to you, *Captain*. Don't get paid enough for that kind of negotiation."

He trekked down toward the docks, his walk resembling a drawn-out march.

"Traitor!" Sol's voice raised. "You don't get paid anything."

Will turned and gave Solomand a quick, two-fingered salute. "Good luck, Captain." He grinned.

CHAPTER 16

RAYN

AFTER SAILING SOUTHEAST for two days, the Spry docked at the seedy port on Trader's Cove. If possible, it was even more dilapidated than the dock at Solomand's hideaway. Fractures zigzagged through some of the scaffolding piles, patched with newer wooden braces that looked as though they'd been scrounged from a scrap heap. The whole construction leaned, swaying and creaking in an unsettling way with the slightest touch from travelers or the breeze. A gray mist hung over the hill-town in the morning, and it looked more like the splintered remains of a ghost town rather than a flourishing trading post.

Solomand was already waiting outside the open bay doors when Rayn came down at sunrise. The rain that had ushered them into port the previous night was gone. The discolored planks were damp from more than water, though. Rayn's boots slid on the splotches of grease, leaked from barrels of oil rolled from cargo ships. She hopped aside when the board sank under her weight; one of the many rotted spots peppered around missing boards. The air was thick with the smell of oil, fish, and a combination of other scents. Rayn held her breath and drew a hand over her nose.

"Coffee?"

Solomand looked a little too cheery for the hour of the day and the atmosphere. He took a sip of his own while pouring her a cup from a dented thermos. He held out the chipped mug to her.

"Thanks."

Rayn had to admit, there was something about the oil-consistency brew that was beginning to grow on her. Besides, the warm steam on her face helped mask the unique odors of Trader's Cove. She took a sip, her eyes passing over the town, emerging as sunlight forced the murky fog away. Dirt streets, muddy from rain, weaved through the town square. The city itself looked more like a conglomeration of elevated shacks, built against one another to keep them from falling down. Dark alleys snaked between the more distantly spaced buildings. Rolling hills sloped down in the distance.

"Why's it called Trader's Cove? Doesn't look like a cove to me?" Rayn remarked.

She took another hasty sip and burned her tongue.

Solomand shrugged.

"Hell if I know. Probably named by a pirate—cove sounds more... piratey than Trader's Hill, I'd imagine." He tipped his mug up, finishing the rest of his coffee. "We'll set off once Zee and Jank get here." He wiped his mouth on the back of his hand and set the empty cup inside the bay on a crate. "Best trading's done in the morning." He rubbed his eyes, moving his hand over his mouth to cover a yawn.

"Depending on what you're trading for, anyway."

Zee appeared beside Solomand, lingering behind him. Jank staggered out. Yawning, he tied the loose sleeves of his jumpsuit around his waist. "About time," Solomand said. Jank gave him a sour look and muttered in a low voice. "Mind your language, Jank."

"Yeah, yeah."

A barefoot boy in tattered clothes strode up and down the length of the docks, carrying a sack of rolled up broadsheets.

He yelled in a grating voice, "Get your latest news—everything you need to know right here. Just the facts."

Solomand scowled and spit on the ground.

"Trash-peddling swindler." He raised his voice, and passers-by scowled at him, crossing to the other side of the street. Hands on his hips, Solomand looked satisfied he had scared the boy's customers away. He wagged a finger in the air.

"The only thing those damn things are good for is—"

"Another High-Brow assassinated by mysterious sleepwalking culprit."

Solomand's eyes narrowed with interest as the boy walked past. "Jank."

The engineer jumped. His face, Rayn noted, was a sickish yellow color. Solomand nodded toward the Broadsheet boy.

"Pay the swindler, will you?"

Mouth half-open, Jank looked like he meant to protest, but swallowed in a pronounced way instead. Digging a coin out of his pocket, he went through a series of movements where he dropped the coin and fumbled to pick it up before finally crossing the street and hurriedly passing it off to the boy. He thrust the Broadsheet into Solomand's hand like he thought it might burn him.

"Here."

Solomand produced a crumpled slip of paper from his pocket and handed it to him. Jank looked at the paper like Solomand was trying to offer him a venomous snake.

"The supply list, Jank."

The engineer snatched the paper, uncrumpled it, and held it to his face as he read, moving his mouth noiselessly.

"Back here by noon," Solomand said. Jank ignored him and kept reading. "Twelve o'clock."

Solomand thumped him on the head with his fist.

"Owe! Sh—." Jank bit back a swear. "I got it," he said, glowering at Solomand. "Come on, Zee."

He shoved the envelope in his pocket and took the girl by the hand, hurrying away.

"Trash?" Rayn glanced over Solomand's shoulder at the scrupulous headlines. "What was it you were going to say those were good for?"

Solomand cleared his throat and smoothed the creased paper.

"Alright. Maybe two things. On occasion, a fact manages to accidentally slip into the endless stream of propaganda. If you know what you're looking for."

"Right." She gazed after Jank, who seemed even more on-edge than usual. "What's wrong with Jank, anyway? Looks like he's seen a ghost."

"More like what he heard."

Solomand's eyes narrowed. His finger following the words to the story about a dead mayor. Rayn rocked forward onto her toes to see over his shoulder:

Mayor of Syracuse murdered in his sleep. The culprit, Samuel McGentry was caught without incident. He claims he was asleep and halfway across the town. This is the third such story in the past five months of similar slayings throughout the Plains cities. Could this be the work of the mysterious Professor Falcon?

Rayn rolled her eyes.

Sensational garbage.

"Mysterious Falcon? Where's the fact slipped into that mess?"

Then again, there was that word sleepwalk again. She finished the rest of her coffee and set the empty mug inside the airship on a crate.

Solomand raised his eye from the Broadsheet to look at her.

"Now see. It's what you'd least expect to be true, that is. Sleepwalker."

He balled the sheet up and raised his arm, gauging his aim before pelting the paperboy on the back of the head with it.

"Now then, off to find you some harmless metal scraps, eh?"

He was already walking into town when the boy turned to see who had thrown the paper at him.

Rayn hurried to catch up, adjusting her gun belt as she went.

"What is a sleepwalker supposed to be?" she asked.

Solomand gave her a sideways glance. "Trust me. You wouldn't believe me if I told you."

"Try me."

Rayn's voice was flat. She wondered if keeping secrets was always second nature to him.

"Alright. It's someone who can be in two places at once while they're sleeping. Not everyone can do it. Only people who have a particular gene."

"Two places at once? You've got to be joking."

He was either crazy or feeding her a line of horseshit to keep her from asking questions.

Solomand gave her a crooked grin and shrugged.

"I tried to tell you."

"And this Professor Falcon?"

She couldn't keep the cynicism from her voice.

A dreadful somberness replaced Solomand's smile. "That'd be Jank's ghost. He's no joking matter."

The uncharacteristic seriousness made a child run up and down Rayn's spine. Whoever this Falcon was, Solomand believed he was real, and—more to the point—he seemed afraid.

"If you believe the stories, he can make you sleepwalk where he wants—offing an official, for instance. The sleepwalker is seen, takes the fall, and he's in the clear. No risk to him." Disgust crept into Solomand's voice.

"That what happened to Jank?" Rayn asked.

Solomand didn't answer, but his eyes raised slightly. If it were true, it would explain the engineer's jumpiness.

As they rounded a bend, rough looking people eyed them with suspicion before turning up their collars and tramping away. Aside from the paperboy, there were no signs of children anywhere. Messenger hawks filled the air with wing-beats as they took to the sky from makeshift, wooden cages; not the most efficient means of communication, but still, the most trusted to avoid interception by authorities.

"Nice place," she said, coughing into her hand, trying to avoid breathing in with her nose.

"Isn't it?" Solomand ducked under a crumbling doorway, which turned down another empty alleyway. Their boots splashing in fetid puddles of water were the only sounds.

"Where are we going?"

Rayn walked faster to keep up, eyeing the dark windows. Her hand moved to grip her revolver.

"Just up ahead."

Solomand nodded towards a door hanging on by one hinge.

Doubt started to play in her head. Maybe it would have been best to stay behind. As Solomand pushed the door open, Rayn eyed the hinge, expecting it to break.

"Down the hall to the left," Solomand said.

Low flames flickered behind cracked and dirt-smeared lamp covers.

Shards of glass crunched beneath their boots. Rayn cringed at the layers of trash. The smell of urine and dead rodents was worse than the colorful aroma of the rest of the town. She swallowed back a gag, trying to stay close to Solomand. She searched his face for any kind of shared disgust but found none. Did nothing bother him? A rat skittered across their path, and he kicked it to the side. It squeaked and burrowed away behind empty bottles and stacks of moldy newspapers.

Oh god!

Rayn clamped both hands over her nose, trying not to look as sick as she felt.

"Well, well, well. If it isn't Cap'n Blacky come to see Old McKlane," a croaky voice rasped. A thin man sat in front of a table littered with oddities at the very back of the room. "Can't avoid a good bargain, eh Cap'n?"

He grinned, revealing a few half-rotten teeth. His watery eyes ran up and down Rayn.

"What's this, then? Dealing inn high dollars now, are ya?"

What the hell does that mean?

Rayn tensed, her heart pounding. Her hands lowered from her face and rested on her gun belt, giving the old man a look that could have cut stone. She had never seen a slave but had heard stories that slaving was a flourishing enterprise on other continents. She pretended to be interested in the mechanical trinkets strewn out before the old man. There was nothing of much value: a variety of knives, solar pocket-watches, and a necklace with a glass pendant caught her eye. A firefly glowed intermittently from within the glass oval.

A mechanical spider made its way across the table. It would raise one ink-colored leg and place it over an item as it navigated through the maze of trinkets. Intricate black gears whirred inside the glass bulb of its body, weaving around a liquid-filled center in the shape of a violin.

Solomand stepped in front of Rayn and slammed his hands down on the table.

"I don't deal in that shit, McKlane, and you know it."

His voice was low and threatening. Rayn relaxed her shoulders, feeling somewhat safer. The spider scuttled behind a dusty bottle with disturbingly lifelike speed. McKlane shrank back as Solomand jabbed a finger in his wrinkly face.

"And it isn't *Cap'n Blacky*, you goat-faced weasel!"

McKlane threw up his hands. "Alright, alright. Didn't mean nothin' by it. Get all kinds here, ya know—'specially these days."

Solomand frowned with disgust.

"I came here to find some parts for a gunsmith," he gestured to Rayn.

The old man shifted his wily gaze to her and back to Solomand nervously.

"Sure, sure—ol' McKlane can get anything ya need."

Rayn dug in her pocket and pulled out the list she'd drawn up before they left the Castle. She passed it to Solomand. He looked from it to her and shook his head, annoyed. She imagined the words running through his mind: *Really Rayn? You couldn't just give this to me?*

No, I wanted to come.

101

She wrinkled her nose at him in return. Rolling his eyes, Solomand passed the list to McKlane.

"Everything on here. I need it delivered to the docks in an hour."

McKlane bit his fingernails, which had a layer of dirt embedded underneath them, as he looked over the paper.

"An hour's a bit tough to swindle."

Solomand cracked his knuckles. "You need something to make it feel less difficult?"

"Not impossible—not impossible! Cost'll be steeper, though."

Solomand glared at him, his lips forming a tight line as he flexed his fingers. Rayn half expected him to haul off and lay the man out. McKlane, for his part, didn't back down, even though fear danced across his face in the shadowy lighting.

"Look here, ol' McKlane'll cut ya a deal, but fair's fair..."

"Alright," Solomand said. "But no payment 'til delivery."

"But come on Cap'n," McKlane protested.

As Solomand stuck his hand in his pocket, he pulled back his coat revealing the handle of his revolver. "You know, I'm always fair. Even with lowlife scroungers like you."

McKlane's scratched his head. It was hard to separate where his grungy white hair stopped and his beard started.

"Alright." He nodded. "Ya got yourself a deal."

Solomand shoved his hand in his pocket and pulled out a large copper coin. He tossed it on the table, and McKlane snatched it up.

"They better be there, McKlane."

He scooped up the firefly necklace.

McKlane bit the coin between his remaining yellow teeth.

"McKlane's guarantee!"

He winked as he tucked his prize into a ragged pocket and scurried away, presumably, to fill their order.

"Let's get out of here," Solomand turned to leave, turning up his collar over his mouth. "Place is starting to turn my stomach."

"Starting to?" Rayn had to take two steps to keep up with a single one of his. Solomand didn't offer any response. His pace quickened as they exited the rundown building and weaved through the dark alleys, taking so many turns that Rayn knew she could never find her way back to the docks without him.

Rayn walked faster until she was walking beside him.

"Where are we going?"

"To see an old silversmith—might know something about your S. L."

He shoved a hand in his pocket and fumbled out a cigarette. Rayn took the hint. He didn't want to talk.

It wasn't long before they arrived at another building, standing alone in the center of what once might have been a courtyard. The remains of a shoddy steeple leaned from the top.

"Let me do the talking in here, eh? Stay in the shadows." He paused. "On second thought, wait out here." He held out his hand. "I'll need your medallion, though."

Rayn frowned but dug the necklace out of her pocket and dropped it in his hand. If the church was anything like the last place they visited, she could wait.

"I shouldn't be long."

Solomand's hand closed around the medallion, and he kicked open the door, unleashing a flurry of dust that swirled into the alley. She glimpsed a black emptiness and heard scurrying as he stepped inside.

Mice or roaches? Rayn's thoughts turned to the mechanical spider, and a chill worked its way up her spine as the door closed behind Sol. She shivered and paced in front of the building in the saturating mist.

CHAPTER 17

SOLOMAND

"I KNOW YOU'RE HERE, Zishay."

Solomand's voice reverberated off the high, slanted walls of slate stone. Then, he spoke in a different language; the language of his mother. It sounded strange on his tongue after all these years; it was lyrical, bitter, foreign.

"*Show yourself, Priest.*"

At first, only the creaks of the floor and the echoing of his own words answered from the vacant building. Then, something scraped against the floor and a low voice answered in the same ancient language. "

"*You tell me to show myself? You are the one hiding in the shadows.*"

A match struck, the flame glowing, then dimming as it bent to the wick of a lamp.

Solomand stepped forward, squinting against the light.

"*I've nothing to hide from you.*"

The thin man stooped over a cane, long, silver hair draped over his black cloak. Bony hands tightened around the cane as he scraped it across the ground and hoisted it up with ease, catching Solomand in the ribs.

"Owe!" Solomand doubled over. "*What the hell old man?*"

He cringed, looking up reproachfully.

Zishay was not the man's proper name. It was the name given him by the Crow Clan during his time with them. It was there Solomand met him.

"*You have not come to see me for many years, Solomand.*" Zishay's eyes were like black marbles beneath thin, arched eyebrows. "*And the paths you travel...*" He shook his head sadly, bringing his cane back down to lean on. "*What would your father say? And your mother? They would expect more of you, Solomand.*"

The old priest was skilled with his use of guilt. His words struck deep in a way that Solomand would never admit. He straightened, still clutching where Zishay had jabbed him. But the real sting burned from the inside and was starting to spread.

Darkness threatened to take control. He fought to keep the memories in check. "*I have not come here to speak of them.*" He *couldn't* speak of them.

Zishay leaned forward on his staff, worn hands coiling on the handle.

"*Misfortune. It still follows you. It is the curse of the Kree.*"

Solomand suppressed the urge to roll his eyes at mention of the curse.

"*I did not come here to talk about ancient superstition.*"

His people were nomads, bound to wander; they could never call a place home or misery would settle on their shoulders. He recalled his grandfather, lying on a colorful, woven blanket in his tent, his eyes burning in accusation at Solomand, then ten-years old.

"*That is why my daughter died!*" The old man insisted, clinging to hurt and disapproval even as he drew his last breaths.

Lemuel Falcon had been there, his hand on Solomand's shoulder—one of the few moments he felt relief at the close friend of his parents being there. Then, his grandfather had handed him a tarnished copper sphere crisscrossed with lines and engraved with cyphered markings.

"*Your destiny.*"

Another thing he had to admit he owed Lemuel, who had later told him in his pervading, yet terrifying manner, *"Your destiny is what you choose it to be."* He dismissed the old man's ramblings as foolishness. *"Stay with the Crow if you wish, or I will return you to Corcyra if you wish. Your life. Your choice."*

Solomand chose the latter, taking the sphere with him. As grandson to the Crow Clan's chief, the device was his birthright. Lemuel explained what it was: an ancient navigational device made by their ancestors. It could interface with any airship or be used as a compass on its own. It could be programed to navigate anywhere on Roanoke. It was also a key to a safely guarded secret of the Kree Clans.

Solomand did not care about what secrets the device held. He only needed it for one purpose.

Zishay scrutinized him, looking like a badly carved statue.

"Why have you come?" He asked.

"I had something sent to you for safekeeping some time ago. I need it back."

"Ahh, the map of your destiny."

Zishay shook his head, looking disappointed. His knobby hands tightened, traveling to the top of his cane.

"It will do you no good, Anim—."

"That's not my name." Solomand stopped him before he could finish.

He breathed in slowly, transferring one hand to his pocket. Lines were more pronounced on Zishay's forehead.

"Even if you gain what you seek, the price will be too great. Even for a pirate."

Solomand's chest felt tight.

I'm not a pirate!

To the old man, he said, *"Are you finished?"* Then, because he couldn't bear the accusatory glint in the old man's eyes any longer, he looked away. *"Where is it?"*

Zishay shuffled forward.

"I will tell you, Solomand, but first you must tell me something."

Solomand raised a hand to his temple, closing his eyes. Sweat trickled down the side of his face.

"*What do you want to know?*"

"*What is it you seek? Revenge?*"

"*Yes. Among other things.*"

It felt almost good to admit it out loud. Almost.

"*Do you even think about what your parents taught you as a child?*"

Solomand's throat went dry. He looked away.

"*I have a lot on my mind these days.*"

Silence. More mice, or roaches, skittered along the wall.

"*Why do you not use the name of your people?*"

Solomand's body tensed involuntarily as anxiety threatened to take control. He knew he didn't need to answer. The old man must suspect it was because Solomand was not going to acquire a black reputation with his Kree name. But more importantly, he resented the Kree and their carefree way of life—the life his mother abandoned to marry a blue-eyed pilot named Silas Black. Even thinking about his parents caused his lungs to constrict. He needed to get out of here.

"*Let it go, Zishay. I walk my own path. Not that of my father, or my mother.*"

"*Alright.*" The old man's voice was resigned, even satisfied.

This only made Solomand feel more on edge. His hands clenched at his sides.

"*Where is it?*"

"*In the bell of St. Marten's.*"

Amusement washed over Zishay's face in the pale light of the torch. "*Should be easy for a man with your reputation to retrieve.*"

Solomand's shoulders slumped, a hand going to his strained face.

Now you're just mocking me. Solomand shook his head.

"*Thanks for nothing,*" he mumbled.

"*Farewell, Solomand Black.*" There was a distant sadness in his eyes. "*I pray you find what you need, if not what you seek.*"

107

"How do you know they're not the same thing?"

"They rarely are," Zishay said, smiling as he blew out the light.

The darkness engulfed him, but the burning of his words remained, working their way through Solomand in a way that was difficult to ignore.

His excuse ready, his thumb rubbed against the warm metal medallion and stepped outside. Rayn was gone. He looked up and down the foggy street.

"Rayn?"

There was no answer. His alarm intensified as he heard muffled cries of pain down the next street, and he sprinted toward them.

CHAPTER 18

RAYN

RAYN COULD HEAR voices: one Solomand's, the other an old man. They spoke in a language she did not understand, but it seemed oddly familiar. Her toe tapped on the pavement, her fingers drumming on her arms as she paced. Why was she so nervous? It was an impossibly long shot, and she had her doubts whether Solomand would manage to gain any useful information based on a solitary piece of forged silver.

What if he did, though? Her stomach fluttered at the possibility, and her mind wandered like it had many times before when she thought about who S. L. was. She imagined him as a tall man, muscular, with worn hands from working. Eyes of smoky brown and short, respectable hair the color of burnt umber. He would be happy she came, taking her at once in his arms to ask why she didn't wait.

Why didn't you come for me? Rayn's fantasy dissolved as the empty feeling rose to the top. *He couldn't be a coward.*

No matter who she may have been before, Rayn was sure she could never love a fainthearted cur. Another question came to her, small and desperate. She asked it to the hollow space inside her where S. L. stood.

What did you run away from?

109

Rayn was so lost in thought she didn't realize she was not pacing anymore, but walking down the street, her hands shoved deep in her pockets.

A hand was on her mouth before she had time to react, firmly pressing down so she could not hope to yell for help.

Dragged off of the street into an alley, Rayn struggled to free herself from the grip, not bothering to waste energy on a stifled scream. There were two of them. One forced her to her knees, holding her arms behind her back as the other tied a gag around her mouth.

Adrenaline rising at a steady pace, she stopped fighting and began to assess her options. The man behind her cinched the rope around her wrists, so it burned and cut into her skin. His partner surveyed her with black eyes, a dark brown scarf covering his head and face. The robes he wore were of the same color and a style she had never seen before.

Slave traders.

She felt her cheeks flush as anger boiled up inside her.

Try and take me, will you?

The bastard would wish he hadn't. The man behind her unbuckled her gun belt and tossed it to his companion, speaking a few obscure words. His hands ran under her coat, up her torso, searching for more weapons. He found a handful of extra rounds and a pocketknife in her coat pocket, then jerked her to her feet.

Neither of the men seemed concerned—a mistake they would soon regret if she had anything to say about it. On her feet, Rayn waited until the man who held her passed her belongings to his companion to look away. Then, she feigned a stumble to the side, tripping the hidden switch on the heel of her boot. When he put his hands on her this time, she twisted to the side and kicked.

The man cried out in pain, releasing her as he hopped on one foot, leaning down to grab his injured leg. When his friend lunged for Rayn, she fell onto the ground, pushing her leg into his stomach as he stopped to take hold of her.

His black eyes widened as his hands went to his middle and her gun belt fell to the ground along with the bullets and knife. Rayn dropped to her knees, bending back, so her bound hands reached the toe of her boots, and sawed through the ropes on her wrists with the blade sticking from her boot.

"Rayn!"

She looked up to see Solomand running toward her down the alley. When he saw the two men, they were bleeding and scrambling to get away. His jaw clenched.

Her hands free, Rayn ripped the gag off her face and spit out the taste of dirt and kerosene. Solomand held out his hand, and she let him pull her to her feet.

"You alright?" He took her firmly by the shoulders, then quickly removed his hands.

"Yeah," she sneered at the retreating slave traders, rubbing her wrists. "Jackasses should have known better."

Solomand's hand moved to his revolver. As a dark look entered his eyes, she thought he meant to go after them. Instead, he spit out a name. "McKlane." Turning on his heel, he bolted down the alley.

"Wait!" Rayn yelled, afraid she wouldn't be able to find her way back without him. But there was no stopping Solomand. Resetting the blade in her boot, she picked up her revolver and dashed after him.

⚙

"McKlane!" Solomand's voice carried through the building as he stormed inside.

Rayn hooked on her belt as she tried to catch up. There was no sign of the old man, and Rayn didn't quite know why she breathed a sigh of relief. If he had sold her out, then he deserved whatever Solomand had in mind. Still, the feral look in his eyes that surfaced... she didn't want to see what he might do.

Looking around at the tables of McKlane's wares, Solomand's brow furrowed, and he kicked them over one by one, scattering

111

trinkets and smashing glass. Rayn found herself edging away from him, suppressing shock as Solomand finished flipping the old man's wares. Chest-heaving, he surveyed the wreckage.

"Dodgy old, goat-faced son-of-a-bitch." He breathed out. "I hate slavers. And anyone that does business with them."

A little breathless, Rayn said nothing at first. She followed Solomand out. His boots found anything that moved, making the gears of the mechanical spider crunch beneath his heel. Rayn tip-toed around the items.

"You sure it was him?" she asked quietly.

"Oh, it was him." Solomand dragged a hand through his hair as they stepped out of the warehouse. "For his sake, what I ordered better be on the docks."

Shaking his head, as if waking from a dark dream, he turned to Rayn and tossed the medallion back to her.

"Let's go."

CHAPTER 19

SOLOMAND

"WH-WHAT DID HE say?" Rayn stammered, clasping the medallion in her hand before returning it to her pocket.

The hope in her eyes crushed him. He tried not to look at her as they stalked out into the street. Movement on the roof caught his eye. He jerked his head to see a sleek falcon watching him, its head tilted to the side. Blue feathers shimmered in the rays of sun that filtered through the fog and played on the roof's peak. A tiny scroll of paper was bound to its leg.

A cold sweat broke over Solomand's skin. The bird's screech cut through the stillness, and it took flight. He pulled his gaze away as it disappeared beyond the buildings into the clearing gray of the sky. That was no ordinary messenger bird. Only one person used a blue myst falcon for communication that he knew of. He spoke to Rayn as they made their way back toward the docks at a pace she struggled to match.

"A gentleman commissioned this, and a separate piece to go with it. He picked up this one first—the second was delivered to the northbound passenger ship, Natasha."

His heart pounded in his ears as he repeated the carefully rehearsed words.

"Wait. Northbound? What does that mean?"

Rayn was trying to keep up with him.

113

"Your charming S.L., more than likely, was headed to the city of Grishtanburg. It was a popular place for people to run after the war—still is, actually."

"Why?" Rayn grabbed his arm, forcing him to stop and look at her.

A tingling sensation crawled up his spine at the touch of her hand. He took a deep breath and met her eyes.

"Because it's so damned cold up there even the airships would rather dive to an explosive, warmer death than freezing to death while chasing ghosts across the ice."

Rayn's hands fell to her sides. As he looked at her distant gaze, the green of her eyes seemed to fluctuate, growing darker, then lighter. The stony look fell for an instant, leaving her looking lost and alone. A pain stabbed at Solomand's heart.

"Sorry," he said more softly. "It's where people go to disappear."

The guilty stabbing grew worse until it was an actual pang, throbbing in his chest, refusing to go away. They walked in silence. Rayn did not seem eager to talk about it any longer, much to his relief.

Enough lies for today.

He worked his finger in between his shirt collar, longing for the clear valley air.

Solomand cleared his throat, praying she would not ask him anything else. He felt sick. Despite what anyone may have thought, he hated lying, especially to her.

Jank and Zee were already waiting for them. Zee sat on top of a huge wooden crate, swinging her legs and munching on an apple. Jank held a pocket watch with a scratched-up face. He squinted to read the time.

"Almost had to send out a search party."

Solomand gave him a dark look which banished the sarcastic grin on his face.

"Everything in order?"

He pried open the two smaller crates and examined the contents. He pulled out one of the ten transmitter cuffs and squinted at the burned-out control panels.

"You sure you can fix this?"

Jank looked offended.

"Of course, I can fix it—as long as I've got the right parts."

Solomand dropped it back into the crate and wiped grease on the side of his pants.

"Did you check that you have what you need?"

Jank rolled his eyes.

"I checked."

He crouched in front of his toolbox, sorting through wrenches and grumbling to himself. "Act like I'm some kid or something."

"And?" Solomand's fingers drummed on the side of his leg.

Jank looked up, the circles under his eyes looking darker as his complexion paled. He dug out a rolled piece of paper from his pocket and handed it to Solomand.

"It's sent." He said.

Solomand stuffed the scroll in his pocket. At least one thing was going as planned.

"Good. Nice work, Jank." He clapped the engineer on the shoulder. "Didn't kill you, either, did it?"

Jank gave him a withering look and shrugged free of his grip. His silence was always a sure way to tell if Jank was actually furious with someone or being his usual volatile self. His seething glare assured Solomand forgiveness for making him send this message would come at a price. He sighed, wondering if Jank would team up with Ivan to take him out while he slept.

"Let's get these on board and get the hell out of here."

Solomand gave a last, distasteful look at the docks behind him as he bent over and shoved one crate up the ramp into the cargo bay.

"Well, well. Solomand Black. Not leaving without me, are you?"

The syrupy voice made his skin crawl.

Oh, hell. Just what I needed.

115

CHAPTER 20

RAYN

A TALL BRUNETTE sauntering up to Solomand. Her confidence was almost tangible, like a magnetic force pushing against Rayn. A rich velvet gown hung off her shoulders, the neckline cut low in a fashion that flattered her figure. Her silky hair was done up in elaborate braids, falling to the side of her bare shoulders without one strand out of place. Tucking her frizzy braid behind her, Rayn shrank away, shoving a crate up the ramp. Glimpsing over her shoulder, she saw the woman arch her perfect eyebrows, dark against her spotless complexion. She gave Solomand a full-lipped smile.

"It has been such a long time since we kept each other's company, don't you agree?" She hooked gloved arms around Solomand's neck and pursing her red lips toward his.

Prostitute. The harsh assumption entered Rayn's mind like a searing arrow. The easy way she sidled up to the Captain, as if all she had to do was bat her eyes and get what she wanted. And Solomand seemed just the type to play into her hands. Rayn gave the woman a savage glare, her reaction of fierce dislike feeling somewhat irrational.

Solomand drew back, removed her arms from around him and took a step back. "Hello, Minuet," he said, his voice dry.

Setting the crate down, Rayn went to get another one. She expected Solomand to easily faun all over the woman. There was no trace of that. If anything, he looked disgusted. Her anger receding,

Jank threw his arms up and groaned. "Oh brilliant, the fu—."

"That's enough, Jank," Solomand cut him off. "There are ladies present." He gestured to Rayn and Zee. "And Minuet, too."

He turned his attention back to loading the crates on board.

Ha! Rayn almost laughed out loud, reveling at the fleeting agitation on Minuet's face. She gave Solomand a mental high-five.

Minuet followed them into the cargo bay, sashaying, her skirts drawn up to not graze the dirtied floor.

"What have we here, Solomand? Found a new toy?" Minuet flashed Rayn a condescending smile as she looked her up and down. "I thought your type was more... blonde." She shifted her weight to one side.

Ugh! What a... Rayn was on the verge of telling this woman where she could go.

"Still..." Minuet tapped scarlet-tipped fingernails on her lips, her eyes narrowing. "She would clean up rather well."

That. Is. It! Rayn's hand dropped to the hilt of her revolver. "I'm not anyone's toy, you..."

Solomand stepped between them before she could finish telling the distasteful woman off.

"Anything other than *you* is my type, Minuet," he said, with a smile that looked like it pained him. "What do you want?"

"You are heading to Blackpool, and it so happens, I am in need of a lift." Minuet's eyes lifted playfully. "Lucky you."

"You're going to... hell?" Solomand feigned a look of confusion and pulled out his pocket watch. "Sorry, I'm not headed that way myself for another... six months, looks like." He snapped the watch shut and swung the chain around his fingers.

Minuet smiled sweetly as she bent forward.

"Nice try, Captain Black. But that goes against our little agreement, doesn't it?"

Solomand's fake smile dissolved, and he returned the watch to his pocket. A crushing disappointment weighed Rayn down when he turned on his heel, relenting with a wave of his hand.

"Fine." He jabbed at the control panel and the doors closed off the sunlight and foul smell of Trader's Cove. "Show yourself to your room." He started up the stairs, raising his voice and saying, "I'm sure the rats will like the company."

"Thank you, Sol, dear. I knew you wouldn't mind." Minuet turned to Rayn. "You and I must have a girl chat later."

She winked before gathering the dark silk of her skirt and sauntering up the stairs. Her high heels clicked on the metal, grinding on Rayn's nerves. Her mouth was hanging open in disgust.

"Excuse me?" She glanced at Jank and Zee and held a hand to her chest. "Was she talking to me?"

Jank cast a menacing glance up the stairs and kicked a crate to the side. "Well, she sure as hell wasn't talking to me—or Zee," he grumbled.

"Who is she?"

"A 'transportation agent.'" Jank made air quotes. "For the Coalition. She steals passage wherever she wants and in exchange, doesn't report our 'suspicious activity' to the Coalition," he started mumbling and jerked a wrench out of his rusty toolbox.

A simple solution to the problem came to Rayn's mind. "Why don't you throw her overboard?" She scowled.

Jank slammed the toolbox shut and laughed. "Would if I could." His face and shoulders fell at the same time. "Sol won't let me," he said in a mournful tone and stomped off towards the engine room. Zee followed after him.

The engines roared to life, and Rayn knew, from past experience, she had better retreat to a more suitable place for Solomand's takeoffs. The image of the prim Minuet flailing around in her cabin made her smile with satisfaction.

I hope she gets knocked out cold.

She darted up the stairs and down the corridor. The airship shuddered and shook as it lifted away from the dock. Rayn was halfway to her cabin when the thought occurred to her that Sol had left out a very important detail about their journey.

How long was she going to be forced to endure Minuet's presence? Rayn rushed down the hall until to the intercom. She flipped the red toggle switch and put her mouth next to the speaker.

"Uh, Solomand."

There was crackling. "Yeah." He sounded depressed.

"How long is it to Blackpool?"

More garbled noise. "Three. Days." He was speaking through clenched teeth in an agonized tone.

Three days? Rayn bit her lip and pressed her head against the hull. The rivets dug into her forehead. Her finger hovered over the button before she jabbed it down.

"How mad will you be if I throw your friend off?" She thought she heard laughter but couldn't be sure.

"I presume by friend you mean Minuet?" The ship jerked upward, and Rayn fought to keep her footing. "You'll have to get in line."

Rayn flipped off the intercom and maneuvered herself along the wall with an unsettling heaviness in the pit of her stomach. Rocks and sways of the airship didn't bother her as much as they had at first. The medallion felt heavy in her pocket, and she pushed it to the back of her mind.

Minuet. What a stupid name!

⚙

Rayn could have spent the time working on the gun in the airship's clandestine armory. The tools and supplies she needed to repair it were packed in the crates loaded in the cargo bay. She had only to go pry them open and get what she needed. Something else put her in a foul mood she couldn't manage to shake. *Minuet.* The woman made her want to lock herself in the cabin. But eventually, the room felt too much like a cage to bear any longer. Besides, why should she be hiding away while Minuet prowled around freely?

119

Flying at a steady pace, the airship was easy to traverse. Solomand must have put it on autopilot. Rayn gripped the railing, making her way down the stairs to the cargo bay. When her eyes fell on Minuet, she came to an abrupt halt.

Damn.

She reminded Rayn of the Highborn ladies who came through Ashbury. Her nose tilted in a stuck-up way as she spoke to Zee. The girl sat on a crate, looking up at Minuet with disdain.

"Have some respect, you dirty, little mud rat." Minuet's venomous words did not match her outward charm. "You shouldn't even be here, you know. Once your precious Captain no longer finds you useful, you'll be on a slave ship bound for Argos."

She flounced past the girl in a huff. Her cheeks were flushed as she squeezed past Rayn without a word, her skirts drawn up in one hand.

Rayn avoided catching her eyes as continued down the stairs. Jank, from a seat in the corner, walked over to Zee and she buried her head in his neck, her shoulders shaking.

Jank's arms closed around the girl. Anger rose inside Rayn on seeing Zee's tears. Her hand clenched at her side, and she spun on her heels.

"Where are you going?" Jank asked, his eyes raised at her when she looked at him.

"Where do you think? I'm going to go rearrange that b—" She cut the word short. "I'm going to rearrange her teeth."

"Don't." Jank shook his head slightly. "She'll make trouble for us, dead or alive." He gave her a look like he knew what she was thinking. "Don't tell Sol either. If he knew she talked to Zee like that… best he doesn't know."

Zee wiped the tears from her eyes. Dirt streaked over her pale cheeks. "It's alright," she told Rayn. "I told her she looked like a horse with rouge on." A devilish grin crossed her face.

Rayn laughed. That sounded like something Solomand would say. Except, for whatever damn reason, he wouldn't say it to Minuet.

Her hand relaxed. "Alright. But let me catch her off this airship!"

Zee hopped onto the floor, her eyes bright. "Only if I can watch!"

"Of Course." Rayn offered a conspiratorial smile.

Jank shook his head as the girl skipped away. "Don't encourage her." He started toward the engine room.

"I don't think it matters whether or not I do."

Jank paused, glancing back. "Stay away from her, if you can help it?"

Aside from making Minuet eat her words, Rayn wanted nothing more than to stay away from her.

"And promise not to, you know, kill her or anything?"

That was harder. "Alright," she agreed with a sigh. "If I *have* to."

⊰✿⊱

She had meant to keep her word, but that evening, on her way down the hall, Minuet was displaying more shrew-like behavior.

Flipping through the pages of a leather-bound sketchbook, her head tilted to the side, she was shaking her head.

"Give me that you—" Jank lurched for her, not finishing his sentence.

"Ah-ah." Minuet held the book out of his reach. "Is that any way to speak with a lady? Not that a mud rat like you would know anything about ladies." She clicked her tongue.

Jank's face was red, his body rigid as she poured through his most personal belonging. Rayn could see the anger and dismay in his eyes.

"Such dark, brooding drawings. They're not very good, though, for all the time I imagine you've spent on them. Pity you didn't have a proper education, then you might have developed genuine talent."

The initial anger Rayn had felt when she first laid eyes on Minuet rose again. She stalked forward and snatched the book out of Minuet's hand. Her heart hammered furiously, her glare daring the other woman to challenge her.

Startled at first, Minuet's eyes narrowed into a lofty glare. Rayn handed the book back to Jank and kept walking.

I promised.

The reminder stopped her from whirling and sending the other women flailing over the railing.

⚙

The kitchen was draped in the sort of stillness that precedes an impending violent storm. Solomand had not seemed keen to leave his post these past days and shut everyone out of the cockpit. Only Zee was occasionally allowed inside.

Rayn didn't blame him. She kept to herself either in her quarters, or wondering about the decks of the airship, glimpsing the passing sky through fogged portholes. This was the last morning before they were due to reach Blackpool, and everyone sat around the table eating breakfast.

The circles under Solomand's eyes were dark, and he didn't look like he'd shaved since they left Lubafell. Minuet stepped through the door, and everyone cringed. Tension hung in the air, thick and palpable.

"Is there any tea?" she asked in a cheery way unfitting for the atmosphere. "I cannot stomach that sludge you call coffee."

Rayn sipped her coffee loudly while pretending to read a long-expired newsprint.

Solomand sighed, slumping over the table. "If there hasn't been the past two days, what makes you think there would be any this morning?"

Rayn's eyes stabbed at Minuet for a moment before returning to the jumble of words she wasn't reading. What was the point

122

of wearing makeup every, single, day? What an insurmountable waste of time!

Minuet shrugged bare shoulders. "I don't know why I would think there would be anything civilized on this airship." She gave Solomand a meaningful look and wrinkled her nose at burned bacon and overcooked eggs before picking up a piece of blackened toast from the tray.

"Be sure to lodge a complaint, will you?" Solomand took a gulp of his coffee and slumped back on the table. "I'll be sure to avoid reading it before I throw it away." His voice was muffled as he talked into the table.

Minuet stuck her nose in the air. "I shall return to my room where the company is better." She banged the door on the way out.

"That toast will ruin your figure?" Rayn muttered.

Jank choked, spewing chewed eggs across the room. Solomand raised his head. "Rayn, if I didn't know any better, I'd swear you didn't care for Minuet."

"How can you tell?" Rayn snatched up a piece of bacon and bit a chunk off of it. "She's..." She chomped on the food, trying to think of an appropriate word to describe Minuet.

"A Coalition prostitute?" Jank offered.

Rayn put the newsprint down and turned to Jank, acknowledging him with the wave of her hand.

"There you go. Good a name as any."

Solomand reached across the table for the pot of coffee and refilled his cup.

"Who knows," he said. "Maybe you and her were best friends and you've forgotten." He looked forlornly at Jank's plate of food, which was un-scorched compared to everyone else's.

Rayn shuddered at the thought of being friends with someone like Minuet, preferring her memories be lost forever. "As if," she scoffed. "What's she after, anyway?"

Solomand's eyes fixed on the splatter of coffee pooled by his fingers.

"An insurgent who called himself the Black Recluse." He took another gulp of his coffee, staring at her over the rim of his mug. "He caused a great deal of trouble for the governor of Corcyra and his men during the war. And even though the bastards won, he was made too much of a fool to let it go." He yawned, waving his hand dismissively. "He's probably dead already, though."

"Black Recluse." Rayn let the name bounce around her head for a minute. She brought the mug to her lips and held it for a pause. "Seems like he could have come up with a better name than that."

Solomand's eyebrows raised. "Oh, really?" He leaned back, tilting his chair with him. "Such as?"

"If he's supposed to be deadly, even a black widow would be more appropriate. Recluses are rarely ever seen." Rayn blew into her mug, sending a puff of bitter steam back into her face.

"Is that so?" Solomand shook his head. "I'll bet you think the praying mantis is a glowing example for women everywhere too, huh? Gives a man one roll in the hay and then eats his head off!" He drew his finger across his neck.

"Well, now that you mention it." Rayn's eyes narrowed into an annoyed glare.

Jank snickered, leaning over his sketchbook but stopped, clearing his throat and hurrying from the room when he caught Solomand's glare, Tearing his gaze from the retreating engineer, Solomand's eyes turned back to Rayn, settling in that searching stare that made her uncomfortable.

"What did this Black Recluse do that they are still wasting time on him?" She asked, her gaze dropping to the table as she shifted in her seat.

Solomand shrugged. "The usual insurgent type shit, I'd imagine."

"Such as?" If he thought his answer was good enough he was mistaken. Rayn enjoyed the way it seemed he was ill at ease, instead of her.

Solomand sighed. "Well, for starters, he'd track their every movement. Intercepting messages and decoded them found out where a squadron would be. Next thing you know, they'd all be dead. Blown up by explosives, or their throats were slit or downed by a sniper's bullet. That sort of thing, you know. Made a general nuisance of himself."

His face clouded over, and he let the front legs of his chair fall on the floor, his face drawn and wary. "That satisfy you?" He stood and shuffled away, looking so cheerless that she felt her heart clench in sympathy.

The medallion and the name S. L. rang through her head like an alarm warning her not to get too close to anyone. Rayn felt dazed. She rose and wandered into the hall and back to her cabin.

"There you are!" Minuet's voice was about as pleasant as a gun blast going off right in her ear.

The ship spinning beneath her feet, Rayn wanted to lie down, not have a conversation with the person she liked least in the world.

"What do you want?" Her hand turned the latch to the cabin door.

"You needn't sound so hostile, my dear. I'm only here to help you." Minuet's look was condescending. She seemed to have missed the signals Rayn had been giving off that she wanted nothing to do with her.

"With what?" A cold rushing sensation rose to Rayn's head. Minuet's face was starting to blur.

"Solomand Black is not what he appears to be." Minuet's singsong voice sharpened.

"You mean a clumsy, jackass masquerading as a smuggler?" It was a strange image to want people to believe if you didn't fit the description.

Minuet's jaw clenched. There was a flash in her eyes as she let her civil mask fall for an instant. "Joke about it all you wish, but Solomand Black is dangerous."

125

"Maybe to himself." Rayn's shoulder pressed against the door. "If he's such a dangerous criminal, why don't you arrest him and be done with it?"

"Because, Rayn, respectable people follow the law—unlike the crew of this ship." Her voice lowered. "The truth is, I'm not after Solomand."

"Is that so?" Rayn edged the toe of her boot inside the cracked door. If Minuet thought she was going to believe her, she was a bigger idiot than Solomand.

"I'm searching for someone important to Governor LeFrost—someone the insurgents took from him."

"And Solomand is supposed to be a part of these *insurgents*?"

Minuet drew closer, and Rayn wanted to gag on the overwhelming flowery odor of her perfume.

"He's no good, Rayn."

Solomand's eyes entered her mind, desperate and cold at the other end of a revolver. Rayn breathed slowly, and the white lights faded with the cool, tingly sensation.

"I hear he once cut a man's eye out for looking at that child who tags along with him."

Rayn realized she was talking about Zee.

"What's your point?" she asked. "Jealous he won't give you attention?

Minuet's cheeks flushed, and she let out a bitter laugh.

"I'm only trying to warn you, Rayn. I would stay away from Solomand Black if I were you. The war is not over in his book, and if you stick around eventually, you shall have to decide where your loyalties truly are."

Skirts gathered up in one hand, flounced away.

Rayn made a point to slam the door before throwing herself down on the bare cot. Where my loyalties are?

"What the hell's that supposed to mean?" she mumbled, hoping that was the last of any chat she would have to endure from Minuet.

126

CHAPTER 21

RAYN

A LAMP BURNED in the window. Rayn lay on her bunk, wide awake, ten-years old in this dream. He said he wouldn't be long. The door burst open, and the shouts filled the cabin. She recognized one of the deep voices.

"Lay him over there, Bek—hurry!"

The floor creaked and shifted under the noise of boots clambering about.

Rayn kicked off the blankets, already dressed in pants and an untucked shirt too big for her. Her bare feet cold on the dusty planks, she pushed the door open and dashed down the narrow hall to the entryway. Once there, she froze.

There was a dark-haired boy who looked to be about her age laid on his stomach on the stretcher her father kept tucked under his bed.

"Lay him over there."

Her father, she realized, was the giant of a man giving orders. He was cutting the boy's shirt off with a curved knife.

Rayn sucked in a breath. The boy's back was riddled with whip marks. Blood spilled over his sides and onto the floor. Rayn looked away as they began cleaning his wounds. The boy cried out, gnashing his teeth and jerking upwards.

"Easy, boy... easy," her father said, pushing him back down with a gentle hand.

The boy started whispering words in a language she did not understand. In between cries of pain, the other man smeared a green salve on his wounds.

"Rayn! I thought you were asleep."

Rayn was so shocked by her father's gruff tone that she jumped. Wiping his hands on a rag, he came and took a knee beside her. The light behind him shadowed his face, and she couldn't make it out. She breathed into his neck, swallowed by the embrace of his massive arms. He smelled of sawdust and oil.

Her eyes were fixed on the boy when the door burst open.

"Sir!" Rayn didn't see the man who spoke. "The boy's parents—they..." The man's voice trailed off. Rayn felt her father's arms tense around her. He stood and turned to the men in the room.

"Let's go," he rumbled, then bent down to Rayn. "Look after him while we're gone."

She nodded, and he kissed her forehead before bolting out the door with the others.

The boy's hair draped over his eyes, long and black and wet with tears. His lower lip trembled, and he clutched on the ends of the stretcher. His shoulders shook as he raised up on his elbows. Rayn took a step forward, nearly stepping in the pool of blood on the floor.

"You should be still," she whispered. "They'll be back soon." Her voice caught in her throat. She laid a hand on his fist. His fingers closed around hers, and he nodded once before slumping forward.

A noise like thunder shook the building, and a sickly bright light spilled in the window. Rayn edged closer to the boy as screams carried through the street.

That's when she woke up.

⊰✹⊱

"Not again!" Rayn pulled a pillow over her head. She didn't want to let the dream go.

The girl started screaming again.

Not a dream.

Rayn's eyes flew open. She threw aside the blanket and sprang out of bed. Bare feet padding down the metal flooring, she dashed down the dark hall toward the screams. Zee's door was cracked open. A sliver of light stabbed into the Corridor. She kicked it open the rest of the way and burst inside.

Solomand looked up from Zee's bunk. The girl's head was buried in his neck as her thin shoulders shook with sobs.

"It was just a dream." Solomand stroked a hand over Zee's silken hair, raising an eyebrow at Rayn. "Alright now?" His voice was soothing.

Zee gave a short nod and hugged him before sinking back into her bed. Solomand pulled a blanket over her.

"No more nightmares tonight, eh?" He ruffled her hair.

The firefly necklace around the girl's neck emitted a dim light as she gave him a grin and curled into the blankets.

Rayn glanced down to her untucked shirt and became aware of her ridiculous half-asleep appearance. Her face burning with embarrassment, she backed out the door. Solomand glanced over his shoulder, motioning her to wait with an amused look on his face.

Rayn stood in the hall, combing fingers through the tangles in her hair. Solomand tiptoed out, easing the door shut behind him.

"Nightmares," he said in a low voice. He scratched his head. "Probably of the day she lost her mother." He took a few steps away from Zee's door.

Suppressing the urge to disappear, Rayn followed. "What happened?" She was glad the hall was dark. It made her feel less ridiculous.

Solomand leaning a hand against the hull. "At the end of the war, the wounded were evacuated—flown to Cierne Island. The Coalition didn't want any high-profile war criminals escaping." He sighed, pushing his sleeves up to his elbows before crossing his arms. "They dropped a bomb on the place. Most of the civilians were killed, including Zee's mother."

"So, you're not…" Rayn stopped herself, biting her lip.

"Her father?" Solomand laughed, making Rayn feel more of a fool. "No. But we're the only family she's got."

"I just thought." Rayn cleared her throat. "You'd make a good one—a father, that is."

She flushed again. Was did she say that? Her eyes, accustomed to the dark, saw his face contort for an instant before becoming lost in a distant stare.

"Did you really cut a man's eye out for looking at her?" She wondered why she kept blurting things out without thinking.

Solomand's eyes narrowed to slits. "You've been talking to Minuet." He said Minuet like the name tasted bad. "I left the bastard one eye—a testament to my good nature." His eyes flashed. "Did she also tell you it was at a trading post where slaves are their primary commodity?"

Rayn shook her head. Solomand glowered at the ceiling.

"Damn if I know why I didn't just kill the piece of shit. Do me a favor, will you? If you plan on having any more conversations with that woman, don't mention anything about Tristan."

Rayn had no intention of speaking to Minuet at all if she could help it. But it was an odd request. "Why not?"

"Because." Solomand's voice raised, and he sounded agitated. Pressing a hand against his brow, he spoke lower this time. "His existence is a privilege only my crew knows about, and I mean to keep it that way."

What the hell is that supposed to mean? Rayn found herself annoyed. "Look, I'm sorry. It's just, I was dreaming, and…" She stopped, unwilling to share any details of her dreams yet. She glared at Solomand, knowing it wasn't his fault, but blaming him all the same. "And now I'm not likely to get any sleep tonight," she whispered through her teeth.

Solomand sighed. "Look, I wouldn't trust anything Minuet says if I were you." He started to walk away.

"Funny, she said the same about you."

Solomand stopped and glanced back, his expression lost to the shadowy corridor. "We're both right."

Rayn traipsed back to her room, her mind a jumble of confused thoughts.

CHAPTER 22

RAYN

BLACKPOOL WAS NOT a shady little conglomeration of makeshift buildings stuck together on a cliff face, providing a means of survival for disreputable types. The buildings here were straighter and not so much newer as properly constructed. Motorcars stirred up dust along the cobbled road that curved down the mountain, carrying goods and travelers to the towns stretched along the valley below. Even the odd motorbike roared past, its rider's scarf flapping in the wind.

Merchant stands were set up along the docks, and the smell of steamed rolls and coffee hung in the crisp air. The road out of town wove downward, disappearing under a cover of puffy white clouds.

Rayn stood on the dock, surveying the bustling city and sipping on a tin mug of thick, murky coffee. Minuet appeared wearing a narrow-brimmed hat over an elaborate, braided bun, a lace veil pulled over her eyes. As usual, not one hair was out of place. Her black corset matched her skirts and was tighter than usual. Men craned their necks as they passed, practically drooling.

Rayn rolled her eyes and tossed the rest of the coffee onto the ground. Minuet made a show of fixing her hair—as if there was anything to fix.

"You know, Rayn, you would be an absolute doll if you did yourself up." She smeared on another layer of deep plum lipstick before snapping her hand mirror shut and dropping it in her handbag. "You can borrow one of my corsets if you like." She smiled. "I always leave a few things in my room for next time."

She winked and blew a kiss at Solomand as he walked out with Jank.

As if!

Rayn wanted to gag at the thought of 'doing herself up,' as Minuet put it. She frowned into her empty cup with distaste, saying, "Corsets are for hookers."

Jank burst out in laughter, holding his sides and stooping over. Even Solomand, who for whatever reason seemed to want to keep peace with Minuet, could not suppress his amusement. His eyes pinched shut, and his shoulders shook as he tried not to laugh out loud. Minuet's ivory cheeks reddened. Her lips formed a tight line, and she regarded them all with disdain.

A sleek black motorcar pulled up to the docks, its engine hissing as it rolled to a stop. Steam lifted from the hood in spindly wisps. Solomand, wiping a tear from his eye, opened the car door for Minuet.

"Glad to see you off, *Lady.*"

He dug a letter from his pocket and held it out, glowing with enthusiasm to be rid of her. It looked like he had even found the time to shave his beard back to a more presentable level.

Minuet sucked in her breath as her eyes fell on the envelope. Then, with a look of pure hatred, she snatched it from Solomand's hand, gathered her skirts in a huff, and climbed inside the waiting car.

Jank leaned against a row of oil barrels.

"Did you see her face?" Still laughing, he pointed after the car as it disappeared around a bend in the road. "That's the best damn thing I've seen in months!" He broke into another fit of laughter.

Solomand sidled up to Rayn, shaking his head. "Did you have to go and tell her off, Rayn?"

"What?" Rayn splattered the remains of the lukewarm coffee to the side of the door. "It's true. I've never seen a hooker who didn't wear one."

She set the mug down and adjusted her gun-belt.

Solomand rolled his eyes upward. "To be fair, Rayn, they are worn by highborn ladies who care about being fashionable."

Rayn shoved one sleeve up to her elbow.

"Yeah, well, breathing is in fashion for me."

A blank stare from Solomand again. "You don't have any female friends, do you?

Rayn cocked her head to one side.

"If it requires me to dress like that and parade around unarmed, I don't want any."

It was easier than saying she didn't have any friends at all. People were complicated.

"I can see that." Solomand eyed her revolver.

"Why do you care whether I told her off, anyway?" Rayn laced her fingers together as she stretched her arms overhead.

"It's best not to burn all bridges in our line of business."

"You mean smuggling or piracy?"

Solomand pinched between his eyes, letting out a sigh. "I don't have time for this nonsense." He glanced around the city contemptuously. "Come back inside, will you?"

Rayn recalled the conversation from the night before. Was he considering her a part of his crew? After living in relative isolation, the thought of being part of something—anything—gave her a strange feeling. She liked it more than she cared to admit.

"It so happens that I have a little business to attend to in Blackpool." Solomand frowned. He kept his voice low. "And it'll have to wait until... after hours."

"After hours, huh?" Jank's eyes narrowed in suspicion.

"Yeah." Solomand hooked his thumbs on the edge of his belt. "I have to retrieve something from the bell tower of St. Marten's chapel."

"What?!" Jank's eyes bulged out of his head. "You mean the old Krishtaren chapel? In the center of the square? Have you gone ace-high mad!" He animatedly waved his arms. "Someone will damn-well see us!"

"There's no *us*, Jank." Solomand took off his overcoat and tossed it atop a crate. "Zee will be on the ship, waiting to gun it when we get on board. All you have to do is stand watch and let me know when you see anything suspicious, preferably before bullets start flying my way."

"Oh." Jank rubbed the back of his neck. "Right, then."

"I knew I could count on your stellar bravery." Solomand gave him a grim smile.

Traces of grease smeared in Jank's reddish-brown hair as he combed a hand through it. He scowled, his eyes dropping to his scuffed boots.

"And what about me?" Rayn felt left out.

Solomand rubbed his chin and hesitated.

"Well. The thing is, Rayn, this isn't something you should get too involved in."

Oh no, you don't!

Rayn tensed, preparing for an argument.

"I'd feel better if you stayed on the ship."

There it was.

I will not!

Rayn had had enough of being left behind. "I'm part of the crew, right?"

"Well, yeah, but..."

She crossed her arms. "I don't want to stay on the ship!"

She bit her lip to keep it from trembling with anger. She was mad at Solomand for dragging her into this in the first place, making her want to be here. But more than anything, she was beginning to suspect, she was mad about being dumped in that godforsaken skyport by the man who ran away to Grishtanburg.

Solomand took a step back, holding up his hands in alarm.

"Fine. If it means so damned much to you, come then. About time you start pulling your weight, anyway."

He meant it as a joke, but still took a step back after speaking.

Rayn's eyes flashed. "I can pull *your* weight off a cliff."

She tilted her head back, trying to look threatening. It was too late, though. Her fury stifled by Solomand's agreement to let her come along, it was difficult to suppress the joy she felt.

"Yes, well, see that you don't pull it off a tower tonight, eh?" Solomand did not look happy.

Jank, whose face was twisted as he tried to hide amusement, managed a straight expression as Solomand turned to him.

"Be at The Pint an hour before dusk."

"What time is that?" Jank asked.

"When it's about to get dark."

"Thanks for being specific," Jank rolled his eyes. "Why the hell can't you learn to tell proper time, Sol?"

Solomand grinned, pretending to take his sarcasm as a compliment.

"You're welcome. Stay on the ship until then. This place is crawling with Pelicans."

Jank groaned.

And Rayn said, "Pelicans?"

"Airmen. 201st blowhards—off duty, but dangerous nonetheless."

Jank stalked away, casting Solomand a begrudging look before he disappeared into the engine room.

"Rayn, you and me are going to do a little recon of the area since you want to be involved."

"Recon?" Rayn adjusted her collar.

"Reconnaissance—military term. Means scout out for possible dangers."

There was a suspicious look about him. What was he trying to do, scare her? It wasn't going to work.

"Fine by me."

"Good." Solomand breathed in slowly, his brow furrowed into a serious expression. "We need to have a talk, anyway."

Rayn's confidence melted. She followed him into the streets of Blackpool, trying to sound disinterested.

"About what?"

"Grishtanburg."

Her stomach turned. The Northland city was a world away. Her chest felt heavy as the certainty of what she wanted became marred with conflicted feelings.

"This is where you'll be flying out of—once you're ready to take the trip. I can get you passage there. Not trying to rush you, but it's something you need to think about."

She only half heard what he was saying.

"Rayn."

He stopped, waiting for her to catch up. What was that in his eyes, sympathy? Rayn looked away.

"He could have had a good reason for running away," Solomand said, his voice softer than usual.

"Yeah?" her face was dark. "It'd better be one hell of a good reason."

Her braid fell over her shoulder as she bent over to adjust the straps on her boot. When she stood back up, Solomand was smiling at her. The crushing feeling lifted, and she felt trapped in the intense gaze of his eyes. Part of her didn't want him to look away.

"Rayn storm." He laughed, but there was a deep sadness in his eyes painful to look at. "I wouldn't want to be your S. L. when you find him."

The spell, or whatever it had been, broke, replaced by a throbbing in her left temple.

"Don't call me that," she muttered, pressing the palm of her gloved hand against the ache in her forehead.

They walked on in silence. Rayn's dark mood blurred her perception of the pleasant city, stirring up an uneasiness. Maybe it was the way all the women dressed in the same fashion. No one made eye contact with them as they pushed through the crowded streets, but she still felt like someone was watching them. Her eyes trailed up the side of a building in time to see gray shutters slam shut.

"Solomand?" she walked faster. "How much further?"

The path turned into a stone staircase as they followed the cracked steps into a courtyard, away from the bustling main streets. This part of the city was old and empty. Sheets hung in the windows, flapping in the breeze. A flock of pigeons took to the sky, filling the air with the beating sound of their wings. Rayn's hand flew to her revolver, her heart in her throat. She relaxed, wondering why she was so on edge. She glanced at Solomand. He hadn't noticed her jump or didn't let on that he had. His eyes were fixed on the church in the center of the courtyard.

"What is this place?" Rayn asked.

Her words echoed in the empty air, and she gulped.

"St. Marten's. It's a Krishtaren chapel." Solomand lit a cigarette. "It's abandoned since the war ended. Governor Jackass makes it hard to follow anything but him. He doesn't like the old ways."

There was bitterness in his voice.

"Governor Jackass?"

Too quiet.

Rayn didn't like it here. She edged closer to Solomand.

"Stefan LeFrost." Solomand spit after he said the name. "He's the governor of Corcyra. Blackpool is just one of the cities under the Coalition's control." He glanced sideways at her. "You really do need a history lesson." He took a pronounced drag on his cigarette. "I'll have to let Tristan see to it when we get back."

He took one last look around the courtyard, his eyes lingering on the bell tower.

"What exactly is it you have to retrieve?"

Rayn leaned closer to him as she whispered.

Solomand ran a hand through his hair.

"Better that you don't know," he finished his cigarette in one long breath and flicked it aside. "Let's go."

Great.

Another unanswered question to file away on her list. They returned to the airship and waited for dusk before going to the place he'd told Jank to meet them.

The Pint was a crowded bar, and despite the pretense of a civilized city outside its doors, it was like any other bar. Smoke curled around the stools in a dense fog, blending with the smell of sweat and liquor.

"Why the hell did we have to come here?"

Rayn turned her nose into her shoulder, coughing.

"To get soaked." Solomand unbuttoned his coat. "After hours work is best not left to the sober." He nudged Jank with his elbow. "Don't go overboard."

"Yeah, yeah." Jank pushed his way through the crowd to join a rough looking group in a game of cards. Solomand took an empty table in the back of the room. A woman dressed in a tight skirt, and a corset that might even make Minuet blush, set a drink down in front of him and took a seat on his lap.

⚙

Men!

Rayn rolled her eyes, her cheeks burning with fury. They were all the same. She planted herself on an empty stool at the bar. What did she care if Solomand wanted to cavort with common tramps?

Sweat glistened on the bald head of the stumpy bartender.

"What'll it be?" his beady eyes watered in the smoky atmosphere.

"Black rum," Rayn said. The man stared at her, toying with his greasy mustache. "Is there a problem?" Rayn leaned forward on her elbows, his suspicious stare rousing her more than she already was.

"That'll be two coppers." The bartender said, his nose twitching.

139

Muttering to herself, Rayn dug in her pocket for the coins, considering the best insult to deliver them with.

"Permit me, Ma'am."

The voice was clear and pleasant. She glanced up as the tall, uniformed figure tossed a bill on the peanut-littered counter. His cropped hair was a toffee brown color, matching his eyes.

He smiled shyly, "That is if I'm not too forward."

The perfect way he filled out his uniform was not lost on Rayn. The black stripes matched the buttons on his jacket, offsetting the navy blue.

"May I join you?"

Anger surged through her as she thought of Solomand behind her, carousing with a bar trollop.

"Sure."

A pleased smile spread over the gentleman's face, and he spoke with a highborn manner of speech.

"I'll have the same as the lady."

The bartender's suspicion dissolved into a pleased smile. He presented them with their drinks.

"It's on the house, Sir." He bowed his head and left them alone.

Looking somewhat embarrassed, the gentleman pocketed the bill.

"Allow me to introduce myself, my name is Reginald London." He held out his hand. Rayn gripped his hand in a firm shake.

"Rayn," she said, then, out of habit, "Just Rayn."

"My pleasure to make your acquaintance, Rayn."

His brown eyes never left hers as, instead of releasing her hand, he bent over and kissed it.

No sarcastic comment—such as Rayn storm.

"Likewise." She drew her hand away and stirred the ice around with her finger before sipping the chilled rum. Solomand's laugh rose above the loud conversations and yelling, and she tipped the glass back for a gulp.

"So, what brings you to Blackpool, Rayn? I have not seen you around." She imagined the suspicion on her face was evident as Reginald quickly added, "I would have remembered if I had."

"Would you?" She brushed loose strands of hair from her eyes.

"I could not forget a face like yours," Reginald said, turning crimson and cleared his throat. He gulped down a swallow of rum. "Sorry," he said. "I'm rubbish at this."

His shoulders slumped in defeat.

Rayn smiled.

"It's alright." His clumsiness somewhat reminded her of a confused puppy. Solomand's drunken carousing grew louder than everyone else in the bar. Rayn scowled.

"I'm passing through..." More yells from Solomand. She rolled her eyes. "With a couple of morons."

She didn't really feel angry at Jank, but it wouldn't be fair somehow to leave him out. She took another drink.

Reginald London leaned closer. His shoulder pressed against her own.

"Would you like to go somewhere quieter?" His cheeks flushed again. "I'm sorry... I meant for a walk or..." He cleared his throat and finished the glass of rum.

Rayn found his blundering had a certain charm to it.

I'd love to.

She couldn't say it. The initials S. L. and the city of Grishtanburg brought her brief moment of enjoyment to a stale halt. She laid her hand on his.

"It's alright." There was a hitch in her voice. "I wish I could."

He couldn't hide his disappointment, but he smiled anyway.

He certainly knows how to lose gracefully.

"Well then, let's have another drink together, shall we?" He held out his glass, which the bartender had already refilled.

Rayn clinked hers against his and gave him a brief smile.

"I'd like that."

141

For a fleeting instant, she wasn't some sad, empty person who didn't know who she was but a girl enjoying a drink with a gentleman.

The room erupted with the sound of breaking glass and splintering wood. She and Reginald turned at the same time, and Solomand appeared in front of the airman, seizing him by the collar.

"Jump in front of me, will you?"

Solomand punched Reginald in the face, knocking him across the bar, spilling the rum all over Rayn and the floor. The startled airman bolted back, but in his energetic swing, missed Solomand entirely.

The entire bar was in an uproar. The bartender screamed at them to leave. Rayn, unsure of what was happening, felt a hand on her shoulder. Her fist raised, but it was only Jank.

"Let's get out of here."

He nudged her towards the door. A few moments after, Solomand and the airman were ejected by the wild crowd, still taking swings at each other.

"What. The. Hell?"

Rayn flung her hands in the air as she and Jank watched the fight continue in the streets. Jank gave her a sheepish shrug. Could Solomand have become this stupidly drunk in so little time? He didn't seem to be. His attack on the airman was too methodical. A vein pulsed in the side of his neck and there was a cold, dangerous glint in his eyes.

Reginald did not fare as well in the fight as Rayn assumed he would. He may have been an inch taller than Solomand, with a more muscular build. But Solomand was the more experienced of the two. It was all over in a matter of moments. Once free of the crowded bar, Solomand lunged upon his opponent, kicking him in the chest. He flew down the street, landing on the pavement with a thud. Solomand was on him again, dragging him to his feet and avoiding his feeble blows. One last swing and Reginald fell to the street in an unconscious heap.

Solomand took a deep breath and cracked his knuckles.

"Gag him, Jank—can't leave him lying about."

"Excuse me?" Rayn barged between Jank and the bloodied Airman. "What the hell are you doing?"

"He's a *Pelican*, Rayn," Solomand said as if it was apparent what he was doing. He pulled her out of the way and stooped to help Jank drag the man off.

Rayn stormed after them into the alley.

"What I *mean*, jackass, is what the hell are you causing trouble for in the first place?"

Huffing, Jank dropped the man's legs to the ground. Without excessive gentleness, Solomand dropped the rest of him and drew a knife from his boot. The blade glistened in the moonlight.

"Hold on!" Rayn maneuvered herself between Sol and the downed airman with a wild leap.

"Look, you can't just go killing people in the middle of the street!" Her voice raised.

"Pelicans aren't people Rayn," Solomand retorted, pushing her aside. "Everyone knows that—even them."

"His name," Rayn hissed through gritted teeth, "is Reginald London, not *Pelican*."

"Reginald London," Solomand mocked, kicking the man's spotless boot. "What a pretentious name. Suits his puffed-up, swank head."

"Why do you have to be such an ass?" Rayn glared at him.

"He's with the 201st." Solomand twirled his knife in hand, the corner of his eye twitched. "You have no idea what they're capable of." There was wild savagery in his eyes. "If you recall, they blew your shop sky high and destroyed your precious rifle."

Rayn crossed her arms. "That was your fault."

"Ah. Well. Best to leave the past in the past." His eyes narrowed. "Why do you care so much what happens to Mr. London here, anyway?" He motioned toward the man's limp form, cringing with disgust.

Rayn stepped toward Sol, jabbing a finger at his chest.

"Because I was having a drink with someone respectable and you destroyed a bar to ruin it and now stand in an abandoned alley trying to *murder* him!"

Solomand shook his head.

"Drinks with strange Airmen. Really, Rayn. What would S. L. think?" He clicked his tongue.

Rayn's eyes widened and before she could even think, her hand had swung to smack Solomand. Her fingers stung, and she could feel the heat of her cheeks. In the pale light, she made out the tears it brought to his eyes.

"I fail to see how an Airman could be worse than drinking with hookers," she snapped.

Solomand wiped a tear away as it rolled down his cheek.

"*Hookers*, as you like to call them, often hear useful information that others do not. Airmen, not so much."

So that's how he was going to play it. He was only hunting for information.

"Although," he raised an eyebrow, "I can't see why it would bother you who I keep company with."

Did it bother her?

"And I might say the same to you."

It sounded petty, saying it aloud.

"I don't like Pelicans hanging around my crew." Solomand gave the man a dark look. "They're dangerous." He slid his knife back in his boot. "But I'll let this one live if it bothers you so much."

Jank looked uncomfortably from Rayn to Solomand.

"The bell, Sol," he prodded. And glanced down at the airman. "This is bound to bite us in the ass, ya know."

"What doesn't?" Solomand leaned over and used the airman's starched coat to wipe the blood from his knuckles. "Let's get on with it, then."

He glanced at Rayn and rubbed the red handprint on his cheek. She thought she caught his mouth turn up in a crooked grin.

CHAPTER 23

RAYN

THE BELL TOWER looked a pale white in the moonlight, instead of its actual color of faded gray. Jank stood watch in an alcove, rifle raised as he scanned the dark windows looking down on them. Solomand leaned his head back.

"Looks taller at night."

He unbuttoned the top button of his shirt and loosened his collar. He tugged at the thin chain around his neck before taking a sharp breath.

"Right."

He and Rayn started to climb.

Stones were staggered within the mortar, allowing enough room for the toes of their boots to get a hold. Rayn gritted her teeth and clutched the coarse footholds with her fingertips.

"How the hell did the old man get up here?" Solomand huffed.

Rayn kept her gaze forward, climbing as fast as she could until she could get her elbows on the edge of the shingled roof. She heaved herself up, swinging her legs and standing triumphantly on the roof before Solomand could offer her a hand.

"Right..." he said again. Perspiration was already heavy on his brow. "You go up that side, and I'll go up this one."

He waved his hand in the direction he wanted her to go.

Rayn nodded, climbing the opposite side as him, clinging to the contour of the tower. The curved stones felt cool through her

145

clothing on the warm summer night. Sweat trickled down her back and soaked the top of her trousers.

Almost there.

The windowsill was out of reach, the shadowy shape of the silent bell taunting her. Her right hand shook as she stretched, gripping with her fingertips. Panting, she pulled herself up. Her boots scraped against the stones as she felt for footholds along the way. She hooked her elbows on the window and pulled herself the rest of the way to the top.

I did it!

A thrill ran through her as she circled the narrow sill, taking in the view. Bracing both hands on either side, leaned out to get a better look.

It was like a pool of flickering lights, some of them moving. The sputtering of motorcars and the distinctive roar of motorbikes mingled with the clip-clop of horses as it rose above the streets. A warm gust of air blew sweaty strands of hair from Rayn's face. Her grip tightened, and she smiled, closing her eyes.

"For the love of god Rayn! Don't do that!" Solomand's voice came from below. He was still inching his way up.

Rayn leaned out further. "Don't do what?"

Solomand clamped his eyes shut and kept moving. "That!"

A wicked smile spread on Rayn's lips.

"Well, if I didn't know any better, Captain Black, I'd think you were afraid of heights." She feigned shock.

Solomand's hand reached next to where she was standing, and she sidestepped to give him room. He pulled himself up, eyes still shut, chest heaving.

"I'm a pilot. I'm not afraid of heights." His fingers never lost contact with the tower as he forced himself to stand. "I just have a problem with falling to my death or being picked off by a sniper—it's a lovely night for it."

The grin still plastered on her face, Rayn leaned out further. Holding herself with only one arm, she swung outside the window.

Solomand made a peculiar noise with his throat. His face looked almost gray in the moonlight.

"It's' rather lovely up here."

Rayn swung herself back to stand next to him. As close as they were, she could feel the tenseness in his arms and see the labored rise and fall of his chest. He was terrified.

"Let's just get what we came for."

"Waiting on you."

She made exaggerated eye contact, extending her arm so she could hang over the edge once more.

"Oh, for god's sake." Solomand pressed himself further against the tower. "Please. Stop."

"Oh, alright." Rayn relented, swinging herself back beside him. "Where is it anyway?"

"There's a compartment under the damned thing that holds the bell up." His hands shook as he slid down to grasp the bottom of the tarnished bell. "I'll lift it up, and you reach under and grab it—and be quick about it, will you? I shouldn't have to tell you, this thing's not light."

He nodded at the bell. Then, breathing out, he took hold of its brim. The vein in his neck bulged as he strained to raise the massive metal dome free of its hook and balance it on his bent knee.

The hook the bell was fastened on stuck through a box-like compartment, which could not be opened when it was in place. Rayn pried the door open with her fingertips. Her hand closed over the metal surface of a spherical device.

"Got it."

She fumbled the hook over the door back into place with her free hand, glancing at the metal ball in her other hand. It was covered with strange markings and had different-sized gears embedded in the surface. A muffled sound cracked from the square, and something whizzed past her head. Rayn's heart jumped. There was a stinging sensation on her cheek, then something warm and wet trickled down her face. The sound rang out again.

Someone's shooting at us!

147

She jerked, lost her footing and fell. For one terrifying instant, she felt like her heart might burst through her chest.

Solomand released his hold on the bell and grabbed her by the arm. He pulled her to safety as the deafening clang echoed throughout the courtyard and the rest of the city. "So much for going unnoticed."

"Hey!" Jank hollered. They looked down to see him flailing one arm overhead, his rifle in the other. "We've got company."

"No shit." Rayn could feel Solomand's hand shaking as he clung to her. Two more muffled shots came from the blackened windows. "And it's about to turn into a regular, high-midnight standoff."

His face inches from hers, he reached up and brushed her cheek. Then, with a look that said, 'I told you so!' he showed her the blood on his fingers. Her heart hammered in her chest, and she gulped.

"Let's get the hell out of this town," Sol said.

Rayn stuffed the geared device down the front of her vest before climbing down ahead of him. More bullets sailed, chinking at the stones over their heads. Gritting his teeth, Solomand whipped out his pistol and fired into the dark.

Rayn's fingers were slipping on the stones. She breathed out in relief and dropped to the roof. Solomand landed next to her, and they dashed across together.

Moving lights approached from the main path. Baying of hounds mixed with a swell of voices.

"Oh, that's brilliant."

Solomand skidded across the last few feet. They jumped together. Instead of finding themselves on the hard ground, there was a thump as they collided with something softer. Jank yelped and shoved at them.

"Bloody, get off!" he wriggled from under them.

"Thanks for the warning, Jank."

Solomand rolled off the engineer. Lights flickered in the open doorway of a building. Without thinking, Rayn drew her pistol, cocked the hammer and fired. Something slumped inside the door.

"Shit." Solomand crouched down, dragging Rayn and Jank with him.

"Can't go back the way we came," Jank panted.

"Then we'll make an alternative way! Come on."

They followed Solomand as he dashed from the lights and voices, skirting around a damp alley as the pursuers converged into the courtyard.

Solomand pushed up his sleeve, exposing the leather transmitter band on his wrist. He jabbed the red button with a shaking finger.

"Zee! Intercept at bearing November, zero, echo, five, eight!"

"Can she really fly that thing?"

Rayn's chest burned as she tried to keep up with Sol and Jank.

"Good as I can," Solomand said, dashing faster down the musty street.

So we're dead.

Their footsteps reverberated against the looming buildings on either side of the path. A small voice crackled over the tiny microphone on Solomand's transmitter.

"That's east?"

"East-ish." Solomand breathed into the microphone.

There was a pause, then Zee's voice came in again. "When?"

Flickering beams of light and shouting grew closer.

"Ten minutes ago!"

Solomand kicked in a door, and they stumbled inside after him.

Rotten boards and debris rained from the ceiling as they burst through a shattered window. Sweating and gasping for air, they followed Sol's lead and paused for a moment, bending and grasping their sides. The barking turned into guttural growls.

"Time to go," Solomand gasped.

He grabbed Jank by the collar and dragged him along until he started running fast enough to keep up. They were going downhill now, away from the city and whoever was hunting them. The path they were on wound down the cliff, beneath the mist.

"Too—dangerous," Jank doubled over, gasping out words between breaths.

Solomand ran harder, and they didn't dare fall behind.

Rayn's hair and clothes clung to her. Their pursuers were getting closer. Rayn drew her revolver, cocking it with a jerk of her thumb.

"Not yet." Solomand eased to the edge of the cliff, searching the clouds drifting by at their feet.

His chest heaved as he closed his eyes, his thumb twitching on the grip of his pistol.

Rayn rubbed the back of her hand on her face, smearing blood and sweat. Lights shone on them through the mist and Rayn's arm tensed. Another sound drowned out the baying of hounds. Rayn never thought the sound of an airship's engines sounded so good. She let out a sigh of relief, still eyeing the lights until the *Spry* was right on them. It rose from the clouds, the bay ramp extended.

Guns started firing. Bullets tore up the dirt, growing nearer with every shot. Rayn squinted and fired back. Someone gave a yelp, and she flicked her thumb, cocking her pistol again.

"Rayn!" Solomand grabbed her by the shoulder. "Let's go!"

Smoke rising from the barrel of her revolver, Rayn sprinted with him. Jank had already made it to the ramp. He crouched there now, waiting with his arm stretched out. Together they jumped across the two-foot expanse between the cliff and the airship. They were going to make it! A gust of wind pushed the *Spry* a few inches out, and only Solomand caught hold of the ramp. Dangling there, his face as white as the moon, he called Rayn's name as she fell. The airship surged forward and away.

CHAPTER 24

RAYN

WIND RUSHED PAST as Rayn plunged into the clouds. One moment she had felt exhilarated, knowing they would be alright. Now, she realized with horror, death was imminent. Much sooner than it should have happened, she collided with the ground and the wind was knocked from her chest. Pain shot through her arms and legs like bolts of lightning, and she struggled to sit.

She gasped to refill her lungs with air. Cool blades of grass touched her fingertips, thick with dew. The pangs lessened in intensity as she crawled forward on damp hands and knees. Her hands felt open space, and she scrambled back with a jolt.

Shit.

There was the unmistakable click of a gun's hammer and the cold steel of a barrel pressed against her temple. Rayn held her breath and froze. The sound of her heartbeat pounded in her ears, drowning out the barking of the dogs and shouts of the search party.

"Don't make a sound," a familiar voice whispered.

"Minuet?" Rayn couldn't believe it was her. "What are you doing here?"

She jerked her head over her shoulder to look at the last person she ever wanted to see again.

151

Minuet wore riding pants, a gray blouse, and a leather shoulder holster with two derringers. On her forehead was a set of infrared goggles with red shields over the eyes.

"Solomand's really made a mess of things this time," she remarked. "One more city he shall have to add to the list of ones to stay away from."

She eased the gun off Rayn's head, a look of triumph spreading across her face.

Rayn's hands lowered towards her belt, not liking the hungry look in the woman's eyes.

Minuet took a step back, her finger twitching on the trigger of her derringer. "Alright, Rayn. Hand over your weapon." The fingers of her free hand snapped repeatedly. Rayn tensed, imagining the sound of Minuet's neck snapping in her hands.

"Don't try anything stupid, either." Minuet arched an eyebrow.

Her mouth drawn into a tight line, Rayn unbuckled her gun belt and threw it at the woman, hoping it would catch her in the face.

"What do you want with me?"

Minuet tossed Rayn's revolver aside. "It's nothing I want of you, per se." Her head tilted to the side. "Solomand has something I want very much, and you will make a very nice trade. Or hang for crimes against the Coalition." A curt smile crossed her lips. "Or worse. I warned you he was trouble. Her hand went to the dial on the side of her goggles, and she adjusted it.

"I barely know him. What makes you think he'd trade what you want for me?"

Rayn figured the more she got Minuet to talk, the better chance she would have at escaping. The ground was too soft to trigger the knife in her boot. Her eyes moved to some rocks sticking out of the ground a few feet away.

Minuet rolled her eyes. "Oh please." She held her hand up to her face. On her wrist was a leather cuff: a transmitter like Solomand's, except it was slimmer. The keypad, with strange symbols rather than letters, was concealed between the linings.

"I suspect he'll stop at nothing to get you back."

Minuet undid the buckle and typed on the coded numbers. Her fingers nimbly worked to reattach the clasp.

Now saw her chance.

"Who says I need Solomand Black to save me?"

She side-stepped, slamming her heel against the rock, then jabbing the protruding blade into Minuet's shin.

Minuet cried out dipping to the side to grasp at her injury. Rayn wrenched the derringer from her hand and hit her over the forehead. She crumpled to the ground as the voices of her men and barks of dogs grew closer.

Rayn slung her gun belt over her shoulder and ran. Her lungs burning, she forced herself to keep going. She was blind in the thick fog. The barking grew fainter, and she suspected they must have stopped where they found Minuet.

Should have used her as a hostage.

The ground tilted at a steep angle and she dropped to all fours, feeling her way ahead in the mist, reaching in her shirt to make sure the device Solomand gave her had not fallen out when she ran. It was still there, and her tension eased as she panted.

How the hell am I going to get out of this?

Her hands found the jagged edge of a cliff, and she stopped crawling, her heart giving a violent jump. A sliver of black sky lit with stars shone through the clearing cover of clouds. Rayn gulped and forced herself to keep crawling down, her hand clutching the cliff's edge, so she could stay clear of it.

The sound of engines grew louder in the mist. Rayn looked up to see a familiar airship speeding toward the edge of the cliff-face.

"Sol." She breathed out a sigh of relief

CHAPTER 25

SOLOMAND

SOLOMAND WATCHED RAYN fall, his heart dropping with her. How could she not have made the jump? Fighting against the airship's forward thrust, he crawled his way to the intercom panel by the door.

"Turn back, Zee!"

"But, Sol, we can't turn back—they'll blow us out of the sky!" Jank yelled.

He recoiled, backing away as Solomand spun around to face him. He might have lunged at the engineer, but a shrill beep emanated from his transmitter.

He looked down to see the coded letters illuminate, revealing Minuet's transmission:

I have her at Rim. You know what I want.

Solomand jumped to the intercom. "Zee—bearing romeo-zero-zulu-five-four!" He turned to Jank. "Make sure the guidance keeps working."

Jank dragged both hands down his face.

"It's not meant to be flown like this, Sol!" he groaned, issuing a final complaint before dodging off to follow the order. "Why can't you learn how to fly the damned thing proper?"

The Rim was the narrow strip of land beneath the clouds of Blackpool. It ran to the outer edge of the cliff, the opposite way of the road that wound into the valley. Solomand secured one end of a rope to a rung on the wall, and the other around his wrist. His fingers quivered, threading the knots. Blood pounding in his ears, he crouched down and eased on the edge of the open ramp.

You know what I want.

He did know. But the fire of hell would be unleashed on this world before he gave it to her.

You go too far, Minuet.

People were not pawns in some game. One would not be exchanged for another. She should have known better than to test him on that. Solomand would never compromise or make deals with anyone that wore Coalition colors. Never again.

The grating shifted under him, tilting as the airship turned. Rushing wind no longer felt cold against his skin. Solomand's boots slipped. The rope tightened, burning his fingers.

If I ever get you out of this…

He tried not to think about what would happen if he didn't get her back.

The engines whined in protest as the *Spry* sank lower, concealed by the white haze of clouds. Solomand spotted her against the cliff; Rayn, with no sign of her captor. He gritted his teeth and got ready.

He nearly lost his footing altogether as the airship lurched forward. Rayn was near the edge now, reaching for Solomand's outstretched hand. His fingers clasped around hers and he yanked her onto the ramp. His arm tightened around Rayn, and he pulled them both inside, slamming the button to close the door before collapsing to the floor.

The ramp creaked shut, closing out the dark night sky.

"What took you so long?"

Rayn rolled onto her back, tilting her head to face him. The blood had all but dried on her flushed cheeks. Wisps of red hair clung to the side of her face.

Solomand felt sick. He managed a relieved smile. "You didn't think I was going to leave you, did you?"

Rayn's eyes closed. The rise and fall of her chest slowed.

"No." She reached inside her vest and dug out the spherical map. "I was sure you'd come back for this." She held it out, her arm resting on the floor.

Solomand's heart gave a painful wrench. Did she really think so low of him?

For you, Rayn! I came back for you!

He wanted to yell it out. But she wouldn't understand. In fact, he meant for her not to—for her own sake. He forced a joking grin, despite the drowning wave of misery that engulfed him.

"Of course." He snatched it from her hand managed a playful look. "It was rather a lot of trouble to get, you know."

Rayn's eyes opened, and she landed a punch on his shoulder.

"Jackass." She grinned.

Jank stood over them. He offered Rayn a hand.

"Hey, Sol—ya want me to add Blackpool to the list of cities to avoid?"

He helped Rayn to her feet.

Solomand stood, slipping the sphere into his pocket.

"Be easier to make a list of places we *can* go," he grumbled, limping away so neither of them could see the morose look he could no longer keep at bay.

He locked himself inside the flight deck, and lay against the door, taking a series of ragged breaths until the smothering pain left and he could breathe once more.

He made excuses to avoid her for the rest of the journey, occupying his mind at the helm, watching the wisps of white cloud pass by the nose of the airship as he checked that the instruments were adjusted even though he knew they were. Even Zee was banished from the helm, left to help Jank in the engine room. His mind would not clear, and he felt like all the years of running had crashed into him all at once.

CHAPTER 26

RAYN

STARS WERE BRIGHT against the clear dark of the sky—silvery light from the moon lit the fields. Her father was out. He always left when the riots broke out within the city walls. The City Forces were growing more brutal in their response. Rayn ran barefooted through the tall grass until she reached the wooden fence bordering their farm. Beyond it, the land gradually faded to desert.

"Rayn, wait!"

It was the boy. They were both older now, nearly fourteen.

Rayn ran faster, but he caught up. He always did.

"He told me to look after you, Rayn. Please come back." He spoke like running was no more effort for him than walking. They were at the fence now, and Rayn paused, her hand on the rough wood.

"I don't need you to look after me."

She turned away, hiding the tears that threatened to fall.

"I know you don't," he put a hand on hers.

The warmth of his touch soothed the pain inside her. His smoky black hair hung over his eyes and down to his shoulders.

"What if he doesn't come back this time?" she choked.

"He will."

And just like that, she knew he would, if only because the boy said it was so. That was how she felt whenever he spoke. He'd lost more than she had, and he still managed to smile in that way that made her heart melt.

"It'll be alright." He squeezed her hand. "Rayn storm."

Rayn's eyes flew open, her heart pounding.

Rayn storm?

She sat in a cold sweat, feeling like a crushing weight had been dumped on her shoulders. What if being around Solomand and the others were influencing her dreams now? They were all she had left of who she was. She collapsed back onto her pillow.

They had gotten back to Lubafell the previous night. Rayn took a shower before collapsing into bed. She stared at the ceiling for a while. It was still dark outside. She decided it was time to pay Tristan a visit before anyone else was awake. She got dressed, leaving her revolver on the bed, and crept up the stairs to his room.

She wrapped on his door, but there was no answer. Thinking it was too early, she started to leave when the door opened. Tristan met her with a cheery smile.

"Good morning, Rayn." He leaned on his cane. "Do come in."

"Thanks." She smiled, closing the door behind her. "I was afraid I was the only one awake."

Tristan sat on his bed and motioned her to a chair next to him.

"I hear you had quite the experience in Blackpool." He shook his head. "I am glad you made it back in one piece." He coughed into his hand. "How may I be of help?"

Rayn gulped. "Remember when you said to tell you if I thought of anything else?"

"Of course," Tristan's eyes narrowed with interest.

"I think my dreams might be memories."

"Really?" Tristan raised one eyebrow. He leaned forward on his cane, his brow furrowed as he listened to what she had to say. She told him about everything; about the boy, about who she thought was her father and the recent development, which she believed to be her new memories blurring the old.

Tristan rubbed a hand across his forehead.

"Do you know the boy's name?"

Rayn shook her head. "No. I always wake up before I find out anything."

"Intriguing…" He rested his chin in his hand, tapping an index finger on the side of his head.

"Do you think they're memories? Or nonsense?" Rayn was afraid to hear his answer.

"Let me do some research and I will get back to you." Tristan appeared distant. Her face fell, and he smiled at her. "Cheer up, Rayn." He walked to his bookshelf, relying much on the support of his cane. "I have all the research of Dr. Galin Highcourt, who… officially engineered the solution." He ran a bony hand along the spines of the books before retrieving a thick, black one. "His work is quite brilliant." He heaved the heavy volume onto the bed and sat down again, looking strained. "One of the foremost minds in the medical field to this day."

Rayn frowned.

"Not a great invention for someone of such a great mind."

"Well, you know, all the best minds are enlisted during a war. Most believe they are doing good."

He brushed his hand over the cover of the book and sighed.

"So." His blue eyes gleamed with mischief as he changed the subject. "I hear you met Lady St. Sebastian."

"Who?" Rayn's eyebrows squished together as she squinted.

"Minuet."

"Oh! Her!" Rayn could not suppress a look of disgust.

Wish I'd have killed her!

Tristan burst out in a good-natured laugh. "It seems that you and Solomand have the same impression of the Lady."

The picture of Minuet and her corsets brought back the barroom escapade, and Rayn frowned.

"Funny, I guess Solomand has a much lower taste in women."

She tried to brush the memory from her mind.

"Oh, no." Tristan leaned forward on his cane. "Sol had only one love. And he never will have another."

He said it with an air of finality that made Rayn believe him. She wondered what sort of woman would capture a man like Solomand's heart.

"Tell that to the hookers in Blackpool," she said, rubbing her forehead.

Tristan laughed again.

"Don't let him fool you. His behavior is a front to find information. He does rather hate not knowing what Minuet is up to. Airmen tend to talk more than they should with nightly companions." He winked at her.

Rayn wondered why this made her feel better. Solomand had said as much, with the wild savagery in his eyes as he assaulted that airman; eyes like a dark sea reflecting stars. Clearing her throat, she changed the subject.

"Solomand said you should give me a history lesson when we got back."

"Did he now? I shall have to clarify on what history he was referring to. He might get unnecessarily high strung if I address unwanted topics."

He leaned over, his breathing becoming more strained.

"Are you alright?"

Rayn thought back to her troubling conversation with Solomand, where he refused to acknowledge anything was wrong with Tristan.

Tristan looked tired. "I'm fine... but I should rest." He reached for her hand and squeezed it. "Everything will be alright, Rayn."

Rayn knew it wouldn't, but she nodded and rose to leave.

"Thank you," she said, her voice sounding small.

On her way down the stairs, she ran into Sol. He looked more of a mess than usual.

"Rayn." He took a step back, combing a hand through his unkempt hair. "Are you alright?"

"Yeah," Rayn said. But the aches and pains were still there, reminding her she had come very close to not being fine. "Why wouldn't I be?"

Solomand came closer. Rayn did not stop him when he ran his thumb along her scabbed cheek.

"No idea. *That*, Rayn, is why we don't fool around when we're hanging off a tower." His scowl deepened.

Rayn placed a hand on her hip.

"You're trying to draw attention away from the fact that you're terrified of heights."

"I'm not terrified of heights," Sol insisted. "I was terrified of..." His gaze dropped. "Getting anyone killed."

"It's not like you were trying to get me killed." Rayn crossed her arms. "I thought you were more worried about your over-the-top compass thing, anyway."

Solomand's jaw tightened. "I wasn't." A grimace lingered on his face. "Have you thought about what I said earlier?"

"About what?" Rayn rubbed her sore arm.

"Grishtanburg."

Why did her stomach tighten every time she heard the name of that city?

"Are you saying you want me to leave?" Her hand moved to the stair railing and tightened.

"No!" Solomand moved forward, then stepped back again, sticking his hands in his pockets. "It's what you wanted, isn't it? And there's nothing more I can do to help you, aside from securing you passage there. I thought you would want to go."

He was sincere now, and it bothered her more than when she knew he was lying.

She didn't speak at first, trying to process in her mind why she didn't want to go.

She never had friends in Port Ashbury, and if there were any before that, she couldn't remember them. Not knowing what she would find in Grishtanburg made the choice more difficult.

"I do," she lied, biting her bottom lip. "It's just, I'm not sure I'm ready." They had made a hell of an exit from Blackpool, anyway. "Besides, how are we supposed to get back to Blackpool after how we barely got out the last time?"

She wondered why the thought brightened her mood.

Solomand's face fell.

"Got a point there." His eyes bore into her, searching. He ran a hand on the back of his neck. "The thing is, we're about to get into something dangerous here. I'll fill everyone in later. You can decide then whether you want to go. I'll get you to a safe port if you decide to go."

Rayn tore away from his gaze. "Sounds good."

She hurried past him and outside to get some fresh air. Almost to the door, she realized she'd left the medallion in her room. For a second, she debated on leaving it. A few weeks ago, she never would have parted with it for a moment. Was it really that important now? Her mind was enough of a mess. She shrugged and turned back to get it. When she stepped into the hallway, she ran into someone she at first thought could only be Will.

"Sorry, Will..."

She looked up, her eyes bulging. It wasn't Will. This man was at least as tall and broad-shouldered, but light-skinned and, unlike Will, frightening. His eyes narrowed into a threatening glower. A spider tattoo poked up from his collar.

"Who the hell are you?" She backed away, hand going to her gun only to remember it wasn't at her side.

More growling than speaking, he muttered a jumble of Slavik words. Then, running a hand on the base of his neck, he said, "Ivan."

162

CHAPTER 27

SOLOMAND

DRAGGING HIS FEET as he walked into the room, Solomand sighed and settled on the foot of Tristan's bed. Tristan looked up from a book by the wretched Dr. Highcourt.

"Sol, why so glum?" He let the book fall into his lap. "Having second thoughts?"

"I don't want to talk about it." He buried his face in his hands.

"Oh, come now. Of course, you do." Tristan's cheerfulness seemed exaggerated, even for him. He leaned forward. "I have some information that you will find of keen interest. Some good news, along with some bad, I'm afraid."

"I can't take any bad news." Solomand groaned.

"But you shall most definitely want to hear the good."

Against Solomand's desire, Tristan told him about Rayn's dreams.

"So. She does remember." Solomand took in the news. An almost alien feeling overtook him. Something he had not felt in a long time—hope.

"Yes. But that could be good or bad depending on whether you intend to ignore my advice and go forward with your ill-conceived ideas of martyrdom."

The accusatory tone was still in Tristan's voice. Solomand willed Tristan's intrusion on his cheerful mood away. He had probably known Sol would react this way, and more than likely

163

told him so he would change his mind. Would he? Solomand wrestled for the idea for a moment. He was beginning to have doubts on what to do when, like a clap of thunder, the bad news dawned on him.

"But, if Rayn remembers, sort of, then maybe..." He sprang to his feet, his heart leaping to his throat.

Tristan gave him a quick nod. "I'm sure it's fine, Sol. I wouldn't even call it *bad* news. However, I should still like to speak with Will."

Sol's mouth felt dry. He dashed from the room, forgetting to close the door. He stepped into the hall to see Rayn backing away from the towering figure.

Oh shit.

A feeling of doom descended on him. He hadn't had time to tell her about Ivan yet.

Rayn spun around. "Solomand!" Her eyes trailed from him back to Ivan.

Sol cleared his throat, doing his best to look nonchalant. "This is Ivan. He's one of us." Ivan gave him a stabbing glare, muttering in Slav something about not playing any stupid game, and Solomand was pretty sure another Kree insult. He glared at him for a moment, thankful Rayn didn't understand. It was no wonder she was startled. Sol had only known Ivan to ever look like some sort of half-starved wolverine with a migraine.

"One of you? I thought you said Tristan was the last of your crew."

Solomand raised a finger. "Almost," he said timidly. "I said almost. You haven't seen him because he's been locked in the basement—*recovering*, I mean."

Why the hell did I say that?

Solomand cringed.

Rayn's jaw hung open.

"In the basement? What. The. Hell. Solomand!"

He eased a step back as she came toward him, unsure who was the more terrifying, Rayn or Ivan.

"Normal people don't keep anyone *locked* in a basement!" She gestured toward Ivan. "Especially if they happen to look like their favorite pastime is murdering someone with an ax."

Ivan did have that look about him. But, for a moment, the corner of his mouth twitched. Was he actually trying not to smile?

"Sorry." Sol cleared his throat and was careful to keep his distance. His voice was timid when he spoke. "He only wants to kill me, though, so you've nothing to worry about."

Rayn threw her arms up.

"I'm tired of feeling like I'm the only one who knows nothing!" She shook her head, giving Solomand one last glare of disbelief before storming away. "In the basement—honestly!"

Solomand breathed out.

That could have gone worse, I suppose.

He stared at Ivan, both hands on his hips. "Who let you out, anyway?"

Ivan puffed his chest out. He had shaved and was looking almost himself again.

"Will give me passcode while you were gone."

"Well, that wasn't the best judgment on his part, was it?" Still, Ivan didn't seem particularly homicidal at the moment. "I'll talk with you later."

Sol didn't so much push past Ivan as slither along the wall as far away from him as possible.

Will was just coming in the front door. Always the ideal soldier, dressed, shaved, ready to go, he offered Solomand a smile.

"Everything alright, Sol? You're as jumpy as Jank."

The Olbian was the one source of steadfast rightness in all the mess that never seemed to end. Will was alright. He had to be.

"Tristan wants to have a word with you." Sol breathed out, leaning against the wall. He dug in his pocket for a cigarette and offered one to Will.

"Sure thing." Will took it. "Anything else wrong?"

"Well…" Solomand let the smoke fill his lungs, then exhaled. "You want to tell me why Ice Man McMurder face is wondering around? He scared the hell out of Rayn."

"Oh. That." Will took a drag on his cigarette. "Tristan's orders."

Tristan. I might have known.

"Ah."

Sol was feeling stupid for being so frantic. They traipsed back down the hall, finishing their cigarettes before they reached Tristan's room.

"So." Will hooked a thumb in his belt. "Any reason you wanted to see me?" He glanced from Solomand to Tristan.

Tristan's brow furrowed as he leaned back on his pillow. Dr. Highcourt's book and an open notebook laid in front of him.

"Will, I would never doubt your character after all these years, but there is something I need to know. Do you have any dreams of before?"

Will's shoulders tensed, but he remained otherwise the picture of calm.

"A few," he finally said.

Solomand's shoulder slumped as he massaged his temple.

"You might have said something, Will."

Will looked amused as he ran a hand under his eyepatch along the white scar.

"If I'd have thought there was any danger, I would have."

"I know you would." Tristan thumbed through his book and scribbled in the notebook. He seemed certain Will told the truth. "Can you tell me about them?"

"Not much to tell." Will shrugged. "It was never anything I longed to return to if that's what you're asking."

"In a manner of speaking, yes. You don't have them anymore?"

Tristan coughed into his elbow and continued to write.

"Not really." Will's face grew somber. "The only memory I have that matters is being shot with that dart by my platoon leader and being left on that burning field with my eye cut out, waiting to die. As far as I'm concerned, whoever I was before died."

Solomand studied him with a probing gaze. It had always been hard to read Will. But they had all come to accept him as one of their own: calm, collected, even when no one else was. There was never any question where his loyalties lay. Solomand knew he would trust Tristan's judgment ahead of his own.

Then why don't you listen to him about Rayn?

He shook his head, dismissing the voice. That was different.

Tristan dropped the pencil on his notebook.

"I believe you, Will. I only needed to know. It helps to have all the pieces when fitting a puzzle together."

Will nodded. "Anything else?"

"Not with you." Solomand turned an accusatory gaze on Tristan. "Why the hell did you tell him to give Ivan the passcode? I'm surprised he didn't stab me to death with a spoon last night."

Tristan started to laugh.

CHAPTER 28

RAYN

RAYN STOMPED ALONG the winding sidewalk, her furious gaze fixed down into the valley. White streaks of clouds turned from pink to orange as the sun rose higher. Right when she was starting to feel Solomand wasn't so bad, she found another skeleton in his closet, or basement, as it were. The hair on her neck pricked up thinking about the menacing-looking Slav. Who the hell was he, anyway? The tattoo on his neck reminded her of the mechanical spider the shifty-eyed peddler in Trader's Cove had in his wares. Imagining the prickly legs skittering across the ground made her skin crawl.

This was an excellent time to bury herself in work, away from everyone. She strode up to the airship and flipped the toggle to the cargo bay. The door groaned open, and she stepped inside as the automatic lights flickered on with a crackling hum. Rayn breathed in the familiar smell of tobacco and her eyes narrowed as they searched around the crates and wooden boxes, eventually resting on the girl in the corner.

Zee sat on a crate, one hand clutching the frayed wooden lid, the other holding a cigarette. On seeing Rayn, she gave a start, dropping the cigarette in a hurry and stomping it out as she slid to her feet.

"Don't tell, Sol," she said in a small voice.

Rayn crossed her arms, looking down at the girl.

"Why? What do you think he'll do to you?"

She was doubtful he would do much of anything.

Zee hung her head, rubbing one arm.

"Nothing. It's just that... he'll be disappointed is all."

Rayn's shoulders softened as she let out a sigh. Part of her wanted to march back up to the castle and tell Solomand—point out one more thing he was doing wrong. While he was busy hiding a dangerous axe-man, the child under his care was off doing things she shouldn't be. At the same time, she didn't want to talk to Solomand at all. Besides, what the hell did she know about filling in as a parent?

"I won't tell," she said. "Provided you don't do it anymore."

Zee's lips pursed together. "For how long?

"Until you're eighteen, at least."

The girl nodded. "Alright." She thrust out her hand.

Rayn grasped it, giving Zee a somber smile before walking past her and toward the spiral stairs to the airship's armory. Plunking sound of boots on metal followed her as the girl clambered up at her heels.

"What are you doing in here, anyway?"

Rayn leaned to the side, catching one of the rivets on the wall with her shoulder.

"Well, I decided it was a good time to do some gunsmithing, since Solomand's prisoner wandered out."

She muttered the last part.

"Prisoner?" Zee heard. "Oh, you mean Ivan. He's not a prisoner. He's an Ice Wolf—they're Slavik assassins. Some people hire them to fight in wars or to be bodyguards—stuff like that."

They were at the landing at the top of the stairs now.

"What's he doing here, then?" Rayn asked, gripping the wheellock of the round door and placing her total body weight on it.

"He's Sol's friend."

Zee pulled at the door, using all her weight to help pull it open. It gave way with a slow grinding noise, letting out the smell of gunpowder and dust.

169

"Friend, huh?"

Rayn stepped inside, eyeing the crate of springs and tools Jank had delivered to the armory.

Didn't look like anybody's friend.

She hoisted the cannon components to the center of the room.

"Sol doesn't like to talk about him. He was sick when we brought him here."

Zee shoved the box of supplies alongside the gun pieces. She hopped atop the black ammo boxes and stood on her tiptoes as she peered out the porthole.

"You shouldn't be afraid of him," she added, glancing back. "He wouldn't hurt you. I met him a long time ago. Sol thought I wouldn't remember, but I do."

She hopped back to the floor.

"Oh, yeah?" Rayn ran her fingers along the rough edge of a file. "What do you remember about him?"

"It was on the island. Sol was sick or something, and the other men in green coats were talking about killing me."

Rayn gave a start at the nonchalant way the girl talked.

"Ivan knocked them all on their... knocked them out." Zee scratched her nose with the back of her hand. "Then he told them he'd teach them something if they ever tried to touch me again. He left after that. Sol was asleep. I don't think he saw what happened." She squatted down. "Can I help?"

Rayn sat back on her heels and caught the girl's eager gaze. Zee showed no signs of being distressed by the idea of men in green coats trying to kill her. Then again, with someone like Ivan taking up for her, it made sense not to be bothered. Tucking her messy braid behind her ear, Rayn wadded a clean rag in her hand.

"Sure, hand me that." She nodded to a tube of oil.

The first thing to do was clean, probably a decade's worth of grime and gunk, from the barrel. Zee scrambled to hand her the oil. It was not unpleasant having the girl help.

She lost track of how long they sat in the armory, her cleaning and Zee handing her tools or helping to run patches through the barrel.

Her stomach had begun to grumble when a voice said, "Mind if I join you?"

She gave a start, then relaxed when she realized it was Will.

"No." Rayn pushed hair out of her eyes, watching as the girl jumped up.

"Hey, Will," Zee said. "Rayn's teaching me how to be a gunsmith."

"Hardly." Rayn laughed.

Will fished a cigarette out of his jacket pocket. "Oh? Maybe you can fix the engine down there with Jank."

Zee scoffed.

"Not a chance." She wiped black hands on her pants, leaving greasy smears. "Is lunch ready?"

Will nodded, and the girl dashed away. Rayn stood up, cleaning her own hands on a rag.

"Sol wanted me to ask you to come to the observatory after lunch?"

Figures he wouldn't tell me himself.

"Have something to do with the mess he talked about getting into?"

"Something like that."

He held the cigarette to his lips. If he knew anything, he wasn't going to tell, but his mild-mannered smile made it hard to hold anything against him.

Rayn let out a sigh, wondering if Ivan would be there.

"Please tell me vodka is on the menu."

Will let out a low chuckle as he tilted his head back. "Anytime you want it to be."

He turned and followed Zee.

Rayn lingered in the armory, putting her tools away and cleaning up the dirty patches of cloth. She bit her lip as she looked down at the cleaned components. There didn't seem to be anything wrong with the cannon that would keep it from firing. All the springs and mechanisms were in functioning order. Did Solomand go to all this trouble to hire a gunsmith to fix a cannon that was dirty as hell? The number of people that didn't clean their weapons drove her mad. She shrugged and left the armory. What did she care if Solomand had made a mistake thinking the cannon wasn't functional when it was? She would be paid for her work, regardless.

When she got back to the Castle, Ivan was nowhere to be seen. Her stomach churned, and her appetite could only stomach a crisp slice of melon left on the kitchen table. The coffee was too cold. She made her way to the observatory. This time she brought her gun, despite what Zee had said about Ivan.

She paused for a moment outside the open sliding doors. Sunlight streamed in from a domed glass ceiling, which combined with the back wall of thick window panes. There was a coating of dust over the few pieces of furniture: a tall, antique looking cabinet, a coffee table, and some dark-cherry wooden chairs. A patched-up sofa of drab brown sat against the back wall, facing the window panes. Solomand had been lying on the couch. He sat up, startling her at first.

"Sorry." He stood and a cloud of dust mixed with the streams of sunlight. He looked like he was trying to gauge if she was still mad or not. "Care to have a seat?"

Rayn walked over and sat down. Hesitating, Solomand eased himself next to her. He cleared his throat.

"Look, Rayn. I'm sorry about earlier." He rubbed his hands on his knees. "I should have told you about Ivan before."

Rayn sighed, sinking further into the scratchy cushions.

"It's alright." Although it wasn't. She leaned her head back, staring at the clouds drifting by overhead. "I'm tired of people keeping secrets from me."

"Well, you're one to talk—you even keep secrets from yourself."

Rayn pursed her lips together, smothering a laugh.

172

Sol edged further away as he continued, "You could have been trying to kill me years ago and not even know about it.

"Still could be." She leaned toward him, keeping a straight face.

The worried look in his eyes caused her to laugh. She liked how he looked when he was more at ease.

"Who is Ivan, then? A hired assassin?"

"He's not for hire." Solomand's grin faded to a distant expression. "He was an Ice Wolf that showed up in Corcyra looking for work. They're specialized assassins in the North, from what I understand. He never talked about his past, and we didn't ask. He's a friend. Only... he got himself hooked on furi a while back."

Rayn had only heard stories about the furi. It was far too heavy a drug for the likes of Port Ashbury. Sol's voice dropped.

"He got carried away with it trying to forget."

Rayn's fingers drummed on her knees. She was torn between wanting to know and being afraid to hear.

"Forget what?"

Solomand worked a finger into his collar and pulled on it, shifting in his seat.

"We were all together in the war. Me, Jank, Will, Ivan... Tristan." His eyes glazed over, and he tilted his head back to gaze out the dome window.

The wind rustled trees outside, lending some comfort to the silence that fell. Solomand's gaze caught hers and she forced herself to ask.

"The war... is that what happened to Tristan?"

Solomand paled as his eyes stared at something far away. He didn't have to answer. Without thinking, she scooted closer to Solomand.

"I'm sorry... I didn't mean." Her hand reached toward him, but she stopped short.

What the hell am I doing?

Voices and footsteps coming up the stairs let them both breathe out a sigh of relief. Jank walked in, looking annoyed, as usual.

Zee was trailing behind Will, biting into an apple, her fingers still stained black. And finally, Ivan lumbered in, fixing a dark, solemn stare on Rayn. Sol gave him a warning look, and he moved to the corner, folding his arms and glaring at Solomand instead.

Sol pulled a cord by the wall, and black drapes closed out the sunlight.

"We're going to go over a few things for those of you who don't already know."

He took the sphere from his pocket and placed it in the center of the coffee table, disrupting the layer of dust. His fingers fumbled for a moment as he turned the gears and buttons in an ordered fashion.

"Our next order of business will be…"

With a series of clicks, the device received the right combination. In a flurry of lights, the compass needle spun, and the projection of an elaborate map formed on the black curtain.

Rayn's eyes widened, and she leaned forward to get a better look. Tiny flocks of birds flew in forms over a cluster of hills; wispy white clouds drifted over bright cities. Solomand pushed another button and one town came into focus. It was like a glittering jewel against a backdrop of the desert.

"We're breaking into Corcyra."

Her eyes transfixed on the airships that flew out of the city port across the black background, Rayn asked, "Why do you need to break into a city?"

Sol cleared his throat.

"Rayn, you may as well know." He made it out like he was confessing a dark secret. "We're not exactly what you would call *upstanding citizens.*" He made air quotes with his fingers.

Rayn rolled her eyes. "No?"

"I know it's hard to believe." Solomand waved a hand, pretending to look ashamed. The twinkle in his eye vanished now as his somberness became real. "It's going to be dangerous." Those eyes bore a hole into her.

Grishtanburg.

She knew what he was alluding to and swallowed, maintaining a collected appearance despite the storm welling up inside.

"Why are you going if it's so dangerous?"

This meeting felt like it was for the two of them now.

"A personal matter. One that I'd rather you not get mixed up in."

So, he was going to send her away. She could tell he didn't want to say it. Her heart sank lower, even though her mind was already made up.

She took a steady breath and exhaled, managing a matter-of-fact voice.

"Well, then, Captain Black. I suppose maybe it's time we parted ways." Her words rang hollow; it sounded like someone else was speaking them against her will.

There was that look in his eye she couldn't place, like a distant storm was brewing. He grinned.

"My friends call me Sol."

Rayn glanced around the room. The others were smiling at her, in a mysterious, stoic fashion. Except for Zee, who looked curious, and Ivan, whose grim expression grew ever more displeased. Rayn assumed it was his natural state of being and nothing to do with her. For all their idiotic stunts, and Solomand's pig-headedness, she realized she could have had worse friends. She gave him a genuine, warm smile.

"Alright. Sol, it is."

Friends.

Rayn stared at the birds flitting about the parapets of Corcyra, not hearing a word Solomand or the others said. She wished he'd told her to go without insisting they be on good terms. It would have made leaving so much easier.

CHAPTER 29

SOLOMAND

THE WHOLE TIME Solomand went over the plan, he felt Ivan's glare burning into him. Not long after Rayn left, the Slav had crossed his arms and stalked away—to his quarters, no doubt. Sol stared at his door now, rubbing the back of his neck. Ivan knew he was holding back, and his brooding nature would not allow him to listen to lies. Sol was glad he had left, rather than forcing him to admit the truth. He breathed out and warily opened the door.

Ivan sat upright on the edge of his bunk, rigid. He did not look to see Solomand before speaking.

"He needs doctor, *Captain*." His voice was a low growl as he turned an icy glare on Sol.

Solomand's throat tightened.

"You think I don't know that?" He took an uneven step toward Ivan.

The slav crossed his arms, his chest rising and falling with every fiery breath he took.

"Why do you come here?"

Sol massaged the deep ache in his left shoulder.

The weather must be shifting.

Whatever the cause, the pain was a welcome distraction from Ivan's accusatory tone.

"I don't need you to remind me of my mistakes, Ivan. I aim to set them right."

"Why now?" His cold eyes were disconcerting.

Solomand shifted uncomfortably at the question. Their run-ins in Blackpool and anywhere else were like child's play compared to what awaited them all in Corcyra. It was the one place none of them should ever go. Solomand, in particular, had been very careful to keep his distance from there for many years.

So why now?

He rubbed his neck.

"Because. It's the only choice we've got."

He briefly relayed the real reason they were going to Corcyra—the reason only he and Tristan knew. Ivan's reaction was expected.

With a look that said Sol was more of an idiot than he imagined, he slowly stood.

"Is stupid plan! Too much risk." He stared down at Sol.

Uncomfortably tilting his head back to meet Ivan's gaze, Sol let his frustration get the better of him. "Would you shut your mouth and listen for once!"

Ice Man! He kept the insult to himself. Ivan looked like he could put up a decent struggle at this point.

Ivan stepped toward him.

"Why should I listen?" His chest heaved. "You only care for you, or you would have found doctor already." He jabbed Solomand in the chest with a finger.

Solomand's tone darkened, anger clawing its way above the guilt.

"You know it's not that simple."

Ivan's chest was against his now.

"You find a way for what matters to you."

Sol's hands trembled as he balled them into fists.

"I'm this close," he said, holding up his thumb and forefinger, "to giving you back your knife."

The vein in Ivan's forehead bulged.

"*Stley eta.*" Do it.

177

Solomand slid one foot back and reached under his coat. He jerked a curved dagger with a polished bone handle from his belt. The blade was covered with a tan leather sheath. He threw it at Ivan's feet, his heart pounding uncontrollably. It was the only thing Ivan said he brought from his past life: the blade of an Ice Wolf. He'd left it behind when he disappeared, and Sol had kept it from him until now. He knew it was wrong to provoke Ivan, but his temper would not allow him to stop.

His lip curled upward, Ivan crouched down, an unblinking gaze looking at Solomand as he took the knife in his hand.

"Oruziy visha." Draw your weapon.

He spoke through clenched teeth, jerking the deadly blade free of its sheath.

Solomand tore his gun belt off and tossed it aside. The fury outweighed the tightness beginning to coil around his chest.

"I don't need a weapon, *khuizda (asshole)*!"

He put up his fists.

Tristan shoved the door open as he yelled at them. He gave Sol a long, pained look that was sharper than any dagger Ivan could have cut him with. He dropped his hands, taking short, deliberate breaths. Tristan turned to Ivan.

"Ivan. He shook his head as he looked from one to the other. "Don't do it."

Ivan's look of anger softened. Tristan looked paler than usual as he slumped against the doorframe.

Tris!

Solomand's chest ached. He sprang to Tristan's side and helped him to the bed. Ivan's brow furrowed and his arms dropped. The knife fell to the floor with a clang.

What the hell's wrong with me?

"I... I'm sorry." He murmured, raking a shaking hand through his hair.

Looking like he'd seen a spirit, Ivan stared at Tristan. He was frozen in place like a hulking statue.

"For the record, Ivan, I agree with you," Tristan said with a wane smile. "It is a rather stupid plan. It's not worth the risk, either."

Ivan's eyes clamped shut.

"How much longer?" It was almost a whisper.

Tristan took a strained breath, and his voice was gentle. "It should have been a long time ago."

Sol leaned against the wall, sickness welling up inside him as Tristan spoke.

"A few months more, I think."

Ivan sank to the bed next to Tristan, shoulder slumped. "There is no other way, is there?"

"No," Tristan sounded sorry. "The risk is still too great. But Sol will not listen to reason."

Ivan cringed, turning a hateful look on Solomand. Unable to stomach anymore, Sol glared at the Slav and stormed from the room.

As he left, he heard Tristan say, "It's not his fault, Ivan." That only made the guilt worse. Sol quickened his pace.

⊰☼⊱

Tristan was wrong. Ivan knew all too well about pain and how to cause it. If his hatred bothered Solomand at all, he didn't care. At least, that's what he told himself. He was an Ice Wolf—a heartless assassin of the Northland. Once one made that choice, there was no turning back on it. But his mind had begun to clear, and the lie was becoming harder to believe.

Faces of two girls, laughing and running in a forest as snow swirled around came unbidden to the forefront of his mind. A shiver crawled up his spine and his eyes closed, forcing the memory back into blackness until only the pain and hate remained.

"I will go to Corcyra." He broke the uncomfortable silence. "This time, Solomand is right. Is worth the risk."

He hated saying it out loud.

179

CHAPTER 30

RAYN

SO THIS WAS it. She was actually leaving. Rayn adjusted the strap of her bag, staring down into the valley. Her fingers tightened around the leather, massaging the cracks and frayed edges. Jank repaired a damaged skiff with salvaged parts. This is what they were flying to Blackpool. Solomand didn't dare take the bulky airship back after their previous escapade. He told her the skiff was faster, anyway. Somehow that didn't make her feel better. Emptiness grew inside her with every step as she walked down to the dock. The sky was a perfect shade of blue to remind her of Tristan's eyes. What would happen to him? And what of the others? Would they ever make it back from Corcyra? She tried not to think about it. Sol and Will were going to escort her to Blackpool.

Will, Solomand, and Jank stood next to the airship, smoking. The icy-eyed Slav was nowhere to be seen. Solomand draped his coat over his shoulder as he strapped the revolver to his side. He dug in the pocket and held out the piece of folded, embossed, paper.

"Your ticket, My Lady." He didn't let go right away as she took it from him.

"Thanks."

Without the heart to return a sarcastic comment on his greeting, Rayn tucked it into her vest, glancing around at the valley one last time. She wanted to stay longer, but it wouldn't do any good to say so. The whole reason she'd left Port Ashbury was to find who she was. Captain Black and his crew were a means of recovering her past, nothing more. She glanced up the hill to see Tristan limping towards them, relying on his cane more than usual. A navy overcoat swallowed his frame. Her heart shrank.

"Can I trouble one of you for a smoke?" Tristan asked, sounding brighter than he looked.

Simultaneously, all three of his friends extinguished their cigarettes and flicked them away.

"You're not allowed." Sol said, slipping on his coat on and turning up the collar.

"Oh, come now. I think twenty-five is quite old enough." A devilish grin spread across his face as he straightened. "Not even as a last request?" Sol's jaw tightened, and he glared at Tristan. "Sorry, Sol. Old habits die hard." Tristan sighed, tipping his head back to look at the sky. His eyes seemed more piercing. "I really only came to bid Rayn farewell, anyway. That is, if she's sure she wants to leave us?"

He leaned forward and took her hand.

"I'm afraid so." Truth be told, she had never felt more uncertain.

His clammy hands closed around hers.

"I shall bid you a safe journey, then. Until next we meet." He held his head high. "Sounds so much better than goodbye, wouldn't you agree?" He winked and opened his arms. She hugged him, startled at the strength of his embrace. "Godspeed," he whispered in her ear, then let go, limping back up the path.

Jank hurried after Tristan, and Rayn's eyes lingered on the pair for a moment, the emptiness inside her expanding. If he'd have looked back once, she wouldn't have been able to get on the skiff.

"Ready?" Sol's voice interrupted her thoughts. Her hand closed around the medallion in her pocket, reminding herself once again why she had to leave.

"As I'll ever be." She tried to sound confident.

"That's the spirit, then." Sol clapped her on the back in an upbeat manner that made her wonder if he really was eager to be rid of her after all.

"Thanks," she mumbled as she climbed on board and secured her satchel of belongings in the cramped compartment below deck. Solomand strapped himself into the pilot's seat, while Will tossed Rayn a cap and a pair of goggles. She pulled them over her head and harnessed herself into the chair behind Sol.

Red and yellow lights flashed on the control panel.

"All clear," Will called, giving Sol a thumbs up.

Solomand took hold of the controls as he pushed the throttle forward. The engines roared to life, drowning out the peaceful sounds of the valley. The skiff shook as they lifted off the support rails and Rayn gripped her harness, her teeth rattling. They drifted up with a burst of power until they had cleared the treetops. Rayn glanced down. The trees blurred together, the castle nothing but a lumpy carpet of vines that melted into the green mountains as the skiff hurdled forward like an arrow into the clouds.

A tingling sensation shot up Rayn's spine. An involuntary smile formed on her lips as she let the exhilaration envelop her, strangling any other emotion. Her eyes closed, soaking in the feeling of clouds on her cheek and wishing the trip would last forever. No matter how long it took, though, it would be over too soon, and she would be on a passenger ship surrounded by strangers, going to a place where people go to disappear. She imagined a dock full of Ivans waiting in Grishtanburg. It wasn't long before the sensation of flying and hum of engines put her into a dreamless sleep, her stomach balled in a nervous knot.

"Rayn." Sol was shaking her. She opened her eyes and pushed the goggles to her forehead. Stars glistened, white diamonds in the inky sky. "I must have dozed off." She yawned behind a gloved hand.

"End of the line," Sol spoke under his breath. Rayn glanced around, unbuckling her harness.

"Where are we?" She stood up, stretching with another yawn.

"An abandoned dock outside of Blackpool." He gestured to the warm glow of light in the distance. "I'll take you to the main docks before we bow out of here."

"So long, Rayn." Will gripped her shoulder.

A lump rose in her throat. "Good luck." She couldn't bring herself to say more.

"Stay close." Sol's voice was a whisper. She nodded again and jumped over the side after him. The answers she wanted were in Grishtanburg. Her feet thumped through the high-grass alongside Sol, sleep still heavy on her eyes. *Why do I feel so miserable?* The cobbled streets rose in front of them, and Sol leaned closer, hooking his arm through hers. "We'll look less suspicious if anyone sees us." She could feel his heart pounding.

They stepped into the shadows of the neatly aligned buildings. "That's your ship." He nodded towards the lighted docks at the Zeppelin, a gigantic, dull mountain; like she expected it would look. "The Victoria. You have your ticket?"

Rayn's mind felt hazy. She dug the brown piece of paper from her pocket to show him. "Good. No one asks about travel papers on that route. I've made sure it's all taken care of." He slipped his arm from hers. "She leaves at daybreak. Once you get to Grishtanburg, I have a contact there who will meet you." He squeezed her hand, breaking her from her daze. "It'll be alright, Rayn. You'll find the answers you are looking for once you get there."

His head leaned in for a moment, and there was a depth of emotion swirling in his eyes she didn't recognize.

"I... I have to go now." His hand was on his collar.

Don't leave! She nodded as he pulled away. "Good luck in Corcyra." Solomand's fingers lingered in her hand. Footsteps shuffled up the alley to their left. "Thanks." he disappeared into the shadows.

Rayn was alone. Muggy air draped itself around her like a gloomy blanket. She traipsed up the ramp and sat on one of the many benches that stood in rows in front of the waiting ships. Gas lamps cast shadows on the wooden planks and crickets sang in the distance. The entire city was asleep, and the airship *Victoria* rested there, ready to sail across the sea to the frozen continent at dawn.

She pulled out her ticket and stared at the foreign writing. The paper wrinkled under the grip of her fingers. She couldn't tell if she wanted to cry or throw up. Then, a scuffling noise in the shadows made her head raise. It was followed by what sounded like corks popping out of wine bottles.

A suppressed rifle. Rayn stiffened. *No, it was nothing.*

But she knew the sound, even if she did not know how she knew. She stood, hooking her bag on her shoulder.

Just wait on the ship.

She fought with herself for a solid minute, looking back and forth from the zeppelin to the shadowed path which lead out of town. She took a quick glance at the black sky.

I have time.

She stuffed the ticket in her coat pocket and darted back the way she had come.

CHAPTER 31

SOLOMAND

SOLOMAND ALWAYS KNEW she couldn't stay. Hours from now, Rayn would be well on her way to the North Continent, out of reach. This should have made him feel relieved. It was everything he intended. Governor LeFrost was persistent. He would hunt every last one of them down. What would happen once he caught them, he didn't like to think of. Hell would freeze ten times over before he let that bastard anywhere near Rayn.

It was this, he dutifully reminded himself as he made his way back to the skiff where Will waited. They would return to Lubafell, carry out the plan and all would be well—or as close to well as it could be. Solomand dragged a hand down his face, his pace slowing until his boots scraped through the grass.

She'll be safe.

He reminded himself over and over to stifle the overpowering urge he had to run back and take her in his arms. A low moan jolted him from his grief.

Pale moonlight lit the surrounding fields, the buildings of Blackpool looming in the distance. Solomand took a knee as the pained groan sounded again, determining where it came from. Even as he pushed his way through the grass, searching the ground, a voice screamed in his head to turn around, get back to the skiff. There was something wrong here. It wasn't until he found the child in the grass that he realized it was a trap.

185

"God!" he fell to his knees, rolling the small form over.

It was a boy of about six years old, dressed in ragged clothes, barefoot—an orphan most likely. Solomand's hands came away warm and wet as he turned the boy onto his back. A clean cut, just under his throat oozed blood. Hands trembling, Solomand felt the small hand for a pulse, knowing it was too late to save him. It was just like all the others.

Solomand was there with Benjamin, the Insurgent leader, on that grim day. It was etched forever in his mind like the scar of blade on an oak tree. Governor LeFrost gloated, the children had been his own idea. The 201st snipers would drug them, cut their throats in such a way they could still make noise when they awoke. Then, when the insurgents heard their distressed cries, the sniper hiding in the distance would take them out. Toward the end, Benjamin had found a young girl which turned out to be the daughter of one of his men.

Trembling, Sol stared at the child, aware that his life was in danger, but unable to move. The child's face grew paler and his pulse stilled. Tears stung Solomand's eyes, and he broke free of the shock, sucking in a breath of air. Forcing himself to stand, he knew he had waited too long. He turned and ran.

I'm sorry, Ben.

It would never be over while LeFrost still lived.

I couldn't save them. His thoughts strayed from the child and into a battlefield in another time. *I couldn't keep her safe.*

The force that ripped through his shoulder came as no surprise, and Solomand fell forward. Another shot cut through the grass over his head as he rolled onto his back. Gritting his teeth, Solomand reached down, pulling a knife from his boot. If that bastard Pelican thought he was going to go down that easily, he had another thing coming! Rolling onto his stomach, Solomand crawled in the direction the shot had come from.

CHAPTER 32

RAYN

SWEAT TRICKLED DOWN Rayn's back. Her overcoat felt heavy, but she stayed light on her feet as she crept along the grass.

The streets were silent, lamps in the street flickered, widening the reach of the shadows as she eased her way out of the city. Had she imagined things? Eyes scanning her surroundings, she took a few steps forward. On the verge of returning to wait for the *Victoria* to open its doors, she tripped over the body.

Letting out a muffled cry, she fell forward over the limp form slumped over a rifle. She rolled onto her back and scurried away, kicking at the man's arm. Her breath caught. It was an Airman. Blood spilled from his neck where a knife stuck in it, forming a sticky pool in the grass. Rayn jumped to her feet and stumbled backward into the high grass. Her fingertips brushed something wet. She held them close to her eyes, her heart pounding faster.

More blood.

It trailed away from the man, back toward the abandoned dock.

Sol!

The muffled sound of a suppressed rifle sounded from further into the fields. No thought to consequences entered her mind after that. Darting across the field, she retraced the steps from earlier. No more shots rang out, but that didn't stop the rising fear that threatened to overtake her. Near the end of the grassy fields, she saw him.

"Sol!" she breathed out, running faster.

He was on his knees. Blood streamed down the side of his head from a deep gash on his left temple. Rayn dashed forward, crashing to the ground beside him. Her arms caught him as he fell forward. His jacket was warm and wet.

"Rayn." Sol spoke through gritted teeth. "Go back... before—"

A bullet cut through the air right next to her head.

Too late for that now.

She dragged his arm over her shoulders and struggled to get him off the ground.

"Come on, Sol!" She strained to keep him from falling as she walked him forward, bent over as more bullets sailed past.

"Damnit, Rayn!" Sol sounding groggy. "You should have... stayed on the docks."

Rayn's foot found a hole, and she lurched forward. A pain shot up her leg.

"Shit!" She crouched down and shifted Sol's weight onto her back, grasping hold of his arms. Grunting, she shuffled forward, knees bent, toward the skiff.

Will saw her coming and jumped out.

"What happened?" he asked, dragging Sol off of her and hoisting him onto the deck of the skiff. In the crisp moonlight, Rayn could see the dark spot on his coat had expanded. Blood covered the entire left side of his face. Her back felt wet where he had laid on her.

"Airmen." She got the word out. "Solomand got one, but there's still..."

A bullet splintered on the deck next to them, and she ducked at the same time Will did.

Will's face was only a few inches from hers as they bent over Sol.

"We have to get out of here," he said, frowning, and Rayn could tell what he was thinking.

You should have gotten the hell out of here, Rayn.

This had been her last chance to find the answers to who she was. But if she'd left Sol, regret would haunt her forever.

"I've made my choice, Will."

Her ticket was gone, anyway—lost somewhere in the blood-stained grass.

Will relented with a nod. He scrambled across the deck as another bullet splintered into the side. Their assailant was getting closer.

"Here." He tossed Rayn a medical kit from below deck. "Try to slow his bleeding. I'll get us out of here."

He jumped in the pilot's seat.

"You need to get him to a doctor!" she called.

"Only doctors worth a damn are in Corcyra—Governor's law. I have to get him to Tristan."

Rayn's hands shook as she tore Sol's jacket open.

But he might bleed to death by then!

She kept the worry to herself and fumbled for some gauze as the engines roared to life.

Will was a much smoother pilot than Sol, but Sol still slid against the mast, smearing the deck with blood. Rayn gulped, working to pack his wounds with gauze and keep them both from flying off the skiff.

Damnit, Sol. You can't die!

CHAPTER 33

RAYN

THE WAY BACK to Lubafell seemed to take twice as long. The engine emitted a high-pitched whine and the smoke scent lingered around them as Will pushed the skiff to its limit. Rayn's hands shook as she packed more gauze into the already soaked bandages. He didn't move, but at least the blood had stopped seeping through his head wound. His pulse grew weak. They were running out of time.

You better make it, Sol.

The skiff rattled as Will pushed the throttle to its absolute limit and turned on Jank's emergency thrusters. It was still dark when they neared the valley. The subtle glow of approaching daylight hung over the trees. The whole skiff shuddered as Will brought it onto the docking rails, and the engine sputtered as he shut it off. Smoke and the tinny smell of hot metal filled the air.

Jank darted barefooted down the path, his baggy shirt untucked and his hair looking wilder than usual. Hands on his head, his face filled with horror on sight of the smoking engine.

"Will! What the f—."

"Wake Tristan!" Will sprang from the pilot's seat to scoop Solomand in his arms.

The look of fury transformed into horror as Jank set eyes on Sol and he dashed, stumbling, up the path without another word.

Rayn's arms ached, and her legs felt wobbly as she plodded after Will and into the Castle. There was a light on in Tristan's room, and Will was already half-way up the stairs before she managed to stagger inside the building. She peeled the cap off her head and leaned all her weight on the banister as she climbed the stairs to Tristan's room. Tristan looked paler than usual, his face lined with worry.

Will laid Sol face down on a tall, silver table lined with sheets. Tristan unrolled a canvas wrap on his bed, revealing knives and other surgical instruments.

"Get his jacket off." Tristan's voice was urgent and severe.

In a daze, Rayn watched as Jank and Will fumbled with Sol's arm, knocking syringes and a glass bottle onto the floor. Something brushed against her arm, and she looked over as the Slav pushed past her. His curved dagger out, he strode up to Sol and sliced his jacket from the neck down and pulled the two halves off him.

Sol's white shirt was red. Tristan was cutting it open already, moving with calm precision.

"He's lost a great deal of blood." He rubbed his forehead, frowning. "Get his shirt off, Ivan."

Ivan cut Solomand's shirt free, exposing the gruesome exit wound on the edge of his shoulder, and long, white scars running all across his back. Blood trickled down his limp arm and dripped from his fingertips into a pool on the floor.

Rayn felt like the room was closing in. It was hot, and the air refused to go into her lungs. She slumped against the wall. Her eyes moved from the scars on his back to the oozing hole in his shoulder.

Tristan's brow furrowed, sweat already streaking down his face. His hands were shaking as he pressed gauze onto Sol's open wound. "He's lost too much." Lines formed on his face as his breathing became heavier.

Ivan's jaw tightened, and he dragged a chair over to the table.

191

"My blood is same." He grabbed a coil of clear tubing and from the table and poked a needle into the bulging vein on his right forearm as he turned to Tristan. "You stop bleeding."

Tristan nodded, his mouth a hard line.

Everything became brighter until there was nothing but a blur and Rayn fell forward to the floor.

CHAPTER 34

RAYN

RAYN SAT UP and groaned as a stabbing pain shot through her right temple.

"What the hell?" She leaned forward, squeezing her head between her hands. Locks of sweaty hair clung to the back of her neck. The room felt stifling. She tore off her overcoat and tossed it onto the floor. Shock shot through her like a bolt of lightning when she saw the dried blood caked on her fingers and remembered what happened.

"Sol…"

How long was I out?

Pulse pounding in her ears, she ran through the door.

Sunlight filtered through a window in Tristan's room. Tristan was nowhere to be seen. Solomand lay on the bed, a blanket pulled up to his chest. Jagged scars poked out from the bandages wrapped around his torso.

"I thought you leave for Grishtanburg."

The low voice startled her at first, and her eyes darted to the Slav who sat on the floor, his back against the wall. A thin bandage wrapped around his right forearm. His eyes were closed as his head rested against the wall. He looked more tired than frightening.

"I… things got complicated." She looked at Solomand and gulped. "Is he…"

193

"Alright?" Ivan's eyes half-opened to give Sol a grudging look. "Solomand is too stubborn to die."

Rayn breathed in the metallic scent of blood filled and her throat constricted. Brightness started to rise in her field of vision, and her knees felt weak. She held back a gag as her eyes fell on a bucket of bloody gauze and rags.

Ivan motioned to a pitcher of water by his side. "Drink."

How long had it been since she had water? Rayn couldn't remember. She slid down against the wall by his side, and he poured a glass. She slowly sipped, cradling the tin cup in her hands.

"Thanks." Her stomach slowly unknotted itself.

"*Pazolustea*," he rumbled, then added after a pause, "You're welcome."

Rayn felt small sitting next to Ivan, but any fear she had for him was gone. She eyed Sol again.

"Do you really want to kill him?"

Rayn was beginning to think Sol had only been exaggerating. If that had been Ivan's intention all along, he was missing a perfect opportunity.

Ivan's face twisted into a glower.

"If bullet kill Solomand, it robs me of the pleasure."

Rayn glanced at the black spider tattoo crawling up his neck. What was the name of the person LeFrost was looking for? Sol had said it was Black Recluse. Did it have anything to do with Ivan?

Rayn watched the steady rise and fall of Sol's chest.

"How'd he get those scars on his back?" She took another sip of water.

For a moment, she thought he would not answer.

"In Corcyra. As boy, Solomand was thief. He steal to survive." His expression darkening, Ivan looked like his thoughts were far from what he spoke of. "I am told that is punishment for such things in Corcyra."

Rayn wished she hadn't asked.

Ivan turned his stern gaze on her. "He will not be happy you are still here."

Rayn shrugged, but the nagging feeling of doubt was already digging its claws in. There was no turning back.

"He'll have to deal with it," she muttered.

Ivan let out a low laugh and shook his head.

"You not like Grishtanburg, I think," he said. "Is too cold."

"Is that where you're from?"

"*Niya* (no). Where I'm from is colder."

"Do you miss it?"

His fingers curled at his side. "No." He looked away, a shadow darkening his expression.

Rayn didn't think he was lying, but she didn't believe he was telling the whole truth either. She looked at his tattoo again.

"Ivan? Does the Black Recluse have anything to do with why Sol is going to Corcyra?"

Whatever he was dwelling on seemed forgotten as he glared toward Sol. "You should know Solomand tells lies."

"So I've been told." Rayn was disappointed, realizing Ivan was just like everyone else: hell-bent on keeping secrets from her. Her shoulders slumped, thinking of her lost opportunity and wondering how long it would take for her to regret it.

Ivan frowned, he pressed a hand to his forehead, looking frustrated.

"I cannot break my word." It sounded more like he was reminding himself than telling her.

Rayn finished the water in her cup and set it on the floor.

"Here's a question you should be able to answer, then. How deep exactly have I stepped in it coming back here?"

She sensed allying herself with Solomand, and his crew meant she was picking sides in a conflict she knew nothing about. Breaking into Corcyra would mean she had consciously chosen to cross the Coalition, which would not bode well. Maybe it was already too late to worry about that. Another thought prodded its way to the top of her mind; did she even care?

One eyebrow raised, Ivan nudged her thigh with his hand.

"Past knees."

"Great. Now I know where I stand."

Ivan nodded, this time an actual smile crossed his lips. "That is always where you stand around here."

Rayn laughed, shaking her head. She struggled to her feet. "I'm going to get something to eat. Want anything?"

Ivan nodded. "Only if not Will's cooking."

"No promises," she called over her shoulder. She found some canned beef and dried cherries, which she took back to Ivan.

Rayn shoveled a forkful of cold beef in her mouth. "Can I ask you something?"

Sitting cross-legged, Ivan lit a cigarette and gave her a hesitant nod.

"Zee told me she remembers you when other men in green coats tried to kill her. She said you saved her."

His brow furrowing, Ivan inhaled slowly, studying her like he did not understand what she was getting at.

"Yes." He breathed out. "She is *chechnye*."

"*Chech—nye*?" Rayn's head tilted as she repeated the word. "What does that mean?"

"In my language, it means little sister." He paused, then added, "I would call you the same."

His hand quivered as he flicked ash into the empty beef can.

"Oh." Rayn took a drink of water. "Why were they trying to kill her, anyway?"

Ivan ran a hand along his neck. "Is complicated."

Rayn rolled her eyes. "That's something Sol would say."

Ivan's dark gaze softened as he looked at her. "Alright. Is because men who have everything taken from them will look for revenge in easiest places."

His eyes closed for a moment, then he offered her his cigarette.

"That's not really telling me anything," Rayn mumbled, taking the cigarette with a sigh. She breathed in the bitter taste of smoke, tired of asking questions no one would answer. "So, if you would call me little sister, what would I call you—in your language?"

"You would call me *Damaychi*, brother."

196

"Brother." Rayn tilted her head to one side. "I like it."

If she ever got to Grishtanburg, she imagined having a brother like Ivan would come in handy.

Rayn washed down the salty tin taste of beef with a gulp of water.

"Do you have any family in the North?"

For a single instant, a haunted look crossed Ivan's face.

"Not there. Not anymore." He answered. His eyes softened as he looked at her. "You should rest." Leaning against the wall, he finished the cigarette.

Rayn nodded.

"I'll be back later." Her gaze lingered on Sol before leaving to go to her room.

⊰○⊱

She stared in the mirror and ran a hand along the circles under her eyes. Smears of dirt and dried blood were splotched across her face. Her hair was mostly torn free of the long braid, an impossible wind-tangled mess. Ivan hadn't hinted at her gruesome appearance.

She undid what was left in the braid and brushed out the tangles. Digging the medallion from her pocket, she ran her finger along the inscription.

S. L. She hung the chain on the corner of the mirror, biting her trembling lip. Unable to hold her emotions in any longer, she started to cry. Long after the water from the shower washed away the dirt and blood from her face, Rayn let it rinse off her tears until she was sure she had none left. Then, she dried herself off and crawled under the fresh sheets, determined to hide until the puffy redness was gone. She would sooner die than let anyone know she'd been crying.

An hour later, she checked herself in the mirror. Satisfied the redness was hidden, she put on clean clothes. Maybe a good cry was all she needed. She felt more resolved to her fate, whatever the

197

hell it might be, and went to check on Sol. If he was awake, she was going to remind him he owed her a rifle. And to think, he almost made her forget!

CHAPTER 35

RAYN

THE SMELL OF coffee drifted through the hall as Rayn made her way to the kitchen. Jank was already there. He stood at the counter, chopping a stack of purple carrots. A soft blue flame glowed beneath the percolator on the stove; steam sputtered out of it. Jank yawned, rubbing his face on his shoulder before resuming his dicing.

"Need a hand?" Rayn asked.

Jank gave her a quick glance and dropped a handful of chopped carrots into a pot of water.

"Rayn! Nah. Thanks, but I've got it."

He wiped bits of onion from his hand onto the side of his pants before flipping his open sketchbook shut before she could get a glimpse of his drawings.

Rayn's nose wrinkled as she glanced at the sink overflowing with empty bowls, sticky cups, and pans layered with grease. Flies buzzed around. Rayn hated washing dishes more than any other chore. Her eyes pinched shut. She didn't want to say it, but feeling sorry for Jank won out.

"Need help with the dishes?"

Jank's face brightened. "Sure."

Holding back a groan, Rayn rolled up her sleeves. "Do you do this every day?"

Dunking her hands into sudsy water, she started scrubbing at encrusted bread dough off a mixing bowl.

Jank shrugged.

"Yeah. We're supposed to take turns, but Sol's a shit cook and Will, well, I think he has it confused with chemical warfare." He scraped the rest of the vegetables in the pot and put the lid in place. "So." His eyes flicked to her while washing the counter. "Why d'you come back?"

Rayn's sleeve fell down to her wrist, soaking up dishwater. She pushed it back up, trying to think of an answer. She didn't have one, not really. Everything had happened so fast.

"Sol owes me a rifle," she said.

Jank snickered.

"You'll be around a long time trying to collect on that debt." He plucked two of the cups Rayn had just washed, shook the water out, and filled them both with coffee. "That'll be about the time Will learns not to poison food."

He handed a cup to Rayn. She took it, wiping her damp hand on a towel.

"Where is Will anyway?"

She breathed in the aroma before taking a sip of the steaming hot coffee.

"He's looking after Tris, in Sol's quarters." Jank leaned over the counter, blowing quick breaths into his cup to cool it off. "It took a lot out of him." His freckles looked darker as his face turned pale. "Patching up Sol like that." He took a worried sip of the cooled coffee.

Tristan.

Rayn swallowed with difficulty. She set her cup down.

"Is he a doctor? Tristan, I mean."

"Tristan could be whatever the hell he wanted to be. His old man is the best surgeon in Corcyra." Jank's voice raised, and he spoke with venom. "Tristan learned alongside him."

Jank took another sip, looking like the thought of Tristan's father made him sick.

Zee's yells for Sol echoed down the hall, and Jank spewed coffee all over the counter.

"Shit!" He dropped the cup in the sink, wiping his mouth on his sleeve. "Tristan said to keep her out of there."

He darted from the kitchen. Rayn tossed the towel aside, set down her coffee and followed him.

Ivan stood outside Tristan's room, holding Zee in a bear-like grip. Struggling, she screamed at him.

"Let me go! I want to see Sol!"

She beat her small fists on his chest. It did not look like Ivan felt her blows at all. He started to carry her down the hall.

"Ivan..." Sol's voice lifted over the commotion, and Zee fell silent. "Let her in."

Ivan stopped in his tracks. Jank's eyes widened, and he shook his head at the Slav, making slashing movements across his neck.

"Ivan." Sol's voice cracked. "Please."

Ivan's face hardened, and Jank's hands moved more wildly. More gently than it looked like he could be, Ivan set the girl down. She dashed around him and into Tristan's room.

"Damnit, Ivan!" Jank dragged a hand over his face and ran past the Slav after Zee. But he was too late to grab her. She ran up to Sol and threw her arms around him.

Sol's face twisted in pain as Zee sobbed into his neck. "Hey, I'm alright." He laid a hand on her head.

He sounded better than he looked. Rayn could see he was fighting to hide the pain he was in.

"Didn't I tell you? Huh?" He took her face in his left hand, wiping away her tears with his thumb. "I'll always come back." He took a long breath. "So, you don't need to worry anymore, okay?"

Zee bit her trembling lip, nodding, and wiped her eyes with her lengthy shirt sleeve. Sol smiled in a forced way.

"Now run along with Jank before you incur the wrath of Tristan."

Zee nodded again, giving him one more hug before sulking away with Jank.

201

As soon as she left the room, Solomand gasped, gritting his teeth. The sheet slid off his chest as he arched his back. His right arm was bandaged to his chest, presumably, so he couldn't move it. The fingers of his left hand were white as he clenched them together.

Ivan went to the table and got a syringe of blue-tinged liquid. He went to inject it in Sol's left arm.

"I don't need it!" Sol drew his arm away from Ivan. "It's only for if..." he stopped to catch his breath, "If someone gets properly... hurt."

"Be still." Ivan's brow furrowed. "Or I properly hurt you then."

"Listen here," Solomand backed away, protesting when his eyes fell on Rayn. Shock spread over his face.

"Rayn?" He jerked his wrist free of Ivan's grip, ceasing to struggle.

She took a few steps closer. He looked like someone who, on the verge of winning a race, had the assured victory snatched from their grasp.

"You should have stayed!"

Rayn felt guilty now. Maybe she shouldn't have left in the first place. If she hadn't, he wouldn't be in this mess.

"I know," she whispered.

There was an ache in the back of her throat.

The look of disbelief still plastered on his face, Sol jerked his arm as Ivan slipped the needled into the bulge of his vein. He gave them both a dejected look before falling back onto the bed.

Rayn frowned, worried.

"Sorry, Sol."

Ivan frowned at him.

"*Idiot.*" He grumbled, throwing the blanket back over Sol's chest.

CHAPTER 36

SOLOMAND

TIME TO THINK was dangerous, and Solomand had too much of it. Pain wracked through his chest whenever dark memories surfaced, intensifying the stabbing from his wound.

"This is our fault!" Ivan's words felt like a bullet.

Eyes clamped shut, he clutched a hand to his heart as it throbbed against his ribs, stifling his breath. Strange that even the vaguest memory of words had such power after all these years.

It was my fault. I was in charge.

One wrong decision meant life or death. He'd made the wrong one in not retreating, and it had sickened him ever since.

"Sol." Tristan's voice dragged him back from the pit he was sliding into.

Solomand's eyes snapped open, and he dropped his hand to his side. Steam wafted from the chipped mug his friend held out to him.

"Drink this. It will help."

"Help what?" Solomand asked, taking the cup.

Tristan held his gaze as he sat in the chair at Solomand's bedside, one eyebrow raised. Solomand's shoulders tensed.

"How long have you known?"

Tristan rested his chin on the handle of his cane.

"Well, it started back then—before this happened." He gestured to his chest. "But they've steadily grown worse over the years, especially as of late."

After all the effort he'd gone through to hide it. Solomand took a sip of the bitter tasting liquid.

"All this time. I thought you hadn't noticed."

Tristan's mouth formed a hard line.

"Honestly, Sol. Did you think I would not discern that my best friend was quietly having panic attacks?"

Solomand took another swallow. The feeling of impending doom subsiding.

"Panic attacks. That's what that shit doctor at Port Bilboa called it." He cast Tristan a sideways glance. "Why didn't you say anything?"

Tristan took a deep breath, looking tired.

"You went through an awful lot of trouble to conceal it from me. "He shrugged. "So, I played along."

"I didn't want you to worry." Solomand gave a short, humorless laugh. "So much for that, eh?" The room stopped its slow spin. Solomand let his head sink deeper into the pillow, balancing the cup of tea on his knee. "How far we've fallen."

"Well, you didn't have very far to fall from, my friend." There was a trace of humor returning to Tristan's voice.

Solomand laughed.

"True. Not like you." He raised his head to take another drink. "What do you think we would have been if all this shit hadn't happened?"

Tristan sank onto the arm of the chair.

"Well, we would both be married to beautiful women, for starters."

Solomand recoiled at the thought of the lady Tristan would be entangled with. "And I imagine we would both have children."

At those words, an invisible punch knocked the wind from Solomand. He tipped the cup back and swallowed the rest of the concoction in one scalding gulp.

Tristan's hand was on his shoulder, his grip anchoring him to here and now. He took the cup from Solomand.

"And we would still be friends."

"Would we?" Solomand jumped at the opportunity to change the subject.

"Of course. Some souls were always bound to end up together. I think ours are like that."

"Like flies to spoiled milk, you mean?"

Tristan felt his pulse, shaking his head. "If that is the analogy you wish to use."

"How about the stupid kid to the smart one? Suppose that's really only when cheating's concerned, though."

Tristan laughed that time. "I cannot imagine anyone would believe your grades if you cheated off of me."

Sol closed his eyes, feeling tired. "You're right, Swank. But I'm the one you go looking for when you get your ass into trouble. What's more important?"

"You see?" Tristan replied good-naturedly. "Our friendship was inevitable."

The thought was comforting to Solomand as he drifted into a heavy sleep. He couldn't imagine a world where he didn't know any of the friends who were with him now, even if it meant taking the pain away.

CHAPTER 37

RAYN

FOR TWO DAYS, Rayn avoided Solomand. Being around him only confused her. Exploring the sunny fields and forest made her feel better. Crisp morning air carried the scent of damp moss, fallen leaves and hinted at the approaching turn of the season. The Kree tribes would be there soon, so Jank said. They stopped briefly before continuing on their way to trade with larger cities to the north. He also said they were secretive about their routes and way of life. Solomand was only welcome because his mother was the daughter of the Crow chieftain.

On her way back from the kitchen one evening, Rayn heard raised voices coming from Tristan's room. She crept upstairs, being careful not to make any noise on the creaky staircase. She pressed her ear to the door. The voices became clearer.

"Too many ways for everything to go wrong!" Tristan's sounded uncharacteristically on edge.

"Be reasonable, Tris." The other voice was Sol's. Inching closer to the door, Rayn felt the coolness of the wood seep through her shirt.

"Do you have any concept of how maddeningly fortunate you are?" Tristan's voice raised. "Your scheming—this is what it ends with! If Rayn hadn't come back with Will—if you had been any later in arriving, Sol... if Ivan hadn't given you his blood. My efforts in saving you would have been futile."

An uncomfortable silence followed.

"I know." The words came in a harrowed tone. Sol sounded beaten.

"If you wonder about it at all, after the trouble we've gone through," Tristan's took a threatening edge Rayne never imagined he could manage. "If you move that arm, Sol, I shall call this whole Corcyra business off."

A bout of raspy coughs followed his warning.

"Alright, Tris. I give you my word." Solomand sounded strained.

Rayn pressed her ear further to the door as Tristan's voice dropped.

"It will complicate things, Sol. Without your right arm, Corcyra will require another man. Even if the Falcon agrees to help us."

Tristan was trying to talk Sol out of the whole thing. Rayn's heart pounded. Corcyra was where the war had been. If it was likely she had been there at all, maybe going back would jar her memories. If she couldn't go to Grishtanburg for answers, maybe Corcyra was the next best thing. She braced her shoulders and pushed open the door, interrupting Sol's protest.

They both turned to her in surprise.

"Lucky I came back then, isn't it?"

Tristan was bent over his cane, his face brightened on seeing her. Sol, however, looked ill.

"No. No, Rayn, don't even think about it!" He raised a finger and took a step toward her.

"Sol." Tristan silenced him with a gravelly tone. "Let me speak to Rayn. Alone."

Sol's mouth hung open. He looked from Tristan to Rayn, a betrayed glint in his eye.

"Fine." He gritted his teeth. "But you're the one who just told me you wanted me to lie around and do nothing."

He limped out, fumbling with the door in his attempt to slam it shut.

Tristan lay back on his bed, struggling as he fought to breathe in. He motioned her over, and Rayn sat next to him. His lips were dry and cracked. She tried to swallow but found it was difficult with the lump lodged in her throat. Was this what it felt like to watch someone you love die? She understood at least one thing about Solomand: that underlying dread in his eyes when he spoke of Tristan.

"Rayn." Tristan reached for her hand. Ice-cold fingers closed around hers. "You think the answers you seek might be there, don't you?"

"Maybe." Rayn's stomach churned. She didn't want to admit she hadn't really thought about it.

Tristan's head moved back and forth on his pillow.

"Corcyra is dangerous, Rayn. For all of us."

"That's not stopping anyone else from going," she said.

"I'm tired." Her hand inadvertently tightened around Tristan's as he took a ragged breath. "Solomand." His eyes opened, slits of pure blue sky looking at her. Despite his harrowed look, his smile was still charming. "Death is not the end of everything, Rayn. I would have let go a long time ago, only…". He turned away, his voice turning flat. "I worry about him… what darkness he would let in."

"Solomand?" Rayn inched closer to Tristan as his eyes drifted shut.

"He's afraid for you to go there." His voice was a whisper now.

"Afraid of what?" Rayn's chest hitched. She wanted him to keep talking, afraid if he went to sleep, he might not wake up.

"He made a promise to someone." Tristan's fingers loosened in her grasp. "A promise he knows he cannot keep."

Rayn allowed his hand to slip entirely from hers now.

A promise to who?

She never had the chance to ask. Tristan was asleep. She watched the rhythmic rise and fall of his chest for a long time, as if leaving him would somehow cause his pulse to stop. At that moment, everything else seemed of little importance. She only wanted Tristan to go on living.

CHAPTER 38

SOLOMAND

IT WAS LATE. Rain gently pattered on the roof. Solomand lay on the sofa, watching the spattering on the windows. The stabbing had started in his shoulder: first a dull ache, now an insistent searing that he couldn't ignore. The painkiller—less potent than the one Ivan had injected into him—had worn off.

I don't need it.

Sol gritted his teeth, slid off the sofa, and crawled clumsily to the cabinet on the other side of the room. With every movement, a new barrage of sharp sensations speared their way through his upper body.

"Ishwa zaswi!"

He muttered the Kree curse with a groan and fumbled open the cabinet door with his left hand. Half-empty liquor bottles clinked together as he rummaged through them. In the very back, he found what he was looking for—a foggy glass bottle of clear liquid which looked like it had been buried in a field for ten years. Hugging it under his arm, Sol crawled back to the sofa.

He slumped on the gritty cushioning and shivered as cold streams of sweat trickled down his back. It was no use trying to open the damn thing with his left hand. He bit off the cork and spit it aside. The stench of distilled Slavik gin rose off the mouth of the bottle, causing him to turn away with a cough before gulping a swallow down. The grating feeling spread like fire down his throat, and he fought the urge to gag.

He braced himself mentally before taking another biting swallow. With great effort, he set the bottle on the coffee table and collapsed back onto the sofa. The pain was still there, but the fuzzy spinning settling on his mind made it easier to overlook.

Why did she have to come back?

She was almost out of harm's reach. He cringed, watching the angry gray clouds roll by in the domed ceiling. The rain fell harder, pounding at the glass for a moment before letting up. The moon peeked out from time to time, giving him an unpleasant dizzy sensation. What time was it anyway? Sol started to reach with his subdued right hand before using his left to dig his watch from his pocket. The first thing he saw was the date: August sixteenth.

Six years ago.

The gin suddenly lost its effect, and he felt unpleasantly sober.

Has it really been that long?

He tossed the watch aside, dug in his pocket once more and extracted a battered bill-fold. He pulled out a brown-tinged photograph and unfolded it. There they were; young, naïve, and hopeful. They all believed they could win. Ben inspired that kind of belief. But it hadn't been enough to save them.

"Stupid," Sol muttered. That's what they had been.

It all came crashing back, like a hammer in his chest: the burning city, the smell of blood and death on the wind. Screams that could never be unheard and sights gruesome carnage burned in his memory forever. His fingers trembled on the photograph and, just for a moment, he wished more than anything he could forget as she had.

"Oh! Sorry. I didn't know you were still here." Rayn's voice startled him.

He looked up, hoping the darkness in the room hid the sorrow in his eyes. Rayn turned to leave.

"Rayn, wait. Stay." He wanted to grab her, imagining the warmth of her hand in his. "Please." There was a desperateness in his voice he didn't want to be there.

Without a word, Rayn sat next to him, keeping a safe distance. He could sense the questions in her eyes without seeing them. He wanted to tell her everything. Maybe it would work out somehow if he did.

No!

He fought back the urge, blaming the fog of gin for lowering his defenses.

Rayn held a hand over her nose and mouth and squinted, leaning forward to look at the aged bottle. "Are you drinking bootleg gin? You trying to kill yourself or something?"

"Or something," Sol mumbled, scooting backward. He cringed as a spasm of pain shot through his shoulder and back. He gasped out, "It's medicinal."

Rayn raised an eyebrow. "Don't make a habit of it, then?"

"God, no!" Sol made a face at the thought of drinking the liquid. "Normally, I hold the open bottle by the airship and let the fumes peel the paint off. What I'd really prefer is a smoke."

"Don't." Rayn fanned a hand in front of her face. "You'll set us on fire."

Sol chuckled, his face twisting in pain at the same time.

"Don't make—owe! Me laugh."

He doubled over, clutching at his throbbing side. Rayn's face was pale as shadowy shapes of clouds passed overhead. A smile flitted across her lips. His heart gave an agonizing wrench, making his shoulder pain feel like nothing.

Rayn, why couldn't you just have stayed on the docks?

She was looking at the photograph in his lap now. Holding his breath, he handed it to her and watched as she smoothed the picture. Her hair brushed the burnt edges.

"Is this your father?" She pointed to Ben.

Solomand's chest tightened.

"No," he said. "But he treated me like he was. All of us, really."

211

He eyed the bottle of gin, wishing it would numb deeper wounds. But Ivan had tried that with something much stronger. No, better to suffer through it. It was no less than he deserved.

Rayn was waiting for him to say more. He took a shaky breath.

"His name was Benjamin Ivers. He was our leader, General of the Resistance and one of the greatest men I've ever known."

"What happened to him?"

Flashes of shouting and streams of blood on cobbles flooded Sol's mind. He bent over, pressing a hand to his forehead as if it would make the memories go away. He didn't want to think about it, much less talk about it, especially to Rayn.

"LeFrost." He forced himself to speak. "He said he wanted to negotiate a truce. Ben took me with him." His fist tightened on his knee. "They let me go so I could tell the others." His voice hitched, and he looked away from her so she couldn't see the demons he tried so desperately to keep hidden away. "LeFrost had him beaten to death."

His eyes pinched shut, trying to block the image. When he opened them, he saw Rayn brushing her hand over the face of Benjamin Ivers, looking sympathetic.

He thought then that he might actually be sick and lurched forward, grabbed the bottle of gin, and swallowed another gulp before shoving the bottle out of his reach. He sank back, trying to focus on nothing but the burning sensation spreading through his stomach.

Rayn handed him the picture.

"Is that why you're going to Corcyra? Revenge?" She tucked a strand of hair behind her ear.

"Among other things." He tried not to look at her. There was just enough conscious unaffected by the tingling warmth to remind him he couldn't tell her everything. Not yet. "You really shouldn't go." His voice was beginning to slur. "It's nothing to do with you."

These last words came with difficulty.

Rayn leaned back on the sofa. He could smell the scent of gunpowder and lavender.

"If you're telling me this to scare me from going, it won't work." Her jaw set stubbornly.

Ah yes. Even if she knew the risks, she wouldn't stay away.

"I'm not."

His hand fell to his side, the numbness weighing heavy on his mind now. Every plan he ever made without Tristan's help ended the same way: disaster. Why should his clever ruse to send her away be any different?

"Just thought you should know."

Rayn eyed him for a moment before reaching across the table for the bottle of paint-peeling gin. She took a drink, grimacing, then leaned her head back, watching the clouds as they gave way to a star-filled sky. Sol's eyes felt heavy, and he laid back, moving his hand. His fingers brushed Rayn's hand—warm against his skin. Without thinking, he clasped her hand. She did not stop him.

CHAPTER 39

RAYN

BRANCHES TAPPED ON the observatory dome as a gentle morning breeze swept across the valley. Birds dove past, shadows against the warm sunlight. Rayn and Sol leaned against each other, still sleeping. Sol's hand draped across her hip, his fingers curled around her thigh. Rayn's head rested on his shoulder, the steady rhythm of his heart beating with hers.

The door slid open with a loud clamber and Rayn's eyes jolted open.

"Sol." Jank's bare feet thumped on the floor as he dashed into the room. His eyes widened when he saw them together, and his face turned beet red.

Rayn's head pounded, and it took her a moment to shake the grogginess.

"S-sorry," Jank stammered, looking away.

Heat flushed Rayn's cheeks as she saw Sol's arm draped over her.

"What is it, Jank?" Sol muttered.

A tingling sensation ran up her spine as his hand dragged across her legs. He sat up and stared at her, one eye open, his smoky-black hair going in every direction.

"Jank—what do you want?" He pressed against his forehead with his free hand, his face contorted in pain.

"Oh, I. Well..." Jank rubbed his arm and recovered his bearings. "I came to tell you..." He glanced uncomfortably at Rayn.

Telling him nothing happened between them would probably make the situation more awkward. She leaned forward, her head feeling like a hammer was beating on it from the inside.

That gin was unforgiving!

"The Crow Clan is back," Jank said.

"Alright." Sol dragged a hand over his face. "Get me a list of what we need and anything that's worth trading."

This seemed an excellent opportunity to slink away. Rayn started to leave.

"Rayn, wait." Sol stopped her, the awkwardness of the situation apparently lost on him. She turned her head, waiting to see what he wanted. "Want to come with me?" His eyes were brighter this morning. "To meet the Kree."

"Alright." She tucked her hair behind her ears again. "Just give me time to wash up."

Her eyes turned to Jank, and the heat spread further across her face. She hurried away.

When Jank thought she was out of earshot she heard him remark, "*Someone* had a good night!" The sound of breaking glass followed. "Hey! You could have hit me with that... what the hell, Sol! You didn't actually drink that shit, did you?!"

⊰✹⊱

Bleached canvas tents dotted the rolling plains where the river widened, dark squares against the waving golden-tinged grass. Horses whinnied, thundering along the water's edge, enjoying freedom from bridle and cart.

"They like the old ways," Sol said as he and Rayn strode towards the camp in the warm afternoon sun.

Solomand seemed almost a different person than the one she'd seen last night. How did he always manage to make her forget how

215

annoying he could be? Getting himself shot was a very drastic ploy.

Taking a long step, Sol's foot found an uneven patch of ground, and he lurched forward. Rayn caught his arm with her shoulder and their eyes locked as he regained his footing.

"Thanks."

There was a quivering in his fingertips as he touched her hand. "Don't mention it."

There was that troublesome warm feeling that spread through her body, and her heart beat abnormally fast.

What the hell is wrong with me?

Seed pods from the grass bristled against her fingertips as they waded through the field and back to the encampment.

Kree children darted about: boys shirtless with leather breeches and girls with colorful beaded dresses. Most of them were barefoot. Their skin was a deep brown, darker than Solomand's, but she recognized some of his features in their faces: the deep-set eyes, dark and beautiful, and black hair with shades of smoky grey.

Some girls rushed to greet Zee, who trailed behind them alongside Jank. Other ran up to Sol, chattering in a language that taunted Rayn.

Where have I heard it before?

Sol laughed, speaking back to the children in the Kree tongue, ruffling their hair and gesturing to his arm. She imagined he was telling them it was nothing and rolled her eyes. He would.

A tall, gruff-looking man with long silver braids stepped out of the main tent and strode up to them. Beads were woven in patterns into his tan clothes.

"Aminaksew! *Anye ashi.*" He spoke in a low, lyrical voice.

The children lowered their heads and scampered away on seeing the Kree Chieftain.

Sol's shoulders squared, and his forehead wrinkled as he bowed his head.

"Iminho. *Anyi manjien.*"

His arms crossed, and the old Kree surveyed Sol gruffly before he laughed and caught him in a fierce hug.

"Still fighting to stay away. You are ever my sister's son."

Sol grimaced, turning slightly paler under the massive force of Iminho's grip. Eyes darker than Sol's fell on Rayn.

"A friend of yours?"

Rayn felt herself blushing the way the old Chieftain looked at Sol.

"This is Rayn," Sol introduced her. "Rayn, this is my uncle, Iminho."

"Rayn." Iminho tilted his head toward the sky. "Your name is like music in our language. Rain brings life to the earth."

He took her head in weathered hands and touched his forehead to hers. Rayn's uncomfortable feeling left when she breathed in the scent of dried grass; it was the same smell on Solomand's coat. It soothed her spirit as it wrapped itself around her, familiar, though she did not know why.

"It is my honor to meet you." Iminho stood back and smiled at them both, amused. "Aminaksew, together you make a fierce storm. Come." He turned back to his tent.

Rayn leaned towards Sol as they followed him.

"What's he talking about?" she whispered.

Sol leaned back. "My Kree name, Aminaksew, it means Angry Wind."

"Angry Wind. Solomand Black, just how many names do you have?"

She was glad to see his mischievous grin returned.

"As many as I need."

They ducked inside Iminho's tent. Bunches of herbs and dried plants hung from a rope stretched from one end of the tent to the other, filling it with an aromatic, pleasant scent. The chieftain sat cross-legged on a grass mat and motioned them both to join him.

"How is your friend? The one with eyes like the sky?"

Sol's jaw tightened. He didn't answer. Rayn suspected he couldn't at this point. Iminho frowned.

217

"You will want the healer again." His long braids jostled back and forth on his shoulders as he shook his head. "It can only do so much, Aminaksew."

"I know." Sol's voice was a hoarse whisper. "But it will be enough."

Iminho's face turned stern. "You go back to the city where misfortune found your family. It will find you again."

Rayn sat close enough to Sol that she could feel him tense.

"Misfortune does not confine itself to any city."

"Ah, you speak the words of Daishee." Iminho's eyes closed. His hands rested on his knees, palms facing up. "A Kree who leaves his people will never be at rest."

"You forget, Uncle. I'm only half Kree." Solomand's tone turned cold.

There was sadness in both their eyes as they looked at each other. The old chief shook his head.

"You are not half our brother, Aminaksew." He pressed a wrinkled hand to his heart.

"That is not what my grandfather thought." Solomand's words were biting. His hand clenched on his knee.

His uncle looked pained at these words.

"You belong with your people. It is the only way your heart can be at rest. You will end up like Daishee, who calls nowhere home." Iminho's eyes flashed as he spoke the name. He sounded angry.

Solomand's gaze lowered. "Have you spoken to him?"

Iminho crossed his arms. "Only the way you do. He only sends a message by his bird." His jaw tightened on seeing Sol's disappointment. "He no longer cares for his people or his past. Careful, you do not make the same mistake, my nephew."

Sol opened his mouth, but a young boy ducked inside the tent, bowing low. He held out a leather satchel to Sol.

"Medicine."

"*Naga maji.*" Sol took it from the boy and rubbed the back of his neck. His eyes narrowed as he watched his uncle.

218

The Chieftain's wrinkled face relaxed.

"Please think on what I say, Aminaksew. We will not stay long here." He sighed.

"I will think on it, Uncle," Sol said.

Iminho grew stern once more. "Not much time is left. The land is restless. A storm is brewing. The Crow Clan will soon leave here to travel to the home of our ancestors across the oceans and will no longer return to this valley."

Solomand looked taken aback. "You already know what I must do, Uncle."

Iminho gave a satisfied nod of the head. "Return to your friend, Aminaksew. But come back when the stars and moon meet this night." His eyes moved to Rayn, and he looked much less severe. "Both of you."

Rayn stood with Sol as he rose to leave.

"We will." He held up the satchel of medicine. "*Naga maji.*"

He bit his lip, the light-hearted glint gone from his eye as they started back up the hill.

"Jank!" He waved his hand toward the path. Jank was busy scrawling on a scrap of paper as he talked with a shrewd-looking Kree elder. He waved back at Sol.

Rayn noticed the way he watched Zee playing in the grass, laughing and darting about with the other children. He became pensive and quiet, and it bothered her not knowing why.

"Sol!" Jank caught up to them, waving the piece of paper. "Bad news." He clutched his side, taking long steps to keep up.

"Yeah?" Sol couldn't have sounded less interested.

"They don't have any salt to trade."

Sol ran a hand along his bandaged forehead. "They have tobacco?"

"Yeah, but,"

"Then any other shortage we can handle." Sol gave Jank a dismissive look and kept on up the hill.

"Sol?" Rayn ventured to ask him a question despite his darkened mood.

219

"Yeah?"

"Who is this Daishee? A friend of yours?"

Solomand gave a sarcastic laugh. "I don't really think he's anyone's friend, unless it plays to his advantage."

There was a bitterness in his words again. He gave her a sideways glance.

"You'll meet him soon enough."

CHAPTER 40

SOLOMAND

SOLOMAND HANDED THE satchel of powdered brown root to Rayn and asked her to take it to Tristan. He wouldn't go himself, not since their heated argument. He thought a long time about what Tristan had said, how Ivan had saved him, and what they would all be risking by returning to the so-called City of Prosper.

He stayed outside, hoping the air would clear his head before he had to face Iminho one last time. Why couldn't anything ever be simple? The Kree leaving further complicated the situation with Zee. He had hoped he could leave her in the safety of the Crow Clan. Zee had no idea what dark piece of her past lay beyond Corcyra's walls. No good could come of her going to Corcyra. Iminho would be more than willing to take the girl in, but she would never go with them, not when she realized they were leaving for good.

Staring broodingly at the ground as he stalked toward the dock, he muttered a heartfelt, "Shit," at his crumbling plans.

When he looked up, he saw Ivan perched on the railing. His thick brown hair was grown out enough for the wind to blow through it. Unlike when he was first dragged here, he looked quite able to take on Sol, and Sol suspected he still desired to kill him with a spoon, even if he had saved his life. He took a resigned step onto the dock and leaned over the railing next to Ivan.

221

"Looks like you're well on your way to throwing me off a cliff now," he remarked, digging in his left pocket for his cigarette case.

Ivan snorted, glancing pointedly at Sol's subdued arm.

"Not fair fight."

"Yeah, well, never was, was it?" Sol's fingers fought to open the silver case, and he dropped it in the process. "Damn," he grumbled, stooping down to pick up the scattered bits of tobacco. When he finally pocketed the case, Ivan held out his own lighter and flicked the flint.

Hesitating, Sol at last held his cigarette to the tiny flicker of flame, then handed one to Ivan.

"Thanks."

Ivan shrugged.

Sol's chest tightened as he took a long drag and held the smoke in his lungs for as long as he could before letting it out. He watched it drift away, into the wind-blown trees.

"Look. Ivan." He flicked ashes over the railing. "Thanks for, you know..."

Ivan replied gruffly, "You do same for me once." He looked at Sol sharply from the corner of his eye.

"So now we are even. Makes easier to kill you."

Sol couldn't tell if he was serious or not. That invisible rope around his chest drew tighter.

Just say it, you idiot!

"For what it's worth, I'm sorry."

He knew he didn't need to explain what his apology was for. Ivan would know. He was an expert of reminding him without even talking.

The Slav's stony expression revealed nothing as he inhaled deeply and let the smoke curl over his lips.

I was having a hell of a rough month!

But Ivan already knew that, and making excuses was not what he wanted to do. Images resurfaced and Solomand could not keep them at bay. Even after so long, it came back as clear as if it were yesterday.

The black smoke had swirled overhead, blocking out the sun and choking the insurgents with its acrid odor. Solomand could see nothing as he stumbled over chunks of rock and splintered wood. The taste of blood and metal seared his tongue, and his lungs ached.

It's over. We're finished.

The realization was just as gut-wrenching now as when he wandered blindly through the rubble, screaming for his men. Whatever faith Benjamin had placed in him was a mistake.

Alarm bells sounded as the enemy airships continued to bombard the city. Dazed, Sol kept moving.

They can't all be dead, they can't be!

"Sol!" Ivan's voice rose over the harrowing noise of the *Pandora*.

"Ivan!"

Solomand waded his way through the rubble, tripping and stumbling until he found his way to the voice. He grabbed ahold of the Slav's arms, dragging him close enough to see through the smoke. "Are you hurt?" He searched him for signs of bleeding.

Ivan pulled away, eyes frantic with a horror that made Sol's stomach turn. The Ice Wolf was never shaken.

"Tristan is hit!"

The words nearly made Sol's heart stop.

Not Tristan!

The highborn son of a surgeon was different. Tristan gave up everything to follow his conscience, they had nothing to lose. He didn't belong here like they did. He was unthinkingly loyal to them all, and if anything happened to him, Sol would blame himself forever.

"Where is he?" Gripping Ivan's collar, he shook him and repeated the question when he didn't immediately answer. "Ivan! Where is he?"

"By downed ship." Ivan pointed to the shadow form of a smoking airship in the distance.

"Shit."

Solomand gritted his teeth and ran, ignoring the occasional bullet whizzing past. The fog lifted enough that he could duck beneath it and make out which of the limp forms sprawled beneath the scraps of a gunship was Tristan. He went numb and didn't feel the bullet that tore through his shoulder, or the shards of glass embedded in his knees as he crashed to the ground at Tristan's side.

Hands shaking, he threw the metal aside, revealing the damage. There were nasty gashes all over Tristan's chest, glass, and smaller shards of metal still sticking out.

Ivan reached them but quickly turned away on sight of Tristan, swearing repeatedly.

"Ivan—I need your help!" Sol practically screamed, digging through the rubble for a med-kit. He finally found one and tore open the contents, looking for anything useful. "Ivan!" His heart raced as he clumsily tried to repair his friend, oblivious to the blood gushing from his own wound. Ivan did not come. But Will did.

"There's an airship evacuating the wounded to Cierne," he said, scooping Tristan in his arms. "If we hurry, we might make it."

Sol nodded and ran after him.

Ivan.

He whirled around and dragged the burly Slav from the ground.

"Move!" he barked, pulling him along as he sprinted after Will.

They clambered up the deck just as the airship was taking off with the wounded.

Ivan stared with a glazed expression as the only surgeon did his best to work on Sol, but he was not known for success. He sank to the floor and muttered in Slav. Sol could only understand a few words of what he was saying.

"He is dead." He was talking about Tristan.

Something inside of Solomand snapped, and he spun around, jerking Ivan to his feet.

"Ivan!" he bellowed. "Don't say that—ever!"

He reared back and punched his friend in the face. His hand instinctively flexed, recalling how much it hurt.

Ivan fell back, holding his nose and fixing a stunned expression on Sol. Solomand knew he had injured more than his nose, but at that moment in time, he didn't care. He gave Ivan an icy glare and turned and collapsed on the airship floor.

The medics had managed to save his life, and Tristan's as well, but Ivan never forgave him—a wedge forever driven between them. They made it to Cierne, and he only ever called Solomand 'Captain Black,' reminding him with no minced words what happened was his fault. Sol had puzzled over his reaction at times—not understanding how someone like Ivan could hold a grudge for so long over the cheap shot he'd taken. If he could have swallowed his pride sooner, he would have asked. But he waited too long. Ivan left. Then he got hooked on furi. One more thing Sol held himself responsible for.

A hawk crying in the forest brought Sol back to the present moment, the damage of the memory already done. He leaned forward, sweat trickling down his neck as his lungs constricted.

"I shouldn't have taken it out on you." He pulled at his collar, fighting to hide the fact he felt suffocated. "I'm not asking you to forgive me." Sol's voice cracked. "I just want you to know you were right. And I'd take it back if I could."

There.

He'd said it. The Slav could do what the hell he wanted now.

Ivan's glare intensified. He flicked the remains of his cigarette over the railing.

A gust of wind tore at the trees. Cicadas buzzed loudly in the bushes. Solomand thought it might make him feel better, getting at least one thing off his chest, but the gnawing sense of loss remained. It felt like a knife was thrust into his ribs. Dragging a hand through his hair, he left Ivan, struggling back up the hill, the remains of the cigarette hanging from the corner of his mouth.

CHAPTER 41

RAYN

A BONFIRE BURNED in the circle of tents, flames flicking and weaving in the warm air. Logs popped and crackled. Drums and chanting swelled over the buzz of crickets as the Kree danced around the rising flames. Beaded bracelets on their ankles clanked together. Rayn sat at the fire, sipping dark tea from a wooden mug. Will and Ivan carried crates of tobacco and dried meat back to the castle, while Zee ran through the fields, chasing fireflies.

Rayn breathed in the oak scent of smoke swirling around her. She could see why the Kree liked the old ways. They were more straightforward, less cluttered. Time seemed to stand still. It was easy to imagine being content here. She watched Sol from the corner of her eye. His restless gaze looked past the flames and the dancers to Zee. There was no peace in his expression. He looked haunted and exhausted.

What's wrong?

She wanted to ask him. Instead, she nudged him with her elbow. "Zee seems to like it here."

Looking jarred from a bad dream, his gaze met hers.

"She does," he murmured.

Flames danced in his eyes. His hair, sticking up from the bandage on his head, looked smokier in the firelight. The strange feeling in the pit of her stomach returned. She squirmed, wanting to look away but unable to.

226

An old woman with long, gray braids stood up and began speaking the old language, her face shadowed by the flames. All the children fell silent, sitting wide-eyed to listen to the voice that was clear and smooth.

Rayn leaned over to Sol.

"What's she saying?" she whispered.

Solomand scowled, flicking a twig into the fire.

"It's an old story." The flames danced in his eyes as he translated for her. "A Falcon, a Crow, and a Bear set sail for Tir Eadon. The Crow could not find his way, so the Falcon gave him a drop of her blood. The Bear could not fly, so the Crow carried him. When they found the place, it was guarded by a great black panther. The Bear killed her so all three could pass through the dawn..." His voice trailed off and Rayn saw that the old woman's eyes were fixed on him even as she spoke to the others.

"What is Tir Eadon?" Rayn asked.

"Tir Eadon. Legend says that the Kree were explorers and when they first found this planet—it is the island they landed on." Solomand scoffed and glanced around as he kicked at the dirt surrounding the fire. "It's just a stupid story."

He motioned for her to follow him, brushing close enough she could smell the smoke from the fire on his shirt. She set the mug down on the dirt and followed him away from the crowd of people.

Zee laughed, running up to a Kree girl her own age, holding her hands out to triumphantly show her a firefly. The two darted off again, chasing another swarm of blinking lights. It caught Rayn off guard when Solomand spoke again.

"When I found her..." His voice was unsteady. "She was alone. I don't think I saved her so much as she saved me. God knows what I would have become back then without her."

She saw his dark expression in the silvery light of two half moons. Solomand was telling the truth now. He didn't have the guarded look he usually did. The same had been true last night. Grishtanburg and S. L. seemed like a distant memory, which was no longer important.

"Your uncle wants you to stay," she said.

"He does." Sol sighed, his eyes closing. He looked tired. He dragged a hand over his face.

"Why don't you? Is revenge so important?"

His eyes shot open then, and the storm had returned. His hands clenched at his side, but he avoided looking directly at her. "Staying with the Crow Clan would only bring danger to them. LeFrost will catch up eventually. He always does." He looked tired. He cleared his throat. "Besides, what I told you is only part of it." His face darkened, and his hand trembled as he clenched it. "Nothing would give me more pleasure than tearing that man's head off with my bare hands!" The fury softened when he added, "But revenge is not our priority. It's not even on the list, to be honest."

Rayn tilted her head back to gaze at the stars. "What is on the list, then?"

Solomand's unbuttoned his collar and tugged on the chain around his neck.

"There is an airburst minefield covering the southern border. To get away from LeFrost for good, we have to make it through that field. LeFrost has a map code which will get us through."

"How do you know?"

His face clouded. "Let's just say I have a *friend* with connections."

"Is that why you needed that map thing from Blackpool?"

He nodded. "Yeah. We're going to steal the code from him, along with whatever amount of money we can get out."

Was he really just running away?

Rayn wasn't sure she believed him.

"Where will that leave me, then?"

"Stuck with us forever." He grinned, the roguish glint in his eye for a second, but she imagined what he was thinking.

I tried to help you, Rayn. I tried to send you where you wanted to go.

He hesitated before putting his hand on her shoulder.

228

"Unless… you could still go with the Kree. Iminho would see that you're kept safe."

Safe. Port Ashbury was safe, too. Rayn shoved his hand from her shoulder.

"No."

The hopeful light in his eyes went out. "Well, it was worth a shot, anyway."

"Mm-hmm." She punched his left arm playfully. "Besides, you're not going to renege on your promise. You still owe me a rifle. Almost got out of it once, not letting you do it again."

Sol laughed then, shaking his head at her.

"I guess we're stuck with each other for a while then."

"Yeah, Jank said something like that."

Sol rolled his eyes. "He would." They started back toward the bonfire. "Well, there's always the chance you'll find the answers you're looking for in Corcyra instead of Grishtanburg."

The grass crunched beneath her boots, and she shoved her hands in her pockets, thinking about S. L. and wondering, if she didn't remember him, did it really matter? After all, whoever he was, he hadn't come looking for her.

CHAPTER 42

SOLOMAND

MINHO'S FAREWELL LINGERED on Solomand's mind as he stared at the crisp lines of gold and pink streaked across the dawn sky. By the time they returned, if they managed to not get killed, the Kree would be gone and would not return to the valley. There were no goodbyes for his mother's people, for they were under the same sky, always. Sol liked the thought, even if it was a childish concept. Death had a way of turning goodbye into something very final. It was best not to dwell long on such things, especially where they were headed.

"That's everything."

The airskiff was staged and ready to go. Not meant for long-distance flights, it looked like a watercraft might—with two masts and sails on a small, open deck. The firebolt engine compartment was below deck and difficult to get to. Tattered sails were attached to the mast and stretched over wing-like airfoils meant for steering. There was no hiding in this craft. If they were hit, they would go down without much of a fight.

Jank climbed on board the skiff, his sketchbook tucked under his arm, a torn satchel on his shoulder. Ivan leaned against a wooden crate secured by ratchet straps. He wore a waist-length coat of a blackish-green color. Stitches in the shapes of circles were on either sleeve where patches had been ripped off. He seemed lost in sharpening his menacing looking dagger Sol had returned to him.

"Sharp enough yet?" Sol tiptoed around the point of the knife.

Ivan bit off his thumbnail and spit it aside, continuing to run the stone along the glistening blade.

"Not possible."

"Here, Sol." Jank tossed him a bundle of thick, navy-blue material that resembled his overcoat. Sol unfurled it, his eyes lighting up.

"My coat!"

Cross-stitching with leather cord bound the two halves of the overcoat together tightly where it was severed. Sol shook it out with his hand, scowling for a moment at his inability to move his right arm.

"Nice work, Jank." He slung it over his uninjured shoulder. "Looks better than before Ivan mutilated it."

Ivan stuck his chin up.

"Next time I leave your coat intact, uh?" He slid his knife back in the sheath before tucking it in his boot.

"Thanks. I'd appreciate it." Sol pretended not to catch the threat. He awkwardly worked to slip his good arm into a sleeve and hang it the rest of the way over his shoulder, leaving it unbuttoned.

"I guess that's it."

He leaned against the pilot's seat and passed out cigarettes to Jank and Ivan. Before Jank lit his, he carefully tucked his sketchbook and satchel in the compartment. Sol sniffed, hoping the metallic smell was nothing to worry about.

"How's the engine?" he asked casually.

"It's good to go." Jank frowned. "Provided we don't have any run-ins with the 201st. Their cannons will tear us apart, you know."

"Ah, speaking of which..." Sol glanced around the skiff, searching for the anti-aircraft gun.

"It's below deck," Jank waved a hand toward the wooden door in the deck. "With any luck, we won't need the damn thing, though."

"Yeah, well, we all know how that goes." Sol rummaged in his pockets. "Is it fixed?"

"It's been fixed. Ages ago."

He looked up as Rayn answered his question. She climbed onto the skiff, wearing her tan overcoat. Her deep-red hair was tied back in a haphazard braid underneath her hat. "All that was wrong with it is someone never cleaned it. Ever," she retorted.

Her head tilted slightly to one side as she pulled her gloves on and slipped into her overcoat.

Solomand's throat tightened. He found himself grinning.

"Haven't changed your mind, have you?"

"What?" She held a hand to her ear, feigning confusion. "Sorry. I can't hear you."

Sol forgot himself for a moment, drowning in the sea-green of her eyes. She always was stubborn.

"Oh." He remembered himself and reached behind the ammo boxes. "I have something for you."

He held up a sleek lever-action rifle in his hand and waited for the stunned look on her face before holding it out to her.

Her eyes raised, Rayn hesitated before taking it from him. Her hands ran along the deep-red stock, tracing the plated blue steel of the receiver.

"Like it?" He already knew the answer.

"An original Drakon with a Slavik optic."

Rayn ran her hands along the barrel, opening the lever action and inspecting the chamber. Pushing her broad-rimmed leather hat back, she closed one eye and shouldering it to look through the scope. She brought it down and glanced at Ivan.

"The best rifles come from the Northland." Her eyes shone.

Solomand noticed the corner of Ivan's mouth turned up in a grin. He cleared his throat, gesturing to the Drakon.

"I figured you have to be good with a rifle if you have one such as the Medved. It might come in handy."

Rayn's eyes narrowed, and she brought the Drakon down to her side.

"Just so we're clear, this doesn't replace the Medved."

Solomand laughed. "A promise is a promise. I'll replace it."

Rayn's expression returned to one of delight, and her hands tightened around the Drakon. "I'll take it then."

Warmth rushed through Solomand when Rayn smiled at him. He would have stolen a thousand rifles if it would make her smile like that just once more.

"Tristan!" Jank hissed a warning, stomping out his cigarette. Sol joined Ivan in flicking the remainder of his over the side of the skiff as Will helped Tristan up the ladder.

He gave Sol a sour look.

"Did it ever occur to you, I actually can smell the tantalizing scent of Kree tobacco, even though you have cleverly distinguished its source?"

Ivan stooped over and helped him the rest of the way on board. His heavy grey coat looked too big, but his color was better—less pallid. His piercing eyes fixed on them all with a hint of grudging.

"A gentleman would share with their friend."

"Sorry Tristan," Solomand patted him on the shoulder. "You ought to know by now, the only gentleman here is you." He put on a mock look of bravery. "But we shall suffer with you."

"Comforting." Tristan sat in one of the four seats, looking strained. Sol pretended not to notice.

Hang in there, Tristan. Just a little longer.

Will pulled Zee on board. The girl was wearing shoes for once but still looked small in her baggy clothes.

Solomand dragged a crate over next to Tristan and produced a browned paper from his pocket. He unfolded it, smoothing it out over the rough wood. The others crowded around. He pointed to an X marked next to an inky ribbon marked 'Red River.'

"That's our rendezvous point. It'll take us two days to reach it."

A gust of wind rattled the sails, and Sol flattened his hand on the map to keep it in place.

"How is the firebolt core going to hold up?" He raised an eye at Jank.

233

Jank took a pause from tugging on his ear to nod.

"Should be fine... unless we take a direct hit to the engine, or..." He stopped as Solomand glared at him. "It'll be fine." He cleared his throat and looked away.

"It will," Sol rolled his eyes.

Thanks for the vote of confidence, Jank.

Failure was not an option, and there were so many things that could go wrong. Even thinking about the possibilities that could throw a wrench in their plans would not be permitted. He smoothed the edges of the map again.

"Why not use your other map?" Rayn asked.

"I'm still working out how to use it. A regular map is simpler." Sol stuffed the map in his pocket. "Can't risk losing that other one. Lemuel would most definitely have me impaled."

Did I say that aloud?

He bit his lip.

"Who is Lemuel?"

He ignored her incredulous stare, strapping goggles into place clumsily with his left hand.

Tristan leaned towards her, tugging at her arm.

"He's the Falcon," he said.

Rayn looked annoyed at this answer. "Who's the Falcon?"

The crew stirred uneasily. Sol glanced at Jank, who had gone a greenish color. Reluctantly, he motioned Ivan to take the co-pilot seat and hooked one of the rigging straps from the mast to his belt. He sat down next to Rayn.

"Remember when you asked me who Daishee was?"

"Yeah."

"Well, you're about to find out.

Rayn rubbed a hand across her forehead.

"Lemuel, Falcon, Daishee—a man of ten names. Like you, huh?"

Sol's stomach tightened at the thought.

"No." He shook his head. "Not like me."

Not even close.

234

Lemuel was a man he loathed, feared, and admired all at the same time. Death followed him, or he followed death. Always lurking in the shadows, he knew things, had ways of unlocking any door, and still showed up when it was too late to do any good. But he showed up and had never ignored Solomand's request for help. The question was, would he agree to help this time?

CHAPTER 43

RAYN

THE RENDEZVOUS POINT was in the mouth of a canyon where the Red River flowed in shallow, rust-colored ripples. Corcyra could not be seen from the canyon, but it was not far away. Water cascaded down the canyon wall of varying shades of red. Will landed the skiff below a protruding rock upstream of the shallow, cascading water. As soon as the airskiff touched the ground, Jank unstrapped himself from the rigging and jumped, red-faced, over the side, dashing out of sight. He returned a few minutes later, sighing with relief.

"Been needing to piss for the last three hours," he mumbled.

"Why didn't you go last time we stopped?" Sol yawned.

"Shut up, Sol." Jank stretched.

Rayn unhooked herself. "Or just go off the side—you men are lucky that way."

Sol's yawn turned into a laugh as Jank's face turned red. He tugged with the buttons on his jacket, cursed and wriggled his right arm.

"Don't think I won't call it off just because we have come this far." Tristan's dark voice warned.

Sol stopped moving his arm, giving Tristan an exasperated look.

"What time is it?"

Tristan checked his pocket watch. "Sixteen forty-three."

His eyes pressed shut, and the timepiece fell into his lap as he coughed into his hand. He drew it away from his mouth wet.

Rayn was standing behind him. Her eyes widened with horror. *Is that blood?*

The others were too busy readying supplies to notice. Sol would want to know!

"Rayn."

She jumped as Tristan looked at her. He shook his head, his eyes pleading. The blood was gone, only a damp smear against his dark coat remained.

She leaned in close to him and whispered, "But, Tristan…"

"I'll be fine." He squeezed her hand. His head leaned back against the seat. She could feel his pulse racing and her heart jolted in response.

What the hell do I do?

She hesitated, looking after Ivan. He was the closest.

Tristan's hand tightened around hers.

"Did Sol ever tell you how we met?" His breathing was slower now, steadier. She knew he was trying to distract her.

"No."

She turned away from Ivan. Was this really the right choice? Her shoulders slumped, and she took a knee beside Tristan.

"Corcyra is divided. Those in the central part of the city are not allowed to associate with those outside the wall—swanks, they call us." Tristan was taking a great deal of effort to keep from coughing. "I was terrible at listening. I went out against my father's wishes and ran into some trouble. Apparently, I stood out."

His shoulders shook as he laughed slightly. He coughed again, this time into his elbow. Rayn saw the moist spot on his sleeve and felt dread tighten its grip.

Tristan kept talking.

"Some rather rough-looking characters were giving me quite a thrashing. I was sure I was done for. But Sol and Ivan showed up with a friend of theirs. Sol told me to go back where I belonged.

237

Tensions were high already between the Coalition. Everyone knew it was only a matter of time before all-out war broke out."

He looked far away—lost in the past for a moment.

"Anyway, I thought about where I belonged for a long while. Then I left my father, the Coalition, everything. I found Sol and the others, and we've been family ever since."

Rayn squeezed his hand, whispering, "Finish telling me later."

She couldn't bear to see him struggle to speak. She decided not to say anything. The way Solomand watched Tristan all the time, surely he would notice.

A grateful glimmer in his eyes, Tristan motioned her closer and whispered, "You made the right choice in staying. You will find answers in Corcyra."

His words, at one time, would have filled her with excitement. Now, tears came to her eyes. If she found everything she wanted in the world, it wouldn't matter if Tristan died.

She hugged him, choking out, "I don't need answers, Tristan. I've found something better."

Gripping the Drakon in her hands, she climbed down the ladder and waded across the river to where Solomand stood. Tristan was a traitor to the Coalition. She'd heard plenty of stories about the examples LeFrost made of anyone who betrayed him.

Her legs felt cool as the flowing water flowed just under her knees. Sol crouched down, surveying muddy three-pronged tracks leading away from the river. She bent down to face him.

"Why did you bring Tristan to Corcyra?" There was more anger in her voice than she meant to let out.

Sol's head jerked up. He looked startled at the question.

"I can't do this without him." He replied defensively.

All about the plan again.

"What happened to it being too dangerous?"

The rifle rattled, and the word dangerous echoed off the canyon walls.

Sol's brow furrowed, and he rose, bringing a warning finger to his lips.

"He's not going into the city—neither are Jank and Zee." His face twisted in suspicion. "Why? What's wrong?" He glanced back to the skiff.

Rayn pulled her hat lower over her eyes, trying to look nonchalant.

If he could keep secrets, so could she.

Solomand studied her, worry lines forming on his face. Her resolve faltered. Was she even doing the right thing?

A shrill whistle echoed around them, and a sleek shadow swooped across the stone, vanishing around a bend in the canyon.

"He's here." Sol gave a last questioning look from Rayn to their ship before calling to Will. "Will, go wait on the skiff."

Will nodded, splashing through the river-bed as he hurried back.

"Let's go." Sol gave Rayn one last suspicious look before following the shadow.

Rayn let out a sigh of relief. She was glad he'd sent Will back. It was better if Tristan were not alone.

Even in the shaded parts of the canyon, there was a steady, baking heat. Sweaty hair clung to the sides of her neck. She clawed it away and tightened her grip on the rifle, tripping forward on the rocky terrain. Her chest felt tight and constrained with every step. Ivan was not far behind them, but Jank trailed back, holding Zee's hand, jumping at every noise.

The whistle echoed again, and more swooping shadows danced around them on the canyon walls. Sol's pace quickened, and she moved her legs faster to keep up. They were following the darkness or whatever was casting it. This was not a comforting thought. She recalled the unnerving silence of everyone when Sol mentioned The Falcon and wondered what exactly they were getting into.

The gentle sound of bubbling water grew louder, and the bird-shaped shadow dove like an arrow into the mouth of a cave. Chest heaving, Rayn wiped sweat from her face and ducked into the narrow mouth of the cavern after Ivan and Sol.

Sunlight funneled into a glistening pool of water, which bubbled up from underground. A sage-blue myst falcon perched on the pond, eyeing them shrewdly. With a screech, it flapped its silver-lined wings and flew up, landing on its master's leather-clad shoulder. Its head jerked from side to side as it continued to watch them.

"Dangerous. How fitting that word heralds your arrival."

Black eyes tinged with blue glittered under the wide brim of The Falcon's hat. The bird snatched a moist piece of raw meat from his fingers. His voice was low. He pushed his hat back.

"*Anye ashi*. Hello, Sol."

CHAPTER 44

RAYN

SUN CAUGHT THE silver lining in the falcon's wings as it swooped over their heads.

"*Anyi manjien*. Lemuel," Sol said, using the same exchange he had with his uncle.

The Falcon wore dusty pants tucked into his boots, and a black gun-belt hung loosely on his hip. A leather satchel was slung over his shoulder, and the sleeves of his rust-red shirt were rolled up, revealing a pattern of intricate tattoos inked around his forearms.

Jank jerked his head up, shifty eyes trailing the myst falcon as it vanished. The man Sol called Lemuel crossed his burly arms, surveying Jank. He scratched at a neatly trimmed gray and black beard.

"Your men are as high-strung as ever."

There was a sleek rifle slung on his shoulder, one Rayn did not recognize. Jank was pale as he hung behind Sol, his eyes stabbing at the man.

"Bodysnatcher," he muttered under his breath.

Bodysnatcher? She remembered the conversation she'd had with Solomand about sleepwalkers, and the mysterious assassin some believed responsible. Rayn had dismissed it as nonsense, but the fear hanging in the air was too real to ignore. Even Zee backed away from the man, fixing her golden eyes in a suspicious glare.

241

White teeth flashed as the Falcon allowed a grin to pass his lips.

"By far my favorite nickname."

Lemuel had a distinguished, yet rough look about him. His age was difficult to place, but he couldn't have been much past forty. He pulled off his hat. Tanned fingers combed through cropped black hair. He shook his head in a disapproving way at Sol's arm.

"Isn't your luck running a little low to be coming here of all places?"

The Falcon's black gaze moved to Rayn, and her fingers tightened around the rifle.

"If this were a game of cards, I'd say it's a good time for you to fold."

Rayn squirmed, feeling the unpleasant sensation he knew everything about her. She also had the nagging feeling in the back of her mind that she'd seen him somewhere before.

"I don't gamble, Lemuel."

Sol's cool manner made Rayn feel a little better. She wondered if he saw the same person they did. He was the type of man who people would probably leave town to avoid. That look in his eyes planted an unsettling assurance that crossing him would be hazardous to your health.

The Falcon's head tilted to one side. A thin scar ran just under his right eye, white against his tanned, weathered skin.

"*I* don't gamble. You and your team, on the other hand, are about to make one hell of a wager." He whistled shrilly. "The question is, what do you need from me?" His eyes were like an animal watching prey. He trained his gaze on Jank. "A sleep walk?"

Rayn glanced at the engineer in time to see all color drain from his face. He looked like he was going to be ill as he tugged inadvertently at his ear. His apparent terror disturbed her, and she renewed her grip on the Drakon, hands soaked with sweat in her gloves.

"Maybe not." Lemuel's eyes moved back to Sol.

"We're going in through the river canals." Solomand said. "We need the grates unlocked. That's it."

Lemuel rubbed a hand along his grizzled chin.

"You know my methods are less than conventional, Sol. The same ones Ben disagreed quite strongly with."

Solomand squared his shoulders, and there was a hitch in his breath before he spoke.

"I'm not Ben. And I don't care what your methods are so long as those damned grates are open."

Lemuel arced his shoulder as his pet collided with him, digging razor-edged claws into the leather guard cinched on his shoulder.

"Striking a blow to LeFrost can only help you, anyway." Solomand looked strained as he wiped sweat from his forehead.

Lemuel reached up to stroke the feathers of his bird. He crouched down to one knee, pushing his hat up.

"I don't hunt pawns, Sol. You know that. I'm only interested in putting the king in check."

His voice was chillingly calm, a man who didn't need help; the thought of it seemed to bore him. He looked as if he wanted Sol to convince him what plausible reason there could be for lending his aid.

Sol's weight shifted to one leg, his hand shaking as it clenched. "You owe it to Ben."

Lemuel's eyes moved to Jank and then back to the bird on his shoulder as he traced a hand through the sand.

"Your highborn friend is no doubt the brains behind this whole suicide venture. Is he with you?"

There was something in his manner that shifted.

Sol's jaw clenched, and The Falcon smiled grimly. Rayn got the impression he only asked questions to bring attention to the fact he knew the answers.

He shook his head at Solomand as if he were a child about to make the same mistake a tenth time. Lines formed around his eyes as they narrowed.

"Alright, Sol." All traces of good humor vanished from his face. "I'll open the grates. But getting out... that is entirely up to you. I'll be gone come sundown."

"That's good enough." Sol relaxed, letting out a breath.

Lemuel returned the hat to his head and adjusted the brim, pulling it low, so it hid his eyes.

"Good luck. You're going to need it. Even with an Ice Wolf tagging along at your heels."

Ivan regarded him with a disinterested look.

"Thanks, Lemuel. I'll owe you one for this."

"Let's hope you live to deliver." He adjusted his rifle sling as the sage-blue falcon took flight. He bowed his head slightly at Sol before turning to Rayn to give her a guarded smile.

"Don't try too hard to be a hero, *Animaksew*."

He held up a hand in farewell as he traipsed through their midst toward the mouth of the cavern. Jank and Zee moved aside, making a path.

As they made their way back to the skiff, Rayn caught up with Solomand.

"Hey, Sol."

"Yeah?"

"Why does Jank call him the body snatcher? Does it have to do with the whole... sleepwalking thing?"

Jank tripped and tumbled the rest of the way down the sloping terrain and fell face first into the river with a splash. Sol cast a sideways glance as the engineer spluttered his way across the Red River.

"Yeah, but best not talk about it in front of him," he said. "As you can see, it's a touchy subject."

244

CHAPTER 45

SOLOMAND

DURING A BATTLE, either your instincts kicked in and you became an unstoppable killing machine, or you choked and didn't make it. But waiting for the fight to start—that was the worst part. The buildup of fear and nerves rose like a swollen storm cloud, rumbling and thick with a tension everyone could feel. It was like that now as the sun faded, a vibrant ball of reddish orange.

Solomand could sense the apprehension of his crew by the somber quiet and the lack of smartass comments from Jank. Will was still placid and methodical. He would do what had to be done without allowing emotion to get in the way, just like he was trained to do. Ivan seemed like he was born for this sort of thing. Having the two of them here eased Sol's worries somewhat.

One hour.

Sol passed out breathing masks to Will, Rayn, and Ivan; red and white tubes jetted out of the respirators, allowing one to breathe when submerged in deep water. Will helped Jank set the codes on their wrist transmitters before handing them to everyone but Tristan and Zee. The girl hugged her knees to her chest. Sol frowned. Zee shouldn't be here. It was too dangerous.

Tristan was helping Jank sync the transmission frequency code of all the transmitters; it was set to alternate every three seconds, making it impossible for the Corcyra interceptors to pick up.

Something about Tristan seemed off. Sol frowned in his direction when he wasn't looking.

It won't matter much longer. He reminded himself, blowing dust out of his respirator tubes. *If all goes well.* That sodding voice of doubt whispering in his ear. *It will—it has to!* He silenced it.

That was that. He would not entertain the possibility of anything going wrong tonight.

Only a faint glow of light remained along the horizons. The sun had given way to the stars. It was time.

"Alright. Time to go," he announced.

Ivan nodded, slipping the bag of Jank's charges on his shoulder. He and Will were going to plant them around the city at strategic positions.

"Rayn, stay with me at all times. Will, Ivan—you know what to do." They nodded. "Stay in contact. If shit goes wrong, let us know immediately." He breathed out, trying to clear his head completely. "Let's go."

Jank's hand tightened around Zee's arm as the others started climbing over the skiff. It would have been so much easier if she'd went with the Kree. Sol ruffled her hair and gave her a reassuring smile.

"It's alright, Zee. Remember what I said? I'll always come back." He winked.

Zee's lip trembled as she stood in the seat, wrapping thin arms around his neck. Jank had to pry her loose.

"Stay safe, Sol." Tristan didn't look at all well. His listless gaze fixed on the stars and he seemed, more than ever, resolved. That frightened Solomand more than anything. He knew this may be the last he saw of Tristan—for longer than he cared to admit. He squeezed his friend's shoulder forcefully.

"You too, Tris." His words came with difficulty. "Look after him, Jank." He clapped the engineer on the shoulder.

Sol climbed down the ladder and tugged the necklace out he usually hid under his shirt. He was afraid of losing it in the river tonight. It was a silver chain with a steel cross from the old world—a gift from his father—and a small silver charm. He kissed the cross for luck and hid it in his shirt before running to catch up with the others.

Coyotes howled mournfully in the distance as they ran at a steady pace along the riverbank. Coursing water shimmered with silver ripples of moonlight and stars. As the canyon narrowed, the river deepened, the walls of rock closing to form a tunnel around it.

"Time to go for a swim."

Sol strapped on his respirator, and the others followed his lead. He stepped into the river, sinking up to his chest. His boots sank into the soft mud at the bottom. The night air was hot, and the water felt good as it soaked through his clothes.

Ivan and Will slid in after him; Rayn was the last to get in the river. She was noticeably reluctant, slinging the Drakon over her shoulder before sliding down the bank into the water. Her feet slipped, and she fell against Sol, digging fingers into his arm with a frantic grip.

"Stay close." His voice sounded garbled through the respirator.

She nodded, easing further into the river, her fingers not loosening their grasp. Solomand knew she was terrified; Rayn could not swim.

Darkness swallowed them as they waded further into the cavern. Rushing water pulled them forward, drowning out the sounds of the coyotes. There was no turning back now. Sol's heart pounded. He held Rayn's hand tighter, fighting against the current to keep her close. Water rose to their necks. A faint golden glow played on the water's surface as they neared the mouth of the channel: the lights from Corcyra.

CHAPTER 46

RAYN

ANYTHING BUT WATER!

Rayn imagined this was how Solomand felt on the bell tower. She regretted how she toyed with him. Water lapped at her chin and mud sucked at her boots, as if the river was trying to claim her with every step she took. Her hand tightened on Sol's shoulder.

If I can't remember anything else, why do I have to be so damned sure I can't swim?

If Solomand noticed the way she latched onto him, he didn't let on.

Her foot found a hole in the riverbed and water sloshed over her neck, filling her ears. Panic clawed at her throat, and she gasped for air. The respirator gurgled, making a raspy sucking noise as it filtered water out.

I'm fine. I can breathe.

She focused on controlling her breathing. In, out. In, out. Solomand's hand closed around her hip and tugged her until her head rose above the water. The water kept rising until she was on her tiptoes, plodding through the mud and tilting her head back.

Sol pulled her toward him until her ear was near his mouth.

"Take a breath." His voice sounded grainy.

Wait, Sol!

She gulped in a swallow of air just before he pulled her under the water. The gap between the river and cavern ceiling closed and standing on the riverbed was no longer an option.

Flailing with one arm, Rayn was more dragged than anything through the water. The Drakon stuck in her back as she kicked it with the back of her legs, trying to pretend the sucking noise of the respirator didn't sound like someone gasping for breath. It felt like much longer than it really was. Her right hand brushed along the slimy walls of the tunnel. She held her breath, and then her head broke the surface as Solomand dragged her up. They were out of the watery cavern, anyway; the trial by river had not yet ended.

She blinked the water from her eyes and stared at the glittering mountain of lights that grew closer. There was a shadowy wall around the layers of golden flickers, which swelled brighter, reaching their pinnacle at the central towers. Small white specks flashed in a series of three as they moved across the sky: airships going to and from the dock on the far side of Corcyra.

An engine roared overhead, its lights floating on the river. Sol tensed and jerked her below the surface without warning. The unpleasant sensation of being suffocated set in as water filled her ears once more. It seemed like forever until the airship lights finally vanished, leaving them in a cloak of darkness.

Solomand brought her up with him as he raised just his eyes above the surface. Her eyes followed him as he turned to look for Will and Ivan; they were not far behind, goggles peeking up from the water like submerged frogs. Solomand's hand tightened on her arm as he swam forward again. Her lungs ached, working harder to pump the warm air through the respirator.

Can't be much further.

She had to keep reminding herself, suppressing the anxiety.

They stayed in the river's cover all the way to the stone wall surrounding Corcyra, where the water was diverted into three different canals which flowed under the barrier. Solomand followed the one on the left. A metal grate barred their way. The black bolt was open; an opened lock hung on the grating. Solomand guided

Rayn's hand to the rusted, grimy bars before tugging his respirator off to hang around his neck. He kicked open the grate just enough so they could both squeeze through.

Rayn's rifle snagged on the barbs of the grating, pulling her back.

"Careful," Sol whispered, unhooking it.

Rayn jerked off the respirator, breathing in short, hungry gasps.

"You alright?"

Sol's hand was on her shoulder. She shivered in spite of the warm air.

She swallowed back the gasping noises and nodded.

He squeezed her shoulder and motioned her forward with the promise, "Not much further."

The canal angled, the water depth slowly dropping until it coursed into concrete trenches; irrigation channels for the fields.

Finally! Land!

Rayn scrambled onto the bank, wanting to lay there on the damp grass and catch her breath. Solomand was already pulling her to her feet, and they were sprinting across the open fields, weaving back and forth to stay in the shadows. It was dark here, though the glow from the inner-city lights shone ever nearer. Just over another wall was a fence of iron and stone which separated the outer edge of the city.

They scaled a shoddy wooden fence around the fields and slid behind a collapsing barn. There was something familiar about this place, something just beyond her reach.

"Where are we?" she panted.

Sol leaned against the rotting wood wall next to her.

His voice was hard. "The Mud."

They were running again.

Damnit, Sol! She felt like her past was only a torch's view ahead of her. *If we get out of here alive...*

She vowed to extract answers from him. He *knew* things. He just wasn't telling. His right arm, she noted, was moving freely at his side. He must have pulled it lose the moment they were out of Tristan's view. She didn't notice in the river, but then, how else would he have been able to swim while pulling her with him?

They reached the second wall; flat iron bars jetted up ten feet in the air, locking the inhabitants of The Mud out of the inner city. They followed the barricade until the empty fields turned into a deserted town square—dark and foreboding. Splintered posts set in the center of broken cobblestones. Rayn stopped, her heart pounding. She'd been here before. This square was once cloaked with an uneasy stillness when a younger version of herself had seen a dark-haired boy being captured and narrowly escape a whipping. They really were memories trying to claw their way back out.

"Rayn!" Sol hissed. "We have to go!"

She had stopped, looking around the empty town in a daze. His hand was on her arm; it felt like he was dragging her away from a part of herself.

"Sol, wait!" She broke free of his grip.

"Rayn!"

He brought his face close to hers. She could see it in his eyes. He understood why she wanted to linger.

"We *have* to go!"

He was right. She clenched her teeth and reluctantly ran after him. Her boots squished, seeping out water. They kept running along the wall until they were on the other side of the dismal town. The bars here were bent and twisted like they'd been melted. Sol kicked at them until the weakened metal gave way, giving them just enough room to crawl through to the other side.

Rayn blinked back, turning away from the blinding spotlight that greeted them.

"Solomand Black."

The cold, familiar voice sent a chill up Rayn's spine. She forced her eyes to open. Minuet stood, shadowed by the lights behind her, and four airmen; their sleek, silvery rifles pointed at her and Solomand.

Well… shit

Rayn felt confident getting captured straight off couldn't possibly be part of Solomand's perfect plan. She fought the urge to snap at him.

We should have stayed back there like I wanted to!

Sol eased his hands in the air, looking nonchalant. "Fancy meeting you here, Minuet."

Minuet raised a hand, and the rifles cocked in unison.

"Hold on—let's talk about this."

Sol leaned over and elbowed Rayn in the side, widening his eyes at her and waving his hands. Grudgingly, Rayn raised her hands, but she gave him a scathing look, so he'd know she wasn't happy about it.

"Get their weapons." Minuet's tone was icy.

Two of the men shifted their rifles to one hand and roughly jerked Rayn's and Solomand's guns away. As her eyes adjusted to the light, Rayn saw they were wearing rust-colored uniforms and gas masks. It was soldiers from the 201st.

She bit the insides of her mouth, practically snarling.

You won't have it for long, you bastards!

She eyed the Drakon. They already destroyed one rifle. There was no way she was going to allow them to do the same to this one.

When Minuet was satisfied they were disarmed, she had them shoved into the back of a waiting motorcar.

The smell of new leather mixed with the earthy scent of river water that permeated their clothes. Minuet sat across from them, a derringer in each hand—one for each of them. The car door clicked shut, and the motor revved as they drove away.

Minuet's coolness was gone. There was savage anger in her eyes. Her chest was heaving as she glowered at Solomand.

"Do you have any idea what you've done?" Her tone was caustic. "How *could* you, Solomand?"

Rayn glanced sideways at Sol. He looked... sorry?

"If you fail to make it out..." Her hands shook as they gripped the deringers, both of them pointed at Sol.

Solomand tugged on his collar. "Luckily, we have you. So, everything should go smoothly." His smile was confident and taunting at the same time.

Minuet's lips pursed together. If steam could have come from her nose, Rayn was sure it would have at this point.

"Damn you!" She hissed. Then sank back in her seat, her hands dropping to rest on her knees. "I've orders to take you both to LeFrost."

Solomand tensed against her, though his face remained expressionless. Minuet's eyes flashed, apparently angered by his lack of reaction.

"You should never have come to Corcyra!"

They rode the rest of the way in silence, and Rayn suddenly noticed something was missing.

Ivan and Will. They must have escaped.

Well, that was some comfort in this rapidly spiraling evening. Maybe they still had a chance.

CHAPTER 47

RAYN

THE CAR RATTLED along, making so many twists and turns Rayn was sure they could never find the way out. Except, Solomand probably already knew, like he knew every other damn thing. Was this part of his plan? Minuet looked like she wanted any excuse to shoot him.

"What's with the gas masks?" Rayn finally had to break the silence. Minuet's eyes narrowed as they jerked to Rayn. "On your Airmen." Rayn shifted on the stiff leather.

Sol leaned towards her, pretending to be discreet. "It's for intimidation." His eyes widened in a mock look of fear.

Rayn bit back a smile.

You're not going to make me laugh here, you idiot.

She cleared her throat and glared at Minuet. "It doesn't work. They just look stupid."

Sol's shoulders shook as he laughed silently. "They really do," he said to Minuet.

Her face reddened. "Well… I'm glad you two adolescents find this amusing. Mud rat!" The insult was directed at Sol.

Holding a hand to his heart, he pretended to look injured.

"Such strong language for a *lady*. I'll refrain from returning a similar one."

"Why?" Rayn crossed her arms. She could think of a few choice things to say if he couldn't.

254

"Because." The sarcasm was gone from his voice now. "One of the best men I've ever known sees something in her. Only God knows what." His voice lowered. "And, if he can see such value in Minuet St. Sebastian, the least I can do is try to. I fail every time, though."

He reached in his coat pocket and brought out a brown envelope, the same kind Rayn had seen him give her in Blackpool. Crimson wax sealed the water-marked edges.

Minuet's face was pale as passing lights streamed through the window. Her eyes were misty. She snatched the letter from Sol. It wrinkled as she clutched it in her hand.

"Bastard." It came out in a choked whisper.

Minuet's veil of composure had fallen. Rayn felt less inclined to hate her when she saw the terror in her eyes, fear for someone other than herself.

No.

Rayn didn't want to believe the implication of Sol's words. She stared at the envelope in her hand, her throat tightening as she wished this ride—this night—was over.

The car rolled to a stop and Minuet tucked the letter down the front of her corset (typical!) before reclaiming her stone-faced appearance.

"You know what's coming, Solomand Black. I only hope you can survive it long enough."

Her eyes were void of sympathy.

Solomand gave Minuet a crooked smile, a flicker in his eyes, a hunger for something.

"That's the difference between you and us, Minuet; we're in the business of surviving things." He closes his hand around Rayn's so hard that her fingers ached. He leaned into her ear. "Be careful," he whispered.

The car door opened, and light spilled in. They were being shoved down a path to the Governor's mansion. Black iron bars surrounded the compound. The green lawn was manicured. Rayn wondered just how much water LeFrost had to steal to keep grass so perfect in the middle of the desert. There was a dome in the center of the flat roof, plus guards with rifles patrolled the many balconies overlooking the grounds.

The sound of pumping blood pounded in her ears, intensifying with every step up the stone path. The manicured governor's mansion gave the illusion of being inviting. Rayn suspected it was the sort of place people went to and never left—at least in the same state they were when they arrived.

She chewed on her lip, longing for one of her guns. She still had her boots, though. Thank god for that. The daggers concealed in the square toes were going to come in handy before this was over.

Minuet nodded at one of her men, and he took Solomand roughly by the collar, jerking him toward the back of the mansion. Dread spreading through her, Rayn stiffened. The hard barrel of Minuet's derringer dug into the small of her back.

"LeFrost wants a word with you." Her voice lowered to a whisper. "Just cooperate, and maybe some of us will live past this night."

Rayn swallowed, her throat dry and constricted. Her gaze lingered on Solomand until he disappeared from view with his escort. Wooden steps creaked under their feet as she was marched up to them and into the front doors. A disinterested-looking guard sat in a chair by the hall. They went past him and into a carpeted hallway. The ceilings were vaulted; lavish artwork was illuminated by gas lamps mounted on both sides of the wall, one at every door. The doors were mahogany, intricately carved with a complicated pattern of loops and swirls. The whole place had a sterile smell to it, like new wood and paint.

Minuet opened the last one on the left and pushed Rayn inside. This room was lined with a dark brown carpet and was drab compared to the lavishly decorated entrance. A lampstand stood next to a tarnished table and two wooden chairs. Deep purple drapes were drawn over a floor length window. Rayn wondered if it was an interrogation room and gulped.

"Wait here." Minuet turned to leave, smoothing her hair; there actually were strands out of place. She shut the door as she went. A key turned in the lock.

Oh, Tristan. Why her?!

Rayn felt somewhat disappointed in him. He felt like a brother that could have done so much better than the two-faced Coalition agent. Solomand was probably right, and she hated admitting it. Maybe there was something more to her than met the eye if a man like Tristan could be interested in her.

Sol.

Her heart pounded again, and she crossed the room with long strides, drawing the drapes back.

The clamber of feet outside the room startled her. The curtains fell from her hand, and she watched the door. When no one came, she paced the room in silence. Pushing damp hair off her forehead, she sat on one of the cushioned chairs, her knee bouncing. A clock on the wall ticked out the seconds, every incessant swing of the pendulum stabbing at her nerves. The only thing she needed to focus on right now was getting out. But she couldn't help but think of Sol's story—how Benjamin Ivers was killed.

What will happen to Sol?

There was an unsettling horror in the pit of her stomach. She had to get the hell out of here and find him, before it was too late.

CHAPTER 48

SOLOMAND

GOOD SO FAR.
Solomand's heart pounded. He was trying not to think of Rayn.

He won't do anything to her. Not yet.

He reminded himself as the guard guided him behind the capital building with the hard point of his rifle.

We still have the upper hand.

The guard lead him into a fenced, stone pavilion. Benches encircled the circular stone platform where a series of posts were embedded into the ground.

Sol's stomach turned as he saw the blood that wasn't there and heard the echoing screams that had long since been silenced. This is where Ben died. It was meant to strike fear in his heart, but it didn't. Rage swelled in him as the guards forced him to his knees and jerked his coat off. It grew stronger as they tied him between two posts. The guard gave the ropes an extra tug before lighting each of the torches around the pavilion, flooding the area with light.

Show yourself you bastard.

Solomand imagined with stirring detail LeFrost's pulse slowing to a stop in his hands, the smug look forever choked from his face. Then he saw him, striding at a leisurely pace, the absolute picture of a gentleman. He wore a crisp uniform embroidered with gold embellishments. His neatly trimmed hair matched the ashen color of his suit. He was accompanied by a man taller than he was, who kept carefully in the shadows. Sol couldn't make him out. He was most likely LeFrost's newest bodyguard. He constantly needed them. It wouldn't be enough to save him, though. Seeing him here now, after what he'd done, Solomand felt nothing but the intense hunger to make him pay for his sins. The knowledge that the governor was playing neatly into his hands was enough to dull what he knew was coming.

"Solomand Black," LeFrost said in a perfectly reasonable sounding voice. "I finally have you." The smirk on his bearded mouth was short-lived.

Sol glowered at him with a devilish smile.

"Took you damn long enough—and I had to come to you in the end."

LeFrost's eye twitched with anger. He snapped his finger and the guard who stepped forward, bullwhip in hand. Sol recognized it, remembering its sting, but he only grinned his defiant smile. No amount of pain LeFrost inflicted on him could ever equal what he had already been through.

"Where. Is. She?" LeFrost swallowed roughly.

"She's nothing to do with any of this," Sol replied darkly.

LeFrost snapped his fingers, and the guard raised his hand. Pain ripped through Solomand's shoulder as the whip cut across the bullet wound. He winced, then leered at the governor.

"Careful. You'll get blood on your uniform," he said.

LeFrost signaled for the guard to continue. It took him longer to interrupt this time.

"You know what's going to happen if you don't' tell me where she is, don't you?" He took out his handkerchief and wiped his mustache.

Sol's split lip stung as he spit a mouthful of blood at LeFrost's feet.

"She'd never have been on that island if you weren't such a son of a bitch in the first place."

His taunt earned him a punch in the mouth, this time from the esteemed Governor himself. The split in his lip widened, but Sol was numb. A thrill of satisfaction ran through him on having made LeFrost angry enough to use his own hands. The untouchable man, usually perched on his lofty chair away from the real world, was pissed enough to come down and get dirty.

He stepped back, flexing his hand, and straightened his tie.

"You forget, Mud Rat. I have nothing but time. You, however, have run out of it."

He turned on his heels and started to walk away, maintain a dignified air, or trying to.

"You think you've finally caught me, swank?" Sol's voice raised. "You've forgotten something!"

LeFrost's shoulder's tensed, and he stopped to listen.

"You don't hunt spiders, especially the Recluse!" Sol raised his head, making sure LeFrost saw his overly confident grin. "By the time you see one, you've already been bitten."

LeFrost looked over his shoulder, trying to look in control, but Sol saw his mouth twitch involuntarily.

"Don't kill him yet, Rollins. I still need answers." He stalked away.

Solomand managed a twisted laugh. Whatever answers 'Rollins' or LeFrost thought they were going to extract, but they were most sorely mistaken. But that's what happened when you took everything that mattered to a man; there was nothing left he cared about losing.

LeFrost's bodyguard stepped into the light as he turned to follow the Governor; disconcerting, pale eyes looked Sol over. His mouth was turned up in an amused grin.

It widened as Sol turned to the guard and spat, "So Rollins... ask me how your face looks with a knife in it? That's about the only question you're getting an answer to tonight."

CHAPTER 49

RAYN

A KEY TURNED in the lock, and Rayn to spring to her feet. A tall, stately looking gentleman in a drab uniform stepped into the room. His neatly trimmed, and the silver beard added a distinguishing touch to his appearance.

"You must be Rayn." His voice was smooth. He closed the door, slipping a hand in his coat pocket. Lines creased his face as he offered her an apologetic smile. "I'm terribly sorry about all this. Oh, where are my manners?" He offered her a hand. "I am Governor LeFrost."

Rayn crossed her arms, ignoring his offered hand. If he thought she was going to win her over with the charming old gentleman act, he was sadly mistaken.

LeFrost drew his hand back awkwardly. "You needn't be afraid of me, Rayn. I only need you to answer some questions for me."

"Like what?"

He motioned to the chairs, curling his fingers into a fist as he returned it to his side. His knuckles were a crimson color—like dried blood.

Rayn's heartbeat quickened. She bit her lip, determined he would not see her growing fear.

Skip the act, old man.

LeFrost strode to the table and poured himself a glass of water. "Would you care for a drink?"

261

"No," Sol was right, again, she noted with reluctance. LeFrost didn't appear to be the villainous type. But real villains rarely did.

LeFrost sipped at the clear water audibly, and she pursed her lips together. When was the last time she'd had a drink? It didn't matter if it had been two days. She would never relent and say she wanted one now.

The glass clinked on the wood as he set it down.

"You know, Rayn. War is a terrible thing no matter what side you happen to be on."

No shit.

There was genuine tiredness in his eyes, which made him look older than he probably was.

"I would very much like to put all this nasty business behind us," he said, sighing.

"Yeah? Then why don't you?" She drummed her fingers on her soaked overcoat.

LeFrost's civilized mask dropped for a moment, and his face darkened. He ventured closer to her, and she could make out more clearly a familiar amber color in his eyes.

"Your associate, Mr. Black, is a very dangerous war criminal. I should think you would be wise enough to not squander loyalty on the likes of him."

"The war is over, don't you know?" Rayn's eyes narrowed. "And, if I'm not mistaken, you won."

She shifted her weight to one leg. There was something eerily familiar in those eyes of his.

"It's not over for Solomand Black," LeFrost snapped, his nostrils flaring. He was dropping the act completely. "If he wanted the war to end, he never should have taken my daughter!"

What?

A sudden gut-wrenching horror hit her like a fist in the chest as she realized where she'd seen those eyes before.

Zee. She might have been able to tell herself he was lying, if it weren't for the same peculiar golden-amber eyes LeFrost glared at her with; so much like the girl's, yet so different.

But why? Was Solomand willing to go that far for revenge? Rayn didn't believe it.

LeFrost's jaw tightened. "You have seen her, haven't you?"

Rayn couldn't have talked if she'd wanted to at this point. LeFrost's hands gripped the back of a chair.

"Sazumay's mother took her to Cierne without my knowing. She wanted to be with her people. If I had known…" his voice cracked, and he cleared his throat. He was good at making it look like he truly cared. His brow furrowed. "Solomand Black took her to exact revenge for the child he lost."

Rayn felt like someone had knocked the wind out of her.

"What do you mean?"

LeFrost picked imaginary dirt from his dress coat.

"Didn't you know? It was an unfortunate occurrence, not intentional. Like I said, war is a very tragic thing."

He's lying.

LeFrost kept talking, but she didn't hear. Her eyes fixed on the door past him, trying to process what he had told her. Zee was LeFrost's daughter. She knew that the island of Cierne was bombed, by LeFrost's command. He really was a bastard. It made little difference whether or not he knew his own daughter was there.

That wasn't what made her stomach churn. *Solomand had a child?*

"Rayn." LeFrost's voice raised, and she brought him back into focus. "Will you cooperate?"

So, he thought telling her this would lead her to betray Sol and the others. Rayn's face twisted into a savage scowl. She may remember only fragments, but those fragments placed her on the other side of Corcyra's wall. She didn't belong here. She belonged in The Mud.

Rayn tilted her chin up, scraping wet hair from her neck with her fingers. "Afraid I can't help you. If there's one thing Solomand Black is good at, it's keeping secrets."

263

It wasn't a lie, she thought grudgingly. Had he really kept the secret of a child?

Her hands started to shake, and she crossed her arms again, trying to hide it.

"I see." LeFrost's face darkened, the last traces of civility vanishing. "How unfortunate."

He turned abruptly and stormed out of the room, slamming the door. She could hear him rattling the keys in frustration as he locked her in. Voices shouted in the hallway, followed by the stomping of feet in different directions. God knows what he meant to do with her now.

Sol had a child.

She remembered the look in his eyes when she told him he would make a good father. Did he really keep Zee for revenge?

She felt light-headed and leaned on the wall by the window.

"No," she managed a choked whisper.

The way he guarded Zee and looked after her. He wouldn't do that. Would he?

The door burst open, and Rayn lurched forward, grabbing a chair and holding it over her head.

Minuet sauntered in, raised an eye at the chair and said, "You're to come with me."

Her heart hammering, Rayn tossed the chair aside.

"Now." There was an unspoken urgency in her eyes.

Am I really going to trust her?

Rayn didn't give it much thought. What choice did she have? Solomand was not likely to be saving her. She was going to have to make her own way out of this mess.

The barrel of Minuet's derringer pushed lightly into her back. Rayn's mind raced. She was going to get out of here, with or without Minuet's help.

Minuet ushered her through another door and up a winding set of stairs which lead to a dark hallway. Their footsteps thumped as they walked to the end of the hall. Minuet glanced around, eyes carefully searching. In a quick movement, she pressed the wall underneath a lamp. A panel slid open, and Rayn was shoved inside another passage.

If one more person pushes me around!

She stumbled forward.

The room was cramped and dark. Minuet lit a lamp and slid the hidden door shut. Rayn held her breath. Her revolver, the Drakon, and Solomand's sidearm lay on the floor. Minuet handed her a folded piece of paper.

"Solomand's map code," she said curtly. She nodded toward the guns. "You're going to need to save him."

"What?" Rayn felt like she didn't have time to breathe. "What the hell are you talking about?"

Minuet arched one eyebrow.

"Solomand will not make it if you don't. And I can do no more to help anyone." She held out her derringer. "Because you shot me when you escaped."

Rayn looked from the pistol to Minuet, her jaw slowly opening. "You can't be serious."

Minuet pressed the gun in her hand, sighing in aggravation. "If I'm not shot, I'll get it worse than Solomand's getting right now."

Rayn's stomach twisted violently, and her hand closed around the derringer, wishing Minuet had told her to shoot her the last time they met. She would not have hesitated then.

"The balcony is through there." Minuet pointed to the shuttered window. "It opened to the back of the compound. You'll see Solomand. Your rifle is silenced, as is my derringer."

Her finger pointed the trajectory through her chest. Rayn knew it would be a non-lethal shot. The bullet was light, and wouldn't expand much.

She cocked the hammer and raised it.

"You're doing this for Tristan, aren't you?"

Minuet's eyes flickered as she tried to hide emotion.

"Solomand should never have brought him here." There were tears in her eyes.

That's one thing we can agree on.

265

Rayn swallowed and squeezed the trigger.

Minuet fell back against the wall, gasping. "Go, damn you! Before it's too late."

Rayn grabbed the weapons, slung them on her shoulder, and climbed out the window into the warm night air.

CHAPTER 50

TRISTAN

TRISTAN'S SKIN PRICKLED as a sultry breeze brushed his face. He leaned forward, inhaling slowly, deliberately. The taste of blood and mucus stuck in the back of his throat. If death knocked on the door in human form, Tristan would have welcomed him in for a cup of tea. As it was, he lurked in the shadows, close enough to feel but just far enough away that the relief he desired couldn't be reached.

Tristan always liked words, especially quotes of wisdom from the ancient texts. They were like music on paper, still gracing the world with their song. They had helped him back in the beginning when he was afraid to die. Now they rang hollow. Fear of dying had vanished long ago; only the insatiable tiredness remained. Gripping that last thread connecting him between this world and the next became ever more difficult. It would be so easy to just let go.

Not yet. He admonished himself. There was a battle still to be fought., wrongs to be righted. His plan was different from Solomand's, and he would need to reach deep to put an end to the mistakes he'd left behind in Corcyra.

"Tris." Jank lay a hand on his shoulder. "It's time."

Tristan raised his head from his arm. The air grated on his lungs as he breathed in. Jank's forehead creased with worry, and Tristan smiled.

267

"At last." He feigned a look of enthusiasm. His stomach rolled, and he bent over, clutching his sides. "Don't look so glum, Jank." He struggled to his feet. "Nothing to worry about."

Jank gave him an uneasy look and took him by the arm. Tristan put more weight on him than he would have liked. All incriminating letters had been handed over to Solomand.

"Keep an eye on Jank, will you?" Tristan gave the girl his best smile.

He gathered she knew something was wrong by the worried frown she gave him. *Be brave, Zee.*

Jank helped him to the ground, unable to hide his fear; he never was good at hiding his emotions.

"Be careful." He clasped his hand. "Are you sure you're alright?"

"Right as rain." Tristan winked. "See you in a fortnight."

Jank was reluctant to release his grip as Tristan shifted his weight to the cane in his hand. He raised his hand in goodbye as he walked away.

Unlike his comrades, he would take the more direct route. Across the endless sands, Coyotes trailed after him, howling to one another and smelling death as it walked hand-in-hand with him. With each step, he could hear them gaining, growing a little braver as his pace slowed. They didn't really bother him, though; they did not deny who they were. The predators within the city's walls were far more terrifying. He felt cold, knowing what they would do to him in the end.

Only a little further.

Corcyra's lights were on the horizon, though the distance he needed to cross may as well have been a hundred miles. Temptation whispered in his ear, taunting him: *Just lie down. Let it go. You have done enough.*

That was the problem, he thought. He had done so much that a weapon, capable of rewriting a person's mind, sat neatly in the hands of the Coalition. If he had not been so eager to impress his father, the E.X. Solution never would have existed. It was his fault, no matter how innocent his intentions were. But it wouldn't remain for much longer.

I will destroy it. Tristan swore with each gasp of breath, his resolve pushing him forward.

He knew he didn't need to make it all the way to the city. A guard patrol would find him soon enough. He sank to one knee, shivering in a cold sweat. His fingers trembled, pressing the buttons on his transmitter. The signal froze, allowing the interceptors to track his location.

He didn't have long to wait. Voices shouted to each other, rushing towards him. Tristan's eyes clamped shut as bright lights blinded him.

"You there—don't' move!"

Tristan held his arms over his head, both knees on the ground now.

"Who are you?"

"What are you doing here?"

Both took turns shouting at him. They were just children, he thought.

One of them wrenched the transmitter from his wrist, but Tristan had already sent a confirmation transmission to Jank.

"Gentlemen, congratulations," he said, maintaining a degree of charm. "My name is Tristan Highcourt. And I have just made you overnight heroes and immensely wealthy, if I'm not mistaken, which I never am."

It was done. They had him now. How they took him in was their problem. With their rifles still aimed at him, he collapsed, drinking in the darkness that engulfed him hungrily. If he had seen the girl coming after him, he might have fought a little longer to stay conscious. But he didn't.

CHAPTER 51

IVAN

IVAN CREPT ALONG the edge of the inner wall. Noiseless, focused, he was finally in his element. Will was making his way around the other side, and they were to meet in the middle. Guards were posted in Sentinel alcoves spaced evenly along the wall; they were too far away to shout a warning to one another, but their station was equipped with alarms to sound a warning which would spread rapidly to the rest.

Light from their electric torches swept the fields and the base of the wall periodically on the wrong side. Those who lived in The Mud were farmers, laborers—subdued and compliant since the rebels were crushed by the Coalition Cities. Corcyra's finest guards were untested by genuine conflict and had no idea that real danger was not the kind to announce itself at their gates. None of them were aware of the two men who prowled beneath their noses.

Ivan took a knee under the first station, slipping his hand into the satchel hung over his shoulder. He pressed the lined gray clay at the base of the stones and carefully pushed the switch on the bottom forward so as not to make even a whisper of a noise. A tiny red light blinked underneath, flashing its shadow on the ground. Once Jank activated the timer, they would simultaneously detonate, keeping the 201st busy—at least for a while. Hopefully, it would be long enough for them all to get the hell out of Corcyra.

The guard's boots scraped overhead as he shifted position. Ivan flattened himself into the shadows of the wall, holding his breath. There was a pronounced yawn, followed by a tuneless whistling. Then, nothing. Ivan shook his head slightly.

Amateur.

The last battle he was in was against warriors. Men. They fought tooth and nail against one another, determined to come out alive. These boys belonged at home with their mothers.

His luck held up throughout his silent lope around the city; a half-asleep amateur manned each alcove. By the time he was their age, he would never make such stupid mistakes. It was always win or die in his line of work, and Ivan never lost. The assassins of his homeland were said to have ice in their blood and fought like the great Northland wolves they were named after. Ivan was not one for romantic tales. A path of blood and ice was merely a matter of survival. But this was all part of a past he never spoke of to the ones he called friend now. They were his new pack. The Ice Wolves and all they stood for could go to hell.

The engine pass was the point where he would meet Will. Black tracks glistened in the moonlight, curving their way out of the Capital Station up to the drawbridge leading out of the city, miles into the desert. It was the primary way of travel between Olbia and Corcyra. Sweat streaked down his neck as he bent to place the last explosive. Will should be up ahead. The city's noises swelled louder here—horns and engines suffocating the sound of the frogs and crickets crying to be heard in the fields beyond the wall. There was no shuffling sign of restlessness from the guard at the station post.

Probably sleeping.

Ivan switched on the last explosive and heard the unmistakable click of a rifle being cocked. He froze.

"Drop to your knees! Move, and you're dead!" The voice was young, maybe eighteen. "Get your hands over your head." The rifle poked sharply in his back.

Ilupai—idiot. First, you say not to move, then order me to.

271

Ivan dropped to the ground and eased his arms up, all the while thinking through the way he was going to whirl around and take this idiot boy's head off. Before he had the chance, there was a scuffling sound, followed by a crunching snap.

"You let a swank sneak up on you?"

Ivan turned to see Will, his arms around a guard's neck. He let the man go, and his body slumped to the ground.

"I was going to handle it." Ivan stood, annoyed at himself. How could he not have heard this noisy child behind him before he had the upper hand?

"Think nothing of it." Will clapped him on the shoulder with a grin. "He left his post, or he'd never have seen you. Had to take out the other one too."

Ivan's face twisted into a scowl.

"Too long." He shook his head. He had grown soft. "I owe you." He slapped Will on the arm. "Glad it was not you who sneak up on me."

He rubbed his neck, glancing down at the boy's pale, clean-shaven face.

Will unbuttoned his coat. "I wouldn't want you sneaking up on me either if it's any consolation."

"Only common sense."

Will grinned as he dug a pocket watch out of his coat and glanced at the time.

"We should go. Sol's probably got himself captured by now."

Sol. Ivan's chest tightened. He was the biggest idiot.

But he could not deny that he respected Solomand's utter lack of fear. He would walk right up into LeFrost's mansion and spit in his face just to wipe away his smirk, totally disregarding the bricks this would bring down on his own head. This is what worried Ivan.

He nodded at Will. "Yes. Has probably pissed off twenty men by now."

"Yeah." Will tucked the watch back in his pocket. "When one would have been more than enough."

"Just one problem." Will rubbed the back of his neck. "We're behind schedule." Will did not look worried, although this was a monumental problem. Even the slightest delay could mean the difference between them all getting out alive. They *had* to get out. Ivan frowned. Tristan's life was at stake. He would not fail.

The train-whistle shattered the heavy silence.

The bridge.

Will and Ivan locked eyes, faint lines of panic drawn on the Olbian's face.

"Shit," he said.

If no one lowered the bridge to let the engine pass, there would be a hell of an explosion—too early.

Will ran to the ladder that scaled the wall and clambered up the iron rungs. Ivan was at his heels. Blinding light of the Olbian Express met them at the guard station, cutting its way through the dark of the night at an unsettling speed. The whistle sounded again—probably wondering why their way hadn't been opened yet.

Will reached for the lever and jerked it with both hands. It didn't move. He put a foot up on the gearbox for leverage and used his weight as he pulled it aft, a vein bulging from his neck. The whistle came in frantic bursts as the light neared.

"Locked!" Ivan pointed to the keyhole on the side.

He broke off in a string of Slavik swears and kicked frantically at it. His head jerked upward.

"Will! The other guard."

Ivan dropped to his knee by the body of the other man Will had taken out by a knife to the neck from the look of it. His hands frisked the man's sides, finally coming across a ring of black keys. He yanked it off the guard's body, ripping his belt loop, and tossed it. Will bent forward to catch it, but they fell. The whistle blared again.

Ivan clamped his eyes shut as Will snatched up the keyring. The keys clanked on the iron as he fumbled to shove the key in place. The ground rumbled as the engine roared down the tracks.

Clink.

The key turned, and Will kicked the lever so hard it stuck. With a massive creak, the bridge lowered. In a still horror, Ivan wondered if it was too late.

The wood barely touched the ground, stirring up a cloud of dust, just as the engine squealed across with a rumble.

The Capital Station. It was headed where they needed to be.

Ivan ran to Will. There was no time to explain.

"Will!" he yelled over the roar of the engine. "Jump!" He grabbed the Olbian by the arm and did not give him time to hesitate. Dragging Will along, he jumped from the guard post onto the moving train.

Ivan had made many decisions in his life, which took less than a second, and it usually began with "what the hell." So far, he had survived them all. Slamming into the moving train car, he hoped this would be one of those. The force of the moving train made them slide backward. Ivan caught hold of the rungs which ran over the top of the car and grabbed Will's hand with the other until he got ahold himself. Looking over his shoulder to make sure Will was secure, he caught the Olbian's expressions.

"For the record, I object. This is the sort of thing Sol would do," Will yelled, then turned his attention to hanging on.

Ivan felt like his hands would be pulled loose. The wind rushed past, bringing tears to his eyes. Will was right. Maybe he had somehow caught Solomand's madness.

If he knew there was a train, he probably would plan for this.

Ivan let a determined grin pass his lips. They shared that, at least; whatever it took to accomplish the mission, both of them would do it. They were running behind, but no more. The capital Station ran behind the Governor's mansion. They could jump off and make up any time that was lost.

It sounded so simple.

"Our stop!" Will's voice carried over the rattle of the wheels on tracks.

Ivan brought his eyes up, blinking through tears to see the lights coming up. The domed capital building rose in the distance, separated from the tracks by an iron fence. Ivan sucked in a breath.

He jumped.

The ground met him with excessive force. After rolling two yards, he landed on his back and looked up, rubbing his jaw and spitting grass. Where was Will? Ivan stiffened. He was lying on a knoll illuminated by lamps fixed all along the fence and didn't know if he should move or not. A hand grabbed him by the collar, and his knife was out in a heartbeat, laying cold against his assailant's neck.

"Easy, Ice Wolf." It was Will. He spoke in a whisper.

Ivan breathed a sigh of relief and brought his leg up to return the knife to its sheath.

"Let's go."

Will's arm was on his, guiding him into the blind spot which ran the length of the fence. They crawled together, inching towards the back of the mansion's pristine lawn. The smell of dirt in his nose, Ivan tried to ignore the various stabbing pains in his limbs.

I am too old for this.

It grew darker the more they edged to the back of the mansion. Here, the lawn darkened. Will stopped, motioning for Ivan to crawl up beside him. He nodded toward the roof.

"Sniper."

"I see them."

Ivan gulped, a lump rising in his throat as his eyes fell on the man tied behind the Governor's residence.

Sol.

When the man struck him, he would eventually look up, a defiant grin on his face and say something which elicited an even stronger blow from the guard. Each time he took longer to raise his head.

Ivan's stomach was a tight ball. He forgot the pains from his fall. He flinched as the man raised his whip and moved to stand. Will held his arm.

"No. I don't see Rayn. He said not to get him out unless she was there too."

The whip cracked again, and Ivan's hands balled into fists.

"You know Sol's plans. Ten things *at least* go wrong!"

"I know," Will said. His hand tightened. "But if we get him out now, we risk losing Rayn too."

Ivan let out a snarling noise.

"Idiot will kill himself."

It made him sick to watch. If Sol would just stop making smartass comments, his life expectancy would significantly increase. Ivan's heart pounded in his ears. That stupid smirk on Solomand's face! He couldn't help but remember all the times Sol had his back and how he stared death down, refusing to show fear or pain. He had done a better job of that than one of the legendary Ice Wolves. Ivan forgot why he was so angry with Sol. His only thought was that he would not let him die like this.

"Enough time." He drew his knife.

"Wait." Will let go of him as a commotion broke out in the courtyard. "Someone's coming."

CHAPTER 52

RAYN

RAYN DOUBTED HER shivering was due to the warm weather. Her clothes, still damp with river water, felt clammy against her skin. Her revolver returned to her side, dug into her thigh, comforting her. Sol's pistol belt was slung over her shoulder. She lowered herself to a prone position, scraping her body across the wooden platform toward the balcony rail. The Drakon felt like an extension of her arm as she nestled the stock into her shoulder. Her left eye closed, she peered through the scope.

A skinny guard, raising his arm, came into focus. She moved the scope to see the man tied between two posts.

Sol!

She didn't have to see his face to know it was him. Her stomach churned, both eyes closing momentarily as she tried to clear her head. Her hands would have to be steady; she couldn't miss. There was nothing else in this present moment but her, and the shot she had to make. She inhaled her right eye-opening, bringing her target into focus of the crosshairs. Her finger squeezed gently as she slowed her exhale.

The stock kicked into her shoulder as the trigger clicked back into place; the suppressed sound of her shot didn't carry far. Her eye to the scope again, she searched for her target. He was on the ground, motionless.

Now, how the hell do I get down?

Her heart raced again.

Without thinking it through, she slung the rifle over her shoulder and climbed over the railing, using the shingles on the roof as footholds. The trouble was when she reached the second floor; there was nothing to catch her boots on. She slipped.

Shit.

One of LeFrost's guards broke her fall as she dropped to the ground. His hands were on her, fighting for the rifle.

Oh no, you don't!

Rayn gritted her teeth

She brought her knee up, catching him in the stomach. Letting out a stifled groan, he loosened his grasp on her arm, drawing his sidearm. If she shot him, the others would hear. She had to be fast.

Rayn slammed the heel of her boot on the ground and the concealed blade shot out of its hiding place in the sole. She dropped the rifle and Sol's pistol belt, bringing her foot into his shin. As he fell to one knee, she jerked a longer knife from her boot and sliced it across his throat before he could scream in pain.

She watched him fall, noting with some disturbance how easy killing had come to her. There wasn't much time for thoughts like that, though. She jerked the rifle and revolver in one hand and dashed to Solomand.

Am I too late?

Sol's head hung below his arms so she couldn't make out his face. His shirt was shredded and streaked with blood. Long, gruesome slashes graced his chest and back where the bullwhip had struck him.

"God, Sol!"

Rayn ran up, the knife from her boot still in hand, still wet with the guard's blood.

She moved to cut his ropes, but her eyes caught the chain around his neck with the cross and unique triangular charm dangling from it. Her heart skipped a beat, and she involuntarily held her breath. She couldn't finish what she was doing. Fingers ice-cold and trembling, she dropped her knife and took the necklace in her hand; there was an 'O' at the point and a compass needle pointing to a name—her name. It would fit perfectly in her medallion, transforming S. L. to SOL.

The charm fell from her hand.

It hurt to breathe.

"Rayn."

Sol raised his head. His lip was swollen, still bleeding. There was a gash across the side of his neck.

"I'm sorry."

She knew she needed to cut him loose, but she couldn't bring herself to move. Lights were coming on now. There was shouting. An alarm bell sounded somewhere close.

"Rayn—look at me," Sol pleaded.

Will rushed up, slicing through Solomand's ropes.

"Was this part of your plan, too?" he asked, pulling Sol's left arm over his shoulder and raising him to his feet.

"I may have gone a little over the top with the insults," Sol admitted sheepishly.

"I hope it was worth it," Will said, sounding uncharacteristically upset.

Sol's mouth twitched in pain, but he still grinned.

"Oh, it was." He spit out a mouthful of blood.

"Rayn," Will said. "We've got to go!" He didn't wait to see if she would follow. He raced toward the gate.

She grabbed Sol's coat from the ground, tucking it under one arm, along with his pistol as she dashed after Will. It didn't really feel like she was the one running.

How the hell are we going to get out of here?

The irrigation canals were a sickeningly long way off, and they would be hunted this time. There was a flash of movement, and something plowed into her. She was on the ground, gasping, as LeFrost's bodyguard stood over her. His eyes looked like frozen lakes, a wildness there that chilled her. A long scar slanted across his lips, giving him a more sinister look as he grinned. His short hair was almost white, but his face placed him as maybe forty. He

279

held a familiar-looking knife in his hand; a curved blade of silvery white attached to a bone handle. It looked like the one Ivan carried.

Something deep inside her was screaming to get away. At any other time in her life, she would have reacted, tried to move. But now, she could barely suck air in her lungs, let alone move.

A blurry figured darted up, colliding with the bodyguard.

Ivan!

Jarred from the daze as Ivan fought to push the vicious-looking man away from her, she pushed herself up on her.

"Ivan!" the bodyguard's eyes widened, and his head tilted back with laughter. "All this time you hiding here!?" He stopped attacking for a moment, pointing his blade at Ivan. "Leave it to you, *Kirno Valk,* to find war and pick losing side."

He laughed again.

Ivan was pale, his eyes filled with an emotion Rayn had never seen on him before.

"Aleksei!" his voice was a whisper. Relief turned to a chill when she realized. Ivan was afraid.

He moved fast, sliding forward and slashing at Aleksei, but the bodyguard was faster. He easily evaded Ivan's attempts to stab him and slit him across the face with the tip of his blade. Rayn's mind slowly cleared, the instinct to survive returning. Ivan would not die on her account! She jumped to her feet. As the Slav moved past her, she kicked in in the ankle with a sweeping movement. The three-inch blade stuck him, and he took a hop back, looking genuinely surprised. He threw his head back, laughing at her and sidestepping another kick.

Ivan was in between them now.

"Get back, Rayn!" He pushed her towards Will. "Leave!"

The shouts grew louder. Minuet's Airmen were close enough to see now, thundering in their direction with guns drawn. Loud explosions started going off, one after the other, growing closer and closer until—in a blast of fire and smoke—a hole was blown into the fence.

Will grabbed her arm. "Get Sol out of here."

He looked at Ivan as he struggled to keep LeFrost's bodyguard at bay. Rayn nodded, gripping his arm over her shoulders, and dragged him through the cover of smoke. Will ran back to help Ivan, keeping the others from following them.

"Rayn." Sol was trying to walk. "We have to get to the river. Jank should be waiting."

He stumbled forward, dragging her down under his weight.

Rayn struggled to get back up. Sol stood on his own, steadying himself with a hand on her shoulder.

"The explosions will keep most of the airmen busy. They won't see the skiff."

That must have been what Ivan and Will were up to.

Yeah, if everything goes as planned.

She wondered just how many things had gone wrong so far. Surely whoever the hell Aleksei was, he wasn't in the equation.

How could it get any worse? She kept moving forward, one step at a time, covering very little ground. A choking ball of fear stuck in her throat. *They'll be after us soon!* The thoughts pushed her to run faster, straining as Sol's strength failed.

CHAPTER 53

WILL

GUARDS FILLED THE streets, circling Will and Ivan. Calculating every move, Will took them out.

One. Two. Three.

He may not remember what he was born to be, but in every battle, his mind cleared. Emotion had no place in a fight. He drew a short knife from his boot and stuck the blade in a man's neck as he lunged past.

Four.

Blood spattered across his coat. From the corner of his eye, he saw the rifle barrel in the window.

"Ivan! Look out!"

Will grabbed a guard and pulled him into his knife. Warmth spread across the front of his coat as the man fell into him. Bullets riddled the man's body.

Ivan spared a glance and slid to the side. The shot grazed his shoulder, but he did not take his eyes from his opponent for an instant more. Will reached in his satchel.

The grenade.

He pulled the pin.

"Ivan!" The Slav looked up and rolled to the side, realizing Will meant to throw it.

Aleksei tore his predatory gaze from Ivan in time to see the grenade fly his way.

"Ha! Good play, Olbian!" he laughed, dashing toward the mansion.

Will turned to run, but something stung his neck. He stopped, drawing his hand to the wound. He pulled it away and stared at the tiny, black dart; panic spread through him like a hurricane ripping up coastal trees.

No.

This is how it had happened before. But last time, the Olbian wasn't afraid. Last time, he had nothing to lose.

"Will!"

Ivan slammed into him as the grenade went off. A wave of heat and searing particles rolled over them. Will knew it was happening but couldn't say he felt it. Already murky coolness entering his mind. Ennea that was his name—a member of Squadron 9.

No. My name is Will!

His hand closed around the dart, and he stood. More guards were running toward them; the bodyguard would soon be too, that was certain.

"Ivan," Will turned to his friend. "Go. I'll hold them off."

"What? No!" Ivan's brows drew together, and he held up his dagger, turning to meet the oncoming men.

"Ivan!" Will seized him by the collar. He opened his hand, exposing the dart. "It's too late."

"No." Ivan's eyes were wide with horror. In many ways, their world had ended when that little dart entered the war. For Will, it had given him a second chance. Now it was taking it back. Everything he was came to a halt.

"Please." The long-held veil dropped from his eyes.

Ivan gritted his teeth, his chest heaving. He gripped Will by the shoulder and gave him a quick nod.

"*Dovednjai, damaychi*—farewell, brother." He rasped out the words.

"Take care of them," Will said.

Ivan nodded again, then tore his gaze from Will as he dashed away.

283

Will's jaw set, and he turned to the men, heart pounding. With a yell, he charged.

If I die, I at least die fighting on the side I choose. I will die as Will.

CHAPTER 54

RAYN

SOL LOOKED UP as Ivan ran to meet them. "Where's Will?"

Ivan's eyes dropped, wiping blood from his hand. "He was hit with dart."

Sol raised his head with a jolt, and he jerked his arm from Rayn's grip and whirled around. Ivan moved to stop him, but Sol shoved him away, trying to get past.

"We're not leaving him behind."

Ivan grabbed him by the collar, dragging him closer. "There is nothing we can do—you know this!"

Solomand jerked free of Ivan's grip. "I'm going to try, anyway."

His face darkening, Ivan drew back and punched Solomand in the face, knocking him to the ground.

"We are going. Or we lose you too." He dragged Solomand from the ground and lay him across his shoulders.

"Follow me," he said to Rayn and broke into a jog.

Will is gone.

If he was hit by one of those memory wiping darts that would mean... Rayn felt like her mind would explode. She ran until she thought her lungs would burst. Her sides ached, and her breaths came in fiery gasps for oxygen. How the hell did Ivan run so fast—and carrying Sol, too?

The 201st airmen, silhouetted in the growing light of the fires throughout Corcyra, rappelled from airships to battle the rising flames.

Guess they need their masks now.

Their boots thudded against the ground. Rayn's foot snagged on something, and she fell forward, the Drakon banging against her back painfully.

"Damn!" She struggled back up and kept running. They were nearing The Mud now. Ivan was just ahead of her. She scrambled through the wall after him, and they made their way through the deserted town.

On the edge of the field she could make out the shape of the skiff, its lights dimmed. Jank jumped over the side, running for them, moving faster than she'd ever seen him.

"Sol!" his voice was panicked. "Is Zee with you? I can't find her!"

"What!" This revelation caused Solomand to find the strength to fight free of Ivan's grip once more. He tumbled to the ground, jumping to his feet, and lurched forward, grabbing hold of Jank with his left hand. "What do you mean?"

"I... I was busy sending the coordinates for the charges to Will and Ivan, and she just vanished. I don't know what happened. I looked everywhere, but I couldn't find her."

CHAPTER 55

SOLOMAND

SOLOMAND TURNED WITH difficulty back towards the city. Somewhere amid the glittering lights and mayhem was Zee: lost, afraid. His stomach a mess of tangled knots, he took a shaky step. He couldn't leave her there.

"I have to find her."

Ivan seized him by the arm. "You will die if you go."

Sol fought to pull away, cringing as pain rippled through him.

"She's got nothing to do with any of this, Ivan—I will not leave anyone else behind!" His voice raised.

Will was lost, probably turned back into one of Corcyra's finest, once again their enemy—either that or dead. He wanted to lie down and puke, but the thought of Zee being caught up in all of this—No! He would get her back or die trying.

Ivan's fingers tightening into a fist. Anger rolled off him like mist off the mountain.

"Let. Me. Go!" Sol clenched his teeth. "You don't care if I die, anyway?"

Ivan drew back, and Sol did not flinch, waiting for the blow to connect with his face. It didn't come. Ivan seized Sol by the collar, lifting him into the air, and hurled him onto the deck of the skiff.

Sol rolled over, coughing, the taste of blood filling his mouth. Rayn was yelling at Ivan as she climbed onto the skiff. There was a ringing in his ear. Ivan and Rayn were both at his side. Ivan had

287

probably been pushed far enough to finish him now. Ivan bent over him.

"I care." he growled. There was a flicker of emotion in his eyes, and his voice lowered. "I will look for her."

He dashed away.

Solomand coughed, arching his back as any movement caused new pangs in the already stinging lacerations.

Damn whip.

It didn't kill him, but it still hurt like hell. He couldn't lay down flat or stand. Everything hurt. The first two fingers on his right hand throbbed. They felt hot and swollen—probably broken.

Jank was kneeling next to him, rummaging through a med kit and handing things to Rayn. He was paler than usual and wouldn't look at Sol.

"Jank." It hurt to talk.

The engineer's eyes were moist.

"Sol, I'm sorry." His shoulders slumped in a defeated way as he held out antiseptic.

"It's alright. I should have made her go with Iminho."

Sol gritted his teeth, biting his tongue as Rayn dabbed antiseptic onto his slashed neck.

"Sorry," she murmured, pressing on a bandage. She was looking at his side now, at the black spider tattoo she had never seen before. "You are the Black Recluse... aren't you?"

"No." He could barely breathe as she pressed on another bandage, a little harder than necessary. She thought he was lying again.

"The Black Recluse isn't one person. That's just what LeFrost thought," he explained through clenched teeth. "We were a special ops team."

Rayn's hand moved to her stomach, her face pale, expressionless.

"The mark where my scar is... it's not a birthmark, is it?"

"No."

The sharp stabs in his body began to numb. This was the moment he had been dreading and trying to avoid. She wouldn't look him directly in the eyes.

"It was a spider tattoo?"

He nodded. "We all have one."

"Who am I, Solomand Black?" There was a coldness in her question that twisted his heart. She already knew or had to suspect the truth.

"You are Rayn... Ivers..." His voice faltered as he finished. "Black. You are my wife, and the daughter of General Benjamin Ivers."

The anguish he was dreading seized him as she asked what he feared she would.

"LeFrost. He said you kept Zee because you lost a child."

Her green eyes locked with his and he felt ill.

"I didn't keep Zee from him." His voice was thick. "I sure as hell wasn't going to go looking for him to return her like some lost, damned puppy." He touched a finger to his split lip, licking blood away. "We didn't know you were..."

Rayn rocked back on her heels, staring off in the distance. Jank took over patching Sol's wounds.

"Rayn, I'm sorry." Solomand struggled to sit up. "Please look at me."

She did, making him feel worse.

"Needing a gunsmith was just a bunch of bullshit. Why didn't you just tell me?" Her eyes flashed. "You acted like this had nothing to do with me when it did! You were going to send me halfway across the damned world instead!" Her hand swept violently, pointing north. "Why?"

"Because." Sol moved to his knees and inched toward her. "You made me promise right after you were shot with that dart." He leaned forward. "You made me swear that I'd kill you before I let LeFrost turn you into one of them!" His heart ached with every beat. "Minuet found out where you were, so we had to act. Grishtanburg would have been safe."

When he looked at her again, tears glistened in the corners of her eyes, threatening to fall.

"Why the hell didn't you just tell me?" Her lips trembled.

Solomand figured the only reason she didn't slap him was because of his current state.

"I wanted to." He scooted forward. "Tristan said if you didn't find out on your own, you might reject the past as reality altogether. That's what happened to Will. He was a Coalition soldier, shot by accident. And now he's..."

Rayn's shoulders rose and fell with her chest. A pain spread through him worse than anything LeFrost could inflict.

"Think, Rayn. When you first saw me in your shop—would you have believed anything I'm saying right now?"

Rayn was fighting to keep the tears from coming. She slowly shook her head.

"Who would want to find out their father was murdered, they'd lost a child, and were married to a man like me." His eyes pleaded with her. "I told you, some memories were better left forgot."

A tear escaped, tracing a line through the dirt as it trailed down her cheek.

"Do you still want me to go?" Her voice quivered, and he felt his heart break the rest of the way.

"Rayn." He took her face in his hand, fingers trembling as he wiped the tear away with his thumb. "I only wanted to protect you. You would have been alright without me."

Rayn moved her head away from his touch.

"I know I don't need you—I don't *need* anyone." Her words were like a dagger. "I don't want to be kept safe—Port Ashbury was safe." Tears of anger flowed freely as she yelled. "That wasn't living, Sol! I would rather die here with all of you than... than..."

He didn't care anymore that she might hate him. He reached forward, curling his hand on her neck. He leaned in, pulling her into a kiss. She didn't stop him. Her hands laced through his hair, drawing his head closer to hers. Her lips were warm, and his mouth stung as she kissed him back fiercely. For one fleeting moment, Solomand forgot about everything else.

She broke away, wiping her eyes.

"How does Tristan know so much about the E.X. solution, anyway?" She looked around, horror spreading across her face. "Sol... where's Tristan?" She looked from him to Jank.

Jank gave her a deadpan look as he stood up. She turned to Sol, anger growing in her eyes. She waited for an explanation.

Sol struggled to stand.

"Tristan's father is Galin Highcourt, one of the most brilliant minds in the medical field. Tristan helped him design the E.X. solution. That's why he knows so damn much about it."

Rayn glared at him. She didn't seem to care about this new revelation. She rose to her feet.

"Where. Is. He?"

Jank saved Solomand from having to answer. "Minuet's men have him." He crossed to the other side of the skiff like he thought she might deck him.

"What?" Rayn turned to him with a savage look. "How could you let that happen?"

Sol cringed at the accusation in her tone.

"We didn't let it happen, Rayn," he said softly. "We needed it to happen. It's the whole reason we came here."

Rayn shook her head in disbelief, pacing back and forth on the deck.

"Why?"

Solomand leaned forward on the side of the ship, cringing as the air stung his back.

"He's dying. Rayn." He hated saying it aloud. "It's a damned miracle he's lasted this long. The only thing that can save him now is a proper surgeon—his father, to be specific."

He hated to admit it out loud. The thought of sending Tristan into Corcyra had never been what he wanted.

Rayn pushed hair from her face.

"But if he's a traitor..." A wild look crossed her face.

"They won't kill him, Rayn. It's not their way." He tried to move his fingers again and was rewarded with sharp pain shooting up his hand like tiny needles. "They'll make him well first." What happened after he wasn't going to think about. It would not come to that. "We will get him out of here."

Jank cleared his throat.

"Sol… Ivan's been gone too long." His voice was hoarse. "We've got to get the hell out of here soon, or we'll be swarmed by jackass pelicans."

He was right. But there was no way in hell Solomand was going to leave Ivan behind.

"Get ready to fly, Jank." He slumped down with a series of winces into a seat. "We're not losing anyone else."

CHAPTER 56

RAYN

I AM A member of the Black Recluse. Rayn's fingers tightened on the edge of the skiff as she peered over the swirl of approaching lights. *My father was Benjamin Ivers.* Her stomach tightened. *LeFrost killed him.* Her hand moved to the Drakon as she drew it close into her shoulder, inching the barrel over the edge. *Focus!* If she got too distracted, she'd be no help in getting Ivan and Zee back. *Zee.* She'd asked Solomand what they would do if she wasn't with Ivan.

"We'll have to leave without her."

There had been a choked kind of horror in his words. She understood why they would have to as much as she shared the dread at having to make that decision. LeFrost would not harm the girl, and they would all come to a nasty end if they didn't get out fast. Zee was safer than all of them now.

As the Governor's mansion came into view, wind stung her eyes. She loosened one hand from the rifle, moving her goggles into place. The Drakon rattled, sliding to one side.

Shit.

She hurried to push it back into place.

"Rayn! On the roof!" Jank's voice carried over the roar of the engine.

293

Sol was trying not to talk if he didn't have to. He leaned forward over the back of the seat, his shirt was plastered to the wounds on his back. Rayn looked away, reminding herself to breathe.

A bullet ripped through the sails.

No, you don't!

Rayn saw him standing in the open. Anticipating his movement, she squeezed the trigger, catching him as he ran. This was who she was: a sniper for the rebels. Not that hard to believe.

"Ten o'clock!" Jank was shouting again.

Rayn swiveled the rifle barrel until the next man was in her sights. He toppled before he could get a shot at them. She did not miss a single mark.

They passed over the twisted iron gate and she saw Ivan, locked in battle with LeFrost's bodyguard.

"There he is!"

Ivan was up against the bars, the bodyguard at his throat. Their blades flashed in the moonlight as they moved together—locked in a savage dance. This was not a fight between the Coalition and Rebel fighters. There was something in the bodyguard's cruel smile that made Rayn's skin crawl. He was enjoying this fight far too much.

Zee was nowhere in sight. Rayn's heart sank. Why did everything have to go so horribly wrong? She looked through the scope again, trying to get Aleksei in her sights; but he kept moving, dodging Ivan's every attempt to reach him with his knife.

Hold still, damn you!

She glimpsed his eyes in the scope as he looked at the skiff. It felt like he was looking right at her. A sinister grin spread on his face. Rayn's hand remained steady as she pulled the trigger.

Shit.

The bullet only grazed his shoulder.

"Son of a bitch!"

She was out of ammunition.

"Rayn! Get the Cannon!" Sol was next to her, crawling across the deck to the compartment.

"But what about Ivan?" Rayn asked, hooking the Drakon's sling over her arm and scrambling across the floor. She wasn't letting it go, even if it was out of ammo.

"I'm going to tell him to get the hell out of the way," Sol said, pulling on the compartment door.

Rayn helped him, hoping Ivan could manage in time. The Skiff tilted as Jank began to circle. And one hand grabbed the mast. Sol's slid into the open door, hoisting the long barrel up to her. He cringed as he bent over, handing her each piece of the gun, and—finally—the wall-destroying rounds.

Rayn wrapped her leg around the mast, using both hands to fit the gun together. She took the rounds from Solomand, and dropped one into the barrel, charging the handle back.

Let's see how you like this!

She let herself go, sliding toward the edge of the skiff, bracing her boots against the side of the deck.

"Ivan!"

Solomand's yell carried down to the fight, and both of the men looked up at him. Ivan nodded in understanding and moved out of her line of sight. The Slav looked up to the thirty millimeter cannon staring him in the face. He laughed, looking unimpressed. Rayn shot it at him, and the cobbled sidewalk exploded, bits of stone flying everywhere.

The bodyguard crouched low, shielding his head from the shrapnel.

"Damn!" She'd missed him, but he wasn't presently attacking Ivan.

She let the gun slide away, leaning over the edge.

"Ivan!"

Ivan looked up, thin lines of blood ran across his face where his opponent had come too close. She reached her hand out.

"Come on!"

Ivan hesitated, glancing back at Aleksei. The Slav was rising to his feet, lunging forward.

"Ivan, now!" Solomand was next to her, extending his right arm over, bracing himself with the other.

Aleksei had almost reached Ivan. Rayn took a knee, raising her revolver. She would not miss again.

The Slav stopped, the grin still on his face. He yelled something in Slavik at Ivan, who turned to face him. There was a pure hatred on his face and for a terrible instant, it looked like he might go back and try to finish the fight. The roar of another airship overshadowed the pathetic noise of their own engines. A high-pitched sound that made her stomach turn accompanied it.

"The Pandora!" She couldn't bring herself to look at its ghostly shape in the sky. *That's it. We're dead.*

"Ivan!" Jank lowered the skiff. He turned, hesitating once more before taking both her and Solomand's hands.

Sol cried out in pain as he and Rayn hauled Ivan into the skiff. The Slav toppled onto the deck.

"Hold on to something!" Jank hollered.

The engines made a horrible screeching noise as they shot up and out of the city. Rayn slammed against Sol and Ivan as the force slid them against the aft part of the airship. A breath caught in her throat as she looked up at the hulking shadow outlined with red flashing lights about to overtake them.

This is it.

A massive weight pressed on her chest. She found Solomand's hand in the dark, her fingers closing around his.

A flash of light shot from the *Pandora's* cannon. There was a terrible splintering sound as the shot ripped through the skiff. Solomand's arms closed around her as their airship shuddered. They were spinning toward the desert, the burning of their ship reflected on the river beneath them. The water swallowed her, sucking her down into its current. She had no breath left to hold. Gasping, choking, she thrashed through the bottomless liquid. Everything faded to a wet blackness.

CHAPTER 57

RAYN

RAYN SLOWLY BECAME aware of a screeching noise in the darkness. She followed it, forcing herself from the black sleep. The sun was warm on her face. She opened her eyes, turning away from the bright light.

"Where the hell am I?"

She used her arm as a shield against the sun, propping herself up on her elbow. Her coat was laid out beneath her over a hard, grainy surface. It felt like something stabbed her in the chest every time she breathed. As her vision came into focus, she saw Sol, Jank, and Ivan were lying in a row next to her.

Groaning, she sat up and leaned forward, her head throbbing. A shadow blocked out the light.

"Here." Rayn glanced up, squinting as her head pounded. The sun behind his back, the Falcon squatted down, holding out a canteen. She took it, cursing at the painful jolt that ran from her lower back up her spine. It faded to a dull throb as she drank. The water was cold against the abrasive dryness in her throat.

Elbows resting on his knees, the Falcon studied her with his dark eyes. She stopped drinking to take a breath, wiping away the water trickling down the side of her face.

"Are they ok?"

She looked at Sol. His upper body was more covered with bandages than not.

The Falcon's eyes flickered to Solomand.

"They'll be fine," he said. His head tilted back, becoming a silhouette in the sun behind him. "I patched him up, but I'm no Highcourt."

Rayn felt ill. Was Tristan even still alive?

The Falcon's eyes narrowed. "Are you alright?" he asked.

Rayn cringed, pressing her aching head with her palm.

"I guess. I feel like... well, shit."

The Falcon's mouth turned up in amusement.

"You have multiple minor abrasions and lacerations, a possible fractured wrist, and you nearly drowned. More than likely, you are dehydrated, and will no doubt suffer from varying shades of blue and purple for the next few weeks." His head tilted slightly, his eyes locking with hers as he scrutinized her. "That's not what I was asking?"

His eyes narrowed further. "I want to know if you are alright."

Rayn's eyes moved to Sol again: her husband. All the information that had ripped through her mind like a tornado the previous night began to settle. Her hand involuntarily moved to her stomach, and she closed her eyes, trying to shut out the disturbing reality. She understood why Sol didn't want to tell her.

"You knew too, didn't you?"

The Falcon's expression did not change. "Yes. I was the one who took you to Port Ashbury for your father."

Port Ashbury.

Suddenly Rayn remembered where she'd seen him before. It was the day Solomand turned her world upside down. Before that had happened, there was a mysterious-looking stranger in the bar that caught her attention.

"You were there."

Lemuel's gaze narrowed. "Yes. Many times."

"Why?"

"I owed your father a favor. We used to work together, but we had a... falling out."

Rayn suspected it was more than that. "You mean sleep walking?"

Lemuel's brow wrinkled. "Yes. He believed it was wrong. I believed that was irrelevant. It is effective." Lines formed on his eyes as they squinted. "So, he left and got himself mixed up in the political dealings of Corcyra, which ended in a senseless bloodbath." He looked like he didn't really want to talk about it and sighed. "He asked me to help him, and I refused. He knew I couldn't compromise myself."

He grew quiet, staring stoically off in the distance before clearing his troubled gaze and turning back to Rayn.

"And that's enough questions answered by me. You didn't answer mine."

Rayn's shoulders slumped, the deluge of unpleasant realities catching up, threatening to drown her entirely differently. She forced herself to meet his eyes and sighed, too exhausted to tell lies. There was no keeping secrets from a man like him, anyway.

"No." Her voice sounded more like a croak. She took a shaky breath, wiping her nose with her sleeve. "But I will be."

The Falcon studied her for a moment longer, then nodded, satisfied. He stood and stepped noiselessly to a black rucksack. Rayn took another sip of water. The bandage on her wrist smelled like flowers and pungent spices-the same scent she had smelled from Iminho's tent.

Kree medicine.

The Falcon rummaged through his bag, pulling out a handful of small, green kanji fruit. He handed one to Rayn.

He took a bite of the fruit in his hand with an amused flicker in his eyes. He walked over to Sol and the others, placing one fruit and a canteen next to each of them. Rayn bit into the smooth rind, savoring the crisp sweetness in her mouth. She didn't realize how hungry she was.

"Thought you had business in Olbia," Sol mumbled, reaching a shaky hand for the canteen.

"Sol!" Rayn's heart jumped.

"It'll wait for me," The Falcon replied.

"Why d'you come back?" Sol croaked between sips of water. Rayn cringed at his swollen, bruised eye.

The Falcon sat on his heels. "You know me, Sol. I won't leave my bet up to fate."

Sol gulped too quickly, and spluttered, choking on a mouthful of water. The Falcon took the canteen from him and set it down.

"Isn't that cheating?" Sol winced with every movement.

"It's called winning, Sol." The Falcon shook his head slightly like Solomand was an idiot for not knowing that.

"Lemuel..." Sol's head was still raised. "Thank you." He sank back to the ground.

The Falcon looked thoughtfully at Solomand. It looked like he wanted to say something, but changed his mind.

He turned to Rayn.

"I have to go." He whistled in a shrill, melodious way. "Make sure the other two drink water while I'm gone." He glanced at Jank and Ivan.

Rayn nodded. The screech of Lemuel's falcon answered his whistle, echoing off the canyon walls as he left through the narrow opening.

Rayn's heartbeat was normal, so long as she didn't think about anything. She crawled painfully to Solomand's side. His eyes opened, and he smiled, slightly.

"Hello, Rayn Storm." He tried to sit up.

"Be still." Rayn frowned.

Idiot. She thought, in a more gentle way than usual.

"Why did you have to get so... tore the hell up?"

Sol let his head fall back to his rolled-up coat.

"I'll heal. But the look on that Airman's face when I told him to stick his head in a cannon... that will last forever."

Rayn laughed, then winced at the stabbing in her side.

"You should have saved it for *after* you got away."

She sniffed, trying to sound annoyed. A fiery ball of anger grew in her chest against her will, knowing what she did now, what LeFrost had done…

"If…" she swallowed, staring into his steel-blue eyes. "If I'd have known, I would have killed him."

There was sadness in Sol's smile. He raised his hand. A warmth spread through her as he brushed her cheek, and the anger subsided.

"I know you would have."

"Then why didn't you tell me before?"

Her voice cracked. Sadness for things she didn't even remember swelled inside her.

Sol's hand fell to his side, and a deep sorrow filled his eyes—so intense she could feel it herself.

"Because sometimes it's not about revenge, Rayn. It's about protecting the ones you have left."

His hand trembled as it laced through hers.

"Why can't it be both?" Rayn whispered.

"There was a time when all I thought of was ripping that man's head off with my bare hands."

"What stopped you?"

He took a shaky breath. "It was killing me, and I needed to live: for you, for Tristan, for what family I had left."

Rayn's fingers closed around his, finally seeing past the secrets and lies to the real Solomand Black: a man who had lost everything and would fly straight into hell if there was a chance it might save his friend. She didn't remember loving him before, but she knew she did now.

"Was it a daughter or a son?"

Sol's eyes closed.

"A daughter." His voice wavered.

Rayn's eyes clamped shut, and she was quiet for a while. Finally, not being able to bear the silence any longer.

"It's not Rayn Storm," she said, blinking back tears. "It's Rayn Black."

Solomand struggled to sit, ignoring the pain as he leaned toward Rayn. He took her chin in his hand.

"You'll always be Rayn Storm to me," he touched his forehead to hers.

Gently, Rayn's hand trailed along his neck.

"I still don't remember you," she whispered. "Except in my dreams, and then it's not as you are now." Her fingers tugged at the chain on his neck. She pulled back to look him in the eyes. "Now I understand why you wanted to kill that Airman in Blackpool."

Sol's head dug into her neck as he laughed.

"Would you have done it?"

"Hell yes," he said without hesitation. "He made me think I might lose you in an entirely different way." He pulled her closer until there was no space between them. "I was stupid to ever think I could be selfless enough to let you go. I'll never make that mistake again."

She ran a hand through his smoky-black hair.

"It *was* a stupid idea, and if you didn't look so damned awful last night, I would have slapped you for it."

Solomand's shoulder shook as he laughed, wincing.

"Oh, I could tell you wanted to. His mouth turned up in his crooked smile.

"There's a reason I call you that, you know, Rayn Storm."

CHAPTER 58

SOLOMAND

SOLOMAND ROLLED ONTO his side. Something felt torn deep in his right shoulder blade, forcing him to keep his arm close to his body. Tristan was right, as usual. He would be lucky if it ever returned to normal. He watched as Rayn shook Jank and Ivan awake, handing them each a canteen of water.

"Where the hell are we?" Jank mumbled, drawing one knee up as he sat. Before anyone could answer, he jerked his head back, glancing around. "How the hell did we get here?"

He held a hand to his bandaged head and went a shade paler. "Shit. It was the bodysnatcher, wasn't it?"

Solomand kicked at him with the toe of his boot. "He saved your life, Jank—all our lives."

Jank cleared his throat, took another drink and muttered. "Still a body snatcher... shithead 201st."

Ivan stared at the ground, listless, barely drinking. Something in his eyes worried Solomand. Ivan's gaze raised for a moment, catching his. The Slav hated losing; Will and Zee's loss would be something he took personally. But there was something else, something Solomand had never seen before. He suspected it had something to do with LeFrost's criminally insane bodyguard.

"What's wrong, Ivan?" he asked.

Ivan's brow was furrowed. Dried lines of blood covered his face.

"LeFrost's bodyguard…"

"Noticed he was giving you a hard time." Sol took a drink of water. "Who is he?"

Ivan rubbed the back of his neck, his shoulders tensed.

"Aleksei. I was his, how you say, protégé." His hand tightened around a hand of sand. "He is no bodyguard." He shook his head slowly.

Sol dug into his pocket for his cigarette case, cringing all the while.

"Lots of Ice Wolves sell themselves out with jobs like that down here."

He pried the case open with his fingernails. There were four cigarettes left, wet and squished. They were still smokeable. He sat up, passing one to Ivan and Jank. Rayn held her hand out, giving him a hard look until he gave her the last one.

"Not Aleksei." Ivan held the damp cigarette to Sol's lighter, puffing until the damp paper finally caught fire. His hand was shaking.

Shit Ivan, what's wrong with you?

"He is not just Ice Wolf. Aleksei was Alpha." He shook his head again. "Frost will regret having anything to do with him."

He finished his cigarette. The others had barely started on theirs.

"He's why you left Grishtanburg?" Sol asked quietly.

Ivan had never been forthcoming about his past, and they had never asked. They all had graveyards share of skeletons stuffed in the closet. Why should he be any different?

Ivan nodded. "Is not good he is here. If not for him I could have got Zee back."

Sol leaned forward, savoring the last bit of tobacco. It tasted like dirt and river water.

"Let it go, Ivan. Will knew what he was getting himself into, and Zee? That's my fault."

Why did Will have to get hit by that damned thing?

A thought entered his mind that it would have been better had it been a real bullet, then he hated himself for thinking such a thing.

And Zee? She was probably scared to death, sure as hell, he'd get her out.

"The cost will be too great," he muttered. Tristan and the priest had been right: both had warned him.

"Did it even work?" Jank spoke up, trying not to sound defeated. "How the hell are we supposed to know?"

Solomand took a bit of the kanji fruit. "Minuet," he answered, his mouth full.

"Why wait?" Lemuel's deep voice interrupted. Jank jumped, causing The Falcon to survey him with amusement. The silky bird was on his shoulder, its head jerking back and forth, eyeing them all with suspicion. He held up a rolled newsprint in his hand before tossing it on the ground in front of Solomand.

Sol gulped, almost afraid to read it. Rayn picked it up, reading as the others crowded around her.

"War Criminal Captured. Long presumed dead war criminal, Tristan Highcourt, was captured trying to enter Corcyra last night. Son of the famed Dr. Galin Highcourt, Tristan shocked the entire allied forces when he chose to betray his family and fellow Corcyrans for the cause of the rebels. It is uncertain how many lives he could be held directly responsible for, but his actions are enough for Governor LeFrost to call for the highest capital punishment: public execution not seen since the end of the war. Though it may be some time before the younger Highcourt sees his sentence carried out, as he was injured during his savage attack of Corcyra's finest. He is currently under the care of his father until he is well enough to face the consequences for his ill choices."

"Horseshit!" Jank spat. "He never attacked anyone—he could barely walk."

"It's just propaganda, Jank." Solomand squinted, pointing to an article further down the page. "Lady St. Sebastian injured by an unidentified invader. She is to be awarded the highest military honor..."

"That propaganda too?" Jank sneered.

Rayn shifted uncomfortably. "No. I shot her."

"What?" Jank's mouth dropped open.

Rayn shrugged. "She told me to."

Jank raked hands through his hair, groaning, "Why the hell didn't' she ask me—I'd have done it years ago, and I would have done it properly."

Solomand took the paper now, ignoring Jank's groaning. He thumbed through the pages, searching.

Nothing.

His heart sank, and he tossed the newsprint aside. He glared up to see Lemuel looking at him.

"What's wrong, Sol? News not to your liking?"

"More what it didn't say." Sol clamped his eyes shut as a wave of misery hit him.

"They wouldn't very well mention Will now, would they? An Olbian mercenary who they turned against themselves with their own weapon."

"No," Sol mumbled.

"He knew the risks. You shouldn't hold yourself responsible." That was typical of Lemuel—no—The Falcon, with his emotional detachment from everyone he worked with.

"Zee didn't!" he snapped bitterly.

There it was: the look he couldn't turn away from.

"She is not in any immediate danger, as you well know." Lemuel's eyes narrowed. "You can't afford to dwell on any distractions."

Anger rose in Sol. "Zee is not just a..."

"You know what I mean." Lemuel interrupted. His voice, barely raised, still carried the weight of a hammer. "You barely got this far, and the hard part is just beginning." He paused now, his shoulders relaxing. "I can get you an airship, but I can't help you with anything else."

Solomand pushed himself up on one elbow and ignored the pain in his side.

"Like you couldn't help us this time?"

Lemuel regarded him like he was a child who did not understand what he was meddling with.

"This is different." His voice changed to that dangerous edge Sol knew so well. "Ivan is right about this Aleksei. He is ambitious. He will be more trouble than you know."

Lemuel had always gone on about a bigger picture. He never was interested in pawns—still hunting the king in some maddening game.

"Still after your chess piece?"

Lemuel's smile was sympathetic.

"More like a puppet master."

"While we play with the puppets?" Solomand sighed.

It doesn't mean your job is any less important. We all have different parts to play.

Lemuel's past words echoed in his mind.

"I know," he stopped Lemuel from repeating the same *gem* of wisdom a second time.

"My business is not yours," Lemuel said, his eyes narrowing. "A war is coming."

Solomand kicked at a rock.

"It's already came, Lemuel. And went."

The Falcon didn't seem to hear. He continued to have that look about him as if they were all children in over their heads.

"You must finish what you set out to do," he said.

"The Falcon is right." Ivan stood, clutching his bandaged side, a rare wave of emotion on his face. "*Toch stalon, to stalon* (what's done is done)." He stiffened, and he recovered his determined, murderous stare. "We waste time here."

"I'm with Ivan," Rayn spoke up. The steadiness in her voice stilled the swirl of emotions inside Solomand. "Let's get them back." She said it like it was the easiest thing in the world, and he found himself believing it would be, if only for a moment.

Once her mind was set, there was no swaying her. LeFrost would never know what hit him.

"Alright," Solomand forced himself to sit. "Get us to your airship, Lemuel. We'll do the rest."

The Falcon crossed his arms, his eyes glittering.

307

"That's more like the Black Recluse I remember."

Sol glanced at Jank. He was the only one who, uncharacteristically, didn't have an opinion. The engineer was hunched over, his haunted gaze fixed on the ground. He slowly raised his head. Sol knew what was bothering him. Jank was one of god knows how many sleep walkers The Falcon had used to accomplish his goals. Most people had no idea what he looked like, only that he was an assassin.

He could pick someone that had a sleepwalker gene, as he called it, and put them into a trance. They went where he wanted. While they thought they were only dreaming, they were actually assassinating some high-brow target. It was a hell of an advantage, but one Ben didn't think was worth using. He especially didn't like how Lemuel left his victims to suffer the consequences.

He had made a mistake with Jank, though. He allowed himself to care. Wherever he was from, he had no family who would miss him. Lemuel took him to Ben, saying he would owe him for taking the boy in. When Jank found out what happened, he was terrified of The Falcon and his body snatching abilities.

"Professor." Jank stood. "I want to do it." His voice quivered. "I'll do whatever it takes."

"Jank, don't," Sol said.

The Falcon surveyed Jank pensively. He bent down, rummaging through his bag. He pulled out a battered leather book and held it out to Jank.

"My sketchbook..." Jank's hand trembled as he took it. "You saved it from the wreckage..." The look of mixed fear and loathing softened.

"You don't need to sleepwalk, Jank. That is my way. Find your own."

Jank's shoulders shook as he hung his head.

As Lemuel walked past him, he said, "Thank you."

"No need." Lemuel grinned. "Just don't let me lose my wager."

CHAPTER 59

RAYN

LEMUEL HAD A ship for them by nightfall. They followed his falcon, nervously, out of the maze of the canyon. They had to go slow enough, so Solomand wouldn't strain himself too severely. He did anyway, limping alongside Ivan and refusing any help. Sweat glistened on his face in the pale moonlight. The Falcon waited for them, a ghostly shape against the star-studded horizon. He stood in the airship's shadow. Rayn's jaw dropped. "Holy hell, Lemuel!" Sol breathed out sharply. "Where did you get *that*?"

It was nothing like the rudimentary cargo ship Solomand had procured. The Osprey had been the kind of craft only a penniless band of desperados would appreciate. This ship would make even the most land-locked individual on a dock turn their heads in admiration. The shape was like ancient flying devices—sleek and aerodynamic. The outside deck was lined with a dull copper, offsetting the flat black coating on the rest of the ship. The bow curved in a narrow nose-shape with two propellers mounted on either side. Three wing-like airfoils angled forward on either side, connected in between by steel beams. At the aft, two shafts containing propellers of tapered length were mounted on either side. Gunner stations were mounted on the top of the airship.

"That, my young friend, is my business." Lemuel strode forward. "You've got your map?" He gave Sol a meaningful look. "Cross the minefield. You'll be safe for a while."

309

"Why can't we go back to the valley?" Rayn asked, scraping sweaty strands of hair from her face. She adjusted the grip on her rifle.

Sol was pale.

"Because of Will." There was a pain in his voice. "We don't know what he might tell them. It's not worth the risk." He leaned forward, clutching his chest.

Will.

It was hard to imagine a scenario where the mild-mannered Olbian might turn on them.

"What about the Kree?"

"Don't let their simple appearance fool you. The Kree have their own ways of vanishing." Lemuel clamped a hand on her shoulder. "Take care of him, will you? You see what happens when he's unsupervised."

"Yeah," Rayn nodded.

"Very funny." Sol clenched his teeth together. "I've been doing just fine without your help, thanks... Gah!" He cried out as Lemuel took him by the arm and escorted him inside the dark cargo bay.

"I can see that."

"Really, Lemuel, I'm not a damn child—I still have one good arm."

Lemuel ignored him. He turned to Rayn. "There's enough medicine on board. Keep him patched up. Keep yourselves patched up." He turned to Sol, a distant expression returning to his face. "Sol." He spoke some words in Kree.

Solomand grew somber, and he bowed his head, repeating the words back to Lemuel

"See you later." Lemuel tipped his hat. Then, The Falcon ducked out of the cargo bay doors, whistling his lyrical call to his pet. The bird answered as it swooped down, catching his shoulder. Rayn watched them vanish into the darkness, feeling like he was more a mystery than when they first met. Still, she trusted him.

Jank hit a button on the control panel by the open doors, and they wheezed shut. Dim lights flickered on.

"The map, Rayn."

Jank held his hand out, and she handed him the scrap of paper Minuet had given her.

"Better make sure he holds onto something."

He took the paper from her and twisted the dials on the spherical device they had received from the bell tower.

"Ivan, give me a hand, will you?" Ivan followed him without a word to the cockpit.

"I'm not an infant, Jank!" Sol yelled after him, rolling his eyes. "I know how to strap myself in when you're the one flying."

"His flying better than yours." Ivan's voiced answered him.

Sol scowled, mumbling, "Ice man."

Rayn stifled a laugh, and Solomand gave her a reproachful look.

"You too, huh?"

"Yeah." He looked injured at her sincerity. The engines came to life with a soft buzzing noise—much quieter than the *Osprey*.

"Come on," Rayn said, brushing against him on her way to the stairwell and caught the look of pain in his eyes. "Sorry." She cringed in sympathy.

"It's alright," Sol half spoke and half groaned, limping up the stairs ahead of her.

The airship lifted, and she suppressed the urge to tell him to move faster. If they ended up slamming against the hold, it wouldn't be the worst thing to have happened in the past day.

He lurched forward, landing on one hand.

"Come on."

She slipped her shoulder under his arm and shuffled with him, leaning on her to the first cabin door. Once inside, she dragged him to the bunk.

"Lay down, Sol," she pleaded, sitting next to him.

"Do I look that bad?" he asked, sinking back. He tensed as his back hit the coarse blanket.

311

"Yeah. You look like shit."

Rayn lay the Drakon next to him and unbuttoned her jacket.

Sol laughed, then groaned, his jaw tightening.

"Don't make me laugh." He settled back, his smile fading as he stared at her. "Are you really alright?"

Rayn shrugged.

Sol raised his hand and brushed her cheek with his finger. His eyes flickered shut.

"I'm sorry. For everything…" His head shifted back and forth on the pillow. "Bad things happen to the ones I love, Rayn. Your father's men, they thought I was bad luck. Maybe he should have listened."

"Don't be stupid." Rayn shoved him. "My father can't have been wrong; I may not remember, but I'm never wrong. And I probably take after him."

Solomand managed a smile.

"It's alright if you don't remember. That just means I can reuse all the love sonnets that I used to get Tristan to help me write, and you'll be none the wiser."

Rayn raised an eye.

"Love sonnets?"

Sol cleared his throat.

"Shall I compare thee to a Medved, straight and true and faithfully there when I need you."

"Ugh—that's awful. No way Tristan helped you with that."

Rayn's ribs ached as she laughed. Then, a still look of sadness fixed on her face. Without a word, Solomand laced his hand through hers. As he pressed his head against hers.

"We'll get him back." He whispered.

She squeezed his hand and leaned in, running a hand through his hair as she pressed her lips gently to his. Pulling away, her heart pounding rapidly, she pressed her forehead to his. "They'll never see us coming."

EPILOGUE

LEMUEL WALKED THROUGH the desert, his boots noiseless on the gritty soil. Moonlight faded and brightened as clouds drifted forward, propelled by a strong breeze. Left hand in his pocket, Lemuel found the tarnished silver ring with Kree markings and returned it to his finger. He never wore it around Solomand; the boy would ask prying questions. Solomand was always *the* boy in Lemuel's mind.

The Falcon's gaze shifted in the direction of the city where, he knew, Tristan Highcourt was struggling for his life, in one way or another. Taunting thoughts sprang up. It would be easy for a man with certain connections and resources to slip in unseen, and leave again with the Highcourt boy. Even as the temptation grew, Mirage shifted on his shoulder, jerking his head to the side and letting out a cry as he spread his wings and took flight.

Lemuel was no longer alone.

Standing still, his hand tightened on the rifle sling.

"I've been expecting you," he said, looking over his shoulder.

A figure stood there, his long, dramatic coat fluttering behind him as the wind blew. A hood of deep crimson shadowed his face. Lemuel shifted his body to face the man.

"Hello, Alaric."

"The Director is not pleased with your... interference here." The man's mouth formed a hard line.

Lemuel offered a grim smile. "Isn't he?"

Alaric's dark hand flinched at his side.

"You tread a thin line that grows ever blurred, Falcon." He paused, his head tilting slightly. "You do recall the terms of your employment?"

"Yes." The Falcon kept his temper in check. "And I trust you recognize my *interference* here has only ensured my future cooperation."

There were the faintest traces of relief in Alaric's voice when he spoke at length.

"The Director may be persuaded by this point."

Lemuel raised an eye. Alaric always was the good-natured one. The others would be eager to throw him to the wolves. It gained Alaric no rapport with Lemuel, however. To him, they were all the same.

Glancing up so his pale blue eyes were visible, Alaric spoke again.

"Nevertheless, your orders are to return to Argos immediately and wait for reassignment there."

"Very well." Lemuel barely concealed his resentment. He turned to continue on his way as Mirage's moonlit shadow circled overhead.

"And Falcon... The Director's orders were quite specific on *immediately*. There is nothing left for you in that city."

Temptation ebbing away, Lemuel did not give Alaric the courtesy of acknowledging his last words before continuing on his way. There was no need to. If he attempted to save the Highcourt boy, they would find out, just as they had found out about him aiding Solomand. The Falcon was not happy with his orders. Still, for now at least, his bargain with the Moirai remained intact.

Mirage's claws dug into the leather guard on his shoulder as he landed, shaking his feathers. Lemuel toyed with the ring on his finger, thinking again of Solomand, knowing any fool plans he made to aid Tristan would link their paths together once more.

It could not be avoided forever. Eventually, the line would be crossed.

ACKNOWLEDGEMENTS

I acknowledge all of those who read this compilation of words and did not find it to be absolute garbage. I do not happen to be one of them. But it has an exquisite cover, don't you think?!

A BONUS SHORT...

THE BOY WHO TRAVELED THROUGH DREAMS

A FRESHLY PICKED ORCHID should not have been clutched in the boy's hand as he sprang from bed. Dampness from dew-soaked grass on his bare feet caused him to slip on the wood floor as he hurried from the room. Morning sun streamed in from the kitchen window, highlighting his small, wet footprints.

"This is for you, Mama!" He placed the flower on the counter. His mother looked up from her drawing as he pushed the half-crushed cerulean orchid toward her. Her breath visibly catching, she set her pencil on the mountain she'd been conjuring from paper with careful strokes. "Oh..." Her honey-colored eyes widened, as she twirled the green stem in her fingers. "It's lovely!" She exchanged a fearful glance with the boy's father. "Where did you find this?"

She was right to wonder. The only flowers within a hundred miles of the Stonecipher were blooms of desert cacti. Orchids like this one grew far north, where the dry land faded into green plains dotted with mountains, cities rested on plateaus and the skies were alive with airships; they were the first heralds of spring and the emblem of new beginnings.

The boy climbed onto a stool before pointing to a painting hanging above the fireplace; it was one of his mother's—a lush field peppered with orchids and cherry trees in full blossom as the sun dipped below distant mountains. "There. I took a walk while I was sleeping," the boy said, proceeding to shovel eggs in his mouth.

"You went sleepwalking again?" The boy's father set his coffee cup down.

"It's fine, Esmond." His mother reached a pale hand and smoothed the child's hair.

"But Everleigh." Esmond's voice dropped. "Maybe we should consider the man's warning."

"It'll be fine." There was a peculiar firmness in Everleigh's tone. Leaning forward, she smiled and kissed her son's forehead. "Now, Jules." Nudging her sketchbook aside, she rested her chin on her hand. "Tell me all about your walk."

A few weeks later the strangers in long, red coats came to their door. Jules did not understand why his parents were afraid, but could feel the tension in their glances and knew something was about to happen. His mother pressed her sketchbook into his hands and hugged him so tight he could not breathe. There were tears in her eyes as she kissed him and gave Esmond a determined nod. Receiving an equally crushing embrace from his father, Jules was unceremoniously slipped out the back window into the waiting arms of a dark-eyed man.

"Keep him safe." Those were Esmond's last words before he slammed the window. A falcon cried overhead, casting a shadow on the moonlit cobblestones as the man tucked Jules under his arm and disappeared down the cramped alleys of the city. He never spoke as he strode with a purposeful step, making so many twists and turns that Jules had no idea where they were. Too afraid to speak, he clung to his mother's drawings and wondered when he would be able to go home.

When at last the man set Jules down, the boy looked up at the sign over a gray-stone building. "Fleet Street Home for Children." He read it aloud slowly before daring to glance up at the stranger.

Eyes like hardened flint stared down. "You'll be safe here." The man dug a folded parchment from his coat pocket and crouched down as he pressed it into Jules' hand. "Your name is Isaac Tobin now." His voice was hard. "Say it."

"I—Isaac Tobin." Tears stung Jules eyes as he realized he was not going back home. His fingers trembled, clammy against the parchment in his hands.

"Your real name." The stranger's voice softened slightly. "Keep it close." He pressed a finger to Jules' chest, and the boy noticed the thick, black tattoo lines that snaked up the man's forearm. "Never forget it."

Hugging his mother's sketchbook, Jules nodded, breathing in the scent of charcoal and graphite.

"Good." The man rang the bell and retreated to the corner of a building, watching until Jules stepped inside the orphanage. Even as the years went by, he told himself this was only temporary. His parents would come for him when it was safe. The alternative was to accept he was the one responsible for whatever unseemly fate they may have suffered. After all, it was his sleepwalking that caused the men to come.

Six years passed and Jules turned twelve. All memories of the tattooed stranger and his strange ability to go travel while asleep had long since been buried. Until the night the mayor of Stonecipher was assassinated.

It was a spring night, like the one long ago, for all that meant in the desert. Wind howled mournfully over, hurling copious measures of sand against the city walls. Most citizens sequestered indoors, hiding from the endless barrage of sand. Others huddled together in dank alleyways and under dilapidated railway bridges, coats pulled over their heads, praying they wouldn't be one of the many who would choke to death from the relentless dust. On the upmost ring of the platform city, twelve-year-old Isaac struggled to maintain his grip on the iron railing, wondering how it was he came to be in his current predicament.

The boy's lungs burned as he breathed. His eyes clenched shut against the cutting wind. He felt like his face was being cut to shreds by tiny knives. His fingers, damp with sweat, slipped on the railing and he re-tightened them. Terror clutched at him like a lead weight. If he fell, he would plummet fifteen stories to an assured death. His panicked heart raced as the wind whipped his body like a kite. Though Isaac's eyes remained shut, a picture began to form in his mind—colors melting together like paint in an artist's hand until the final stroke—when it took on the quality of a photograph so lifelike he could have stepped into the scene. As the wind faded, he found himself no longer on the balcony, but in the bedroom that had come to him as a fragment of his imagination. Velvet carpeting was soft on his hands, dark in the light from a firebolt lamp.

Isaac struggled to his feet, sucking in a breath when he saw the man coming towards him; he was pale, with a hooked nose and beady eyes. Thin lips pursed together in a condescending scowl. He recognized the mayor's face from the broadsheets and video broadcasts in the town square.

"What the blazes are you doing in my bedchamber?"

Feeling like someone else was in control of his body, Isaac backed up, drew out the revolver tucked in his waistband and squeezing the trigger with alarming precision. A scream pulled his attention to a maid standing by the door. She locked eyes with him before dashing from the room, yelling for help. Staring in wide-eyed horror as the mayor collapsed with a heavy thud, the boy stumbled, tripped over a stool in the room and fell. On the ceiling, a camera lens pointed down and the reflection of his own face looked back.

Jerking his head up with a gasp, Isaac shook. Cold seeped into him and there was the peculiar taste of dirt and grit in his mouth. He was leaning against a building where he had fallen asleep hours ago. "It was just a dream." Hands pressed on his head, he rocked back and forth, trying to convince himself this was true. Images of a sky-blue flower and his mother's face pushed to the front of his mind.

Remembering the incident of his childhood and losing his parents caused a tremor to work its way through his body. "It was just a dream." he said it aloud, hoping it would solidify into reality. No one can really go places in their sleep. One hand on the rusted metal of the building, he stood. Something fell to the ground with a clank. Thinking his watch had fallen through a hole in his pocket again, he leaned over, feeling along the ground in search of it. His fingers brushed across the warm barrel of a pistol. Anxiety seizing his chest, he snatched it up, holding it close to his face to see it better in the storm-blackened night. It was the same one from his nightmare.

A siren blared; low at first, then rising above the noise of the wind and maintaining steady at an ear-splitting decibel. "I've killed the mayor..."

Heart pounding, Isaac could hear security forces running through the streets and sank against the shadows of a building as they dashed past. When they were gone, he clambered off in the opposite direction.

Until tonight, he had been nothing more than an orphan no one would give a second look to on the crowded roads; scrawny, covered in coal-dust like all the others. But all that was over. Now, he was being hunted for a murder; one he committed in his sleep.

Whistles sounded as he ran down a dead-end street. Footsteps of his pursuers neared. Chest heaving, he took a step backward and let out a cry as he fell. The noise of his yell was stifled by a rough hand clasped over his mouth. A heavy grip pinned his arms against his body. "Be still, boy," a low voice ordered.

Isaac obeyed, listening in a heightened panic as the footsteps receded.

His captor slowly let go. Boots clambered on the rungs of a ladder, followed by the scraping of the manhole cover being slid into place. A match struck and the flame of a gas lamp illuminated the man's face. Dark hair framed the man's tanned face, his neatly trimmed beard flecked with silver. Lines formed at the edges of familiar dark eye.

"Tell me you didn't drop the gun." The falcon on the man's shoulder cocked its head, stretching wings of shimmering blue.

Isaac eased away, his knees quivering.

"You did." The man sighed, setting the lamp by his feet. As he reached in his coat pocket, Isaac whirled and fled. Above the sound of his own footsteps echoing, the man's voice raised.

"Jankyn Jules Lee."

Hearing his name spoken for the first time in six years brought back the image of his mother smiling while she tucked him in at night; of his father teaching him how to tie his shoes. The memories were happy, but the feeling they awakened was that of deep, aching loss. Thinking of himself as Jules for the first time in many years, the boy turned around.

"You." He remembered the man's eyes and the shadow of the falcon on that night long ago. Worse than longing was the hope the stranger's appearance evoked. Hope was a dangerous thing to meddle with when the threads of reality promised a very different outcome. And yet, Jules found himself gripped in its hold. He walked back to where the stranger stood. "Who are you?"

The man unbuttoned the top button of his sable duster. "I am called many things. You can call me Falcon." Taking off the coat, he draped it over one shoulder and rolled up his sleeves. Dark tattooed lines twisted from the tan skin of his wrists up the length of his arms.

Jules blurted out the question before he lost his nerve. "Are my parents alive?" Dripping of water somewhere in the tunnel compounded the silence.

"I'm sorry."

A hard knot formed in Jules' stomach. He kicked a loose rock. "It's all my fault. This stupid curse." Every place he visited in his childhood dreams, every step he took, only proved to forge a path to his parents' demise.

The man called Falcon crossed his muscular arms, frowning down at Jules. "Not your fault. It is a rare gift you have. Only, you don't know how to use it. You have no idea how hard it is to find sleepwalkers." His coat fell to the ground as the bird adjusted itself on his shoulder, and, as he stooped to retrieve it, documents fell from the leather satchel slung over his shoulder. On top of the papers was the photograph of an ornately decorated bedchamber; the only thing missing was a corpse on the dampened velvet carpet.

All relief fading, Jules recalled the Falcon's comments about the gun. How could he have known about it? He eased away, trying to put as much distance between him and the man as possible. "It was you—you did this to me!" He pointed an accusatory finger as his heart worked to keep up with the racing in his mind. "You bodysnatching murderer!"

Collecting his papers from the ground, the man gave Jules an amused look. "A colorful way of putting it."

Before the boy had time to react, the man reached out and pushed him to his knees with a firm grasp on his shoulder. The tip of a metal rod pressed against the base of his neck and a jolt of electricity shot through his body, knocking the breath from his lungs. Letting out a cry of pain, Jules fell forward onto his hands, his whole body shaking as the feeling of a thousand stabbing pins crashed over him in waves. "What did you do to me?" he gasped.

The Falcon collapsed the steel rod in his hand and concealed it in his pocket. "There was a cordycep inside your nervous system."

"A *what*?" Beads of sweat trickled down Jules' neck as he took slow, precise breaths. Vaguely aware of the stranger digging in his satchel, he pulled his gaze from the spinning ground.

"It's not important." There was a detached look of amusement on the man's face as he offered Jules a canteen. "I deactivated it. So you can rest easy knowing your body will no longer be… s*natched* from you again."

Jules yanked the canteen from the man's hand and grudgingly took a drink, wiping water from his mouth with the back of his hand as he gave the Falcon a savage glare. "You used me."

Tell me all about your walk. His mother's words came to his mind, a painful reminder of what he had lost. It was alarming how raw the wound was after all these years. The canteen fell from his hand, its contents spilling out and soaking the leg of his pants. "You killed them too, didn't you?"

A dark look clouded the man's face and Jules pressed himself further against the hardness of the tunnel wall.

"Careful, boy." Offense hinged on the Falcon's words. "I had nothing to do with the fate of your parents. And my modus operandi rarely involves tampering with the fate of a sleepwalker."

Anger roiling inside him, Jules voice raised. "You took away my parents, my childhood—my *name*. And then you were going to leave me to take the fall for your assassination? And you don't play with fate?"

"Correct." The Falcon's voice was hard. He shook the dust from his coat and slipped his arms back through the sleeves.

"Now what? Are you going to kill me?" Jules rested his head against drawn-up knees, willing the nausea to pass.

"Kill you?"

Jules glanced up to see the man reaching into his pocket. Scrunching against the wall further, he cringed with one eye open. The older man's eyes narrowed as he drew out a watch and held it up for the boy to see before glancing at it. "No."

"Why not?"

"Do you wish me to?" The watch chain coiled around the man's finger as he swung it in the air.

"No!" Jules jumped to his feet.

The assassin returned the watch to his pocket. "You have two options. Remain here and live out the rest of a very short life in the sewers. Or keep up."

"Keep up?" Jules wanted to believe in the possibility his life was not moments from ending, but he was having difficulty accepting it to be true.

"Yes." The Falcon's brow furrowed as he hoisted the lamp in front of his face, giving a slight shrug. "Your choice." He was already walking down the tunnel, stooping so his head did not touch the top. His falcon careened its head to look at Jules as he passed.

Jules' heartbeat slowed as the distance between them grew and the lamplight faded. He would soon be left in darkness. Glancing up at the entrance to the city, he knew he must decide. Where the assassin was going was unclear, and his intentions more so. He was the one who got Jules into this mess. But if he stayed here, he knew how it would end. Leaving, even with uncertain odds, was better than the alternative.

"Wait!" the word echoed down the tunnel as Jules dashed after The Falcon. "Where are we going?" He asked as he fell in step behind the man.

"Far from this god-forsaken desert wasteland." The man reached into the satchel and produced a familiar leather-bound sketchbook, which he held towards the boy. "Your father asked me to keep you safe. I'll give you a fresh start. That is the best I can honor his request and my debt will be paid." He sounded like his thoughts were miles away as he spoke.

My mother's book.

Taking it, Jules was too grateful to care how the Falcon had come to have it in his possession. The book fell open where a faded blue orchid was pressed between the pages and its scent mixed with the smell of graphite and paper.

"What do you wish to be called, boy? Is it Isaac or Jules now?"

Running his fingers along the flower's crisp edges, the boy allowed a smile to escape his lips as he looked at his six-year-old face preserved forever by his mother's hand. Using his proper name did not seem right somehow. Not now. He thought of his years as Isaac Tobin, the lost child who kept to himself at Fleet Street Children's Home.

"Jankyn," he said, sounding a little surer of himself. "Jankyn Fleet."

ABOUT THE AUTHOR

ANNA ENJOYS WRITING adventure stories with airships and sarcasm. She lives in an unnamed town in South Carolina with her husband, three sons and imaginary friends. Although her female lead character is a strong, capable woman, Anna sometimes enlists her husband to open jars and reach things off the top shelf.